PIECES OF DARK, PIECES OF LIGHT

A Novel

Endorsements

Pieces of Dark, Pieces of Light is a futuristic international mystery/adventure novel that will keep you turning the pages, unable to put it down. Linda Rooks has written a combination science fiction, mystery, adventure, and romance that will appeal to teens and adults alike. It is a timeless tale of good and evil where God tests man and faith and values prevail. I highly recommend it.
—**Bill McCollum**, former Florida Attorney General, US Congressman

This novel has a realistic foundation in Washington, its diplomatic structure, and serious international challenges. The author takes the reader through a journey in time with unique twists and cleverly crafted turns into the future. Linda Rooks has a talent for developing captivating characters who face dramatic personal challenges, and international intrigues which cause the reader to devour one page after another. Wonderfully written, it truly captures the title from darkness, there is light. It clearly reminds us with faith and hope, there is light.
—**Congressman John L. Mica**

A compelling journey through decades past, present, and future, *Pieces of Dark, Pieces of Light* inspires the reader to appreciate that our life's everyday decisions are part of a bigger design than any one individual can understand, but that faith in God's plan will save ourselves, loved ones and perhaps civilization writ large. A moving tribute to the power of faith.
—**Tom Feeney**, former US Congressman and Florida House Speaker

Linda Rooks has provided a fast-paced, exciting story that expertly blends international intrigue with science fiction. Anyone that enjoys a tale with characters who entice the reader to keep turning pages will enjoy *Pieces of Dark, Pieces of Light*. I strongly recommend the book for anyone who enjoys an exciting tale.

—**John M. House,** PhD, Colonel (USA Retired) and Desert Storm combat veteran

Linda Rooks's latest book—*Pieces of Dark, Pieces of Light*—is a richly engaging novel set thirty years in the future, but with its tentacles reaching back into the twentieth century. Her ingredients in this compelling story are international espionage, time travel, family secrets, betrayal and restoration, faith and integrity. Her characters are finely developed as the story unfolds, revealing lessons that we need to be reminded of today, long before the future she describes so eloquently.

—**Darryl M. Bloodworth**, former Air Force pilot, author of *We Who Remain*, and trial lawyer

Linda Rooks's debut thriller ticks all the boxes: international intrigue, compelling characters with plenty of heart, and a fast-paced plot that kept me reading through the night. Rooks hooked me with her well-developed characters and their respective spiritual awakenings—and she pulled me in with a creative mix of science fiction, suspense, and just enough romance. This is your next best read!

—**Catherine Finger**, award-winning author of the Jo Oliver Thriller series.

Those who enjoy the writings of David Baldacci will love *Pieces of Dark, Pieces of Light*. I could not put this book down.

—**Captain George Daniel Prettyman**, USNR, Retired

Pieces of Dark, Pieces of Light is a page-turner that will keep you up all night until you finish it! Award-winning

Linda Rooks has written another certain best-seller, only this one is filled with intrigue, long-held family secrets, and a major worldwide crisis. If you like suspense and can read while holding your breath for long periods of time, dive into this book!

—**Martha Bolton**, Emmy-nominated writer for Bob Hope and the author of eighty-eight books

Linda Rooks has created a fascinating, intricate plot in this sci-fi and political novel that will keep you on the edge of your seat. Although I'm not into reading a lot of fiction, I couldn't put this book down. Rooks communicates relevant spiritual truths on topics that reach across the world from our country to Tajikistan, both now and in the future. Don't be surprised if this novel makes it to the Big Screen.

—**Ginny Dent Brant**, author of *Finding True Freedom: From the White House to the World.*

I have always enjoyed an action-packed novel. In *Pieces of Dark, Pieces of Light*, you will be drawn into Linda Rooks's characters and fast-moving dialogue. Suspense at its best with a bonus of inspiration and life lessons. An intriguing read that both entertains and gives you something to think about. You won't be disappointed!

—**LeAnn Weiss-Rupard**, president of Encouragement Company & best-selling *Hugs* author

Pieces of Dark, Pieces of Light

A Novel

Linda W. Rooks

ELK LAKE PUBLISHING INC

PUBLISHING THE POSITIVE
Plymouth, Massachusetts

A Christian Company
ElkLakePublishingInc.com

Copyright Notice

Cover and Interior Design: Kelly Artieri, Derinda Babcock, Deb Haggerty
Editor(s): Mary W. Johnson, Cristel Phelps, Deb Haggerty
Author Represented By: Jonathan Clements of Wheelhouse Literary

PUBLISHED BY: Elk Lake Publishing, Inc., 35 Dogwood Drive, Plymouth, MA 02360, 2022

Library Cataloging Data

Names: Rooks, Linda W. (Linda W. Rooks)

Pieces of Dark, Pieces of Light / Linda W. Rooks

460 p. 23cm × 15cm (9in × 6 in.)

ISBN-13: 978-1-64949-671-3 (paperback) | 978-1-64949-672-0 (trade hardcover) | 978-1-64949-673-7 (trade paperback) | 978-1-64949-674-4 (e-book)

Key Words: international intrigue, chemical weapons, Tajikistan, time travel, romantic suspense thriller, weapons of mass destruction, marriage reconciliation, life

Library of Congress Control Number: 2022944198 Fiction

DEDICATION

To the late Andy Merritt, whose vision spread the light of love, hope, and caring far and wide across our land. He will be remembered as a man who pierced the darkness with the light of hope and will continue to be esteemed for his humble dedication, loving perseverance, and inspirational outreach that gave hope to hurting souls.

ACKNOWLEDGMENTS

As this book gets ready to go to print, my thoughts and thanks go to a number of people who helped *Pieces of Dark, Pieces of Light* come to full fruition.

First and foremost: The men in my small critique group—John Leatherman, Tracy Lesch, Bill Geary, and Greg Kriefall—who labored with me month after month as *Pieces of Dark, Pieces of Light* took shape. Many thanks for their valuable contributions to the military, action, and technology portions of the story as well as to some of the futuristic elements. This wouldn't have become the story it is without their participation in hammering out the details (and I mean details) of each and every chapter during our many late night sessions.

Sunny Rinker, who helped me create transparency in some of the more delicate scenes of the book, but most of all for her unrelenting faith in me and the book's potential. Her early enthusiasm for *Pieces of Dark, Pieces of Light* encouraged me to take the book seriously enough to seek a publisher, and her faithful partnership in bringing it into the light ultimately got it into the hands of readers.

Because it was important to me to make this story as realistic as possible, I appreciate the counsel and advice of many others as well who helped me bolster the realism and authenticity of the various scenes. In this regard, my thanks goes out to:

Dr. Greg Samano, who helped me create the Ichiban Syndrome, a fictional neuromuscular disease we hope no one ever experiences.

Chris Wolf, who offered a number of insights into the future possibilities of computer and weapons technology, and for his tips on how to skillfully incorporate nanotechnology into the time travel sequence.

Lyle Cain, who came through for me once again on my technology questions, this time by envisioning a future phone based on quantum entanglement, resulting in a quantum communication device or Q phone for my characters to use in 2052.

Congressman John Mica and his staff—Stephanie, Gary, Josh, and Rusty—who provided tours of the White House and State Department so I could realistically portray the scenes taking place in the halls of government.

Congressman Tom Feeney, who met with us in DC, gave us access to government areas, and helped us envision a future America in 2052.

Roger Franks and Ginny Gentles, who educated me on residential communities and suburbs in the DC area so I could create a believable home environment for my characters.

Ken Mikesell, who helped me envision the TV technology of the future.

Colonel John M. House, USA Retired, who took the time to help me give my military characters added credibility.

Thanks also to the friends, family, and neighbors who rallied around me, taking my phone calls and emails to answer strange and inquisitive questions as a prelude to my applying their expertise to the making of this book, including Laura Jackson's medical advice, Julie Wolf's relationship tips, Tommy Thompson, Pat Short, and John Wieck's ideas about life in the future, and Bob Lehn, whose honest encouragement as an avid suspense reader spurred me on to believe in the book's potential.

Most of all, I can't adequately begin to express my huge appreciation to my husband Marv, who always believed in this story and was the first to identify it as a thriller. His willingness to always be my sounding board when I needed a second opinion and his enthusiasm and wit in throwing out a clever line now and then to liven up a scene provided a sweet encouragement throughout my writing. He has been there each step of the way, from traveling to DC with me to scope out the landscape for the story, reading chapters as they came to life, hashing out ideas with me for a plot twist, continuing to believe in me when disappointments came, and rejoicing with me over little successes.

My appreciation also goes to:

Deb Haggerty at Elk Lake Publishing for believing in my story and giving me the opportunity to share it with the world.

Mary W. Johnson, my editor at Elk Lake, who pushed me and made me stretch (in spite of my protests) so we could partner together to bring the book to perfection.

Kelly Artieri, cover artist, who created this incredible cover.

My agent, Jonathan Clements, who has continued to believe in me as we've persevered together through the ups and downs of the publishing world.

Finally, I thank God for giving me the opportunity to write this story and for guiding me through the process.

PROLOGUE

Clouds of dust spiraled above the young man's feet as he raced along the road, shoving aside a yelping dog that blocked his way. Heart hammering, his dark eyes locked onto the five-story brick edifice ahead.

In long seconds he was there, bounded up the steps and charged to the opposite end of the corridor. Knuckles poised to knock, he changed his mind and grabbed the knob, pushing his way inside.

Across the room, the gray-haired man turned at his desk, scowling at the interruption. His fierce eyes bored into those of the intruder.

The young visitor tensed, out of breath and gulping air. With quivering hands, he shut the door and waited to hear it click.

The man's chair creaked under his weight. His voice carried his gruff irritation.

"What is it?"

"Father, they've been found."

"What's been found?"

"The weapons. They found the weapons."

CHAPTER ONE

WASHINGTON, DC
THE NEXT MORNING

Apparently the new mind-activated coffee maker was not working. By now the aroma of brewing coffee should have reached the bedroom. Janssen tried it again and waited while he trimmed his mustache. The hum of his razor was coaxing him back to sleep. And still no smell of coffee.

He craved it. That uneasy tremor from within, that longing for the taste of roasted brew and the accompanying rush from the first sip grew stronger by the minute.

Half shaved, Janssen slid his quantum communicator onto his wrist, tromped down the stairs to the kitchen, and turned on the coffeepot. His Q watch said 6:42.

Charlie sure left early. Wonder what she's up to.

Wrestling with the quiet of early morning, he spoke to the theater-sized screen on the family room wall across from the kitchen bar.

"ITV. News on."

Voices hummed from the speakers, joining him now as he grabbed a box of cereal and searched for sugar. The words "Tajikistan," "weapons," and "found" bit into the shaky fog of his mind and stopped him. Cereal box in hand, he turned to see a dour ITV news reporter standing in a dusty field, surrounded by austere desert mountain ranges with a darkening sky behind. She was half-turning to face the mountains as she spoke.

> Somewhere behind us in these mountains, the weapons were discovered in a cave this morning. Tajik authorities are not releasing the identity of those who found them, to protect both the persons involved and the location of the cache. The weapons appear to have been concealed there for years, perhaps decades. It's a surprising find, as Tajikistan is a peaceful country, not known for any past or present involvement in terrorist activities. And since there have been no known weapons of mass destruction on the planet since the WMD Treaty of 2032, where these came from is a mystery. The weapons are reportedly active, which means for the first time in twenty years the world must once again deal with the threat of weapons of mass destruction.

Janssen gaped at the ITV screen.

Weapons? In Tajikistan?

The invigorating smell of coffee filled the kitchen as Janssen stood with his eyes riveted to the images flashing across the screen. The words of the newscaster rattled around in his head. "A danger no one would have expected in a place no one would expect to find it."

He poured himself a tall mug of coffee, took the first sip, and then sat on a barstool.

The scene on the ITV screen switched to the city of Dushanbe. A man spoke at a lectern in front of the Parliament Building. As the cameras closed in on him, the reporter identified him as "Prime Minister Jumakhan Oqilov."

And that was his name. Officially, of course.

But for Janssen, a far more personal relationship with the man on the screen drew him in. He knew him as more than the official spokesman for a country most people knew little about. He was a kind man, a man of integrity, a man who had mentored Janssen as a boy. He was Janssen Aryan LaMarche's uncle.

Jumakhan's voice faltered as he explained about the guards posted around the weapons cache and as he read a statement explaining the official Tajik position. Lines of stress streaked his face.

Janssen tilted his mug back and forth and stared at the black liquid swirling around inside it. Other than occasional emails, he hadn't been involved with his uncle or Tajikistan for quite a while. In the last few years, life had been all about Paris and India and trying to strengthen the position of the West and its African allies in world affairs.

And lately, if he was honest with himself, life was also about trying to ignore these blasted pains that intermittently troubled him.

The scene shifted back to the States. President Gelford's press secretary reported the president and his staff had been delving into the situation since early morning and declared Gelford's intention to fully check things out in Tajikistan.

"ITV off." Janssen grabbed his cup and headed back to the bedroom. Secretary Tomlin was going to have his hands full. The office would be abuzz, and there was no telling how this morning's events in Tajikistan might spill over into other sectors of the State Department. Janssen needed to get to the office.

He was three steps from the top of the stairs when a sharp pain jabbed him in the side. Janssen groaned. *No. Not again.*

He gripped the rail, trying to steady the mug in his right hand, then took a deep breath and steeled himself for the pain he knew would follow. His body tightened, then grew suddenly weak. The long flight of stairs beneath him lengthened in his vision as he fought for control.

Sit.

He thudded onto the marble stair, his left hand sliding down the rail post, the cup in his right clanking against the hard step. Sprays of the dark liquid splashed onto the ivory surface.

Need to get a handle on this. Need to see those lab tests. Why did I wait so long to go to the doctor?

The pain lingered a few moments. When it subsided, Janssen breathed deeply several times as his body eased and relaxed. He rose, retrieved his cup with its few remaining drops, and continued to the top. He hobbled to the bedroom, where he dropped into the velour cushions of the armchair beside the bed. Janssen scrolled through the phone book in his Q watch, looking for the doctor's name. When Dr. Monnihan's number appeared on the screen, he selected it. The ring tone sounded and quickly went to voice mail.

"This is Janssen LaMarche. Checking to see if my tests are in yet. Give me a call at the office or on my Q phone and let me know. Thanks."

He punched off his quantum communicator, then closed his eyes. The episode on the stairs had taken a lot out of him. He was already tired and couldn't shake the picture of his uncle from his mind. *Tajikistan.*

What was happening in Tajikistan?

Leaning back in the chair, he sipped the last bit of coffee and faced the mahogany cabinet. "ITV. News on," he said.

The cabinet doors separated. Janssen straightened his shoulders as the news anchor began repeating the same information about Tajikistan he'd heard earlier. He glanced at the time. The morning was going fast. He needed to grab another cup of coffee and something to eat, clean up the mess on the stairs, go by the Pentagon, and make some other stops before going to his office at the State Department for a meeting at eleven. And he was meeting Charlie for lunch.

As he rose and grabbed the shirt hanging on his closet door, he glanced back at the ITV screen, where the segment of his uncle making the statement from the podium in Dushanbe played once again.

Weapons of mass destruction in Tajikistan? Questions flooded Janssen's mind.

And doubts.

It'd been a long time since his last heartfelt conversation with his uncle. What did Uncle Jocko know about this? *Concealed there for years, perhaps decades.* Or did his grandfather know, when *he* was prime minister there years earlier?

How had weapons of mass destruction made their way into Tajikistan without either of them knowing about it?

When his Q watch rang, Janssen was changing lanes on Interstate 395, but his mind was locked into the memory of Iran's 2029 bombing of Los Angeles. Vivid images of blown-out buildings, bodies in the streets, and mass devastation replayed through his mind. The words of the reporter on the morning's news and the sight of his uncle had reignited those long-ago fears.

The phone went into voice mail, then informed him a call was waiting from Leslie Ann, his office receptionist.

What kind of weapons were they? Nuclear? Chemical? Biological? If they were either of the latter, odds were they'd be inert after all this time. But nuclear weapons would still be active, even if they'd been there since the treaty.

The treaty. Thank God for it. After the devastation in both LA and London, the international community had finally come together. His father had been part of the negotiations that brought peace from the constant danger of WMD, something that made Janssen proud.

He watched in his rearview mirror as a Coca-Cola truck from the right lane maneuvered in behind him. The car behind slowed to give him room. *There are still some gracious people in the world.*

"Call office," he said into his Q watch. The youthful face of his secretary mushroomed beside him in a hologram when she answered. "Hi, Leslie Ann. What's up?"

"White House Deputy Chief of Staff Robertson called. He wants to meet with you at ten this morning, Mr. LaMarche."

"Robertson? Hmm. That's in just over an hour. Did he say what it's about?"

"No, only that it's extremely important."

"Where?"

"The White House Office."

"Thanks, Leslie Ann. You'd better reschedule my eleven o'clock. What else is happening in the office this morning?"

"Just lots of talk, Mr. LaMarche. You know ... about the weapons they found."

Janssen sighed. "Yeah, I heard."

"It ... it's scary."

"Yes. It is. Very."

The cars in front slowed to a crawl. A horn honked somewhere behind him. "Gotta go. Traffic's bad. See you this afternoon."

The traffic in all lanes had come to a standstill, and the beguiling feminine voice of Cool Navigator spoke through the radio. "Traffic congestion next two miles. Collision between two cars."

PIECES OF DARK, PIECES OF LIGHT

Janssen stared across the Potomac at the DC skyline where the Washington Monument glinted in the sun, then shifted his gaze toward the White House.

White House Deputy Chief of Staff Randall Robertson wants a meeting with me? He's never even met me.

CHAPTER TWO

"LaMarche, one thing making this situation so urgent is that within the last two hours, sources have told us some unknown entity is attempting to get these weapons for themselves." Robertson leaned forward. "We don't know who it is, but the offer to buy the weapons is coming through the Islamic Revival Party. From what we understand, that's not a good sign."

Janssen frowned and shook his head.

"No, it isn't. The IRP has been friendly to radical Islamic fundamentalists in the region for decades. Doesn't sound good at all. Even though they're not in control of the government, they still hold significant sway." Janssen stroked his fingers across his mustache. "But you say we don't have any idea who this entity is?"

"Nothing substantial. It could be Iran, Syria, the Saudis ... we just don't know. Some rogue group even. Or China."

"Robertson, do we know what kind of weapons they are? If they're active, it sounds like they'd be nuclear. If they're chemical or biological, I'd think the weapons would no longer be viable. Not after so many years."

Robertson leaned back and crossed his arms. "We don't know what kind they are. But our sources tell us they're active weapons of mass destruction, and they emphasize 'active,' saying they're potentially *very* dangerous. So they could be nuclear." He shook his head. "We just don't know."

"And who is this 'source?'"

"An unofficial government employee."

"A spy?"

Robertson raised his eyebrows and avoided Janssen's eyes. "An unofficial government employee. That's all I can say." He smiled. "Part of the ground crew, I guess."

"I see." Janssen visualized a mole digging a hole in the side of one of the mountains.

Robertson rose and paced to the long mahogany table in the center of the room, then walked to a credenza and poured himself a cup of coffee. "Want some?"

"No thanks. I'm good." Janssen observed Robertson as the young-looking chief of staff stirred cream into his coffee. Janssen wondered how he'd risen to this position so early in his career.

Finally, Robertson took a seat again on the opposite couch, leaned back, and unbuttoned his jacket.

"LaMarche, your name has come up as someone who not only has close family ties to the prime minister of Tajikistan and speaks the Tajik language, but has also proven himself a very capable diplomat over the years." Robertson continued. "In fact, one person on the Joint Chiefs called you 'brilliant.' Another referred to you as 'charismatic, and a man whose active listening skills can,' and I quote, 'pull harmony from a nest of black widows.'"

Janssen laughed and uncrossed his legs. "That's quite a tribute."

"We pulled up your records, and we found your achievements quite impressive."

"Thanks, but there must be a little luck mixed in there somewhere."

Robertson chuckled. "Actually, I'm surprised your name hasn't risen to the top sooner. To cut to the chase, LaMarche, the Chiefs are looking at using you in this Tajikistan crisis. But first they wanted me to ask you a few questions. We know Jumakhan Oqilov is your uncle, but what kind of relationship do you have with him? Are you in contact with him? What kind of man is he?"

Janssen crossed his legs again. "Our relationship is good, but I haven't seen him for quite a while. We occasionally exchange emails. We were particularly close in the past."

"Could you tell me more about it?"

"As a young boy, I used to visit Tajikistan often, since my father was a diplomat and my mother's family was there. I would stay sometimes for a couple of months at a time. Jumakhan Oqilov is the youngest of my mother's brothers and was only a few years older than I, so we spent a lot of time together. We both loved the outdoors and shared many youthful adventures." He chuckled. "And some youthful pranks too, I might add. He liked the idea of having an American nephew who was close to his age, and we used to talk for hours about politics and philosophy and so on. We always had a great deal of respect for each other."

"And how would you describe your uncle as a person and a leader?"

Janssen's mind flipped from the scene of his uncle on ITV that morning to cameo recollections of his uncle as statesman and to memories of conversations they'd had in the past.

"He's a very honest, caring man. He loves the people of Tajikistan and can be extremely resourceful in their behalf. He's even-keeled, and a good negotiator himself."

"Must run in the family."

Janssen laughed. "He can be a bit stubborn once his mind is made up, but all in all, he's a reasonable man and open to new ideas."

"I need you to be honest with me here, LaMarche. If you were in charge of negotiations, would that make him more receptive to US concerns, or would he try to put you off ... would familiarity breed contempt, as they say?"

In charge of negotiations? Janssen leaned back in his chair and felt a flush spread from his chest to his face. Given his connections, he could understand the government using him in dealing with Tajikistan. But this would indeed be a fast-track elevation in status from his usual mid-level responsibilities.

"As I said, we have a very good relationship. He respects me a great deal. I don't think he'd be less inclined to take me seriously because I'm his nephew." Janssen paused and drank from the glass of ice water on the table beside him. "Actually, I have a feeling our relationship might prompt him to go the extra mile in trying to understand the US perspective—if that's what I was representing."

"That's what we were hoping to hear. And how about you? Would you feel compromised in any way because of the family connection? If things get tough, where would your loyalties lie?"

"I'm afraid I don't know much about what the US intends to do, but I've always prided myself on keeping my personal life separate from my professional responsibilities." Janssen shifted on the sofa and recrossed his legs. "But if I'm going to be completely candid with you, Robertson, I need to know more about the objectives of our mission. I know better than to make blind promises in this kind of situation."

"I respect that." Robertson tapped his fingers on the table and studied Janssen carefully. "It would be best for

President Gelford and Secretary Tomlin to fill you in, but of course, generally the main objective is to keep the world safe from WMD. Beyond that, from what I understand, the Chiefs of Staff have already determined the Tajik government won't just relinquish the weapons to us, and they themselves don't have the technology to neutralize the weapons. Tajikistan is a poor country, as you know, and can probably use US financial help. As I understand it, the US mission will be to try to purchase the weapons and neutralize them."

"That makes sense. With those objectives in mind, I feel certain no personal concerns would interfere with my carrying out the mission in good conscience."

Robertson nodded.

"Of course, Secretary Tomlin will be the prime negotiator anyway," Janssen said, "so he'll have the final call."

"Actually, no. Tomlin will oversee it, but the Chiefs of Staff all agreed a softer, more personal approach would be the best way to go here. You're the man they're looking at."

A caution light flashed in the recesses of Janssen's mind. His hands felt sweaty. Why was he feeling uneasy? "I see. That's quite a responsibility."

"Yes, it's an enormous responsibility." Robertson rested one of his elbows on the arm of the couch and clasped his hands together. "LaMarche, your credentials seem to make you the perfect candidate. The president will have the final word on it after I report to him, but if it's a go, you'll need to immediately clear your calendar of everything else in order to lead the mission. Have you pretty much wrapped things up from your Paris assignment?"

Janssen nodded. "Just a few odds and ends left to do."

"Good. Seems we caught you at a good time, with you being stateside right now. If we go ahead with this, you'll need more staff—a press secretary, another aide. But first tell me what you think. Are you up for this?"

Are you up for this?

Janssen looked across the table at Charlie munching on her sandwich, then allowed his eyes to wander to the blank wall behind her.

Are you up for this?

The question had echoed through his mind with haunting regularity after his meeting with Robertson, even as he celebrated the possibilities of the promotion and pondered the mission's responsibilities. Why was the question nagging at him like this? He rattled the ice cubes against the sides of the glass and took a drink.

Because you're not well.

Janssen groaned inwardly. These pains couldn't be anything serious. He'd always been healthy. It was just a pain that came and went.

Wasn't it?

He certainly didn't need a health issue interfering with things now. But it was nothing. It wouldn't interfere.

"Janssen, you're a million miles away," Charlie said, and took another bite of her chicken sandwich.

"Yeah. Sorry. Can't stop thinking about the meeting with Robertson." He took another drink of iced tea, then chomped down on his roast beef sub.

"It's quite an opportunity for you—an honor they would choose you for the job."

"The situation in Tajikistan is serious, Charlie. It's a responsibility that can't be underestimated. It would all be up to me."

"Who could negotiate better with Jumakhan and Rajanov than you? You're the right person for the job, Janssen."

"Jumakhan and Rajanov trust me. I know that's true."

"And that will make the difference," she said, raking her fingers through the ash-blonde hair at the nape of her long neck.

She took out a burgundy lipstick and ran it over her mouth. Janssen was always amazed at how his wife could do that without a mirror. She returned the lipstick to her purse and looked at her watch. "Incidentally, how was your doctor's appointment yesterday?"

He stared at her in surprise. "Fine." He set his glass on the table. "How'd you know I had an appointment?"

"Doesn't Leslie Ann give you your messages? I called yesterday. She said you were at the doctor's."

"Hmm."

"Everything all right?"

He shifted in his chair, then nodded. "Yeah. Fine. Usual routine stuff, that's all."

Back at the office an hour later, the president of the United States called Janssen to invite him to head up the diplomatic mission to Tajikistan. If he was agreeable to accept the position, the president wanted Janssen to meet with him and Secretary Tomlin the next day to iron out the details. The day after that, he would make the announcement to the public. Janssen was to be prepared to give a press conference an hour afterwards.

No call had come in yet from the doctor's office.

CHAPTER THREE

Janssen could hear the buzz of conversation through the closed doors of the Thomas Jefferson Room. He needed to get in there. The media was waiting.

Gripping the doorframe, he leaned against the jamb, taking slow, deep breaths to better control the waves of intense pressure bearing down on his abdomen. His pain would pass in a moment.

"Mr. LaMarche?"

Hearing the voice of his new public relations assistant behind him, Janssen stared down at his notes on the pretext of rehearsing the statements he would soon make to the press.

Of all times for this to happen.

"Are you ready?" Danny prodded gently. "They're all in there now."

Janssen took a deep breath, squared his broad shoulders, and nodded.

"Ready. Let's go in."

Pushing through the mahogany doors, Janssen was momentarily taken aback by the large number of reporters and cameramen crowded into the mid-size room. Global Illusion TV crews in their standard camera helmets gathered in the back between marble columns. Semicircular rows of brown metal chairs cut across the mahogany floor, where reporters busily tapped on trans-information receivers and arranged camera settings. He recognized a few of the faces from the Washington Press Corps and nodded to Dillard Trekker, the foreign correspondent he'd often seen while serving in the Paris embassy.

In the large video clouds hovering in each corner of the room above the jade-green walls, he saw himself from different angles—in bigger-than-life dimensions—approaching the lectern. In place of the usual antique mirror mounted above it was the large gold seal of the State Department. The flags of the United States and State Department flanked either side.

Striding to the lectern, he laid his notes on the polished surface. The pain was almost gone now. Briefly, he leaned onto his hand planted on the lectern and took another deep breath to clear away the remaining pangs of discomfort coursing through his body.

"Ladies and gentlemen of the press," he began, trying to straighten his back. "I appreciate you being here this morning. After I make my statement, I will entertain questions." He took another deep breath and looked around the room. The mass of reporters clicking on their TIRs jarred against the quiet elegance of the room's glittering chandelier and marble statuary.

"As President Gelford informed you earlier, he has asked me to travel to Tajikistan to meet with President Rajanov regarding the cache of weapons allegedly discovered there last week. I am honored to represent the United States in this important undertaking. Unfortunately, the Tajik government has not yet disclosed to us the exact nature of the weapons—only that they are active weapons of mass destruction. As you can imagine, we are very concerned, since this discovery has the potential of reopening a serious danger which we thought had been laid to rest twenty years ago."

In the back room of her consignment shop, Evie LaMarche had retreated to watch the unfolding press conference on ITV. Sitting in the mauve club chair with a glass of soda, she watched her father march to the lectern. The imposing images of his stalwart figure and chiseled, resolute countenance belied his age of fifty-six years. She lounged back as he began his statement and the cameras closed in on his face.

He flinched, and the color drained from his cheekbones. Evie bolted upright, grabbed the controls and hit the magnification button. Something was wrong. He looked so pale. She scooched the chair closer to the ITV screen.

His shoulders now appeared hunched over, a sharp contrast to his usual stately bearing. He attempted to straighten them without success.

"Miss LaMarche?"

Evie jumped when she heard Helen's voice behind her. Her assistant's head poked through the opening from the shop's showroom.

"Did you say *Miss LaMarche*? Goodness, where did that come from? Call me Evie, Helen. Do you think I'm an old woman?"

"No, but I—"

"Helen, I'd especially like to watch this press conference live. If you could take care of the store for a few minutes, I'd appreciate it. That's my dad. He's heading up the diplomatic mission to Tajikistan. It's his first press conference."

"Oh really? Your dad? Oh, I see. Well, I ..." Helen shifted a yellow checked baby blanket from one arm to the other, sighed and continued to stand by the door. "I'm sorry to interrupt you, Evie, but there's a man out here who wants to talk to you."

"What does he want?"

"He didn't say."

"Tell him I'm occupied at the moment. I won't be available for about fifteen or twenty minutes. And see what he wants. Maybe you can help him, okay?"

Evie turned back to the ITV. Her dad's face had a little more color now. Maybe he was just nervous. Not like her confident dad, though. This press conference was a big deal for him. He was now answering questions and pointing to a reporter with round wire-rim glasses.

"Dillard."

"Since there've been such strict prohibitions on WMDs, and careful monitoring throughout the world for twenty years," the reporter began, "where do you believe these weapons came from? Do you think they were hidden there by Iranians before the WMD Treaty of Nations went into effect? Or could the weapons possibly have come from North Korea or Syria?"

"Right now we have no way of knowing with any certainty where they came from. Iran, Syria, and North Korea are certainly possibilities. It's also possible the weapons were taken there by Al-Qaeda or Hezbollah operatives early in the century, or hidden by a rogue rebel group such as El-Azizun prior to the WMD Treaty of Nations of 2032. The WMD that went missing during Libya's regime change could even figure into this."

A slim-faced African-American woman on the right side of the room raised her hand. Janssen recognized her as the CNN correspondent. "Maddie."

"Sir, are the weapons secure now? I understand they're in a very remote part of the country. Is the US government satisfied with the way they're being protected? Can we rely on the Tajiks to keep them safe?"

"At this time, the Tajikistani government has armed guards protecting the cache. They'll do their best to keep the weapons safe, but we feel it's imperative to negotiate with them as soon as possible so the weapons can be moved to a high-security area and then dismantled. The weapons were found in the northern region of Tajikistan, which is dominated by the Islamic Revival Party, an extremist political faction commonly known as the IRP. The People's Democratic Party is in control of the country, however, and they're our friends. But the IRP still wields enough power to keep us concerned, primarily because of their friendliness to some of our adversaries."

Moving to the left side of the podium, Janssen felt a stab of pain in his groin. He winced and steadied himself with his hand against the lectern while trying to maintain his composure. He nodded to a reporter standing at the corner of the room beside the triple-sashed windows. "Victor."

"What does the treaty have to say about how a situation like this should be handled? What is Tajikistan obligated to do?"

Ignoring the rising pain, Janssen continued. "We've been looking at the language of the treaty, and although there is some disagreement over interpretation"—the pain bumped up a notch, and his breath hitched—"the general consensus seems to be that it is up to the local government to"—another sharp jab—"to dispose of the weapons." He paused for a beat to lay his hands along the edges of the lectern. "That could include handing them over to another government. Only if they refuse to do so would the UN get involved, which could take time. Dragging out a resolution to this crisis could have serious consequences." Janssen turned to his right. "Frazier."

"Sir, what kind of relationship do we have with their government at the present time? What has their response been toward our overtures to speak with them? Do we have any reason to believe they would trust us, or prefer our advice over that of their neighbors in the Middle East?"

"Tajikistan was our ally in the war against terrorism in the early 2000s and was helpful during the US withdrawal from Afghanistan. We have had friendly relations with them ever since. Their closest relationships have been with"—he inhaled deeply to repress a new spasm of pain, then exhaled—"Russia. And India. India is our ally, and of course we hope the new Russian regime will cooperate. Tajikistan is a poor country, however, and there are those in their government, particularly those in the IRP, who see a chance to make a great deal of money by selling these weapons. This is where we must intervene. I believe we can be successful." He nodded to a woman in the back who sat directly in front of the pedimented glass doors that led to the State Dining Room. He lifted his shoulders in a stretching motion. "Yes."

Got to get control over this thing.

"Mr. LaMarche, with all due respect, even though you have the reputation in the Department for being a smooth negotiator, many of us were surprised the president chose you rather than the Secretary of State to tackle such an important mission. The research we've been able to do in the last hour since your appointment was announced by the president indicates your mother is from Tajikistan, and you may even have family ties in governmental positions there. I somehow suspect that's not coincidental. Do you have family ties in the Tajik government? And if so, how big a part does that play in your appointment?"

Knowing how sharp these reporters could be, Janssen had anticipated the question. When he explained the Tajik prime minister was his uncle and described their relationship, a ripple of surprise resonated among the notepads of those who had not yet done their homework.

"Also, my grandfather was prime minister in Tajikistan for a number of years earlier in the millennium, so there's a lot of family history." He pointed to a reporter at the end of the first row. "Johan."

"Mr. LaMarche, how will this personal relationship with your uncle benefit these negotiations? When did you last speak with him?"

Janssen felt an intense tightening in his middle again, and he raised his eyes to catch a glimpse of himself in the hologram to his right. Deep lines furrowed his forehead. He blinked back the pain and continued.

"I ... uhh ... spoke with Uncle Jocko ... excuse me ... Prime Minister Oqilov ... a few months ago on another matter. We've arranged an official telephone meeting for this week." Janssen licked his lips and reached for the glass of water on the shelf midway between the top of the lectern and the bottom. How could he have stumbled over his uncle's name? He quickly gathered himself together and continued.

Somehow, other than that one gaffe, he managed to stay coherent and answer questions with his usual poise, despite the aches and cramps coursing through his body. He knew these reporters had more questions. He also knew a nation was watching, a nation on edge with fear. He needed to give the people of the US confidence in his ability to handle the situation and keep the world secure in this time of crisis. He needed to hold himself together and stay strong.

Just when he thought the questions were drawing to a close, a reporter to his right jumped up and thrust out his hand to get Janssen's attention. It was Trent Garrison, Investigative Reporter from the *Washington Tribune*. Janssen nodded to him.

Trent stood with a scowl across his face and cocked his chin. His tone was brittle.

"I'm not sure I see your relationship to the prime minister as positive. In fact, I see it as a possible conflict of interest. What if you're forced to take a tough stand with the prime minister? I presume the Administration is counting on your personal relationship to make him more agreeable to your terms. But what if he isn't? Can you be a tough negotiator with your Uncle *Jocko*—as well as a caring nephew?"

Collecting himself from the verbal lunge, Janssen's nerves tightened for the parry and riposte. He measured his words carefully.

"A good question, Mr. Garrison. And it would certainly be a mistake to rely solely on the family relationship. I know what is at stake here, and I know what must be done. World security must supersede any personal feelings I might have. I will do whatever is needed to contain these weapons. But because of our personal relationship, I know Jumakhan Oqilov to be a very reasonable, responsible, and honorable man. He will want to be a part of keeping the world secure."

Janssen shifted his gaze to a woman who was raising her hand in the back.

Still standing, Trent intercepted him. "Then why did President Gelford select you—Oqilov's nephew—to carry out the negotiations? If Oqilov is so reasonable, couldn't the Secretary of State or someone else have done the job?"

"The Secretary of State is an integral part of the decision-making here, Mr. Garrison, and his role is certainly not diminished by the president calling upon someone who has had a very close and intimate relationship with the region. I don't expect my uncle to make any concessions contrary to the interests he represents simply because of our relationship. By the same token, I will not require a great deal of time in establishing my credentials in a part of the world we don't deal with on a daily basis. And his is not the last word. President Rajanov and the representatives of the Majlisi Oli will have to concur.

"We are facing an international crisis, Mr. Garrison. I'm sure our president wanted to take advantage of every possible resource at his disposal to insure a positive outcome. He apparently saw me as just one more gigabyte to strengthen the diplomatic hard drive."

Trent closed a window on his Q watch, then resumed his seat.

Janssen pointed to a reporter in the back corner, who was raising a blinking stylus in the air. "Yes."

"As a follow-up, does the Secretary of State have an Uncle Jocko too?" Laughter erupted among members of the press, and Janssen felt the room relax.

I owe that reporter one. Need to get his name.

"Seriously," the reporter continued, "what is the agenda, and who else will you be meeting with?"

The hands on the ornate wall clock at the rear of the room seemed to be moving backward. Surely he'd been answering questions longer than it indicated. He was beginning to feel weaker. With his voice growing fainter, he inventoried the order of meetings and officials he would meet with.

"I'm sorry. That will have to be the last question. Good day." Quickly Janssen turned and steered himself toward the mahogany door he had entered a few minutes earlier.

Danny held it open for him and scanned his face with concern as he passed by. "You don't look well, sir," he said.

"I'll be fine. Just stress. Would you get my hovaway, Danny? I need to get back to the office."

Danny retrieved his mobile transport from the hallway and brought it to him. Janssen grabbed the handlebars, pushed the lever, then felt the sag of lift-off as his transport lingered momentarily above the ground.

As it moved forward, his Q watch rang.

CHAPTER FOUR

"ITV off," Evie said, as she gathered together some papers from the end table and rose to rejoin Helen in the boutique section of the store.

"Where's the man you told me about?" She looked around and saw only a woman and small child browsing through the racks.

"He left."

"What did he want?"

"He wouldn't say. He just walked around the shop looking at the baby things—occasionally picking something up to examine it, then putting it back. He was talking to himself under his breath—or maybe he was talking on his Q, I don't know. I did see him make one call. Then he left."

"Hmm. I'm sorry to put you in that position, but I didn't want to miss seeing my dad live. It's a big moment."

Janssen's Q watch rang again. He slowed his hovaway, clicked on the phone, and touched the patch at the back of his ear. The round face of a red-headed, middle-aged woman formed a hologram beside him.

"Mr. LaMarche, this is Kate Mitchell from the president's office. President Gelford has put the mission team together and wants you to meet them. He's scheduling a meeting for tomorrow at two p.m. in the Oval Office. Can you make it?"

"Certainly. How long will we have?"

"About forty-five minutes."

"Sounds good."

"I'll tell him you can make it then."

Moments later, Janssen thrust open the door to his office and made his way past the cheerful congratulations of his staff to his private office. Charlie perched tentatively on the edge of the sofa. Poised and self-confident in her plum-colored suit and amethyst earrings, she sat with chin cocked, narrowing her blue eyes to stare out the window, apparently lost in thought.

When Janssen entered the room, she turned and drew her lips into a supportive greeting. "You were impressive as usual," she said, smiling up at him. "You're a natural for this."

Janssen could tell she was in a hurry, but appreciated her support, however brief it had to be considering the pressures of her own job. He leaned down and brushed his lips against the side of her face. "Thanks. That means a lot. I know I can count on your honesty."

The ringer on his Q watch went off. "It's Jenn."

Dropping into the plush leather of his chair, he loosened his tie, reached for the glass of minted iced tea on his desk, and punched a button. It felt good to be off his feet.

"You forgot to say cheese," Jenna teased, as the animated face of his sister billowed in front of him in a hologram.

"Yeah, well, it was kind of a serious subject." He took a swallow of the tea. The cool, tangy liquid felt refreshing on his throat.

"You sure? I thought it was a little lighthearted there for a minute." Her voice mellowed. "But are you all right? Your face looked awfully pale ... and strained. I've never seen you look quite so fragile."

"I'm fine."

"Don't lie to me, Janssen. I'm your older sister, don't forget."

He laughed. "I can't forget. You always remind me."

"Well, you did a great job. You're a celebrity now, you know. My students were watching and are very impressed you're my brother. Maybe sometime soon you could do a virtual with them?"

"I'd like that. Let's do it."

When his Q watch signaled again, he clicked it on and winked at Charlie. In the hologram before him the winsome image of a beautiful young woman's face appeared, deep brown eyes gazing out from beneath lush lashes.

"Daddy, you were wonderful," she cooed. She blinked her eyes and paused awkwardly. "But is something wrong? You didn't look like you felt good. Your eyes ... you looked like you were in pain."

"I'm fine, Evie. I'm fine. Just kind of an intense conference, that's all."

"All the women in your life." Charlie laughed when Janssen clicked off his phone a few minutes later. "Remember now, the kids are coming over for dinner tonight. Evie's picking up your dad."

He nodded and pursed his lips in mild surprise. He'd forgotten. "Shall I ... "

"You're welcome to invite Jenn if you like."

Accompanying Charlie back into the outer office, Janssen saw members of his staff standing in front of the large screen of the Global Illusion TV in the sitting area. Danny sat in one of the blue high-back chairs. Turning to see what they were watching, Janssen was startled to see his own face on the screen. "So much for staying under the radar."

Charlie grinned at her husband as he shook his head in resignation. She pointed a well-manicured index finger at him. "See, you're a celebrity—like Jenna said."

A Global Illusion TV news analyst trumpeted the latest from the nation's capital.

"A few minutes ago, in the press conference given by Janssen Aryan LaMarche, it became clear why the president chose him to go on this important mission, now dubbed Operation Jocko. Although Janssen LaMarche has only held mid-level positions in the State Department prior to this time, he apparently has close ties to leaders in the small nation of Tajikistan."

After recounting Janssen's credentials and personal relationships in the Tajik government and describing pivotal moments in the press conference, the moderator asked his cohost to chime in.

"Well, Mat, Janssen LaMarche is reputed to be a man with great charisma, one who listens and not just talks, a man with a great deal of wisdom and a way with words, although in an awkward moment in the press conference he fumbled a few of them today. He has served in the US Foreign Service for nineteen years and speaks several languages, the Tajik language apparently being one of them."

"I'd say it sounds like Janssen LaMarche may be one of the State Department's best-kept secrets, Emily. In this world crisis, it may be he's not only the best man for this mission, but the only one who can quickly restore a sense of security to our planet. As he said, he will not have to take additional time to establish his credentials in a country we don't deal with every day. He's already got the respect of the Tajiks."

The moderator resumed. "Now on to other news. The US decline in population has brought about a controversial move to ... "

"There you go." Charlie patted Janssen on the arm. "I've got to get back to work. See you tonight."

Shaking his head, Janssen walked back into his office, closed the door, and collapsed into the comfort of black leather. The pain was gone now, but he felt weak from the intensity of the morning's ordeal. He pulled off his tie, leaned back, stretched out his legs and stared vacantly at the ceiling.

Tajikistan. The weapons. Where did they come from?

Questions rolled across the screen of his mind. How long had they been in that dark cave? Was his relationship with Jocko strong enough to secure them for the United States? What did Jocko know about them? He recalled the scowl on Trent Garrison's face and his accusatory tone. What if he *did* have to take a tough stand? But he didn't anticipate that happening.

He lowered his eyes and allowed his gaze to rest upon a picture of his mother standing on a cliff overlooking the Pacific. Jenna had taken the portrait and texted it to everyone in the family. Later, when he visited Tajikistan, he'd seen the picture atop a cabinet in his grandparents' living room.

Janssen rubbed his fingers along the edge of his chin, then slipped his fingers down his neck and inside the collar of his shirt, where he felt for the familiar links of coarse metal. He hooked his forefinger around the gold chain. Cocking his neck a little to the left, he unbuttoned his collar and drew the chain through the opening at his throat. A gold medallion swung from the chain, and Janssen brought it up in front of his face, turning it around in his hand to stare for a moment at the rose engraved in the middle. He dropped it back inside his shirt just as his intercom buzzed.

"Sir, Sandy from Dr. Monnihan's office wants to speak with you."

The warm feelings of anticipation that engulfed him a moment earlier evaporated into a dull slithering dread. His breakfast felt like lead in his stomach. "Put her on."

"Mr. LaMarche?"

"Yes."

"Your lab tests have been completed, and Dr. Monnihan would like to meet with you as soon as possible. Would one o'clock this afternoon work for you?"

"Could I talk to him by phone?"

"He wants to see you in person."

CHAPTER FIVE

In spite of the cool air circulating through Dr. Monnihan's office, beads of perspiration spread out in waves from Janssen's throat into his face and down onto his chest. His dark eyes searched the doctor's compassionate but steady gaze, their eyes locked in reluctant mutual understanding. He sat motionless for one full minute before he spoke.

"So you're saying this ... Ichiban Syndrome is a disease that moves quickly and has no cure. But ... is it terminal? Or is it a crippling disease that lingers on indefinitely?"

Dr. Monnihan sighed and shook his head.

"It's terminal, Janssen. I'm sorry." He pushed back his brown leather chair and repositioned it so the two of them were facing each other. He watched Janssen, his face a blend of professional composure and abject sympathy.

"How long do I have? And what can I expect?"

"The first stage can last quite a while. From what you've told me, you've apparently been experiencing these pains for the past year. I believe you may have now entered stage two. Ichiban Syndrome is a progressive neuromuscular disorder. The pains are intermittent, gradually growing in strength and duration. In the second stage, you feel intense cramping and contractions of the smooth muscles. But the third stage is the worrisome part."

He paused, and Janssen felt his heart dropping into his groin.

"You know you're Stage Three," Monnihan continued, "when you experience a triad of symptoms—the pain and muscular contractions, plus various visual disorders."

"Visual disorders? What, for instance?"

"Dizziness, vertigo, twitching of the eyes—what we call nystagmus. It can take a variety of forms." He pressed his lips together and searched Janssen's face. "When these symptoms begin, you will have two weeks at most. After that ..." He lifted and then dropped his hands in a helpless gesture. "I hate to do this, Janssen, but I know you want to be prepared."

Jansssen took slow, short breaths to steel himself. "Yes."

"At the end there are seizures, vomiting, maybe an inability to swallow, and then in forty-eight hours, it's all over."

Janssen inhaled deeply and held his breath to steady the emotion rising from his gut. He didn't want to call it fear, but he could feel his heart pounding against his rib cage. His throat constricted into a tight knot. "I see."

"I'm sorry, Janssen." Dr. Monnihan shook his head. His eyes filled with compassion. "I wish there was something I could do. I know you're getting ready for an important mission abroad. We'll hope things hold off for a while." He swiveled his chair back to the desk. "I can give you medication for the pain." He leaned toward his left, spoke into his TIR, pressed a button and watched some words pop up on the screen.

"You can pick up the prescription in twenty minutes. And here..." He turned once again to his TIR, said something indistinguishable into it, and pressed the button. "I'm also prescribing an herbal supplement and a multi-vitamin heavy in vitamins B and E. They might help. And drink lots of water." He ran his hand through his salt and pepper hair, leaned against the back of his chair, and sighed. "Most importantly, whenever you feel the pain coming on, be sure to rest, Janssen. Don't push yourself."

Janssen felt bolted to his chair, his body like lead. Sweat soaked his collar. His mind swirled.

Now. Now this would happen.

Deep down in his innermost soul, an urgency took a firm, unyielding hold.

The mission must go on.

He had to accomplish this task. Too much was at stake. There was an answer somewhere, and he'd find it.

He reached over and grabbed the doctor's hand. "Thanks, Jim. I'll make it. Somehow I will."

"If anyone can, Janssen, you're the one."

The balloons bobbed about against the back window of Evie's car, making it difficult for her to see out the rear window.

I hope Grandfather's ready, Evie thought anxiously. *I want to get back before Daddy gets home.* She turned onto a side street and pulled into the driveway of a stately white two-story house. Hurrying up the walkway, she rang the doorbell and listened as the chimes rang out the tune to "Anchors Away." As it ended, the door swung open, and a handsome elderly man with white hair and mustache stood before her, his back as straight as a ship's masthead.

"Hi, Grandfather."

"Hello, Evie. You're right on time."

"So are you," she laughed. "I'm glad. I need to get back and get ready for Daddy's homecoming."

Evie waited as Phillip LaMarche pulled the door shut and jerked it back and forth several times to convince himself it was secure.

"Did you see Daddy's press conference today?" Evie asked as she took his arm and proceeded down the walkway to the car.

He stopped in mid stride, turned to Evie, and slowly nodded his head. "Yes, I did. I imagine Uncle *Jocko* saw it too. And I dare say he may not have received it warmly. I was appalled at Janssen's use of his nickname. Uncle *Jocko* indeed!"

"Oh, nobody cares." Evie shrugged her shoulders. "It gave a light tone to the press conference. Everyone laughed." She pushed her blonde hair back off her face and tossed her head. "Hopefully, Uncle Jocko isn't that uptight. I thought Daddy was marvelous. He did look a little peaked though."

"Yes, he lacked a little of his usual vitality."

Evie popped the lock on the passenger side of the blue Volvo. The door sprang open and she reached in to push a purple balloon out of the way. "Here. Be careful of the balloons. They're flying all over the place."

"What in heaven's name do you have all these balloons for?" Phillip asked as he slowly clambered inside.

Evie cocked her chin upwards and narrowed her eyes at her grandfather. Shutting his door, she circled to the driver's side of the Volvo, climbed in, and began backing down the driveway. "I got the balloons to celebrate Daddy's press conference, Grandfather. It's not every day someone has a major press conference on Global Illusion TV."

She turned on her blinker and waited as two boys on air skates sailed by in front of her, then made a left turn onto the highway. "Have you heard the news anchors talking about Daddy? He's become a national hero overnight."

"I just hope he goes over as well with Jumakhan." Rubber tires squealed and Phillip lurched forward, reaching out to brace himself against the front console and window frame.

"Car in right lane," an automated voice warned as the car lurched to the left.

"Evie! Watch what you're doing. You almost pulled in front of that car."

Evie straightened the wheel. "I didn't see it. He must have been in my blind spot."

"You have a lot of blind spots, I'd say—red ones, blue ones, yellow ones, green ones ..."

"Okay, Grandfather, I get the point."

Janssen was not prepared for balloons. Nor for the air of celebration throughout the house. With his luck reversing itself so suddenly, he'd almost forgotten the high point at the beginning of this day. But he was glad for the festivity, because it reminded him he had choices. He could look down into the doldrums of his recent misfortune, or up toward the noble goal of helping to create a stable environment in the world. He had an important role to play, and he planned to play it. What took place after that was beyond his control. But today was his.

As he shut the door behind him, Evie emerged from around the corner to the hallway in a white tie-front blouse and breezy black and white gingham skirt that swished about the tops of her ankles. She slipped her arm through his as he approached the family room. "I was so proud of you today," she said. "You were wonderful, Daddy."

"Thanks, honey. Are you responsible for the balloons?"

"We all did it. We wanted to celebrate your wonderful success."

"Ahh. But you have a way of making things a little more special." He smiled into her eyes and squeezed the hand she draped around his arm. Just the sight of her always cheered him up.

Stepping into the wide-open family room area, he spotted his elderly father sitting in the armchair near the fireplace. "Dad. It's good to see you. Glad you could make it."

"It was nice of your wife to invite me."

Janssen perched on the edge of the slipcovered couch opposite his father. "What did you think of the press conference? Did you see it?"

His father looked at him sideways, and drew his lips down to a thin line. He nodded.

"Fine, Janssen, fine ..." His voice trailed off with an air of aggravation. "I have some doubts about that Uncle Jocko remark, however."

Janssen frowned, shook his head, and brushed his fingers along the soft bristles of his mustache. "I don't know why I said that. I ... I was distracted ... had a sudden cramp, and you know, I'm not used to all those cameras. How do you think Jumakhan'll react if he watched it?"

"If? I think you can be assured he *did* watch it, or will watch it on the Web if he didn't see it initially," his father retorted. "I haven't talked to Jumakhan for some time, so I'm not sure what his disposition is these days. But I know the officials of Tajikistan do not take their positions lightly. He could be the brunt of some jokes over there. That might not bode too well for you."

Janssen grimaced. "I don't know what got into me. Do you have any suggestions as to how we ... I ... can make it up to him?"

"Let me think about it." Phillip shook his head again and crossed his arms in front of his narrow chest. "I just can't believe you made a blunder like that."

Jenna was smiling at Janssen from the other side of the granite-faced fireplace.

His peripheral vision caught her standing there in a red print dress, the twinkle in her green eyes immediately stealing his attention away from his father. He looked up and saw her smirking at him. A hint of dimple bit into her cheek.

"When did you come in?" Janssen said, jumping up and taking a step toward her. "I didn't see you."

"Oh, you know me. Sneaky as always. Big sister is always watching, you know."

Janssen laughed. "Big sister definitely is sneaky. I'll agree with that."

Jenna giggled and grabbed his arm, leaning closer to whisper in his ear. "I take it Dad wasn't too keen on your remarks about Uncle Jocko."

"Hardly." Janssen bent over the gray marble coffee table and took a potato chip from a ceramic bowl. He listened to the crunch and enjoyed the sensation of the salty morsel, then reached for another chip and turned back to his sister.

"Why did you call him that anyway?" she asked.

"I dunno. Really don't. Just slipped."

"That's not like you, Janssen."

"I know."

She tilted her head to the side and drilled his eyes with her gaze. "Square with me. Something's wrong."

Janssen stared at her silently.

He had decided not to tell the family about his diagnosis. He didn't want to feel obligated to explain why he was proceeding with his responsibilities in Tajikistan. The women in his family, loving as they were, would try to talk him into a more sedentary existence to hopefully postpone the inevitable. Jenna, however, had a way of boring into his soul, and he felt his resolve weaken a little.

But not now.

"I'm okay," he finally said.

"How about lunch Wednesday?" Jenna suggested. "We have a work day at school and I need to go to the Smithsonian to plan a field trip. I could meet you at one."

"I've got a heavy schedule, Jenn. I'm meeting with President Gelford tomorrow, and Wednesday, I expect to be getting into some serious negotiations. I don't know. I'll give you a call."

"Lah di dah. Meeting with the president. Well, I guess if I have to take a back seat ..." She giggled.

Charlie's slim, tall figure slipped from the dining room to stand by Janssen's side. "Dinner's ready, if you've come down from the clouds yet."

"Thanks, Charlie."

As they strode beneath the sprays of multicolored balloons above the doorway and passed into the classically styled dining room, the rich aroma of well-seasoned meat greeted them. Janssen inhaled deeply.

"Ahhh, let me guess. Rack of lamb."

"Your favorite," Charlie said with a knowing smile. "Of course."

Janssen walked to his place at the head of the table and stood behind his armchair as the family streamed into the room.

"Everyone, help yourself from the credenza, then take a seat wherever," Charlie instructed.

"In my day, we always used to sit at the table and pass the food around," Phillip said with a superior air as he dished some creamed spinach onto his plate. "It was more elegant. But I guess everything is casual now."

Charlie pushed her hair behind her ear and fingered her earring. "I could get one of those new android butlers," she said. "Then we could sit at the table and be served. But I think they seem a bit pretentious."

"Ach," Phillip said, moving along to the mashed potatoes. "What is the world coming to? Android butlers!"

Janssen finished filling his plate, then took his seat. As he shook the folds out of his napkin to place it on his lap, he felt a hand on his shoulder.

"I hear you did a great job, Dad."

"Alexander. I didn't see you." Janssen shifted his body so he could see his son over his shoulder. "Glad you could make it."

Alexander stood behind him. He was a tall young man with wavy dark hair and deep-set eyes. "Didn't get to see all of your press conference. Had clients at the time. But I recorded it." Alexander spoke rapidly and decisively as if accustomed to giving high-pressure sales pitches. "But what I saw was very impressive. You were the featured story on the news tonight."

"With twenty-four-hour news, they need to talk about something. Did you just get here? I didn't see you earlier."

"I was in the study. Talking to a client on my Q."

"Oh, I see. How's business?"

"Real good. Real good." Alexander eased himself over to the credenza and stabbed the meat fork into a large portion of ribs, then dropped it onto his plate. "We're talking about expanding some more to take advantage of the slow economy. Rates are low."

"Expanding? You mean ..."

"Buying up businesses that are going under."

Janssen nodded.

Where does my son's zealous ambition come from? Certainly not from me.

He took a bite of the lamb and quietly savored the juicy, delicate flavor of the well-seasoned meat.

"To our rising star," Charlie said, raising her goblet of wine toward Janssen.

"Hear, hear." All eyes converged on Janssen as together everyone raised their glasses in his direction.

He smiled at the clinking of the crystal and nodded his head appreciatively. "And may there be no falling stars over Tajikistan."

A mixture of subdued laughter, giggles, and guffaws spread around the table.

Phillip took a sip of wine, then shook his head. "I still can't believe you made that comment about Jumakhan. *Uncle Jocko*. How could you call him that in a national press conference? It sounds so—common."

"Probably because I didn't go to the Academy. Lack of breeding, you know."

Janssen took another sip of his wine and set the glass on the table. Jenna stifled a laugh and pretended to cough.

"You joke about it," Phillip said, "but the discipline learned at the Academy does enhance your professional demeanor."

"No doubt, Father."

"Charlie, this rack of lamb is absolutely fabulous," Jenna interjected. "I love what you do to it."

Janssen shot her a look of appreciation. He could always count on his sister to come to his aid.

"Mom has the gift of entertaining." Evie paused with her fork in the air. "I need to get some of your recipes, Mom."

"Any time." Charlie swallowed and cleared her throat. "Say, Evie, how are you doing with Sweet Peas? Is your little store making any money yet?"

"Well, not quite." Evie put down her fork. "But it should start turning around before long."

"It could start turning around sooner if she'd stop giving everything away," Alexander added sarcastically.

Evie sighed. "I'm selling things too. But sometimes people come in with such need. I just can't turn them out into the street with nothing."

"Like what?" Charlie asked.

"Well, like the other day this young mother came into Sweet Peas with a newborn baby. She was a single mother—no husband, no family, nothing. She had no money, a one-room apartment, and no place for her baby to sleep."

"So what did you do?"

"I gave her a crib."

Alexander groaned, and a look of disapproval spread over her mother's face.

"But it was an old crib," Evie added quickly. "Not one of the better ones. Couldn't have gotten much for it anyway. After all, I am running a thrift store." She paused and began running her finger along the base of the crystal wineglass. "The things aren't new anyway. And that's one of the pitfalls of having a thrift store for children. Mothers come in who don't have any money, and they need stuff."

"And they know where to find a soft touch," Alexander interjected. He picked up a rib and took a sizable to-the-bone bite. "Ummm. Delicious."

"That's why we have charities—to help people like that. A business isn't expected to give things away," Charlie said. "Evie, you have a good heart, but you're too sentimental. You need to learn where to draw the line."

"Well, it's hard not to help people when they need it." She pulled herself up more erect in her chair. "Anyway, I'm not apologizing for helping people. I want to do it."

"I help people," Phillip commented, forking up his creamed spinach. "I give to United Way every year."

Janssen felt his body tensing. He hated this. Why did everyone have to give Evie such a hard time for her generosity? At twenty-four years old, she'd get a good learning experience from it.

Charlie tossed her head, making her earrings bob. "Janssen, I think we should have set Evie up in a business that has less philanthropic tendencies."

"It makes Evie happy to do this. She'll be fine," Janssen took a swallow from his wineglass, set it down, and picked up his fork. "I love the name of her shop. 'Sweet Peas.'"

"Dick Tracy, Sparkle Plenty and Sweet Pea. Always one of your favorites," Jenna laughed.

"That's where we got the name," Evie said, brightening. "Daddy and I used to love reading those old comics we got at the antique shop. Li'l Abner was another of our favorites."

"It really is a cute name," Jenna observed. "You'll get the hang of things before long."

Evie shot her aunt a look of thanks for the encouraging words.

"Well, to change the subject," Charlie said, readjusting the neckline of her sweater and directing her conversation to Phillip. "How is Sarah doing? Is she any better?"

"No," he responded matter-of-factly as he bit into a piece of lettuce. "She's dying."

Jenna set her glass down on the table with a thud, causing drops of wine to splash on the tablecloth, a look of deep sorrow gathering over her face.

"Dad! I didn't know."

Sarah had worked for their family for years as a housekeeper, and later as a caregiver for their mother when she became sick. Sarah had always been there for family emergencies, and had earned the affection of them all. Janssen, watching Jenna, felt his sister's reaction as if it were his own.

"What's wrong with her?" Jenna asked.

"Cancer, I think. Her condition worsened in the past two weeks."

"But they have a cure for cancer."

"Yes, well, they apparently diagnosed it incorrectly at first. Now it's too advanced."

Jenna rubbed her palms along the edge of the table in agitation. "That's terrible."

"It's a part of life," her father said in the same matter-of-fact tone. "When it's your turn to die, it's just your turn to die, that's all."

The blood drained from Janssen's face. The skin of his forehead and neck grew clammy. Where was his father's compassion? In his mind's eye he saw Sarah scurrying about his mother when she was sick, fluffing the pillows, bringing her tea, sitting at her side and reading to her from the Bible. Now she was dying.

And so was he. But who knew? He wondered what his father would say about him.

When it's your turn to die, it's your turn to die?

Is that how it was? He looked around the table, first at Evie, the apple of his heart. It would be hardest to leave her. And Jenn, his kindred spirit. They'd always been able to read each other like a book. Charlie would miss him and grieve, but she would move on. She was a strong and beautiful woman. They had a great friendship, but she was a survivor. She'd be fine. And Alexander? Well, Alexander was Alexander.

He looked at Evie, her blonde hair pulled back in a bun, then at Jenna's pixie face. He was not going to leave them. He was not going to die. He had too much to do. The doctor was wrong. He was not going to die.

"Janssen." It was Jenna who brought him out of his reverie. "You look like you ate too many mashed potatoes. Your face is absolutely white."

CHAPTER SIX

Evie couldn't sleep. That night she tossed and turned, seeing her father's face as he'd looked at the dinner table that evening. Every bit of color had drained from his countenance. She remembered him at the press conference, stopping in the midst of his response, stumbling over his words, leaning on the podium. It was not like him.

Later, in the middle of the night, she awakened from a fitful sleep to find herself crying out, "God, help my father. Please help him." Her heart pounded, and her breathing was heavy. She had no idea why she was so troubled, but certainly something was wrong. Finally, towards morning, she fell into a deep slumber.

When she awoke, bright sunlight streamed through the bedroom windows. She'd overslept.

THE OVAL OFFICE

Janssen LaMarche strode confidently up the steps of 1600 Pennsylvania Avenue. With his impressive stature and self-possessed demeanor, he looked completely at home in the White House. Against the foundation of a square jaw and high cheekbones, his olive complexion was accentuated by a shock of dark hair beginning to gray at the temples. His thick mustache and heavy eyebrows enhanced the depth of expression in his dark eyes, giving Janssen a rugged but handsome appearance.

At the top of the steps, Janssen paused. This was the third time this week he'd been invited to the White House. He glanced up at the marble columns beside him and tapped the edge of an ITV disc against the palm of his left hand. Who would have thought the path he'd chosen in life would lead him here? If he had pursued his father's dream for him—accepted an appointment to Annapolis, played by the rules, joined in the political game—one might have foreseen his new role. But even though Janssen had chosen to do life his own way, here he was, right in the place his father had hoped for.

He nodded to the Marine guard who opened the door to admit him to the building, and chuckled to himself as he thought back on the night before. His father couldn't stomach the idea he was actually proud of his son. That would negate all his former admonitions and denunciations of Janssen's unconventional choices. His 'Uncle Jocko' gaff *had* been unwise, but his father would be full of bravado when he met with his friends at the club that evening for dinner. *"Did you see my son on Global Illusion TV? Yes, Janssen LaMarche. That's my son. The man the president has chosen for the mission to Tajikistan."*

As Gelford's aide opened the door to the Oval Office, the atmosphere of the majestic room steeped in over a century of history caused him to pause. He was no longer just an observer, but a player. The mission he would lead was wrapped in the drama of history. His leadership could bring the country, and the world, into a place of safety or danger—even demise.

Hesitating a moment longer and straightening his tie, he passed through the door and into the destiny awaiting him inside. Dr. Monnihan's words of portent from the day before nibbled at his mind, but he shut them out as he caught the eye of President Gelford.

"LaMarche. Excellent." Collin Gelford strode across the room, extending his hand. "I believe almost everyone is here now. Let me introduce you." He paused. "Good job with the press conference, by the way."

Janssen steeled himself, waiting for the president to allude to the Uncle Jocko incident. He felt a surge of relief when, instead, Gelford waved him over toward one of the blue striped chairs.

"Come meet the members of your team. You've already met Chip Neely, our Ambassador to Tajikistan."

Janssen cordially shook the hand of the elderly gentleman. "Ambassador," he responded amicably. "I'm looking forward to our working together."

The thin lines at the corners of Neely's narrow eyes crinkled into an affable smile. "Same here. I know your input will be most valuable, especially since your history with this country appears to be quite extensive."

Janssen nodded. Approaching retirement, Chip Neely had a long tenure in the consulate. The weapons discovery in Tajikistan had brought unexpected drama to what was to have been an easy last ambassadorship.

"Here, meet Bradley Jones." The president turned and introduced a muscular African-American man who walked up to join them. "Jones is a chemical weapons specialist from Sandia National Laboratories and a former Ranger. With his background, he'll add a wide range of talent to the munitions team."

Janssen nodded to him and took his hand. "I'm sure your expertise will be greatly appreciated, Mr. Jones."

"I hope to be of service, sir."

Gelford turned to peruse the room. "Where's Quigley?"

Janssen heard the name as if in a fog. "Quigley?" Janssen surprised even himself with his tone of bewilderment and looked quizzically at the president.

"Yes, Michael Quigley. He'll be going with you to head up the munitions contingent of your team, to identify and contain whatever weapons are over there."

His mind whirling, Janssen saw the president study his changed expression.

"Do you know him?" Gelford said.

Janssen stared at the president for a second, letting the name settle into his brain.

Michael Quigley.

The name bounced around inside his head, and for a moment his mind froze.

"Yes," Janssen said finally. His gaze drifted downward from the president to the colorful presidential seal woven into the carpet. Ghosts of Jenna's tear-stained face floated before his eyes, diminishing the great seal into a swirl of colors and images. He pushed those thoughts away now as he'd always done, and once more focused his attention on President Gelford.

Not appearing to notice Janssen's temporary mental absence, the president turned to a young redhead sitting on one of the gold brocade couches. "Let me introduce you to your media coordinator, Bethany Chambers. I guess you know you'll be accompanied by a contingent of media correspondents."

Forcefully bringing his mind under control, Janssen nodded, smiling at the woman studying a screen on her Q watch. He had forgotten this part of the negotiation process. The private meetings and then the public explanations, interpretations—the spin.

"And you know Secretary Tomlin, of course," Gelford said, as he continued around the circle of those in attendance.

"Yes." Janssen took the hand of the Secretary of State and shook it firmly. They'd spoken extensively at their prior meeting, and despite the man's brusqueness, Janssen appreciated the man's openness and honesty in sharing the important role before him, and the glory—or infamy—accompanying it.

"And you met Randall Robertson the other day." The young aide approached from the president's desk. "Randall is a Deputy Chief of Staff. He'll be the liaison between you and the White House. He'll keep me abreast of things in general, so you can focus on negotiations with President Rajanov and your uncle ... Jocko, is it?"

The laughter was polite, but the mutual sentiment of amusement was genuine. It was the light moment Janssen had expected. After the laughter subsided, everyone seemed more relaxed.

But Janssen felt the dark clouds rising into his mind once more. Jenna's face rolled before his eyes, followed by Michael's.

You can't separate them. The personal and the public— the role we play, and the real person who hides inside. Somehow it all runs together.

Just as Evie locked the door to her shop, rain pelted her. She thought of her umbrashield wand lying on the back seat of her car and sighed. *Where is my wand when I need it?*

Well, not with me.

Holding her purse over her head, she raced through the driving rain to her car and pressed the button on her key ring to activate the rain awning. The hood of the trunk popped up. She groaned as she ran her finger over the wet key fob to find the correct button. This time the translucent gold rain awning spread out to protect the driver's door. With rain splashing against her face and beating down against her shoulders and back, Evie hurried to the back of the Volvo and closed the trunk lid. A cool wetness hugged the skin of her arms as heavy raindrops seeped through her lightweight shirt jacket, penetrating the turtleneck underneath.

She slipped under the rain awning, clicked the doors open, then jumped into the driver's seat—water dripping from her clothes and puddling on the floor at her feet. She looked at herself in the rearview mirror. The hair hanging at her shoulders had soaked up the rain like a wet mop.

Nothing had gone right today. Because she'd overslept this morning, she'd missed her appointment with Mrs. Annabelle Danamaker, who wanted to donate an entire wardrobe of upscale children's clothing to Sweet Peas. Now Mrs. Danamaker was angry with Evie for standing her up. *And understandably so. Who wouldn't be?*

At noon, Sweet Peas had been swamped with customers when the computers went down. Evie'd had to do all the transactions by hand, and the repairman couldn't come and fix her computer till the next morning. Not wanting to throw the inventory system any further out of whack, she decided to close shop early and check on her dad. She was worried about him, and now she was soaking wet.

A deep growl rumbled through her stomach.

And she was hungry.

She decided to get some fast food at a drive-through before leaving Alexandria. She could wait in the car at the State Department Building and eat lunch until the rain stopped. Maybe she could even dry out a little before she went in to see her dad. Pulling out of the alley, Evie saw a man parked in a green Toyota staring at her.

Men.

Seeing the familiar yellow and red logo of her favorite chain up ahead, she pulled into the drive. The greasy aroma of hamburgers wafted through her car's ventilating system. Her stomach churned in anticipation.

Just as she rounded the building to enter the drive-through for Burger World, a black Honda with a University of Kansas sticker on the back cut in front of her, splashing mud over her front window. Her anti-magnetic bumpers prevented a collision, but caused the Volvo to jerk badly.

"Car cutting in from right front side," warned the car's mechanical voice.

"I know," Evie responded to the automated warning device. "Believe me, I see it." Resisting the temptation to lean on the horn, she glared piercing arrows at the driver instead.

Several minutes later, with the rain still drumming on her roof, she pulled into a parking place at the top of 22nd Street near the State Department's C Street entrance. The hamburger was still nice and hot. Everything she wanted at that moment caught up with her on this one bun, and she purred her approval as she settled comfortably on the seat and watched the rain stream in narrow rivulets down the windshield.

Hovaways puffed along the sidewalk. People scurried by in the rain. A tall young man beneath his translucent umbrashield walked past her car, crossed the street, and breezed along the walkway toward the heavy glass doors of the State Department. The wind blew open his tweed jacket and buffeted his umbrashield just as he approached the covered entrance. Closing the umbrashield, he put the wand in the pocket of his jacket and disappeared inside.

Evie checked herself in her mirror and groaned. *What a mess. I hope Daddy doesn't have anyone important in his office when I come in looking like a drowned street woman.*

CHAPTER SEVEN

Janssen did not see Michael Quigley when he first entered the Oval Office. Michael had entered unobtrusively, and was standing beside the marble fireplace talking to Bradley Jones when Janssen first spied him. His former brother-in-law had not changed much, except his sandy hair was now thinning and mixed with gray. He had the same prominent cheekbones, fair skin, and a wide, firm-set mouth.

"Oh, there you are, Quigley. We were just about to start without you." The president looked around the room to get the attention of the others and pointed to the sitting area. "Why don't each of you take a seat over here. Then we'll begin."

Janssen strode to the empty couch and sat down at one end. He set an ITV disc on his lap and unbuttoned his jacket.

Robertson joined him at the other end, smiled at Bethany Chambers across from them, and opened a screen on his Q watch.

After Secretary Tomlin and Bradley Jones took hardback chairs near the front, Michael Quigley slipped to a blue striped chair beside Ambassador Neely. Grabbing the back of it, Michael stepped to the front and sat unevenly, angling his body to the left. He crossed one leg over the other, leaned back, and folded his arms across his chest.

Halfway between the sitting area and his desk, the president unbuttoned his coat and stood with legs apart, hands folded behind his back.

"Each of you, I'm sure, understands the importance of this mission," he began. "Weapons of mass destruction have been unheard of for twenty years. We are unprepared for the devastation they could cause. Whether they are nuclear, chemical or biological, their discovery in Tajikistan has shocked the world into the realization that danger still lurks in the unknown hiding places of the past."

Gelford cleared his throat and glanced at Bradley Jones. "What makes the situation particularly ominous is a top secret report that came to my attention the day before yesterday regarding a discovery in Syria in 2038." He turned to Bradley Jones and relaxed his arms to his side. "Jones, I believe you can articulate this information more clearly than I. Would you please explain briefly what was in the report? The ramifications will be obvious."

Jones nodded. "Yes, sir, Mr. President." Jones placed the palms of his hands on his knees, then rose tentatively to his feet and turned to face the others. "As the president said, about fourteen years ago, US Special Forces found the remains of a chemistry lab in an underground bunker in Syria, where they discovered encrypted notes from a Lithuanian scientist. They sent the notes back to be analyzed by the Stanford University biophysics lab, and after more than three years of research, the lab issued a report, stating the formula was a preservative that would not degrade when combined with chemicals or biological products."

The brisk, rhythmic tune of a samba caused Jones and the others to look towards Bethany, whose face colored as she pushed a button on her Q watch. "Sorry."

Jones chuckled and continued. "Further testing confirmed this compound was a preservative that maintained the potency of both chemical and biological weapons and would prolong their shelf life indefinitely. Since then we have found references to weapons called Sarin X50 and Anthrax Lilliputian LD."

Over his left shoulder, Janssen noticed movement from Michael, who had uncrossed his arms and shifted in his chair.

"I'll skip the technical explanations," Jones continued, "but we believe the references pertain to enhanced versions of the originals, which were mixed with the preservative formula and in theory would last indefinitely. Although we have never found such weapons, intelligence points to strong evidence of their development and production. One of my roles over the past few years has been to track down any leads which might help us find them." He glanced back at Gelford. "That's why I was chosen for this mission. After the weapons were found in Tajikistan, it seemed a good idea for me to go along ... just in case." He nodded to Michael Quigley. "And I am honored to be on this team." Jones turned toward the president again, then sat down.

Gelford took two steps closer to those assembled.

"Thank you, Jones. I want to remind you all, this is top secret information." The president assumed his previous stance with his hands folded behind his back and continued. "But you can see it doesn't matter what kind of weapons these turn out to be. Until they are safely in our hands, the world sits in the shadow of danger. It's a danger hovering just beyond our grasp, but close enough to unleash unspeakable horrors upon us, should we fail in our mission. It won't be a simple task, and the stakes are high."

He paused and scrutinized each person in the room, weighing the impact of his words. He put his hands on his hips and frowned, his eyes growing darker and more intense as he continued speaking.

"But we're approaching our goal with our hands tied behind our backs. Unfortunately, we're not moving forward out of the same position of strength the US once enjoyed. We can't risk a military operation. We must achieve victory through diplomacy." He emphasized each of these last words with an emphatic gesture. "World peace has become increasingly fragile."

"Amen to that," Tomlin said, crossing his legs in the opposite direction, left over right.

President Gelford slid his hands into his pockets.

"Unfortunately our maturing population demographics, diminishing tax base, and sagging economy weaken us further. The foundations of our world leadership have shifted precariously. Now, as the only superpower truly devoted to peace, the challenge we face in Tajikistan must be won on the diplomatic front. And I emphasize *must*."

Bradley Jones peered over his shoulder at Michael Quigley, then at Secretary Tomlin, who sat rubbing his palms together.

"We're fortunate to have a gifted and well-connected man to carry out this mission—Janssen LaMarche." All eyes shifted toward Janssen. "A lot rests on his shoulders, but the rest of us in this room have the responsibility of giving him whatever support he needs to help him accomplish the goal. Tomlin swiveled in his chair to indicate his approval.

"I repeat," Gelford continued, "and I can't emphasize it too much—this mission must be carried out through my policy of soft power, and thus this negotiation process. There is no alternative."

He scanned the expressions on their faces, apparently waiting for nods of understanding and consent, then directed his gaze toward Quigley.

"There will be three phases to the mission. For those of you who have not yet met Michael Quigley ..." The president motioned towards Quigley with his right hand. "He will lead the munitions part of the team, which will be dispatched as a preliminary envoy to check out the weapons' location, what exactly is there, how large the cache is, and how safe they presently are."

Janssen and Michael quickly exchanged glances. Both men looked away.

"After the first group returns and their findings are analyzed, the entire team, headed by LaMarche, will return to Tajikistan for the primary negotiations. This group will be accompanied by the fanfare, the press, and all the rest." He nodded to Bethany Chambers. "Finally, once an agreement has been reached, the Secretary of State will join you to put on the finishing touches. Of course, I'm sure much of the negotiating will take place before anyone sets foot on foreign soil. Am I correct, LaMarche?"

"Absolutely, Mr. President. I have arranged phone conferences with Rajanov and Oqilov early tomorrow morning."

"Excellent." Gelford took another step closer to the group, placed his hands on the back of his hips and leaned forward. "Part of the challenge, of course, is to offset any financial gain the Tajikistan government would make from dealing with militant states or terrorist groups. We must be prepared to match whatever they are offered." He looked around at those assembled to see if he had made his point. Several of them nodded in understanding.

"Would you like to brief us now and share your thoughts, LaMarche?"

Janssen stepped to the spot being yielded by the president. He nodded at the assembly as he slipped the ITV disk from its package and slid it into a digital receiver, then watched a map fill the freestanding screen on the other side of the room.

"First, I want to give you a little geography lesson," he said. "How many of you are familiar with the country of Tajikistan?"

Ambassador Neely nodded his head, Michael gave a crooked smile, and Secretary Tomlin nodded and cleared his throat.

Looking out at the group assembled before him, Janssen attempted to push away the shadows of memory lurking in his mind. Regardless of where he focused his eyes, he could not get Michael Quigley out of his line of vision. Michael Quigley—the man who had abandoned his sister and broken her heart—was a member of his team. His discomfort with the idea of working with him continued to unnerve him.

Janssen cleared his throat to regain focus. "I want to give the rest of you an idea of the geography of the region, as that plays heavily on the strategy we must use for the mission."

Robertson leaned forward, head cocked to one side, chin leaning on his left hand.

"The tiny country of Tajikistan is shaped like the profile of a sick moose on his knees. The capital of Dushanbe is where the moose's eye would be, here in the south. Soghd Province, where the weapons were found, is in this northern area up here where the horns would be."

Everyone laughed. Janssen noticed even Michael could not restrain a chuckle, although he quickly caught himself and stiffened his back.

"Sorry," Janssen said. "You know I always used to fail those inkblot tests."

A couple of guffaws and chortles lightened the heavy atmosphere once again. Satisfied, Janssen continued.

"Tajikistan is surrounded by the countries of Afghanistan to the south, Uzbekistan to the west and north, and Kyrgyzstan and China to the east." Janssen waved his hand over the large land mass at the top of the map. "Russia has always been a significant player since the twentieth century, when Tajikistan was part of the Soviet Union."

Gazing at the map, Bradley Jones touched his fingers to his lips as he leaned forward and tilted his head to the right.

"While a moderate government is currently in control of Tajikistan, a radical Islamic group exerts a great deal of influence in this northern region. Since Soghd Province is separated from the rest of Tajikistan by high mountains, Soghd's culture and economic life are actually more similar to those of the neighboring country of Uzbekistan than Tajikistan."

"And I believe there are some militant Islamic groups in Uzbekistan," Ambassador Neely added, moving his stout body closer to the edge of his chair.

"The Ambassador has just touched on the key problem." Janssen pointed a finger in his direction. "For the past fifty years the Islamic Revival Party, known as the IRP, has had various degrees of influence in the government. In recent years it's become more of a threat to the People's Democratic Party, or PDP, which is the party in control. In the northern region of the Soghd Province there's continued to be civil strife because of Islamic radicals, some of whom cross over from Uzbekistan"—he nodded to Neely—"and others who are part of the IRP. It's a tense region, and the fact it's here the weapons were found is disturbing." He looked at the president, then at Secretary

Tomlin. "In the early 2000s, three terrorists apprehended by the US came from this northern area of Tajikistan."

Secretary Tomlin leaned back and raised his hands toward his face, the fingertips of both hands lightly touching in a steeple position. "Have you been in this northern region? Or just the capital?" he asked in a low gravelly voice.

Janssen's mind did a quick flashback. *Tall jagged mountains. Trails winding through underbrush. The laughter of olive-skinned boys.* "I spent time in the north with my grandfather one year. He was Prime Minister during that era, and he was determined to resolve a water dispute that had caused serious problems."

"And did he?" Bethany Chambers asked with a twinkle in her eyes.

"Yes, he did, eventually. It's what earned him the love of the Tajik people." His eyes involuntarily wandered to Michael, who blinked, turned his head away, then looked back and pursed his lips.

"He was a wise man. Kind of a Solomon, you might say." Janssen ejected the ITV disc and removed it from the receiver.

The secretary lowered his hands and moved to the edge of his chair. "Thanks for the briefing, LaMarche."

Janssen slipped to his earlier seat on the couch as the secretary rose and took his place in front of the team.

Standing erect with legs apart and hands again raised in front of his chin with fingers touching at the tips, the secretary immediately continued in his characteristic gritty voice.

"The first thing we must do is gather information and find out who we can rely on. I will contact the Saudis to see if we can get their support, and then do whatever is necessary regarding Russia, China, the British, and the EU. Ambassador Neely"—the secretary looked toward the elderly gentleman—"will undoubtedly have a take on Uzbekistan and Kyrgyzstan, since he has been stationed in that region."

The Ambassador nodded appreciatively. Janssen was glad the secretary was treating him as more than a figurehead.

The secretary turned once more to Janssen. "Do you have a plan for dealing with the internal workings of the Tajikistan government and the different factions there?"

"I'm working on that, Mr. Secretary. I'll keep you informed."

"Any questions for LaMarche or the secretary, or me?" the president asked, rising once again to his feet as the secretary moved back toward his chair.

Michael Quigley uncrossed his legs, gave the bridge of his nose an agitated rub, shifted his weight again, and moved closer to the front edge of the chair. He cleared his throat and looked from Janssen to Secretary Tomlin, then to Gelford.

"Questions? No. Except if Sarin X50 and anthrax are contained inside these weapons, we can't—I mean, *can't*—let anyone else buy them. Period."

CHAPTER EIGHT

If Danny leaned back in his chair, he had a clear line of vision right through two doorways to the front entrance of the office where he presently worked as public relations assistant to Janssen LaMarche. It intrigued him that when he sat close to his desk, working on the computer or hunched over while talking on the phone, he couldn't even see the outer office, but now, leaning back, he was staring straight at the front door.

Earlier he had downloaded several messages. A number of others lay on his desk. Phone calls had been pouring in while he was at lunch, all wanting interviews with Mr. LaMarche. *Who should I call back first? Time? CNN? Fox? How will Mr. LaMarche work all of these into his schedule?*

As he sat viewing the front entrance, the door swung open and in walked a totally drenched creature, straw-colored hair plastered to her head. A red, white and black plaid shirt hung heavily from her shoulders, while black slacks clung to a pair of skinny legs. Leslie Ann greeted her.

He rolled his chair back under his desk and punched some numbers on the phone. *CNN first.*

Okay, he said to himself after he had hung up from his third phone conversation. *CNN wants ten minutes at least. Fox wants fifteen, Time an hour—oh, boy. I don't know about this hour stuff. US News will probably want the same thing.*

Maybe I should wait till Mr. LaMarche gets back before I call the rest ... get an idea of what he's willing to do.

He leaned back in his chair once more, letting it roll back to where he could see the outer office again. He needed to think.

LaMarche had two weeks before his trip. Danny knew he planned to spend a lot of time on the phone negotiating before he actually left for Tajikistan. Maybe Shannon, his aide, could suggest ways to fit these lengthy interviews into their boss's schedule.

Danny stood up and was almost into the hallway when the front door flew open again. He blinked, then stared. Was this the same girl? Big, beautiful brown eyes smiled even before her mouth did. She breezed into the room, shaking her head to fluff out the golden hair streaming down her back. A dry red turtleneck was neatly tucked into her black pants, still damp and shiny enough to fit the contour of her shapely silhouette. Her plaid shirt was draped over one arm. She handed the key to Leslie Ann, smiled, and then let her gaze drift about the room. When her eyes got to Danny, her smile seemed to brighten. He had no idea how dumb the expression on his face must have looked, but his knees grew weak and began to buckle under him. His only thought was whether he could successfully fumble his way back to his chair and sit down.

When Danny finally gathered himself together, Shannon had already escorted the beautiful creature over to the chairs in the reception area. The sound from the ITV blared through the office. Shannon must have turned up the volume for her. Who was she waiting for? LaMarche? He threw on his brown tweed jacket and shuffled into the outer office, stopping at Leslie Ann's desk. "When will Mr. LaMarche be back?"

"Hard to say. He's meeting with the president. It was only supposed to last forty-five minutes or so, but you know how those things go. He's meeting his team, so things could get more involved than expected."

"Oh, uh." He stood awkwardly at the desk, trying to think of what to say next.

Leslie Ann looked up at him. "Anything else?"

"Who's in the reception area?"

Leslie Ann glanced in the direction he indicated. "You mean Evie? That's right, I guess you probably haven't met her yet. That's Mr. LaMarche's daughter."

"Mr. LaMarche's daughter?" he parroted back to her.

"That's right." She grinned at him. "Mr. LaMarche's daughter."

He squared his shoulders and tried to maintain an air of confidence. "In that case, it might be appropriate for me to meet her, don't you think? After all, I am PR. I need to know as much about Mr. LaMarche as possible, including meeting members of his family."

"I'll introduce you."

Evie was leaning her damp head against the back of one of the navy blue high-back chairs with her eyes closed. She jumped a little when she heard them coming, but quickly recovered her composure.

"Evie, I want to introduce you to the newest member of your dad's staff. Danny Saunders. He's your dad's new PR director."

Danny's heart hammered in his chest. She was even more beautiful up close. He caught his breath and nodded.

"Nice to meet you, Miss LaMarche."

Evie smiled up at him, her long lashes fluttering. "Yes, good to meet you too. I'm sure my dad will have a lot for you to do—especially now."

"Yes, I have no doubt about that. I—I've already received calls from about ten media groups," he stammered.

"Oh, really? Who?"

Okay, Danny, pull yourself together. This isn't the time to look like an idiot. He cleared his throat and jumped in. "CNN, Fox, *Time, US News,* the *New York Times, Chicago Tribune, LA Times,* and uhhh—*Wednesday's Word, News Flash Today* .... Actually, I think it's more than ten."

"Sounds like it. And I guess they all want interviews."

"Yeah." He shook his head. "I don't know how we're going to work them all into his schedule."

Evie chuckled. "Dad's going to hate that. He really dislikes being in the limelight. A little is okay, but he dreads the idea of celebrity status. He always felt sorry for his friends when they became the *major story*. But that's what happens when you're as good as he is."

"Speaking of the major story," Shannon said as she entered the room, "there he is." She nodded towards the ITV in front of them. Janssen's face appeared in the teaser as the voice of Morgan Thomas introduced the topics for the upcoming segment of news.

"Who is the man who has been chosen to be top negotiator in the new world crisis in Tajikistan? That story's coming up. But our top story today shows how visits to the past can possibly solve problems in the present. Sean Richards reports."

The picture switched to a lithe young man standing in front of the Headquarters of the New York Police Department. He spoke energetically.

"Recent explorations into time travel have given law enforcement authorities new hope in resolving some of history's most baffling unsolved crimes," the reporter said. "New York Police Chief Judson James believes in just a few years investigators will be able to travel back in time, where they may serve as first-hand witnesses to infamous crimes—crimes such as the murders committed by the Boston Strangler and Jack the Ripper, as well as the assassination of President John F. Kennedy."

"Goodness," Evie exclaimed. "That's amazing! Wouldn't that be wonderful if they could go back and find out who killed that young mother and her two little children? You know, the ones murdered and left in the park next to the Potomac a couple of years ago?"

"Yeah," Danny said scratching his head. "I doubt they'd probably do that one, though. They'll probably want to go back and find out who was responsible for some of the high-profile cases."

"Whoever committed those crimes are dead themselves now," Evie said, as though astounded someone could disagree with her. "They took place decades ago. I'd think they'd want to solve crimes where they could actually find the killer and prosecute him."

"Yeah, well, you know how things go," Danny said. "If they're going to spend that kind of money, I'm sure going back in time would be like space travel, in terms of the bucks involved."

A frown settled over Evie's face, growing darker with every word Danny spoke. Clearing his throat again, he went on as though his words were set on automatic pilot and he couldn't shut them off. "If they're going to spend that kind of money, they'd probably go for the big cases."

"Probably so," Shannon agreed.

Evie stood and impatiently shook her head, her hair swinging back and forth on her shoulders.

"That's what's wrong with all of us," she said in disgust. "All we think about is money and glamor and fame. Maybe we should think about protecting innocent young women and children and finding their killers. That would discourage people from doing these atrocious things." She took a step towards Leslie Ann's desk, then spun around. "Going back and identifying Jack the Ripper isn't going to help anybody." She tossed her head again and tramped towards the hallway leading to the inner offices.

"Well, you're right, but—" Danny flushed. He'd blown it. What had he said? He was just being logical. He spoke to her retreating figure. "I'm sorry. I didn't mean to get you upset."

"Oh, I know. Don't worry about it."

She returned to retrieve the plaid shirt she'd left on the blue chair. "I'm sure most people would agree with you. I just don't understand it, that's all." She turned and headed back across the reception area toward the hall door leading to Janssen's office. "It ... it's just been kind of a rough day today, and ... I think I might just go back and wait in Dad's office." She half-heartedly looked over her shoulder, as if remembering her manners at the last minute. "It was nice to meet you, uhh—"

"Danny."

"Danny. Good luck with the PR job."

He watched her disappear down the hall. When he turned back to Shannon and Leslie Ann, they were grinning at him.

"What?" He sighed, then trudged back to his office, picked up a Burger World bag sitting beside his chair, and popped a cold French fry into his mouth.

CHAPTER NINE

Hearing voices outside the door of her dad's office, Evie turned from the walnut bookcase to the right of Janssen's desk where she'd been looking at her grandmother's picture just as the door swung open.

Janssen stood in the threshold, a look of pleasure on his face. "Evie. What a surprise."

"Hi, Dad." She smiled as her father shut the door and strode toward her. Although he was smiling at her, a heaviness hung over his face. "How was your meeting with the president?"

"Fine. Fine." He laid the ITV disc on the bookcase and placed his strong hands on her shoulders, giving her a squeeze and kissing her cheek. "It's great to see you, honey." He loosened his tie. "What brings you here?"

"Just ... wanted to say hi. So you met your team?"

"Yes, I did." He took a step backwards and retrieved the disc, then slipped to the credenza behind his desk where he placed it on a shelf near the bottom.

"Well, what do you think of them?"

Her dad turned to her and shrugged his shoulders.

"Oh, they'll be fine." He frowned and looked downward, appearing to stare at the top of his desk.

Evie cocked her head to the side. "Hmm. You don't look fine. Everything okay?"

He looked up at her again and pulled his lips back in a tight smile as he moved to his chair and sat down. His fake smile. A deadness dulled his eyes.

"Everything's good."

Evie blinked and took a deep breath. "You're not well. That's it, isn't it?"

"Oh no, I'm fine," Janssen said with a sudden cheeriness. "It's just—" He looked back at her dubiously and started rubbing his chin.

Evie took a step toward him. "It's just what?"

He licked his lips and shuffled some papers on the edge of his desk. "The team isn't exactly what I had in mind, that's all."

"What's wrong with it?"

He heaved his shoulders in a sigh. Then he told her about Michael Quigley being selected for his team.

Evie stared at him in shock. "Does President Gelford know…?

"I don't know. I somehow doubt it."

"How did he get picked to go?"

"He has an outstanding background, Evie. When you were a baby, Michael almost single-handedly saved the Golden Gate Bridge from a terrorist attack. That was in 2029." Janssen pushed his chair away from the desk and paced to the other side of his office, where he stood with his back toward Evie and looked out the window. "He's a sharp guy professionally. It's just in his personal life he stinks."

"He's a rat."

"He may be a rat, but he's a smart rat." He turned to face her. "Anyway, he's hopefully learned a few things about women in the last eight years."

"At Jenna's expense." She tossed her head and tromped to the bookcase where she studied a five-by-seven photo of Jenna and her family.

"Yes, to be sure."

Evie didn't have to sell him on the notion of the great hurt Michael had caused her aunt. Her father was Jenna's main support at the time. "I don't know how anyone could hurt her like that, let alone her own husband. How can someone do that to his family?"

"I have a feeling he wasn't thinking about them ... at all." Janssen stepped back to his desk and dropped into his chair. He downed the glass of water sitting there and began raking his fingers through his mustache.

Evie replaced the picture. "Dad, have you talked to him much since then?"

"A couple of times, off and on."

"About Jenn?"

Her dad hesitated, then took a breath. "No."

She wanted him to say more, but wasn't surprised when he didn't. Her father hated to get in the middle of sticky personal problems. Was this the reason for her dad's ghostly appearance the last few days? "Did you just find out about Michael today?"

"Yes. At the meeting."

Leslie Ann knocked on the door and cracked it open. "I've got your coffee, sir."

Janssen nodded to her, and Leslie Ann crossed the room, placing a mug on the desk in front of him.

"Evie, what would you like? Coffee? Tea?"

"Nothing, thanks. I'm good."

As Leslie Ann left, Evie turned to him again. "What will you do now?"

"Nothing. Act civil. Do my job. Be professional." He took a quick sip of coffee.

"Poor Jenna. What do you think she'll say?"

Janssen stared into his coffee mug. "Jenn's a good sport. She'll handle it okay—at least on the outside."

"It's the inside I'm thinking of." Evie moved to the chair opposite his and perched on the edge. His face appeared pasty, his eyes dull. An uneasiness swept over Evie once again. The foreboding that had haunted her through the day returned. She thought of her dream the night before.

"Dad ... the reason I came over ... " She sighed.

Her dad was watching her, waiting.

"Dad, I'm worried about you. You don't look well."

He laughed. "I'm fine, Evie."

"You don't look fine. You look ... terrible."

He shook his head and laughed. "I'm not quite sure how to take that. Do I need a haircut? A shave?" He rubbed his chin as though looking for bristles.

"Dad." She pursed her lips in pretended annoyance. "You know that's not what I mean. You looked so pale at dinner last night, and at the press conference you just didn't look like yourself."

"You worry too much." She caught his eyes unprotected for one moment, and tried to read what she saw there. He rose from his chair, slipped around his desk, and stood behind her chair, rubbing her shoulders affectionately. "Thanks for caring, honey."

Evie felt her resolve weaken. But she had to know.

"Dad." Putting her hand on top of his, she turned to face him, "Don't put me off. Something's wrong. I just feel it. Last night I woke up from a deep sleep and found myself praying for you. I was sweating. My heart was pounding. That's not like me. It was spooky."

He laughed again and removed his hand from Evie's shoulder. "That *is* spooky. But it's nice having someone pray for me. I can probably use it. But waking up in the middle of the night like that ..." He walked to the side of his desk and reached over to get his coffee mug, then looked over at her and winked. "Maybe you're just getting a little too much religion."

"Dad, don't tease me." Evie rose from her seat, crossed her arms, and stood looking at him with a worried frown gathering across her face. "I'm serious. I'm worried about you." Her voice rose in intensity. She took a breath to calm herself.

Janssen smiled knowingly and took a long drink of his coffee. "I hear you impressed my new young PR assistant out there."

"Impressed? Hardly. You're just trying to change the subject, Daddy."

"No, no. He told me I had a beautiful daughter."

"He's just being nice. Believe me, he can't be impressed after the big argument we had this afternoon." Why wouldn't he give her a straight answer?

"Argument?"

"Yes, about time travel." She uncrossed her arms and sighed, then ran the palms of her hands up and down the sides of her black pants.

"Time travel? You argued about time travel?" Janssen settled again in his chair behind the desk and leaned back.

His apparent composure was making her a little crazy. How did he do this? He could turn a conversation on its edge before she even knew it and change the tone so she felt foolish to continue.

"Yeah, time travel." She shrugged. "He's just a typical guy. Likes the flashy, dramatic stuff. No depth."

"How does that relate to time travel?"

"It's a long story, Daddy. But I think we were talking about your health."

He looked at her and smiled that familiar smile that said, *I love you, but you're not going to get what you want.* From experience, she knew pursuing these questions any further would be useless. She looked again at her father, trying to look upbeat, while a dark heaviness crept into his face and sallowness dug into his cheeks. He tapped his Da Vinci ball and began scrolling through his email.

Evie walked to the window. On the street below, the rush hour had begun, and a snag of cars had already clogged 23rd Street. A blue Ford GT inched out of the parking lot across the way, attempting to push into the line of cars creeping along the street. Cars honked at him. Evie sighed and turned back to face her dad. She felt empty, defeated like the blue Ford.

"I know you have tons of stuff to do. I won't keep you. I—I was just concerned." She took a step toward him and searched his eyes. "Let me know if I can do anything. I love you." She went over to him and planted a kiss on his cheek.

He stood up and drew her into his arms, holding her and rubbing her back affectionately. "Thanks, honey. I love you."

Evie breathed in the familiar woodsy scent of his cologne and rested for a minute against his shoulder. Then she left.

Janssen shut the door behind his daughter and walked to the expansive picture window overlooking the Lincoln Memorial and the Potomac. Shadows gathered over the city as nightfall approached. He gazed out, wondering. Why did Evie have to press so hard? She was the child of his heart. But the world was bigger and meaner than she comprehended.

He couldn't afford to think about his illness now. He had important things to do. He was her father. She needed to trust him.

CHAPTER TEN

At six a.m. the next morning, Janssen put his imprint onto the thumb pad on his office door. Although his suite of offices was dark, the strong smell of coffee welcomed him inside. He pushed a button on his watch. A surge of light filled the reception area, and he strode toward the coffeemaker. *Bless Leslie Ann's heart. She remembered.*

Cup in hand, he went down the hall to his private office and sat at his desk, looking at the notes spread out neatly before him on the rich walnut surface. After bringing up the contact screen on his Da Vinci ball, he touched the Oquilov logo and heard a ringing phone from the speaker on the handset. A voice answered in the Tajik language. His brain switched gears as he converted his thinking from English to Tajik. A familiar warm sensation brought back pleasant memories of a former time.

"Janssen!" The animated face of his uncle billowed up before him in a hologram. Strands of gray had crept into the thick black hair at his temples. Creases had formed on his lower cheeks. "I've been looking forward to your call. You still look like young man."

"Hello, Uncle. My fond memories are always with you. Many are the hours we spent together in our younger days."

"Yes, yes. How I remember. And now you have important role in United States."

"And you in Tajikistan."

"Yes, separate paths in separate countries bring us back together again now."

"The world grows smaller all the time."

"Increasingly so. How's my Jenna? And your family?"

"They're doing well. Jenna teaches school."

"Oh, yes. I remember now. I thought she would be artist. She always painted pictures."

Janssen laughed. "Yes, she did. But she loves children. She is a good teacher."

His uncle smiled. "Yes, yes." He nodded his head. "So, you will be in Tajikistan soon? In one, two weeks?"

"That's the plan. But I want to spend some virtual time with you on the phone first, to get an idea of where the hearts of the Tajikistani people lie at this time. I don't feel as connected as I once did. I'd like to know what is transpiring in my beloved Tajikistan."

"Ohh, Janssen. As always there is good and there is bad. Our economy begins to get stronger, but resistance movement continues to cause divisions among people, particularly in north."

"That's been a longstanding problem. What's happening in the economy?"

"New corporations and investments from some of our neighbors along with oil discoveries make things better. More jobs."

"A welcome development."

"Yes, yes. I understand I'm famous in America now."

Janssen thought he saw a twinkle in his uncle's eyes. "Famous? Oh, you mean—"

"Uncle Jocko." He laughed.

"Uncle, I'm so sorry." Janssen leaned forward and shifted his weight in the black leather chair. "I hope I did not embarrass you."

"Actually, you make Rajanov envious. It seems I am more famous than he. I think you need to give him nickname too."

The two men laughed—deep guffaws joining together over the fiber optic wires to reconnect two lives separated by time and distance.

"Jocko. It's so good talking with you again. But of course, you know I have a very serious reason for calling."

"Of course, Janssen. Weapons. You want to talk about weapons found in north. I know. I know."

"They're very dangerous, Uncle."

The silence on the other end disturbed him. In the hologram hovering before him he could see the lids of the older man's eyes drop. He was staring vacantly at something.

"Uncle?"

"Yes, Janssen. I am here."

"I know we all want to see these weapons disposed of safely ... so no one will get hurt."

"Yes. We all agree to that."

"The United States would like to help in having that done."

"That would be good. I would like United States to help us dispose of weapons safely."

Janssen was relieved to hear those few words from his uncle, but he knew they were just beginning. "Do others in the government feel as you do?"

"It is hard question, Janssen. There are many considerations. Tajikistan has been friend to world. We do not want trouble. We want to do what is right. But there are many considerations."

"What are some of the others?"

"Our people. We need to do what is right for Tajik people."

"Uncle Jocko, I also want to do what is right for the Tajik people."

"I know, Janssen. I know, and if it were not you coming to speak with us, Rajanov and others might not be so ready to have conversations. The Oqilov name is still strong in Tajikistan. Your lovely mother was an Oqilov, and you are not a stranger to our people. But there is great pressure."

"Where is the pressure coming from?"

"Those with influence."

"Who?"

"We are poor country. We do not want to lose recent gains."

"Nor would I want you to."

"We know, Janssen. We know you care. That is why Tajik government will talk with you."

"The United States is prepared to give Tajikistan a great deal of money, Uncle. We will match whatever is being offered to you."

"Can you give our people jobs?"

"Money can provide opportunities for jobs. We will do whatever is needed."

"Can you? United States has economic problems now—money not available so much. That is what I hear."

"We have enough, Uncle. We will do whatever is needed."

"But can you keep our people from losing jobs they have already? When our people go even one month without job, their families suffer."

"I understand. I do. We all learned that back in the times of the COVID 19 pandemic of 2020. It's hard to recover. We have ways to help with that too, though. We would do our best. But there are bigger issues even than economics."

"For us, Janssen? Or for United States?"

"For all of us." Janssen paused as he and his uncle tried to read each other's eyes in the holograms hovering before them. "Uncle, where are the weapons—exactly? I know they are in the north, but where?"

Jumakhan blinked several times and looked away. Again, there was a long silence as he ran his hand over the top of his head. He was not looking at the hologram now. Janssen felt the distance—not in geography, but attitude. His uncle did not want to tell him where the weapons were.

"I'm putting you in an awkward position."

Jumakhan's virtual looked back at Janssen, his eyes sad and confused. "It is difficult."

"We will be sending a man over there to inspect the weapons. Will he be able to see them?"

"Can he be trusted, Janssen?"

Janssen felt jolted, the way one might when smacking his face into a sliding glass door. Could his uncle trust Michael Quigley? How could Janssen say yes? The shadows rose once again into his mind. *Michael on his team.* He had to have confidence in him, but could he?

"The president picked him very carefully for this mission. He has a strong background in munitions analysis."

"But can I *trust* him, Janssen?"

"Yes," he lied. "Uncle, I don't want to put pressure on you. I know you're in a difficult position. We can talk again. But would you find out for me whatever you can? What the United States must do to be given a receptive ear from Tajik officials? And who it is who opposes us?"

"It is you, Janssen, that brings receptive ear from Tajik officials. They respect you. They listen to you."

"But there is opposition ...."

"Yes, there is opposition. But your coming makes difference."

"Will you find out what you can, Uncle? Let me know what else we can do? And what should I say when I talk to Rajanov today?"

"Just have friendly conversation. Tell him concerns. Tell him United States is prepared to help Tajikistan with economic issues. I will see what I can do, Janssen. I will call you back."

"Thank you, Uncle. You have my email address, don't you? And my Q number? We can communicate by email and text too, if it's easier."

"Yes, Janssen. Goodbye until later."

The hologram withered, and once again Janssen was alone in the quiet of early morning. Janssen rose from his chair, walked to the window, and watched a pink glow wash over the Lincoln Memorial as shadows fell away. *Just as the sun sets over there, it rises over here. Abraham Lincoln.* A bigger-than-life man who met history at the moment of its need and turned the future in a better direction. Could he—Janssen LaMarche—make a difference in the present crisis? The danger seemed even greater than he had at first comprehended, his role more urgent. In the wrong hands, these weapons were a dire threat to peace in the world.

And Michael. Could he trust him? Securing these dangerous weapons was imperative. But he had a loyalty to his uncle too. He had to make sure his uncle and the people of Tajikistan would not be hurt. And what was Uncle Jocko trying to tell him? He talked about jobs, recent gains— those with influence. Who was trying to buy the weapons? Where they came from seemed to be a mystery. Janssen turned from the window and began to pace randomly about the room, his eyes glazing over as he stared absently at the familiar objects of his office. *Can you be a tough negotiator with your Uncle Jocko—as well as a caring nephew?*

Could he? What if it was a conflict for Jocko—how would he react? Would Jocko confide in him? He'd seemed close-mouthed, reluctant to say too much. Perhaps the next thing to do was to telephone Rajanov—see if he could discern anything from the Tajik president. Anyway, it was growing late over there. He needed to call soon.

Just as he began to make the call to Rajanov, he heard the phone ringing in the outer office. The caller ID said unidentified, but taking a chance, he picked it up anyway.

"I thought I'd find you there." It was Ambassador Neely. "About the only time you can get through to Tajikistan before night. Been on the phone with them?"

"Yes. I've talked with Jumakhan, was just about to call Rajanov."

"How'd it go?"

"Okay. Say, what is the source of the economic upturn in Tajikistan of late?"

"Textile corporations and investments, mainly from Iran. Of course, their oil reserves have made a difference for a number of years also."

"Iran?"

"Yes, it's quite a breakthrough for the people. Provides thousands of new jobs. But I wanted to tell you—I've also been on the phone. Just spoke with Reicker, our ambassador to Uzbekistan. He promised to keep a watchful eye out for anything unusual. Isn't aware of anything at this point. But he will get in touch with CIA operatives over there and others who have an ear to the ground."

"Good job, Neely. Thanks."

Disconnecting the call, Janssen rose and strode once more to the window. The city was now bathed in a subdued light. "Iran?" A sharp pain shot briefly through the muscles of his left thigh. He ignored it and deep in thought, remained gazing out over Washington.

The pain bit at his leg again. He flexed his knee several times, hoping to dull its effect. Without success. He shook it vigorously. Deep in his groin area he felt a cramp grip his insides. Another twinge, this time sharper and more acute. The gnawing pain widened. Involuntarily, he tensed his body. *Here we go again.*

Janssen hunched his shoulders as new pangs curled through his chest, then into his shoulders and upper arms. The pain in his abdomen tightened. The nerves in his legs pinched and squeezed together. His leg quivered, and he began to lose his balance. He grabbed hold of the back of the chair next to the window and worked his way around it until he dropped awkwardly onto the cushions. Racked with pain, he gripped the armrest and slowly drew in a breath, trying to subdue the sharp crescendos overwhelming him.

The phone rang in the outer office. Despite the physical battle he waged with the unseen forces ravaging his body, his mind was drawn to the battle outside. Thoughts of Iran and Quigley and the vapid response from his uncle continued to swirl through his mind. He wondered who was calling. It wouldn't be Neely again. But who at this early hour?

He flinched as the pain intensified.

CHAPTER ELEVEN

No one answered. Jenna switched off the phone and strolled to the closet.

I hate to bother Janssen. I know he's busy, but I'd sure like to know if we're doing lunch today. She shuffled through the clothes hanging on the rack. Especially so I'd know what to wear.

She studied a blue rayon dress on its hanger. About right. Dressy enough for the Capitol, but casual enough. Jenna strolled to the mirror and smoothed the fabric over her hips. The loose fit made her look slimmer.

Climbing into her Jeep in the coolness of the early summer morning, Jenna rolled down her windows to breathe in the fresh, clean air. As she pulled out, a gust of wind blew in the window and caught a stray wisp of hair. She shook her head back and forth to throw it back in place and caught a look at herself in the rearview mirror. *Yes, it definitely has that tomboy look.* She smiled, remembering her brother's unmerciful teasing when she cut it short. "I think you always wanted to be my older brother instead of my older sister."

"Particularly when we got older and I couldn't beat you up any more," she chided.

Secretly, she knew Janssen liked her hair short so he could come up behind her and mess it up. He liked teasing her like that, he said, because he loved watching the natural gleam in her eyes grow and dance into the twinkle he'd loved since childhood.

She smiled at the memory, then gazed back at the road.

The cheerful memories suddenly faded. Her heart skipped a beat. Why did Janssen look so pale lately? What was wrong with her brother? Hopefully, she'd find out today at lunch.

Janssen lay on the couch recovering from his latest bout of pain and idly scanned the room. Evie had forgotten her plaid shirt, leaving it on the armrest. A wave of guilt swept over him. He hated brushing Evie off like he'd done the day before and seeing her dejected face when she kissed him goodbye.

Her beautiful face, her beautiful heart.

He'd have Leslie Ann call her—or maybe he would call her himself—to let her know her shirt was here.

He closed his eyes again, Evie and the red plaid shirt evaporated from his thoughts as the different faces he'd encountered via virtual phone that morning paraded through his mind.

The last call had been with Rajanov two hours earlier, while he was still in early recovery from the pain. Since Rajanov expected to hear from him that day, Janssen felt pressed to call him while it was still daylight in Tajikistan. Sweeping the discomfort from his consciousness, he'd made the call. He did more listening than talking, encouraging the Tajik president to share any concerns he had about the upcoming negotiations. Rajanov had been fairly candid, and Janssen hoped he'd been able to reassure him about the ability of the US to deliver on promises of economic aid and intentions to keep things peaceful. Rajanov offered no information as to who was trying to buy the weapons or where the weapons had been found, and Janssen did not ask. He would wait till he felt more clear-headed to discuss these more compelling issues.

His body still ached as he repositioned himself among the sofa's plush cushions. He looked at his watch. Ten o'clock. Time to call Secretary Tomlin to give him a report. Pushing himself up, he rose and limped to his desk, punched a code on his computer and spoke the name: "Secretary Tomlin."

He heard the varied pitches as the computer dialed his phone, then a portly woman's face ballooned before him. Her voice was businesslike but warm. "Secretary of State Tomlin's office."

"This is Janssen LaMarche. Is he in?"

"Mr. LaMarche. Yes. I know he'll want to talk with you, but I'm afraid he's in a meeting at the moment. Can I have him call you back?"

"Certainly. I'm at my office." He disconnected, clicked his DaVinci ball and said, "Today's schedule." The screen filled with lines and words and numbers. He scrolled down to look at the rest of his day.

He'd almost forgotten the evening portion of his schedule. Live interviews with CNN and Fox News. There was an asterisk beside them with a note from Danny. "Question: where would you like the feeds to come from? The office or your home?"

Janssen clicked *Reply,* spoke the word "Home," then hit *Send.* After coming in so early, he knew he'd be ready for some R & R before the interviews this evening. He lifted himself out of his chair and picked up Evie's shirt, then shuffled to the door of his office. Pulling it open, he came head to head with Shannon on the other side, her outstretched hand reaching for the knob.

She took a few steps backward into the hallway. "Oh. Sir. I peeked in on you earlier and you looked like you were asleep. I ... I just wanted to see if you needed anything."

Janssen shifted Evie's shirt to his left arm. "I was just resting. Thinking. Got in very early this morning."

"I know. How did your phone calls to Tajikistan go?"

"Fine. Fine."

Shannon moved aside to give him room as he eased into the hall and faced her. "Shannon, I want you to do some research for me. See what you can find out about textile companies in Iran—particularly those that have expanded into Tajikistan. Find out who runs them—and whatever you can about the company executives. See if there's any link to rogue political groups."

"Yes, sir. I'll do it right away." She turned to leave.

"Shannon."

"Yes, Mr. LaMarche?"

"Is Leslie Ann in?"

"Yes. Shall I get her?"

"No. That's okay. Need to stretch my legs. Been a long morning." Janssen wandered down the hall into the reception area, which was empty. Turning back, he peeked into the kitchen and found her at the coffee maker.

"Leslie Ann, thanks for remembering to make the coffee last night. That little bit of caffeine may be responsible for any success I may have achieved in our negotiations with Tajikistan this morning."

Leslie Ann laughed and turned to face him. "You're welcome. Just doing my job."

He held Evie's shirt out to her. "Would you call Evie and let her know she left her shirt here yesterday? She can pick it up, or I can take it home with me tonight. Whichever is easier for her."

Leslie Ann took it and nodded. "I'll call her right now. By the way, you have some messages. I'll send them to your computer." The phone was ringing as she walked to her desk. "Janssen LaMarche's office … yes, he's here." She looked at Janssen. "Secretary Tomlin."

Janssen retreated into his office and shut the door. In the picture ballooning before him, he saw the secretary sitting with his elbows on his desk, his fingers below his chin lightly touching in a steeple position. "LaMarche. What have you found out?"

Janssen filled him in on his conversations and told him about Iran.

"Interesting connection. We'll look into that. Whether or not they tell us where the weapons are isn't absolutely crucial though, you know. Our quantum technology can locate them with even the rough parameters you've already given us. In fact, we're already looking."

"I see." Janssen's mind was feeling crimped around the edges. He wasn't sure he felt completely comfortable with this technological invasion of Tajikistan. Perhaps his uncle would expect it. The Tajik officials might already be ahead of him on it.

Secretary Tomlin lowered his hands and took a more relaxed posture, then smiled. "I talked to the Ambassador from Tajikistan this morning. He makes one thing very clear."

"What's that?"

"With the high respect you have in that country, you're definitely our man. Stay healthy."

CHAPTER TWELVE

The first time Jenna saw the man watching her, he stood beside the large African elephant in the Smithsonian rotunda. From within the niche of the faux rock pedestal on which the elephant stood, a short, slender Middle Eastern man stared at her. When he saw her look his way, he quickly averted his eyes.

She shrugged it off until she noticed him again at the opposite end of the Dinosaur Room, standing in the eerie yellow light around the long-necked *Diplodocus longus*. He was half-hidden below the tail of the T-Rex, his dark eyes following her every move while he spoke into his cell watch. Jenna nervously moved towards the fossil lab, then into the adjoining exhibit of fossil mammals.

As she zigzagged from room to room, trying to lose the dark stranger among the maze of exhibits, a musty odor hung in her nostrils—the odor intentionally introduced by museum designers to produce more realism. The smell intensified her uneasiness.

She crossed into the Ice Age exhibit and spoke questions into her Q watch, noting the names and historical information of the mammals before her. Tomorrow her aide would transcribe it and print it out for the students to use during their upcoming field trip.

A half hour had now passed without incident.

Relieved, Jenna turned to the next set of animals, then gazed around the room to pick the next subject.

Through the legs of the Irish elk in the case beside her, she spotted the strange man once again, hovering in the orange haze on the other side of the railing. He quickly lowered his arm, as if he'd just taken a photo of her. Jenna's heart rate shifted into a higher gear. Why was he following her?

Janssen's mission.

The thought struck her like a meteor exploding in midair.

But why would they be interested in me? Does anyone know I'm his sister?

Jenna pictured Uncle Jocko, the house in Dushanbe where she and her family had visited when she was a child, the faces of children she had played with in Tajikistan. She straightened her back, took a deep breath, and blew out an enormous sigh.

Yes, there are people who know Janssen has a sister.

She scurried to the entrance to the next exhibit, wondering if it was possible to elude this man without leaving the museum. *Was he really after her? Why?* Surely she was safe with crowds of people around. She'd try to work fast.

"Now, where are the giraffes, elephants and tigers?" she asked herself. "The modern mammals?"

Pulling the museum map from among her papers, she stopped to trace her way through the diagram. "Ah. Over on the other side."

With one eye on the map, she threaded through the maze of rooms. She was simultaneously walking and glancing down at the map to check her position when she bumped into the same short Middle Eastern man, standing in the greenish light of a glass exhibit case. He reached toward her and said something in an unfamiliar language. Jenna recoiled from his touch, spun around, and dashed back the way she'd come. Her heart hammered. Her breathing nearly matched her heart rate.

Jenna whipped through the Asian exhibit, then Africa, until she once again found herself in the Ice Age exhibit. Beneath the snarling mastodon, her small Middle Eastern stalker stood watching her. She reeled backward, trying to decide which way to go. *He couldn't have gotten here this fast.*

Unless there's two of them. Panic ripped through her veins.

She finally emerged into the spacious rotunda where the giant elephant guarded the museum entry. She still didn't know if she and Janssen were having lunch, but it was getting close to noon, and she had the air shuttle to navigate.

The light from the exit drew her. She'd had enough. She scurried toward the door and down the steps of the museum.

On the sidewalk in front of the Smithsonian, Jenna inhaled the summer air and felt a deep wave of relief spread through her body. She glanced back at the doors from which she'd exited, shook her head to even out her hair, then adjusted her jacket as she crossed Madison Drive and hurried to the entrance of the air shuttle. Her heart still thumped hard. As she cut through the grass and gravel of the Mall, her pace quickened to a run. At regular intervals she turned to make sure no one was following her.

I'll call Janssen as soon as I'm on the air shuttle. After all this, I hope he's going to have lunch with me. I need some good company.

"Tell her yes. But she has to pick the place. And it has to be nice. And I'm buying."

He was smiling as he turned from the speaker to give his attention back to Danny sitting in the chair opposite his desk. "My sister."

"You seem to have a close-knit family, sir. That's nice." Danny leaned forward and rested his forearm on the desk.

"Yes. She's a delightful person. Now about tonight. You say Fox is at eight-twenty and CNN at ten?"

"Yes." Danny turned to his Q watch and scrolled down the screen. "The camera crews will start arriving at seven-thirty to hook up the feeds. I'll get there about seven, if that's okay. We'll need to do your makeup, and make sure everything is set up right."

"I'd better give Charlie a call and coordinate things with her. How long do you think it will be?"

"They're only fifteen-minute segments, so it shouldn't run late."

"Sounds good. Do you have my address?"

"Yes, Leslie Ann gave it to me earlier."

"Fine."

Janssen reached for the phone, then paused and looked back at Danny. "Anything else?"

His new PR assistant clambered to his feet. "No."

"I'll see you at seven then."

"Yes, sir." Danny turned and exited, closing the door behind him.

Janssen picked up the phone, tapped his Da Vinci ball, and pulled up his contact screen. "Charlie ... office." He listened to the ringing on the other end.

"Office of the Interior."

"Charlie LaMarche, please."

"Oh yes, Mr. LaMarche. One moment."

Charlie's confident, handsome face appeared before him. He heard the crisp low voice of his wife. "Hello, Janssen. How's your day going?"

"Okay. Challenging. I'm pretty tired. Just wanted to touch base about my GITV interviews tonight. Danny's setting them up from the house."

"From the house? I didn't know ... I'm not sure we left things camera-ready. You should have told me." Her mouth retained a static smile as she listened to Janssen's reply.

"Sorry. We just decided this morning. I'm running to keep up with myself. And I'm really tired. Need to rest before my interviews."

"You have a heavy responsibility, Janssen. I know."

"Can Donna clean things up? It'll only be one or two rooms. Just straighten things, dust a little, turn Floor Vac on."

"What room will you be using?"

A pinpoint of pain shot through his head, causing a light dizziness. Then it was gone. He paused and looked around. Everything was as it had been before.

"Janssen?"

"Oh, uh, what did you say?"

"I asked you what room you'll be using."

Janssen's eyes twitched, and the pain began again in his abdomen—and now a slight nausea too. He struggled to stay focused on their conversation as a subtle dread crept into his subconscious. "I, uh, was thinking of either the family room ... in front of the fireplace, or the study .... What do you think?"

"I think your study would look nice. With the bookcases behind. And the model ship on your desk as an accent piece."

Janssen heard her words, but they weren't connecting with his mind. "Okay ... sounds good." A strain crept into his voice as a strange tension seized his body.

"I'll give Donna a call," Charlie said. "See if she could run over there and do a once-over in the front living areas—and your study."

"Thanks, Charlie." He disconnected the phone and turned back to his Da Vinci ball, fighting back the nausea and ignoring the pain. He chose 'Steno,' then stared with unrelenting concentration at the light filtering through the window on the opposite side of the room.

"This is a confidential memo to the file. At 6 a.m. spoke with Jumakhan Oqilov. Cordial conversation. No hard facts, but ..."

The pain in his stomach grew stronger, its muscles contracting into knots. He gazed back at the screen and realized after a moment his eyes had begun to twitch. Refusing to give into his rising fear, Janssen tried to straighten his body, but the cramping worsened and he felt his insides lump together into a giant, excruciating ball. He placed one hand firmly on the desk for support and tried to continue his dictation.

"Oqilov expressed concerns ... that negotiations with US could result in Tajikistan ... losing ... recent ... financial gains." The words on his monitor fuzzed over. His eyes continued to twitch. He squeezed them shut, trying to gain control. Dizziness swept over him, and the room began to gyrate. What had Dr. Monnihan said about visual changes and vertigo? *There will be a triad of symptoms ... after that you have two weeks at most.*

Janssen's heart froze. *The Ichiban Syndrome.* He'd had the pain ... and by now was used to coping with it. But the visual thing and the dizziness were new. The whole screen jumped and blurred before him. The room began to spin. It dropped, then pitched, yawed, and spiraled upside down. A queasiness overtook him as he watched the room tumble erratically around him.

The pills. He reached toward the desk drawer, pulled it open, and felt for the bottle.

An enormous crescendo of pain wracked his body. He grabbed for the desk, gripped it tightly. Pain and nausea swept upwards. He was hot—so hot. He shuddered with uncontrollable spasms as his muscles contracted and pulled together. His insides felt as if they were imploding. Trembling, he fumbled for his satellite phone but only succeeded in knocking it over, sending it clanking onto the hard surface of the desk.

Everything reeled uncontrollably now in convoluted somersaults. The room was growing dark. He felt himself falling. The last thing he remembered was his head pounding against the hard surface of the desk. Then everything went black.

CHAPTER THIRTEEN

On the air shuttle with the summer tourist crowds, Jenna stood squished between a large heavy businessman and a stocky young mother with a three-year-old. When the air shuttle approached her stop, Jenna inched toward the exit, but a teenage boy, oblivious with his handheld techno-entertainment, elbowed past her. Jenna recoiled and stepped backwards onto the foot of an older man, who swore at her.

She sighed as the air shuttle slowed to a smooth stop. Hopefully having lunch at a nice place with Janssen would make this crazy day worthwhile. The doors slid open, and the crowd behind pushed forward in one huge mass, shoving Jenna through the opening. She scrambled down the steps and out onto the platform with a press of passengers crushing her from behind.

Standing on the platform in her blue dress, Jenna felt disheveled. She smoothed her skirt, tossed her head, and ran her fingers through the hair at her temples.

At the State Department, the security guard couldn't find her name on the visitors' list and called Leslie Ann in Janssen's office to confirm Jenna was cleared for entry. Jenna stood in line behind a tour group going through security, shifting from foot to foot in her impatience.

Jenna looked at her watch. She was late. She didn't want to mess up Janssen's schedule, and she wanted to spend as much time with him over lunch as possible. The tourists finished filing through the z-ray, and Jenna headed for the elevators.

By the time she got off on the sixth floor, her anxiety about the man at the Smithsonian was replaced by her anxiety about being late for her lunch date with Janssen. She smiled as she remembered his insistence on going to a "nice" place. Should she choose The King's Grill or Barnaby's Place? Both were wonderful.

Leslie Ann looked up from her desk when Jenna entered her brother's suite of offices.

"Hello, Ms. LaMarche. Haven't seen you for a while. Having lunch with your brother today, huh?"

"Yes, the country schoolmarm is being treated for lunch in the big city by her famous brother." She waggled her shoulders and grinned. "Is he ready?"

Leslie Ann chuckled and pushed a button. "I'll buzz him—Mr. LaMarche, your sister's here." She winked at Jenna and covered the mouthpiece. "Where did you decide to go?" But before Jenna could answer, Leslie Ann frowned at the intercom and rolled her eyes toward the ceiling. "Mr. LaMarche?" She turned back to Jenna. "He's not answering. One of the lines is lit. He must be on the phone."

The other phone rang, and Leslie Ann picked it up. Jenna stepped backward and glanced around the room. She wandered to the antique roll-top desk to her right and ran her fingers along the rim of a brown earthenware chalice.

"I'm sorry," Leslie Ann said after getting off the phone. "But I think I heard a grunt when I buzzed him." She grimaced. "He's probably seething at my interrupting him."

"Oh, but he's a pretty benign dictator," Jenna said laughing as she walked back toward the desk. "Anyway,

I'll make sure he doesn't have you for lunch. After all, he's got to hold his appetite for going out to a nice restaurant with me, right?"

Leslie Ann laughed. "He *is* a very benign dictator. He's a great boss. I love working for him." She motioned toward the chairs in the waiting area. "Why don't you take a seat for a minute till he's off the phone?"

Jenna walked to the blue armchair. Setting her purse on her lap, she scrolled through her phone, looking at the notes she'd taken at the Smithsonian. She shuddered, remembering the man who had followed her. She closed the note screen and picked up a magazine. Leafing through the pages, she stopped to scan an article on space flight vacations. Fidgeting, she put the magazine down, stretched her back and stood up. "Is he still on the phone?"

"Looks like it. The light's still on."

"Hmm." Jenna paced about the room for a minute and strolled back to the roll-top desk, looked at her watch, then ambled past Leslie Ann's desk. "I think I'll just meander back there and look in on him."

Leslie Ann's face shifted into a doubtful frown. "I don't know. He's been on some pretty important calls today. I don't think it's a good idea to interrupt him."

Jenna hesitated and adjusted the collar of her jacket. "I don't believe he'll mind. He's used to me being his pesky sister. I won't bother him, I promise. I'll just look in."

Ignoring Leslie Ann's look of silent protest, Jenna strode confidently down the hall and quietly turned the handle of the door to Janssen's office. She cracked it open and peeked around the edge. The room appeared empty. The smell of stale coffee hung in the air.

She scanned the sitting area. The desk and credenza. The bookcase. The butler's table.

The desk.

Her eyes flashed back toward the desk. The telephone was lit. She took a step closer.

Draped over the corner of the desk beside the phone. Rumpled dark hair. Flattened jaw. Mustache squished into the shiny walnut surface. Formal sleeve wrinkled and stretched awkwardly over a contorted forearm.

Janssen's head lay scrunched onto the hard surface of the corner, partly cradled into the crook of his elbow. Jenna's stomach sank into a sick wad. Her mind swirled in a shock of confusion. When she finally caught her breath, it erupted in a frightened whisper.

"Janssen! Oh no!"

Jenna was at his side, although she didn't remember crossing the space between the door and his desk to get there. She leaned down, and he slowly raised his head to look at her, his face drawn, his eyes hollow, his pupils tiny dots. Dozens of small pink pills lay scattered on the floor beneath an open drawer.

Jenna reached her arm gently about his shoulder.

"Janssen." Tension gripped her body. She reached for the phone. "I'll call 911."

"No." He jerked his head up in a forceful, determined gesture, but it fell back onto his forearm. "No," he said in a hoarse whisper.

"But Janssen ... " The pain in his eyes was unbearable to see.

Janssen twitched his hand toward the Da Vinci screen. "Doc ... "

"Yes, I'll call your doctor. It's in your contacts?"

Janssen twisted his head toward her in an affirmative motion, grimaced and closed his eyes. "Yes."

Jenna put the phone back on the hook, and pulled up his address book. "Doctor," she said.

"I do not recognize your voice," a mechanical voice responded.

She reached for Janssen's Da Vinci ball and scrolled to the Ds. "Dr. Lake?" she asked.

"No," Janssen whispered, his eyes still shut.

She scrolled down again. "Dr. Monnihan?"

Janssen briefly opened his eyes and nodded. Jenna touched the screen, reached for the phone, then patted the screen again. She heard ringing.

"Dr. Monnihan's office. Can I help you?"

"Yes. I need to talk to Dr. Monnihan. I'm calling for Janssen LaMarche." Her breathing was heavy, her voice scratchy.

"He's with a patient."

"This is an emergency." The nerves in her body bristled. The desperation in her voice had to be obvious.

"One moment."

Jenna looked over at her brother, and with her free hand pushed back a lock of his dark hair. What had happened to him? Over the last couple of months she'd seen signs of sickness, but he'd denied it. He always had an excuse ...

On the other end of the receiver, she heard a man's voice. "Dr. Monnihan."

"Dr. Monnihan, this is Jenna LaMarche. I found Janssen in his office slumped over his desk in great pain ... and there are pink pills strewn all over the floor."

Janssen touched her arm. "Tell him ... tell him ... it's my eyes."

Jenna wrinkled a bewildered brow. "Dr. Monnihan, he said to tell you it's his eyes."

"I'll be right over. State Department, right?"

"Yes, Suite 600." Jenna clicked off the phone. "He's coming right now, Janssen. Why don't I get somebody to help me move you to the couch?"

"No." His eyes squinted into a frown, and he reached out to Jenna. "Just ... stay ... here. Wait." He pointed toward the door. "Is the door open?"

"Yes."

"Close it … please."

Jenna hurried across the room and shut the door, then came back to his side and gaped at him as she stroked the hair at his temples. His skin was clammy, his face sunken, his complexion sallow. She picked up one of the pink pills and inspected it, then pulled the bottle from the drawer. Dumapril.

A pain pill.

She'd heard of it. What had Janssen been trying to cope with? What secret was he keeping from his family? She'd been concerned about him for a while, particularly since the press conference. Today she'd hoped to have the answer, and now she feared what that answer might be. Her heart pinched into a tight wad.

Jenna retrieved a small pillow and offered it to Janssen as a buffer for his head. He nodded, and she gently raised him just far enough to slip it underneath. Crouching down beside him, she put her arm snugly about his shoulders and smiled at him compassionately, her heart trembling with a combination of love and fear.

"I love you, dear brother. I'm right here. You'll be all right."

CHAPTER FOURTEEN

Jenna heard the front door slam, then heavy footsteps moving briskly up the hall. Dr. Monnihan thrust open the door and immediately rushed to Janssen's side. He knelt down and looked in his eyes.

"Did you take the pill?"

"Yes," Janssen said weakly.

"How long ago?"

"I ... don't ... know."

"He's been in here at least thirty-five to forty minutes," Jenna offered.

Dr. Monnihan reached into his bag and pulled out his body scanner. "Let's get him over to the couch." With Jenna and the doctor on either side, they helped Janssen limp across the room.

"What's wrong with him?" Jenna asked anxiously.

"The couch, please."

Dr. Monnihan positioned him horizontally on the sofa, and Jenna arranged the pillows comfortably behind Janssen's head, then tugged at his shoes and raised his feet. Her mind churning, she eyed Dr. Monnihan as he ran the scanner over different portions of Janssen's body, stopping periodically to read the monitor.

"Now," Jenna urged when he was done. "Please. What is it?"

Dr. Monnihan caught Janssen's eyes as he lay on the couch. "Janssen?"

Janssen nodded his head. "Yes. Tell ... her."

"Why don't you sit down," Dr. Monnihan said to Jenna, motioning her to the striped chair near the sofa while reaching over to drag one of the black leather chairs to a spot beside her.

Jenna sat and gazed at the doctor fearfully. She had a sour taste in her mouth. Her heart pounded against the wall of her chest.

"Who are you to Janssen?" he asked her.

"I'm Jenna LaMarche. His sister."

"Do you know anything about this?"

"No. Nothing." She scrunched the fingers of her right hand. Every nerve ending stood on edge. "I thought there was something wrong. He's looked so peaked lately." She drew in her breath and bit her lip, then locked eyes with the doctor's. "It's serious, isn't it?"

The doctor inhaled, then blew out a long breath. "I'm afraid so, Jenna. Your brother has Ichiban Syndrome. He's a very sick man."

"Ichiban Syndrome?"

"It's a neuromuscular disorder. Have you heard of it?"

"No."

"IS is a progressive disease where large amounts of fibrin builds up in the muscles. It causes serious muscle shrinkage and painful contractions, eventually affecting the smooth muscles of the organs as well."

She stared at him. "Is there ... a cure?"

The doctor met her eyes compassionately and drew in a deep breath. She heard the brief tolling of the clock beside Janssen's desk. It struck only once.

Dr. Monnihan shifted in his chair, then leaned toward her.

"The good news is Janssen should recover from this particular attack in"—he looked at his watch—"probably another fifteen minutes. The bad news is ... I don't want to scare you, but I feel the need to be honest. His family should know the truth." He looked at Janssen lying motionless against the pillows. He sighed and shook his head. "Jenna, he's in the final stages of this disease. He's been battling intense seizures of pain for quite a while. The muscles, including the smooth muscles of the organs, begin to harden and lose their elasticity. Then they contract, causing a shriveling effect along with more pain. In the final phase, the eyes are affected. Dizziness and so on."

Jenna was numb. Janssen's words whirled through her mind.

Tell him it's my eyes.

"Final phase?"

"He has maybe two weeks, Jenna. I'm sorry."

Jenna felt as if a load of bricks had crashed into her skull. Her eyes glazed over. She stared at Dr. Monnihan, unable to respond, frozen in her seat, her mind blank.

Her shock finally gave way to fear, and she steeled herself enough to turn and look at her brother. He peered at her through the slit of his eyes, then closed them. Pain still wracked his body. She could see it in him, in his head, his eyes.

She leaned toward the doctor. "You said two weeks?"

The doctor nodded.

"You mean until—?"

I should never have asked that question.

But she knew. She saw the words in Dr. Monnihan's eyes even though he was too compassionate to utter them. She couldn't let herself say them or even think them, because then she'd have to acknowledge them as truth.

She leaped from her seat and reeled across the room, her head thumping in time with her heart. She paced to the bookcase, then back toward the ship's clock. Janssen's eyes were closed, but she knew he could hear her. She needed to rein in her emotions. She shook her head to clear it, and blinked back the tears that stung the corners of her eyes.

She returned to the doctor, her agitation barely subdued, and perched on the chair beside him. "You mean ... there's no cure? None at all?"

"None." Dr. Monnihan shook his head. "Not ..." He sighed. "Not unless you're a child in the womb."

Jenna gave him a look of utter puzzlement. "A child in the womb? What do you mean?"

"When women become pregnant," he said, "they undergo a battery of tests to identify a variety of potential problems in the fetus. Ichiban is one of the diseases that can be detected at that time. If it's discovered in the very early stages of pregnancy, IS is easily treated and eliminated. It's a congenital disease, Jenna. Janssen was born with a predisposition for it." He looked back at Janssen.

"But once the person's born there's nothing you can do?"

"I'm afraid not."

"If there's a cure before a person's born, there has to be a cure later. They must know enough to do something."

"No. It all has to do with the development of the fetus."

Jenna had been sitting beside Janssen on the sofa for almost half an hour when she noticed him looking at her. His eyes were clearer. The pain pills were beginning to work.

"How do you feel?"

Janssen quirked one heavy eyebrow and smiled weakly.

"Better. Queasy, but better." He looked at Dr. Monnihan sitting across the room. "Thank you both for being here."

The doctor's furrowed forehead belied the smile on his lips as he nodded in response. He dragged his chair closer to the couch, his face grim.

"Janssen, you know this is just the beginning. I want you to be realistic. Get things in order. There will be more attacks. And they're only going to get worse."

Janssen averted his eyes and looked toward the window.

"I really thought I'd be able to complete this mission ... I thought I'd have that much time anyway."

Jenna squeezed his hand affectionately. She gazed at his face. "How long has this been going on?"

His eyes darkened with regret, and perhaps sorrow. "Quite a while. A year, I guess."

"Why didn't you tell me?"

"I didn't want to worry you."

"Worry me? Janssen." She saw the pain and disappointment in his eyes, those brown eyes that had so often comforted her and given her strength when she needed it most. The very same man who was so strong in helping others shrank from seeking help for himself. "Janssen, I'm your sister. I love you. I want to support you in this."

"I know. But there was nothing you could do. Not really. I thought I could conquer it." He looked at the doctor with a wry smile. "Isn't that right?"

"Yes, it certainly is. He tried his best. He's a fighter."

Jenna's heart was tearing apart as though it was being ripped from her body. The words were pressing into her mind once again. She stood up and paced across the room in agitation, trying to catch her breath. For Janssen's sake, she wanted to stay in control. But the tension mounting within her screamed for release.

Janssen was looking at her from the couch. Although he seemed more stable than he'd been earlier, his face was pale and drawn. A helplessness sapped the characteristic aura of strength from his countenance. She saw him struggling to project his inner resolve onto her, trying to find words of comfort. Over the years, she'd watched his rugged fortitude grow into a mighty sheltering tree, seeking always to protect the ones he loved.

A horn honked in the street below. From the couch, she heard his voice. His brown eyes followed her as she rambled about the room. His voice, now anxious, reached out to her.

"Hey, Sis. It'll be okay. We'll get through this together. Jenna. Help me with Evie and Charlie, okay?" He lifted his head, his eyes pleading as he attempted to distract her from her fear.

The heaviness within her chest rose to her throat, ripping and pulling at her heart. The reality she'd kept at bay for almost an hour now forced its way to the forefront. The words would no longer wait, but printed themselves in her mind.

She hastened to his side, choking back tears. Jenna swallowed hard and took his hand.

"Jenna, I need your help in telling the others—especially Evie. Will you help me? Please?"

"You know I will, Janssen. You know I will."

The unwelcome words flashed before her eyes, taunting her, blaring through the silent fear crushing her heart.

Janssen is going to die.

An avalanche of pain burst from its stranglehold. Tears spilled over and streamed down her cheeks. Jenna buried her head on Janssen's chest and sobbed.

"I'm sorry. I'm so sorry. I should be brave, I know, but I'm not. You can't die. I won't let you."

She felt Janssen stroking her hair, fluffing the short locks that encircled her head, as he'd done since the earliest days she could remember. Her brother. The one constant in her life she could always count on. She felt his fingertips smoothing away the tears from her face. "We'll fight this to the end," he was saying. "I won't give in to it. Miracles still happen sometimes, you know. Maybe we'll get Evie to praying."

Several minutes had passed when Janssen felt Jenna slowly disengaging herself from his embrace. She looked down at him, wiping her face with her hand.

"Janssen, you do need to tell Evie and Charlie and Alex. I don't know what to do about Dad. He seems hard, but losing you—" She shook her head. "You're his pride and joy, whether you realize it or not."

"Yes. I'll have to do something … soon."

His strength was edging back to him. The hopelessness of a moment ago slipped into his more familiar and comfortable bent toward action. Janssen smiled at his sister, whose passionate devotion seemed to ease the deep ache of impending calamity. Her pain had diffused his.

"And I need to tell the president," Janssen said. "I'm afraid the situation in Tajikistan is growing more urgent. He'll need to find someone to replace me."

Dr. Monnihan cleared his throat and walked across the room toward them. "Would you like me to go with you when you meet with the president? I don't know how much it would help, but perhaps I could answer some of his questions."

"I would like that very much … for you to accompany me. I'll give him a call now." With Dr. Monnihan's help, he limped to his desk and dropped heavily into his black chair. Janssen touched the Da Vinci screen. "President Gelford."

In a moment, Kate's easy-going face hologrammed before him. "Office of the President."

"Kate, this is Janssen LaMarche. I need to speak with the president today if at all possible. Or if not today, tomorrow morning."

"It's urgent then?"

"Very."

"Would you like to speak with Randall Robertson?"

"Yes, that would be good."

Soon he heard the smooth baritone voice of Gelford's aide. The visual was turned off. "Randall Robertson."

"Randall. This is Janssen LaMarche. Something very serious has come up, and I need to speak with the president. Today, if I can. Do you know if he has ten minutes to spare?"

"His schedule is packed. Can I help? Or what about Secretary Tomlin? No, his schedule is almost as bad as the president's, but we could check ...."

"I know how busy they both are. I ... I hate to interrupt anything, but this could affect a very important aspect of the mission to Tajikistan."

"Let me check with Kate." He heard the click of the phone as Randall pushed the hold button. Music from a stringed symphony played "America the Beautiful." A hologram of Mt. Rushmore followed by the Grand Tetons appeared.

"He has an awards ceremony at four o'clock," Randall said on his return. "If you can get here by three-forty-five, he may be able to squeeze ten minutes in. Would that work? Doesn't give you much time."

"Yes. Three-forty-five it is. Will you be there?"

"Yes."

"Incidentally, I'm bringing a Dr. Peter Monnihan with me."

CHAPTER FIFTEEN

"You say the only cure that exists for this disease—at all—is for a fetus in the womb?"

"That's right, Mr. President." Dr. Monnihan nodded as he sat beside Janssen in one of the chairs opposite the president's desk. Gelford swiveled his chair around toward his window and gazed absently at the gardens beyond. A full minute passed in silence.

Turning back to his guests, the president's eyes roved from one to the other. He had exhausted all his questions. Now he stared at Randall Robertson, his deputy Chief of Staff. "Any suggestions?"

Randall pinched his lower lip and nodded reflectively.

"Well, this may sound pretty farfetched. But I have friends at the Health and Human Services Department. There's a lot of new developments—experiments." He looked at Gelford, then at Janssen. "With time travel."

With eyes closed, Jenna sat on a swing at the north end of Janssen's front porch in Bethesda, waiting for his return, when he stole up behind her and rumpled her hair.

"Janssen." She jumped and looked back at him, the usual brightness of her eyes quickly dissolving to tears.

"I'm sorry." She sniffed and dabbed at her eyes. "What did the president say?"

"First of all, he asked me not to say anything about this to anyone unless I feel it's absolutely necessary—even family. He wants me to hold off as much as possible until he checks into some things."

"What kind of things?"

"He and his aide Randall Robertson want to talk to some people at the Health and Human Services Department."

"That sounds encouraging."

"Crazy is probably the better word." He shook his head. "Here, let's go inside." He held the door open for Jenna and ushered her into the marble tiled entryway.

"Crazy?" She stopped beneath the crystal and antique brass chandelier and turned back to face him. "If there's anything in the works, they'd probably know. They should have the latest information."

"No doubt. I'll try anything at this point."

"So you're going ahead with the interviews tonight?"

Janssen nodded. "That's what the president wants. I'm just following orders. Things are certainly out of my control." He slipped down the short hall to his left and into his study. "Looks like Donna was here all right," he said, inspecting the room. "Charlie's okay."

"I think you should tell her."

"Charlie?"

Jenna nodded.

"Yes. You're right." He strode across the burgundy and gold Persian rug to the built-in mahogany cabinets behind his desk, picked up an intricately constructed model of the Cutty Sark from the bookcase, and placed it on the corner of his desk.

"What time are the ITV crews getting here?" she asked.

"Seven-thirty. My public relations assistant will be here at seven."

Jenna glanced at the brass wall clock across from his desk. "It's five-thirty now. How do you feel?"

"Tired. Brain-dead."

"Did you have any plans for dinner?" Jenna asked as the two of them turned and headed back into the hall.

"Not that I know of. Charlie may have something in mind."

"Why don't you rest, and I'll get Chinese takeout. I imagine you're as starved as I am, since neither of us had any lunch."

"Actually, I'm more tired than hungry. But I should probably eat something before the interviews." He pulled off his blue, rope-striped tie and headed for the stairway curving up to the second floor.

Lying on the king-size bed in the master bedroom, Janssen heard Jenna's car pull out of the driveway. He closed his eyes to sleep, but his mind was a jumble of faces and questions and memory sound bites. Was his life really about to end? There was so much he still wanted to do. He'd never thought a lot about God, but if there was a God—and he believed there was, somewhere—why would God allow him to die just when he could do so much good? He thought about President Gelford's words that afternoon. *Wait... until we check into some things.* What did he mean by that?

Evie saw a Fox News truck parked in the driveway as she pulled beside the curb at the end of a row of cars lining the street. The front lights blazed. *Dad must be having some interviews tonight.* In a striped shirt and blue jeans, she climbed from the car and walked toward the gabled house.

A black Honda with a University of Kansas sticker on the back was parked in front of her. The car looked faintly familiar, but she couldn't recall where she'd seen it.

She smiled as she passed Jenna's Jeep. She always enjoyed seeing her aunt. Remembering her conversation with her dad the day before, she bit her bottom lip and frowned with a pang of uneasiness. *I wonder if Dad told Jenn yet about Michael.* She shook her head in disgust as she thought about the inappropriateness of the situation. *Poor Jenn.*

Evie passed her mother's tan Mercedes in the driveway, then swung open the gate and strolled past the birch tree up the front walkway. She hesitated a moment at the door before she knocked gently. No one answered. She knocked again. Still no answer. Unsure whether it would still work, Evie placed her thumb on the access pad to test it and heard the door click open. *Hmm. That's nice.* The memory of late-night entries into the house after a date flashed through her mind. *Mom and Dad still have my print on the lock.* She turned the knob and slowly pushed open the door.

From the kitchen, Jenna heard the click of the front door just as she watched the rack in the micro-fridge swivel back to the refrigeration compartment. She walked down the hallway expecting to see another member of the Fox News crew, and instead saw Evie standing in the foyer under the light of the chandelier.

"Evie! I didn't know you were coming over tonight."

"I was surprised to see your car outside too. Is Dad having an interview?"

"Two. One with Fox in about"—she looked at her watch—"fifteen minutes, and another with CNN at ten."

"Goodness, I hope I'm not in the way. I just came by to pick up a shirt I left in Dad's office."

"You're fine. You can be part of his cheering squad. Have you had dinner? We have lots of Chinese food."

"Yum. You sure you have enough?"

Jenna grinned at Evie. "More than enough. Charlie and I came up with the same idea tonight. We both brought Chinese takeout for everyone."

"Oh no." Evie chuckled as she followed her to the kitchen. "How do you happen to be here tonight, Jenn?"

Jenna rearranged the stacks of plates on the black granite counter as she grasped for a rational response. "I had lunch with your dad today ... er ... at least I went to his office to have lunch, and I was with him at the office, and he invited me to come watch the show." She'd blown that. She knew she sounded awkward.

Evie looked at her curiously. "So you and Dad spent some time together today?"

"Yes."

Evie hesitated a minute, studying her as if she were trying to read the look in Jenna's eyes. "Dad told you, didn't he?"

Jenna bristled and stared back at Evie. "Told me what?"

"It's okay, Jenn. I know. Dad told me yesterday."

Jenna knit her brow and blinked back the fog slithering through her brain. *Jenna, I need your help in telling the others—especially Evie.* "He did?"

"Yes. Are you okay? How do you feel about it?"

Jenna's head felt like a tight canvas drum with a mallet banging against it. The conversation was suddenly going down some weird track.

"Awful. How could I possibly feel anything else?" She looked at Evie again, surprised at her calm demeanor. *Did she know? But she said she did.* "I'm surprised you look as calm as you do ... as close as you are to your dad."

Evie seemed taken aback by Jenna's response. She stared at her again. "My dad?"

Jenna felt a cold sweat break over her face and neck. "Y-yes." What was happening? Was Evie talking about Janssen's illness? For a moment the two women stared at each other, each seemingly baffled by what was transpiring between them.

Jenna tried to think of a way to take back what she had just said, to turn it around inconspicuously. *If Evie didn't know … but how* could *she know?* Janssen specifically told her he hadn't mentioned it to anyone. *But Evie just said …*

She frowned and decided to play it safe. "Your dad and this mission. It's really getting to him, you know. It's such a heavy responsibility."

"I've never known that to bother Dad. What do you mean 'as close as I am to my dad?' Are we talking about the same thing?"

"I don't know. Are we?"

Transfixed by one another, Jenna saw mirrored in Evie's eyes the same apprehension she felt herself. What was her niece talking about? Was Janssen hiding something else? Jenna could see the wheels turning in Evie's head, just as they were turning in hers.

The door to the kitchen burst open as Danny entered the room. He hesitated as he spotted Evie in the kitchen with Jenna. His face flushed. "Oh, ah, I'm sorry. Did I interrupt something?"

Relieved at the rescue, Jenna stepped toward him. "No, no. You're fine. How are things in there? You all ready to go?"

"Yes. We're all set up. Just waiting for the feed. Should be in about ten minutes. You're both welcome to come in and watch." He turned to Evie, who still looked perplexed. "It's nice to see you again, Miss LaMarche."

Evie nodded. "Yes."

Noting Danny's discomfort, Jenna smiled and touched his arm. "Would you like something to eat now? I don't think you got anything when you first came in."

"Uhh, actually yes, if you don't mind. That's really why I came in here ... to grab something to eat. If that's okay."

"Sure. The food's in the micro-fridge. Dinner will be served in no time." She stepped to the row of stainless steel appliances and pressed the touch pad. "Evie was going to eat something too, I think. Right?" Jenna turned back toward Evie for confirmation.

"Yeah. I'd like to. But ... I think I'll say hello to Mom and Dad first before they start the interviews. Are they in the family room?"

"The study," Jenna said, as she reached for a plate from the top of the counter.

Surrounded by GITV cameras, video screens, and the noisy prattle of crew members, Janssen LaMarche sat motionless before the bookcases gracing the west end of his study. The surface of his desk was cleared of all but a few sheets of paper in front of him. The model of the Cutty Sark, which his father had brought from New England when he was young, stood on the desk's left-hand corner. Immediately behind him on the lower shelf of the upper bookcase were pictures of his wife, his children, and his parents. In a strategic place where GITV cameras were certain to capture its image, Danny was positioning a large photo of his mother's family from Tajikistan.

"That's good," Charlie said. "Leave it right there." She slipped back to the bookcase where she joined Danny in rearranging books and knickknacks to achieve the best photo shots for the camera. When she finished, she cocked her head toward Janssen. "Remember to lean slightly forward. You'll come across better on the cameras."

Janssen leaned toward his desk and lifted his head, craning his neck around to see if she approved.

"That's good." She came around in front of him and observed him carefully. "You know I have to do this all the time with members of the Department. So take advantage of me."

He nodded and smiled weakly. Charlie—a good woman—a great companion. How was he going to tell her? But he needed to. Tonight, after the shows.

She patted him on the shoulder. "You look good. Keep that position." She threaded her way through the cameras and crew and took up a position against the wall in the back.

Janssen rubbed his eyes. He was still tired, and his body ached. He focused on the plasma monitor of the ITV screen in front of him where the host, Mat Christopher, who would soon be interviewing him, was now drilling physicist Paul Richards on a subject which had recently captured Janssen's interest.

"But my question is," Christopher continued, "what are the ethics of time travel? How do we know when we send these people back—even though it's for a noble purpose—we won't actually change something in the time continuum?"

"In crime-lab time travel, people will have the role of observers only. They will not interact, so they should have no effect on their surroundings. Other types of time travel could pose that threat, but that's not what we're talking about here."

"And how do they get back in time? Worm holes? Is that it?"

"Yes ..."

The producer held up his right hand with fingers extended. "Five minutes till air time."

The audio from the ITV immediately muted, and Christopher's mouth continued moving in silence.

Danny entered from the kitchen, wiping soy sauce from his mouth. He motioned to Janssen. "Ready?"

Janssen nodded.

The producer counted down. "Five, four, three ..." He raised two fingers, then one, continuing to mouth the countdown. He pointed a firm finger to Camera One, staring at the lanky camera girl over red-rimmed glasses. The red light on her camera lit up, and the voice of Mat Christopher, already into his introduction, resonated through Janssen's earpiece.

"And now we have the man of the hour, Janssen LaMarche. Janssen, welcome to the show."

CHAPTER SIXTEEN

"You were wonderful, Daddy."

Except for Danny, who was standing next to the cameramen in front, Evie was the first to move through the tangle of workers and camera equipment to congratulate Janssen when the fifteen-minute segment ended. Janssen smiled at her and fumbled to remove the earpiece as he attempted to push himself out of his chair.

"Here, let me get that." Danny leaned over the desk at Janssen's right, but as he grabbed for the earpiece, he accidentally bumped Evie's arm. "Oh, I'm sorry." He recoiled quickly and reached out to her.

She smiled at him tolerantly. This guy was in public relations? Most of her encounters with him seemed to end with his apologizing to her.

"Good show, LaMarche." The producer lumbered toward Janssen with hand extended. "We look forward to more interviews in the coming days and weeks. I'm sure this won't be the last."

"Glad I could accommodate you, Ralph. It was a pleasure."

The producer nodded to Danny and Evie, then went back to one of the cameramen.

"I was surprised to see you out there amid the ITV cameras," Janssen said, turning back to Evie. "It's nice having a cheering section."

A memory flickered across Evie's mind. *Cheering section.* Jenna's words when Evie first arrived that evening. Evie was always amazed at the melding of minds between her dad and his sister.

Jenna emerged from the right. "Janssen, you were great."

"Yes, you were ... as usual," Charlie added, coming up behind Evie.

"I feel very affirmed." Janssen chuckled. "I appreciate each of you being here. But seriously, Evie, what brings you here tonight?"

"Oh, I really just came by to pick up my shirt. I didn't know you were doing interviews. But once I was here, I figured I might as well watch. By the way, while I'm thinking of it, where is my shirt?"

Janssen stretched his chin and curled his lip. "You know, I don't have it. Things got ... busy today, and I forgot it. But ask Danny. He may have brought it."

"When's the next interview?" Charlie asked.

"At ten."

Charlie eyed the brass wall clock opposite Janssen's desk. "In that case, CNN will be here any minute to set things up." She touched Evie's arm and gave her a half-anxious, half-hopeful look. "Will you help me clean up a little before they come?"

"Sure, Mom. What do you want me to do?"

"When the Fox crew leaves, pick up any papers or things you see lying around. Put the chairs back in order. I think Jenna already cleaned up the kitchen."

"I hope there's still some food left. I'm famished."

"I'm sure there's still enough for you," Charlie said. "It's all in the micro-fridge."

When Evie had done everything she could to straighten up, she headed for the kitchen. Although the tangy aroma of Chinese still clung to the air, Evie saw Jenna had indeed cleaned up everything. Evie opened the refrigerator and let the frigid air blow in her face while she looked on the shelves for the delectable little containers. The cold air felt refreshing after she'd emerged from the crowded study, muggy from the hot lights and thick throng of people. She pushed #5 on the door of the micro-fridge and watched the interior rotate. An arm extended the shelf with the Chinese food into the heating section. Evie set it on warm and listened to the soft whirr of the microwave.

After piling lo mein, egg foo yung and Mongolian beef on her plate, she sat down and took a bite, purring in contentment. From the front hallway, she heard the commotion of equipment and people moving through the entrance of the house, some leaving, some coming. CNN had arrived.

"Could I have some of that?"

Evie looked up to see her dad standing in the doorway. She glanced down at her plate, then up at him. "Of course, Dad. Didn't you get to eat?"

"I wasn't hungry before. But now I'm starved."

"Here, have some of this and I'll heat up some more."

"I don't want to take your food."

"You have to go on the air soon. I don't have anything I have to do." She stood up and pushed the plate at him. "Here."

He took it gratefully, pulled out a chair, and made audible moans of approval as he wolfed down the food.

With her stomach churning in anxious anticipation, Evie warmed up another serving for herself. "How are you feeling tonight?" she asked.

"A bit tired, to be honest. I'll be glad when these interviews are over. It's been a long day."

Evie brought her plate over to the table to join him. "Dad, did you tell Jenna ... ?"

"Well, I see you both found something to eat." Charlie stood at the kitchen door with her hands planted firmly on her hips. "Things seem to be going according to schedule, Janssen. The Fox interview went great. CNN is here. Got things cleaned up. Had plenty of food, thanks to Jenna and I having a joining of the minds tonight. Do you need anything else?"

"No. Thanks, Charlie. Everything seems to be under control. Thank you for your help."

"Okay then. I'm going to watch your CNN interview, but as soon as it's over, I'm heading for bed. I have a big day tomorrow."

"Uh, Charlie. I was hoping to talk to you for a minute afterwards."

"Can't it wait until tomorrow, Janssen?" A frown etched into her forehead. "I'm really tired. I hadn't planned on all this tonight."

Janssen's face clouded. "I'm not sure ... "

Charlie tossed her head and laughed nervously, then sighed. "Well, talk to me now, then."

"I can't right now."

"Janssen, really, I'm tired. We're meeting with Senator Goodman from Florida and the Senate subcommittee to try to get something worked out on this bill to solve the water crisis in Florida, now that the aquifers have given out down there. It's hard to believe greed can kill a state like it did there. Too much construction. Everyone wanting property on the water. It's really come to a crisis now, and I need to be fresh."

"I know, Charlie. It's an important issue—"

"We can talk tomorrow, okay?"

Janssen rubbed his fingers roughly over his chin as Charlie left the room. He brusquely stroked his mustache.

Evie could always tell the seriousness of her dad's thoughts by the intensity with which he rubbed his mustache. On a scale of one to ten, this was a nine-and-a-half. "Something wrong, Dad?"

Janssen exhaled and let his shoulders droop. Their eyes met unabashedly. He was looking at her with more vulnerability than Evie ever remembered seeing before.

"I'm okay. Just have to get through this next interview." He squeezed his eyes shut again, then widened them in an apparent effort to erase the frown lines from his forehead.

"Are you sure you're okay?"

"Yeah." He smiled weakly.

Evie knew if there was something to talk about, this was not the time. He had to be up for CNN. She forced her face to brighten and nodded cheerfully. "I'll be watching, Dad. Just remember to look at the birdie."

They both laughed. Janssen's eyes lingered on his daughter as shared memories from Evie's childhood photo ops danced to the surface of their minds.

"Just so he doesn't fly over my head," he said wryly.

They laughed again in unison, then rose, carried their plates to the sink and strolled arm and arm to the study.

Danny was walking toward the front door with the producer after the interview when he heard Evie calling his name. He turned to see her hastening toward him, the crispness of her colorful striped shirt adding to her bounce and vivaciousness. Flustered by the sudden attention, Danny's face flushed. He twisted his neck back and forth and tugged at his blue and yellow tie. He smiled at her before returning to his conversation with the producer.

"It was great working with you, Tom," he said, as he pulled out his card and handed it to the small burly man. "Call me if you need anything more."

The man shook Danny's hand. "I'm sure I'll be getting in touch again."

"Anytime."

When the producer left, Danny turned back to Evie, who now stood beside him. He was amazed she actually wanted to talk to him.

"Do you have my shirt?" she said.

"What?"

"My shirt. Do you have my shirt?"

Danny stared at her. "Your shirt? I'm not sure I know what you're talking about."

"Dad thought you might have my shirt. Leslie Ann called me today and told me I could pick it up here tonight. Dad thought Leslie Ann gave it to you."

"Nooo. I'm sorry. I ... I don't have your shirt. I don't know anything about it. No one told me to bring a shirt. At least I don't remember anyone telling me to bring it."

"That's okay." Evie shoved her hands in the pockets of her jeans and made her way toward the living area.

"I'll ask Leslie Ann about it tomorrow," Danny said weakly.

"It's really not that important," she said over her shoulder. "I'll talk to Leslie Ann myself. I can get it later."

Danny watched Evie's willowy figure retreat toward the dining room while he dodged a cameraman bustling through the front hallway. But he immediately bumped into a second one close behind him.

"Does Evie know?"

Jenna's whispered question took Janssen by surprise. He'd already told her that afternoon nobody else knew.

"No." He finished untying the knot in his tie, slid it from around his neck and placed it on the dining room table beside him.

"Are you sure? She acted like she knew. Are there other secrets flying around out there I don't know about?"

"Secrets?"

"Yes, Evie acted like she knew something I didn't."

Michael. He darted a glance at Jenna hovering close beside him. *He'd forgotten to tell her about Michael.*

His daughter's voice startled him. "Do I know what?"

Janssen looked over to see Evie standing in the doorway on the other side of the room. "Evie!"

Evie strode to the end of the credenza and stood before the siblings. "Do I know what?" she repeated.

A numbness crept through Jansen's brain. "I—uh—this isn't a good time, Evie."

Evie's eyes widened in bewilderment. "What do you mean?"

He shook his head. "I don't know. Nothing."

Evie stared at him. "What kind of secret are you and Jenna talking about?"

"It's nothing," Janssen said.

"Nothing? But I just heard Jenna ask you if I knew, and you said no."

"Uhh. I don't know." Janssen groped for the right words an excuse, a diversion. "I need to talk to your mom."

Evie frowned. "Where *is* Mom?"

"She went to bed. You heard her. She has a big day tomorrow. She went to bed." Janssen saw Evie staring at him as though he was withering into a hologram specter. He was losing control. He had planned to tell Charlie and Evie together. But Charlie was in bed, and Evie ... He looked at Jenna, dread and uncertainty unraveling his usual calm demeanor.

Jenna linked her arm through his and drew close.

"Janssen. Each of us has our own part to play. You're not going to get complete control over this thing. Charlie's in bed, but Evie is here now. I think you ought to tell her."

He wasn't prepared for this. He didn't want to tell his daughter he was dying before he told his wife. He rubbed his fingers over his mustache in agitation and glanced from his sister to his daughter.

"Let's sit down." He moved to the table, slumped into his armchair at the head, and continued raking his fingers through his mustache.

Perched next to her father in one of the Chippendale side chairs, Evie leaned forward and gazed at him uneasily.

A sick anxiety clawed at Janssen's heart. His daughter's eyes—so trusting. He knew he was about to shatter her world. And only yesterday he'd lied to her, denied the truth she so uncannily suspected. But he couldn't protect her any more. He had to tell her.

Janssen reached for Evie's hand and held it tightly.

Evie felt her father's fear through the firm grip of his hand, saw it in the shrinking scope of his eyes. Evie's heart pounded. Maybe it was better the other way. She'd always wanted the truth from her father. Now she knew she was going to get it, and she was terrified.

"Honey, some things happen we have no control over," Janssen began. "This is one of those times. If there was anything I could do to change this, I would. But we have to face the truth. Evie, you must be brave. We must all be brave. This isn't going to be easy."

His words hit her like hieroglyphic symbols spattering against her mind. She had no idea what he was saying. A chill ran through her body. She shivered and began to tremble. "What do you mean?"

"Honey, you were right." Janssen swallowed hard. "I'm a sick man. Very sick."

Evie's mind froze. She knew it—*had* known it—ever since two nights ago when she awakened in a cold sweat and found herself praying for him without knowing why.

Her father took a deep breath and swiped his hand across his mustache. Anguish bled from his brown eyes as he opened his mouth to continue.

"Evie, I—I may not have long to live."

Evie gaped at her father, the ashen drooping of his face, the dark puffiness beneath his eyes. He was the one man in all the world she really looked up to.

She felt Jenna's hand tighten against her shoulder. Tears welled up in Evie's eyes and spilled onto her cheeks. Looking up, she saw Jenna's face contorted in an agony matching her own. The sight of her aunt's face tore into her heart.

Wild crescendos beat against her breast.

"No, Daddy. No. This can't be true. I won't let it." She grabbed him around the neck and pressed her face against his, her chest heaving in sobs as the torment ripped at her body.

He drew her close, wrapping his arms securely around her. "I love you, Evie. I love you. Be strong. Be strong."

Jenna smoothed Evie's hair with her hand. Finally, Evie disengaged herself and sat erect. "Where's Mom?"

"She went to bed," Janssen said.

"You may be dying, and Mom's in bed?" She jumped up and paced to the credenza. "What on earth is she doing in bed?" Her voice was growing louder with each question. "Does she know?"

"Evie. No, your mom doesn't know." Jenna went to Evie and placed her hand comfortingly on her arm. "But we need to keep quiet. Some of the news media might still be here. Your father is an important man. If this gets out, it could cause problems, more than any of us want to deal with."

"But why isn't Mom here?" Evie asked, her voice cracking in an effort to talk quietly. "What is she doing in bed?"

"Evie, don't blame Mom. You're hysterical." Janssen stood and faced Evie. "Your mom had no idea what I had to tell her. She has no idea I'm sick. She's been running herself ragged to help me with my interviews tonight, and she has an important job herself. She's done her best. Don't be angry with her."

"Yeah, well, Mom is probably the only one who didn't realize something was wrong with you." Tears splashed down her cheeks, and she wiped them with her hand. "You knew, didn't you, Jenn?"

Jenna nodded her head slightly.

Evie choked back a sob. Her eyes were bleary as she looked back at her dad.

"What exactly is wrong, Dad? What do you have?"

CHAPTER SEVENTEEN

Shrill ringing from the telephone awakened Janssen at six-thirty. That, and the cheerful voice of Kate in the president's office, seemed out of place somehow after a night of tossing and turning and thinking about his future—or lack thereof.

"President Gelford would like you to meet him and the Secretary of State this morning at eight o'clock," she said. "Can I tell them to expect you?"

"I'll be there."

Charlie, rattling around in the bathroom getting ready for the day, peeked around the threshold.

"Did I hear the phone? Who was that?"

"The president's office."

"Oh? What did they want?"

"He wants me to meet with him this morning."

"Hmm. Another meeting. Janssen ... "

He waited for her to finish her sentence. "Yes?"

She stood in the doorway watching him, took a few steps toward the bed, then walked to the window and gazed out at the scattering darkness.

"When I went downstairs, I happened to look out the window and saw Evie's car." Charlie turned. "Did she spend the night here?"

"Yes."

"Why?"

"She—ah—wasn't feeling well."

Charlie stood scrutinizing him, then came toward the bed, her eyes fixed on his face. "What is it you wanted to talk to me about last night?"

"You have a big day ahead of you, Charlie." He threw off the woven ivory duvet cover, pushed himself to a sitting position, and moved to the edge of the bed. "Let's talk about it when you're through with your meetings."

"It's serious?"

"Nothing you need to think about now." He stood and went to the closet. "Just call me when you're through with things, and we'll get together."

"All right, then. I'll get in touch with you as soon as the meetings are over."

Janssen turned and faced her. "I'll look for your call."

Showered, shaved, and dressed, Janssen slumped onto the side of the bed as he heard Charlie's car pull out of the driveway. He was exhausted. All night he'd lain in the darkness, half dreaming, half awake, as the previous day's events swirled in his head. He remembered lying for what seemed forever with his face mashed into the hard surface of his desk, his body wracked with pain. He saw the president swiveling in his chair, heard Randall Robertson's smooth voice speaking the words "time travel" while the raucous talk show host prattled on about wormholes. Superimposed on the rest, the grief-stricken faces of Evie and Jenna continued to flash across the cinema of his mind all night. Once again he felt the heat and anguish of Evie's tears against his cheek.

Around three o'clock in the morning, he had gone downstairs for a glass of water. When he passed Evie's bedroom door, he heard her talking, and he looked in to see her kneeling on the floor, her eyes raised toward the ceiling. A light from the lamp outside her window cast a glow on her upturned face. She looked like an angel.

"God, please don't let Daddy die. God, I know you have more for him to do. Please, God. Let him live."

He thought about it now—her praying. Did prayer really work? Was there a God who actually heard people's prayers? He sat there and stared at the floor. His mother used to pray, he recalled, like Evie had done, on her knees. Sometimes she prayed just sitting up. He remembered once seeing her standing at the sink, praying and scrubbing potatoes. Strange he'd forgotten that.

He reached for his watch on the nightstand and wrapped it around his wrist, then rose from the bed and started for the stairs. Evie met him in the hall, and they embraced.

"I have a meeting with the president at eight o'clock. You can pray for me if you want. We'll see what he has to say. It'll either be a conversation about who we should get to replace me—or maybe they've discovered some new experimental cure." He smiled down at Evie, then rescued a stray lock of hair and brushed it back from her face.

Janssen found something incongruous about the sight of Dr. Edgar Bryant and Dr. Naomi Pruitt sitting amidst the majesty and sophistication of the Oval Office.

Dr Edgar Bryant was a middle-aged man with a large potbelly and an unkempt auburn-and-gray-streaked beard. His gray-brown eyes behind his heavy dark-rimmed glasses seemed unfocused, and, as he spoke, his eyes continually seemed fixed on nothing in particular—or something far away, Janssen couldn't decide which. When he spoke, the nasal quality of his voice almost drowned out his words.

His colleague, Dr. Naomi Pruitt, was a heavy woman with frizzy reddish hair. Her mouth stayed in the shape of a round O regardless of whether she was speaking or listening. Her pale blue eyes, topped by light brown lashes, offered scant contrast to her milky freckled complexion.

They seemed a ragtag pair, but the hope they offered made them the most beautiful sight Janssen had ever seen, and, as he listened to them speak, he conjectured they were undoubtedly the most brilliant as well.

Dr. Edgar Bryant was a renowned physicist and professor at Princeton University. Dr. Naomi Pruitt specialized in molecular medicine at Brigham and Women's Hospital at Harvard.

"Time travel sounds like science fiction," began Dr. Bryant in his almost theatrical nasal voice, "but today it is a lot more science than fiction." He chuckled at his own ironic humor. "For years, scientists have explored the possibility of traveling through time, even while the world scoffed at us. Today, we believe we have crossed barriers that will serve as an entrance into new dimensions."

Janssen sensed he was hearing Bryant's opening lines from the classes he taught at Princeton, but he hung on every word, as he imagined his life did as well.

"What you will be most interested in is what we call 'therapeutic time travel.' It differs from the time travel you hear discussed on the news, because it more closely resembles time *reversal*. In other words, as you go back in time, you actually travel through your own life in what we call a 'time womb,' briefly revisiting physical states of your own body."

He paused and stared blankly at the great seal emblazoned on the ceiling above him, then lowered his head and scratched the back of his neck.

"At the same time, my colleague here"—he looked toward Dr. Pruitt, and his mouth curled upward in a half-smile—"has been experimenting with a great deal of success in administering medical treatments to those whose healing can only have been accomplished at some remote time in the past." He adjusted his glasses. "In your case, Mr. LaMarche, the disease you have is congenital, and a cure can only be administered before birth, so the sole hope of a cure involves your being healed before you were born. Obviously you are already born. But with therapeutic time travel you can be sent back in time to the precise period when healing could take place, and the remedy can be successfully administered."

"Whew!" Janssen shook his head in disbelief. "You mean you've devised an actual system where I could go back to—the womb, be healed of this fatal disease, come back here to this time, and lead a normal life?"

"That's what I'm saying."

"Has it been done before?"

"Well, yes, it has been done. But you would be the first human." He scratched his head. "We have experimented with mice and monkeys, as I said, over the past fifteen years. The last subject was a monkey, Selma, who'd lost her leg to gangrene. We sent Selma back to the point when her leg could have been saved if treated properly, and Dr. Pruitt here was able to administer the drugs through time release capsules, dispensed by nanobots. Selma came back completely healed with two legs." His heavy eyebrows twitched up and down as he readjusted his glasses. He cleared his throat. "My understanding is you were born in 1995. Is that correct?"

"Yes."

"What month?"

"November."

"Perfect. 1995 is stupendous."

Janssen rubbed his chin, then raked his fingers through his mustache while he let the words sink in. "I hate to ask, but how does one get back in time?"

"Oh, that's the elementary part. We use a wormhole. It's wonderful. The genius of science and the wonder of the scientific mind through the ages. A number of years ago, we unearthed the journals of a physicist by the name of Sean Blanchard, who did his work in New Mexico. By studying his writings, we discovered he had created a minute wormhole in space in 1995, but thought it was worthless because it was too small for any known use. But today, through the use of lasers, high-powered mirrors, and a system of reflectors which separates out the negative parts of the laser beam, we have been able to inflate his wormhole to a completely traversable passageway to the past."

President Gelford leaned back in his chair and crossed his arms.

"Fascinating. I had no idea this was going on." He leaned forward again. "Of course, the age-old question with time travel is the same one I have now. Will anything be altered, other than Janssen being healed? In other words, if he, or anyone else, goes back in time, can anything happen where history could be changed?"

"Naturally, that is the question we always have to deal with," Dr. Bryant said. "The answer is not exact. But with the time womb, I don't believe we have to worry. Unless something is altered by Mr. LaMarche's going back, nothing will change in the future. To put it more plainly, if his going back does not cause anyone to do anything they did not do the first time around, then there will be no change in the chronology of events. If for some reason someone *did* alter their behavior, then everything is opened up to the possibility of change, which could cause problems. But I don't foresee that happening here."

"I see." The president turned toward Janssen. "So, LaMarche. What do you think so far?"

All eyes turned to Janssen, who sat on the couch envisioning himself being thrown down a black hole, arms and legs flailing as he sailed into pitch-black nothingness. "What is this wormhole like?"

"It's a tunnel through time," Dr. Bryant answered.

"You mean I would merely walk through it?"

Dr. Bryant's throaty phlegmatic laugh was interrupted by a spasm of coughing.

"No. You will travel through the wormhole in a soft plasma vehicle which we call the time womb. Your DNA is injected into the cushiony substance of the time womb to ensure you are locked in your own history in time. Because your individual DNA controls your destination, you can't get off the track."

Bryant paused, and everyone looked once again at Janssen.

"How do you feel about this, LaMarche?" Randall Robertson said, perusing Janssen's face. "It's your life, after all. The decision rests with you as to whether or not we will proceed."

"I don't seem to have a lot to lose. I'd like to talk to my family first, but barring anything dramatic, I think I would say yes."

"I was getting to the family thing," Randall said. "I'd hoped to hold a family briefing this afternoon. Unfortunately, the president is entertaining a number of foreign dignitaries, and I'm searching for an appropriate conference room at this point."

"You can use my conference room," Secretary Tomlin said. "I'm positive it's free later this afternoon. Say around three?"

"Perfect," Robertson said. "The president is hoping to involve only your immediate family, or those you are closest with. We need to keep this as confidential as possible."

"I understand."

Secretary Tomlin cleared his throat, leaned forward and steepled his fingers. "Now, how long will all this take?"

"Two days," Bryant said, "once he's back in the womb."

"How long altogether? From now until he returns?"

"I'm assuming you want the shortest time possible?"

"Expedited in as short a time as can be carried out successfully. This man has an important mission ahead of him, and we have no time to waste."

"Pruitt, I yield to you," Dr. Bryant said. "I believe you will be able to explain the time sequence of the procedure more clearly, since much of it is medical in nature."

Dr. Naomi Pruitt stretched the roundness of her mouth into a wider circle. She spoke haltingly, as though she needed time for her thoughts to catch up with her words.

"First—I will need to run a battery of tests on Mr. LaMarche. I have the records from Dr. Monnihan—but we must be very precise. Also, I plan to consult with a Dr. Meyers from Texas who has published papers on Ichiban Syndrome. I have already placed a call to him. But I believe we would get quicker response, Mr. President, if your office placed a call as well."

"I'll take care of it personally," Gelford said.

"I need to receive his expert guidance as I prepare the intrauterine treatment."

"Just fly him here and let him take part in the whole thing," Secretary Tomlin inserted. "We don't want to take any chances."

"Is that what you want?" With eyebrows raised, Pruitt looked at Tomlin, then the president.

"Yes."

Pruitt looked at Bryant. "We also need some advance time to send the scouts on ahead."

"Scouts? What's that?" Secretary Tomlin asked.

"The scouts are nanobots carrying magnets. They proceed ahead of LaMarche to scope out the exact destination in time and space we are aiming at," Bryant said. "They wait at the front end. Meanwhile, the time womb carries polarized magnets which are drawn into place by the scouts when they meet."

The secretary shook his head. "If it works, that's all I care about. So how long?"

"We'll have to prepare the time womb." Dr. Pruitt looked thoughtfully at Dr. Bryant, who nodded in response. "Preparation time could easily take two days."

"Can it be done in one?"

"Possibly."

"Do your best."

Dr. Pruitt looked at Gelford. "So your office will call Dr. Meyers, Mr. President?"

"I will call him personally. Just get his number to Kate. Anyone know what his party affiliation is?"

CHAPTER EIGHTEEN

It was a quaint old house, converted into a secondhand store. In alternating colors of blue, rose, yellow and green, childlike letters spelled the name "Sweet Peas" on the large sign above the door. A garland of miniature flowers scrolled about the edge.

Danny pulled alongside the curb, thrust open the door of his black Honda, and stepped around the car to the store's entrance. Slung over his arm was a red, black, and white plaid shirt. The windows of the shop were dark, and a "Closed" sign hung on the door, but he pulled on the handle anyway. It didn't budge.

The sign showed the hours as "9:30–5." Danny looked at his watch. It was now ten o'clock. He shrugged his shoulders, got back into the Honda, and headed back to the office.

"I can't find it here anywhere." Leslie Ann looked perplexed as she returned to her desk where Evie waited in the gold leather chair. "You know, I think Danny might have taken it with him when he left a little while ago. He was probably trying to escape the phone. The media have been hounding him all morning, and with Mr. LaMarche not here to consult about scheduling appointments, he said it would be better to just be out. Apparently Mr. LaMarche told him last night not to schedule any other interviews until they had a chance to talk."

Evie's shoulders drooped as she watched Leslie Ann drop into the chair behind the desk, causing it to swivel back and forth. "You haven't heard from my dad this morning?"

"No, and I have no idea where he is. There's nothing on his appointment calendar."

Evie heaved a sigh. "He had a meeting with the President at 8:00, but he should have been back by now."

"What?"

Evie shook her head. "Nothing. Nothing. Well, I guess I'll be going. Tell Dad to give me a call when he gets in, or if you hear from him."

"Sure will. What do you want me to tell Danny? Shall I have him call you about your shirt?"

Evie sighed again as she stood to her feet. "It doesn't really matter." She headed toward the entrance. "Thanks, Leslie Ann. I'll talk to you later."

As she closed the door to her father's office, a heavy lump formed in her throat. The sound of the door shutting behind her felt like an odd foreshadowing. Fear overtook her, and tears blurred her vision as she headed toward the elevators. She leaned on the down button, hoping to restrain her emotions until getting to her car. One of the elevators coming up from the first floor stopped on Two, then Five. When the doors opened, she moved toward the elevator and almost collided with a young man hurrying from inside.

It was Danny.

"Ohhh, sorry." He swayed backwards and stretched out his hand to keep from running into her in the corridor.

Evie slid to the side, dazed, still preoccupied with her thoughts. "Oh, it's you."

Danny smiled. "Yes, it's me."

Evie lowered her head to hide her tears and stepped past him to enter the elevator, but the doors closed before she reached them.

"What brings you up here—" Danny's question trailed off as he stared at her swollen and tear-stained eyes.

"I came to get my shirt. Leslie Ann said you might have it." She struggled to maintain a normal tone of voice.

Danny stood quietly watching her for several seconds. "Yes. I do have it." He shifted awkwardly from one leg to the other and began to stammer. "I didn't mean to upset you. Looks like I messed things up again. I'm sorry. Your shirt is in my car right now. I can go get it for you, if you'd like."

Evie looked up at him with mournful eyes. He was trying to be nice. "Thanks, Danny. I don't need it right now. I can get it later."

"It's no trouble. Are you on your way down? I'll go with you and get it out of my car." He pushed the button on the elevator, which was already descending from the upper floors. The bell dinged and the doors opened. "Come on. I'll get it for you now. Where are you parked?"

Chatting happily on the elevator and along the walkway into the parking garage, Danny seemed lost in a kind of euphoria. Evie uttered a few appropriately-timed ohs and mm-hmms, but wasn't really listening to him. Her mind was somewhere else.

On the third level of the parking garage, Danny beamed brightly. "Here we are. Now let me get your shirt."

Evie stopped suddenly and stared at the car Danny headed for. A black Honda with a University of Kansas sticker on the back. She looked from the car to Danny and back again. It had been in front of the house last night. But before that ...

The drive-thru line at Burger World. The picture flashed before her mind, and she saw the University of Kansas sticker. A slender young man. Black Honda.

"Do you ever go to Alexandria?" she asked.

"Why, yes," he responded agreeably. "It's a nice change from DC. I go over there sometimes just to get a break at lunch."

"Do you ever go to Burger World?"

Danny looked at her quizzically. "Yeah. I was just there the other day."

"For lunch at the drive-through?"

"Yes. Why?"

Evie rolled her eyes and shook her head. "Where's my shirt?"

Danny reached into the passenger side of his Honda, retrieved the shirt, and was about to offer it to her when she grabbed it out of his hand and turned on her heel.

"You are so rude."

He stared at her, his mouth open. "What do you mean? Because I gave you your shirt?"

With her emotions so raw, it felt good to turn her deep burning sadness into anger instead. "Do you happen to remember cutting off a blue Volvo in the drive-through line at Burger World on Tuesday and splashing mud all over the windshield?"

Danny turned white as his eyes grew round with a look of horror. He stared at Evie in disbelief. "That was *you*?"

"Yes, Danny. That was me. If it hadn't been for my automatic bumper guard, I'd have a dent in my right front fender to prove it." She glared at him in total disgust, shook her head, and tromped across the parking garage to her Volvo. Danny called after her feebly.

"I didn't mean—I was playing music—didn't see you ..."

Charlie's narrow blue eyes were fastened on Janssen as she spoke, her forehead furrowed.

"If there's any possible way out of this, then we have to take it, Janssen." She reached across the small round table in the coffee shop and took his hand. She was biting at her bottom lip, trying to stay strong for him, but her eyes gave away her fear. Janssen knew Charlie was not a woman to cry or let her emotions get the best of her. "What did they say are the odds of this therapeutic time travel being successful?"

"I didn't ask. But Dr. Bryant and Dr. Pruitt acted fairly confident. Of course, they're probably excited about having a human guinea pig to test out their theories." He laughed sarcastically. "But they want to have a briefing with the family today at three in the conference room of the Secretary of State's office complex, so you can ask any questions you have then."

Charlie nodded and looked away. "Who will you have there? I mean, who from the family?"

"They only want me to include family I'm most involved with on a day-to-day basis. Those I'm closest to. I thought I'd just have you and Jenna and Evie. Alexander has too many other things on his mind. And I don't think it would be wise to involve Dad."

"It's probably enough to tell Alexander and Dad you're having a fairly serious medical procedure and will be inaccessible for a couple of days."

"Yes, I guess we should at least prepare them, in case the worst—"

"But we'll believe for the best."

He nodded. "Charlie, as a side-note, I think you may need to do a little fence-mending with Evie. She was pretty upset you went to bed last night."

Charlie sighed, staring long into his eyes before she spoke.

"Janssen, I'm so sorry about that. I didn't realize the seriousness of what you were going to tell us last night. I'm not surprised Evie's upset with me." She shrugged her shoulders. "I've got so much on my mind, I guess I can seem a little cold at times. But we'll all get through this—together."

"I'm encouraged, Quigley. Sounds like you're on top of things. I'm impressed you've already managed to locate the weapons in northern Tajikistan."

Michael Quigley leaned back in his chair and crossed his arms in front of him.

"Technology, Secretary Tomlin. There was a time I might have taken credit, but I'm smart enough now to know it's the technology that does it, not me. I just know how to use it."

"Hmm. Well. Sounds good. Can you tell what kind of weapons they are?"

"They don't appear to be nuclear. Satellites have picked up no sign of radioactive decay. My guess is they're chemical and biological. The optics and photonics sensors should be able to tell us soon."

"Not nuclear though?" Tomlin asked in apparent relief.

Michael frowned in concern.

"No. But that doesn't lessen the danger, Mr. Secretary. With today's technology, and the chemical compound Jones spoke of at the meeting in the Oval Office, even chemical or biological weapons developed forty years ago could have more devastating and far-reaching effects now than they did back then."

"How's that?"

"It would be nothing today to develop delivery systems to launch these weapons into distant reaches of the globe and disseminate them over large geographical areas."

"Frightening prospect."

"Yes, particularly since we don't even know who we're competing with to obtain them. Has LaMarche made any progress?"

"They're talking." Secretary Tomlin looked at his watch, then rose from the high-back chair behind his desk. "I'm going to have to excuse myself. Another appointment at three." He reached across the polished walnut surface stacked with papers to shake Michael Quigley's hand.

Quigley got up and stood opposite the distinguished gentleman.

"Keep up the good work, and keep me abreast of any new developments."

"Absolutely, Mr. Secretary. I'll continue checking the coordinates to make sure we've pinpointed the location as precisely as possible."

Tomlin nodded, then shook his head. "Quantum physics and modern technology never cease to amaze me. What can't we do these days?"

Michael ambled across the room to the door and made his way down the long hall toward the reception area. He pushed open the outer door and quickly stopped. Janssen LaMarche stood at the front desk.

Michael winced as he considered his options. At the meeting in the Oval Office, he'd managed to arrive late and leave early to avoid a confrontation with his former brother-in-law. But now he couldn't leave the Secretary of State's office without walking directly past him.

He had to admit it. He was embarrassed and ashamed. He and Janssen had spoken only briefly on a couple of occasions since his divorce from Jenna, but he could tell the usually amicable Janssen LaMarche did not have fond feelings for him. Their exchanges had been courteous but cool. Being on his team to Tajikistan was awkward for them both—probably a shock for Janssen, he surmised, but a real opportunity for him.

Michael squared his shoulders, took a deep breath, and headed toward the front desk. Seeing Janssen spotting him as well, he extended his right hand.

"Congratulations on this assignment, Janssen. Everything I've seen so far looks very positive. I expect to see good results from the mission." He almost said "our" mission, but quickly restrained himself.

Janssen returned the handshake politely. "Yes, I hope it will be successful—all the way around."

"Yes." Michael felt a little off-balance from Janssen's chilly response. Did he have a hidden message of some kind in the words *all the way around*? Or was Michael being paranoid and oversensitive?

"Uhh, how's the family?"

"Fine." Janssen observed Michael with a penetrating gaze.

Feeling his former brother-in-law's eyes boring into his, Michael shifted his weight from one foot to the other and crossed his arms in front of him.

"Are you having any luck in locating the weapons?" Janssen asked. "With quantum technology, I imagine you can do it remotely."

Michael relaxed his arms to his sides as his nervousness eased up. Quantum technology. Safe conversational ground. He felt the air clear somewhat.

"Yes, as a matter of fact." He lowered his voice to avoid being overheard by staff in the vicinity. "I believe we've located them."

"Already? Good. It should help in the negotiations."

A wave of relief and satisfaction spread through Michael's tall frame. The conversation was going well. He straightened. "Hopefully we'll have more detailed information soon."

Janssen nodded. "Very good, very ..." Janssen's eyes strayed, and Michael heard the door from the hallway opening behind him. Janssen's face brightened, then clouded just as suddenly. "Jenn!"

Michael felt the color drain from his face, the confidence of the previous moment quenched by a numbing dread. He turned toward the door, toward the woman who'd been his wife for sixteen years and his ex for seven. A woman he'd not seen since a few months after he divorced her.

Jenna LaMarche.

CHAPTER NINETEEN

With only candlelight in a few windows along its narrow, winding streets, the village was dark at one o'clock in the morning. In a small room beside the craggy cliffs at the edge of town, a muffled droning awoke the man sleeping under a blanket on a thin mattress. His hand groped in the blackness toward the sound. At once the noise ceased, and a light emanated from a belt buckle lying on a rough table beside his makeshift bed. He flipped up a brass ring, punched a button, and watched words scroll across the screen encased within.

"Coordinates located. Call home."

When Jenna opened the door, she spotted her brother standing near the reception desk talking to a tall man with thinning blonde hair. Their heads were close together as if speaking confidentially. Janssen's eyes met hers with a look of surprise.

"Jenn!" A smile flickered across his lips, then faded. When his companion turned around, Jenna froze, her hand still on the door handle. After the events of the past two days, her mind was in a whirl. Her first inclination was to turn around and leave immediately, but she couldn't seem to move.

Coming to her rescue, Janssen cut across the reception area to stand by her side. He patted her shoulder and brushed his face against her cheek. "It's okay. I'll explain," he whispered.

She peered up at Janssen in confusion.

"I hadn't had a chance to tell you yet, Jenna," Janssen said in a normal voice Michael could hear, "but Michael is on my team to Tajikistan. He'll be heading up the munitions inspection."

"Your team." Her voice was flat. "To Tajikistan." She felt two worlds colliding inside her head.

"Yes." His eyes begged her to understand.

Jenna swallowed hard. She drew in her breath and turned to face Michael as she tried to muster a smile. "Hello, Michael."

Michael nodded and crossed the room to stand before her. "How are you, Jenna?"

"O-kay." She let her voice lilt upwards in her response, trying to sound cheerful, although she felt anything but.

"You're looking—really good."

Jenna flushed. *A compliment from Michael?* Now she knew this was a dream. She swiveled her shoulders with a sassy lift and tossed her head. "I *am* really good."

Both men laughed.

"That's my Jenn," Janssen said.

One corner of Michael's mouth turned upward. "Yeah."

Evie slid into the chair beside her father, who was already at the table in the conference room next to Jenna. She slipped her arm through his.

"How are you, Daddy?"

"Doing okay." Janssen reached over and patted Evie's hand.

"You said the president is going to explain a plan that might be able to cure you?"

"That's right." Janssen tried to smile encouragingly, even as he wondered how his family would feel about the proposed cure. "Actually, I don't think the president will be here. It's his deputy chief of staff, Randall Robertson."

Charlie's tall trim figure appeared in the doorway, followed by Randall Robertson. Jenna moved over to let Charlie sit between her and Janssen. Robertson shut the door, then shook hands with each family member as Janssen introduced them. He circled to the opposite side of the conference table, where he stood with hands behind his back.

"I know this has been a hard time for all of you, but some answers have surfaced which may offer the miracle you're looking for." He paused for a moment, choosing his words. "However, it probably doesn't come in a form you would expect."

As Robertson introduced the subject of time travel, Evie and Jenna gasped and looked at Janssen wide-eyed. He smiled and nodded to let them know he was fully attuned to what was coming. Thankfully, he'd already filled Charlie in on the prospect when he first told her about his illness earlier in the day.

As Robertson concluded his opening remarks, the door eased open and Drs. Bryant and Pruitt entered, along with a tall, distinguished gentleman. Robertson motioned them to his side and extended his hand. "Dr. Meyers?"

"Yes."

"Pleased to meet you. Randall Robertson. Won't you three have a seat?"

Robertson introduced them to the family and explained their roles, credentials, and backgrounds, then turned and faced the doctors.

"I've given these folks a brief description of what will happen, but perhaps you would each like to elaborate a little. Dr. Meyers, I don't think any of us exactly understand the medical procedure. Why don't you begin?" Robertson pulled a chair out for himself, positioned it where he would have a clear view of everyone, and then sat.

"I guess I'm kind of the newcomer here," Dr. Meyers said, looking around the room. "I'll have to tell you, I have no experience whatever with time travel." He motioned to the family members sitting on the other side of the table. "What I know, however, is there is absolutely no known cure for adults with Ichiban Syndrome. It's a fatal disease. But there is a cure if it's identified in the womb, early in gestation. When we do DNA testing right before the beginning of the third month of pregnancy, the disease is easily identifiable and easily eradicated. But it's important we treat the child during the eleventh week of gestation. At this point, he's fully formed, but it's still early enough to make DNA alterations."

Meyers looked at Dr. Bryant, then at Dr. Pruitt. "My question to you would be this. Are you able to pinpoint the time in the gestation period so precisely in the therapeutic time travel process? It seems it would be difficult."

Pruitt spoke up. "You just brought up the biggest challenge for me, Dr. Meyers. If we knew his was a full-term birth, it would be fairly elementary. However, Mr. LaMarche doesn't seem to know if he was full-term or not."

Janssen looked at Jenna. "You don't happen to know, do you?"

"Hmm. Maybe we should have included Dad. He should know."

"I didn't think including him would be a good idea with his age and his health and ..."

Jenna nodded her head. "I know. You're right. Maybe I could just call him and ask him the question. Of course, he'll think it's a bit odd, but he thinks lots of things are odd."

Spontaneous chuckling spread among the LaMarche family members.

"Why don't I do it?" Janssen offered. "It would seem more natural for me to ask."

"Good point," Jenna said.

Robertson spoke up. "Then you'll call your father, LaMarche, to get the information? Sounds like pinpointing the time would be helpful." He looked at Meyers and Pruitt.

"Yes, the more precise we can be, the less opportunity exists for error." Pruitt stretched her mouth into a wider circle. "But with the camera taking visuals of the fetus, I think we can probably pinpoint it visually anyway."

"Oh, you have cameras?" Meyers looked at Pruitt. "We'll be able to see the fetus?"

"Yes."

"Well, then it shouldn't be a problem. The eleven-week fetus is pretty easy to discern. He's completely formed down to his fingers and toes, even fingernails. All the body systems are working." He spoke proudly, as though he were speaking of his own child. "He breathes, swallows, squints. He can make a fist, and he can even bend his fingers around an object. All in one tiny package. We should be able to pinpoint the target time quite easily."

Evie ran her fingers under the blonde hair at the nape of her neck and tilted her head as she listened to the doctors. "Uh ... can we be present during all this?"

The four on the other side of the table glanced at each other. Dr. Bryant pulled on his beard and spoke up. "Seems reasonable to me."

Pruitt looked at Bryant. "I don't see any reason why they can't be there."

"We'll be able to see my brother in the womb?" Jenna said.

"Yes, with our optical scan cameras, you'll be able to follow him through the entire procedure."

The three women looked at Janssen. Jenna smirked, and a dimple dented her cheek. "Well, little brother, we'll have your number after this."

Randall Robertson laughed and ran a glance over the three women sitting beside Janssen. His gaze lingered on Evie.

"We'll also have audio," Pruitt continued. "You'll be able to hear everything Mr. LaMarche hears."

"Even in the womb?" Jenna asked.

"Even in the womb." Pruitt said. "We will have a microchip implanted in LaMarche from which we can hear everything he would be able to hear. The audio chip in the womb will be similar to a fetus hearing the surroundings of his mother."

"You're not going to tell me the fetus can hear," Charlie said.

"Yes, he can," Meyers said. "We know for a fact a thirteen-week-old fetus hears many things—his mother's voice, loud noises, music. Some believe even in the eleven and twelve-week-old fetus, the auditory nerves, brain functioning, and memory patterns are developed enough for him to hear some of these noises."

"In addition," Pruit said, "we've enhanced the microchip program to filter out the distortions that may result from the amniotic fluid to clarify what is heard. It's quite amazing. You'll literally be able to hear a pin drop."

Meyers grinned disarmingly at Jenna, then at Charlie and Evie. "Could prove rather interesting for you ladies ... you'd get a peek into your mother's life when she was a young woman." Everyone was silent for a moment.

Randall Robertson leaned forward and looked at the three women. "Do you have any questions?"

"Yes, I do." Charlie straightened herself in her chair and cleared her throat. "What are the actual odds of success?"

Drs. Pruitt and Bryant looked at one another, motioning with their eyes for the other to go first.

"As for the success of the medical procedure," Dr. Pruitt said at last, "I'd say there is at least an eighty percent chance of success, once Mr. LaMarche arrives at the correct time and place. The most difficult part of the procedure is what we have already discussed—making sure he gets back to exactly the right time, which is the eleventh week."

"It could work all right in the twelfth week too," interjected Dr. Meyers. "There's a little leeway."

"We will be giving him a time-release capsule designed to begin when he gets back to the proper destination. But he will also be monitored remotely by us, and we can either delay or speed up the delivery of the serum."

"How's that?" Charlie asked.

"We are sending nanobots back with him. One hive will be a medical team whose function is to make sure the medicine is administered on time—or when we tell it to."

"Hive? Nanobots?" Evie's forehead crinkled in puzzlement. "Exactly what are nanobots? I know they're real small. Aren't they supposed to be smaller than a hair?"

Bryant spoke up. "They are, in fact, a thousand times smaller than the diameter of a human hair. They operate in swarms or hives. By themselves they can do nothing.

But put a million of them together and program them for a specific function, and they can accomplish amazing feats. There will be several hives of nanobots on this mission, each charged with a different responsibility. One hive will control the audio we were discussing. One will control the video, another will administer the medicine, and three will be in charge of the time womb."

Pruitt pursed her lips with a look of amusement. "We've even given them names."

"Names?" Janssen said. "Like what?"

"The swarm going ahead of the mission is called Scout," she said. "The group which goes along to guide the time womb is called Ranger. Bell will control the audio, Actor will control the video. Doctor will be there for the medicine administration, and so on."

Janssen chuckled. "Well, I'm glad I'm not going back in time alone. Sounds like I'll have plenty of company."

"Dad," Evie said, shaking her head. "You're amazing."

Bryant was watching Pruitt with a glint in his eyes. She looked back at him roundly. "That's all I have to say. Dr. Bryant. You have the floor. What are the odds of success from your perspective?"

"Ummm, yes, the odds." His eyebrows twitched twice. "In terms of the mission back in time being successful, I'd say the odds are seventy percent. That's still good, wouldn't you say?"

Jenna frowned and fidgeted with her collar. "What are the dangers?"

Bryant stared blankly at the cornice above the doorway for what Janssen thought was an exceedingly long time.

"One danger would be virtual particles popping up around the time womb and damaging it. But we are taking every precaution to eliminate anything which would attract them, like metal. Mr. LaMarche will be meticulously dressed in a decontaminated substance which will not interfere with the magnetic forces of hyperspace. Also a failure in the lasers or reflectors could cause the neck of the wormhole to constrict so tightly that Mr. LaMarche would be unable to make it through. But this is *highly* unlikely. We have tested the lasers and the mirrors and the reflectors quite extensively. They are working perfectly. "

"What would happen to him if he couldn't make it through?"

"According to Einstein's theory, the intense force and near-infinite space time curvature would stretch him like a piece of spaghetti. It would not be an agreeable experience. But that's not going to happen."

Bryant scratched the top of his head. "Asking what would happen if he doesn't come through is like asking what would happen to you if you were hit head-on by a Mack truck. The experience would be terrible—but chances are very slim it will ever happen to you."

"We've tested this procedure a number of times with animals," Dr. Pruitt interjected, "and there have been no problems with the lasers." Dr. Pruitt then proceeded to tell them about their success with the monkey Selma.

"And one other thing I want to mention to you, Mr. LaMarche," Pruitt continued. "We don't know how the trip in the time womb will affect your physical comfort. Consequently, we have tried to provide for different possibilities. In the pocket of your robe, there will be a packet with two pink pills and two blue pills. If you experience nausea, take one pink pill. If the pressure feels too intense, take one blue pill. The second set of pills is for your return trip. The pills are fastened into the decon robe, so they will disappear and reappear along with the robe."

"When and where will this time travel take place?" Jenna asked.

"Our laboratory is in the basement of an annex of Walter Reed Army Medical Center," Bryant said. "We'll give you the address. As far as when it will happen, we will proceed as soon as everything is ready. Secretary Tomlin asked us to expedite the mission as quickly as possible."

Randall Robertson moved to the edge of his chair.

"Dr. Bryant is exactly right. We'll move as soon as they give us the green light. If any of you want to be there when Mr. LaMarche departs, I suggest you be ready at any moment. We will not wait for anything or anybody." He looked at each family member. "I'll be responsible for making phone calls to you at the appropriate time. Just be sure to give me your contact information."

Robertson raised a forefinger. "One more thing. Do not tell *anyone* what we are doing here. This is highly confidential."

Evie was exhausted when she drove into the driveway of the Georgian townhouse she called home. After leaving the family briefing, she spent a few hours at Sweet Peas, organizing things for the next couple of days so Helen could handle the store without her. The techs were still trying to get the computer back up, and Evie wanted to make sure it would not cause problems while she was away.

She trudged up the walkway to the front entrance of her apartment. The emotional roller coaster of the last twenty-four hours had left her numb. The only thought she could focus on was whether to bother getting undressed for bed or just fall fully clothed onto the bedcovers.

As she climbed the steps, the front light beamed down on a large bouquet of flowers on the front porch. Coming closer, she saw all her favorite blooms. She leaned over, breathed in the sweet fragrances, and turned the arrangement around to find a name.

A card dangled from a thin blue ribbon fastened in the middle. She drew it closer and saw "I'm sorry for the things I've done. Most humbly and apologetically yours …Danny."

At the sight of the flowers and the card, the strain of the day, along with Evie's fear and simmering grief, lessened and gave her hope for tomorrow. She picked up the flowers and carried them inside to her bedroom. Setting them on the table beside her bed, she crawled under the covers and fell asleep.

By the time Janssen and Charlie turned into their driveway, it was late. Janssen's body ached with fatigue. His mind was numb.

When the meeting with Robertson and the doctors ended, it was almost evening, and he'd had another episode of pain, intense muscle contractions, and dizziness. Jenna and Evie had already left, and it was the first time Charlie had witnessed the disease's effects. Thankfully he had brought his pills, and Dr. Meyers was quick to give him a shot which immediately relaxed his muscles, preventing his symptoms from reaching the severity of the day before.

Later, he called his father to see if his dad remembered whether his birth had been full term. It was no surprise to Janssen when Phillip grew irritated with a question seemingly irrelevant fifty-six years after the fact. But not only did his father sound annoyed, his tone hinted at defensiveness. Finally, Phillip told him as far as he could remember, Janssen's birth had been full term.

When Janssen called Alexander, he could tell from his son's preoccupied tone that his call had interrupted something important. He tried to make it brief. He simply told Alexander he was going into the hospital to have a procedure done.

"Anything serious?" Alexander asked.

Janssen didn't think he really wanted to know all the details. "Oh, it's some long, drawn-out thing the doctor wants to do. I've been having a little pain. You know how doctors are. They want to probe everything that's ever happened to you—almost from before you were born."

Alexander's nervous laugh betrayed his relief that it wasn't something critical requiring his undivided attention. He sounded anxious to get off the phone. "Yeah. They get carried away," he said.

"Well, I just wanted to let you know."

"Yeah, thanks for calling, Dad. Hope you get some rest in the hospital."

"Oh, I'm sure I will. I have a feeling I'll be sleeping like a baby."

Now, as he stepped out of his car, he had a surreal sense he was entering a kind of twilight zone, where whatever happened next was out of the range of known expectations. He was too tired to try to comprehend it. Sleep sounded like an attractive option.

He pushed through the back door with the intention of heading directly for the stairs and bed, but then hesitated at his study door. He hadn't checked his email all day. He collapsed onto a chair and rotated the screen on his Q watch to 'Email.' Into his mailbox came the name Oqilov.

An email from Uncle Jocko. The subject line read *Confidential.* He highlighted the post and read the message. It was short, consisting mainly of one name—

Tahad Abdul Azzadafa. Nothing else, except an abstruse admonition.

Please no response by phone, email, or text.

CHAPTER TWENTY

He was reading an e-book, a suspense-thriller. Gripped in the conflict of the intensifying drama, he expectantly clicked to the next page. Only one phrase was printed there, but it appeared over and over and spread across the holographic screen, multiplying and filling the entire window—Tahad Abdul Azzadafa.

Advancing to the next page, he encountered the words again—line after line of the one name streaming down the page. Scrolling from one screen to the next, he saw the name running down the pages without end. "Where's the rest of the story?" he heard himself ask. He clicked to other programs, but the only phrase that appeared on his display was Tahad Abdul Azzadafa. It was like a virus, taking over his communications system. He closed the folder in frustration, climbed out of his chair, stepped backward, and plunged headlong into the nothingness of a black hole.

He awoke in the middle of the night, drenched in sweat.

The sun streaming through the windows the next morning jolted Janssen from his uneasy sleep. He shuddered, the nightmare's specter still clinging to his mind. He fought back a tumult of mental images as the cobwebs of sleep slowly scattered.

The aroma of sizzling bacon brought him into a full state of consciousness. Charlie had let him sleep. She was making breakfast. He looked at the clock. Obviously they hadn't gotten the call yet. He heaved a heavy sigh. Would this wild adventure bring the cure they expected? He could only hope. But it was a hope that was tethered to a portentous, constraining fear.

The morning light from the windows dimmed. Through the windows he spied dark clouds drifting across the sun. Janssen threw back the ivory comforter and jumped out of bed. He was anxious to get going with everything and have it over.

He and Charlie were in the kitchen having their third cups of coffee when the phone rang. It was Randall Robertson.

"We're ready to go."

As they turned off the highway and headed down Missouri Avenue to Georgia Street, the sun, which had been slipping in and out of the clouds all morning, finally faded away. A heavy cloud cover descended upon the city.

Janssen looked up at the sky. "Hurricane Ophelia."

"I gather the hurricane is still trying to make up its mind where to hit," Charlie said. "It's beginning to look nasty. We may be in for a storm."

"To look at the bright side, I won't have to worry about the hurricane," Janssen quipped. "A storm here today won't have much effect on me when I'm back in 1995."

Charlie smiled bleakly and reached for his hand. "You're something else."

She turned on Columbia, then again on 14th. After taking a few hills and winding around some curves, Charlie slowed the car and turned her head to look out the window at the dilapidated neighborhood. "You sure we've got the right street?"

"That's what Cool Navigator said."

"Hmm. Which building is it?" She looked at the screen, then back out the window. "Doesn't look like an area where we'd find a hospital."

"Nooo, it doesn't." Janssen looked at the address printed on the paper he'd been given and the one he'd entered on his device.

At the top of a hill, a mammoth edifice loomed above the surrounding structures. As they approached it, Cool Navigator began to blink. "Arriving at destination."

"That must be it."

Charlie pulled the car in front, and they both scanned the façade for an address. "There it is," Charlie said. "See? Behind the ivy."

"Yes. 1259. That's it."

Charlie maneuvered into a spot at the side of the building. Janssen straightened his shoulders. "Well, here we go."

The structure was old with grime-caked windows. Janssen pulled hard at the handle on the massive front doors. Charlie entered first. Janssen followed.

"Which way do we go?"

Janssen perused the paper. "This way, to the right."

At the first intersection, Janssen shook his head. "Not this one. Let's try the one up there."

They turned right again, then took an immediate left. Charlie cleared her throat. The air was musty and stale. She coughed. "I can't say this building has been kept up too well."

Together, they wove through the narrow hallways, their footsteps on the marble floor echoing.

At last, they arrived at a steel door at the end of a small alcove. A sign said "Private: Research Personnel Only."

"This is it." Janssen punched a code into a pad on the right. The lock disengaged with a quiet click.

He stepped back to let Charlie enter first, then followed her down another passageway to an elevator.

He pressed a green button and waited. The elevator doors opened, and he pushed the button marked "B."

When the doors opened again, they stood motionless, staring at the enormous space stretching out before them, its floor bustling with activity.

The laboratory was a monotone room—its only pop of color a red couch near the elevators. A lounge with five round tables, each encircled by four chairs, took up part of the far wall opposite the doors where they stood. Muted newscasts flickered across a plasma video screen mounted high on one wall. A gigantic monitor dominated the room's center, encased by speakers and surrounded by groupings of sofas. The underground lab was as modern, immaculate, and sophisticated as the building's entrance was drab, dingy, and unkempt.

To their right was a row of instrument panels and monitors. Men and women dressed in uniforms walked around, some wearing goggles and virtual gloves, others with wire headphones and microphones. The other end of the room was divided by a wall of glass. Beyond the glass, Janssen saw a white vehicle about the size of a small car, made of something that looked like foam rubber—all enclosed, girdled by a clear transparent substance which Janssen assumed to be windows. The vehicle had no wheels, but appeared to sit on a kind of track. To the right, at the end of the track was a partitioned entryway. Janssen could see nothing beyond the first few feet.

"Within the next two hours, we expect to receive the signal from Scout that the magnet has reached its destination." Janssen jumped at the sudden sound of Dr. Bryant's voice. He had not seen Bryant when they first stepped out of the elevator, but suddenly Bryant was there beside them, explaining the schedule for the day and describing the varied apparatus assembled throughout the facility. "We intend to have you ready by the time we hear from Scout, so we can send you on your way." Bryant's obvious enthusiasm made Janssen a little nervous. Charlie looked at Janssen, nodded, and squeezed his arm.

Bryant escorted Janssen to a secured door marked: *Decontamination Area.*

"This is where your voyage begins. The assistant inside will describe what is to follow. Be advised, however, once you enter here, you cannot exit until your mission is over."

Evie and Jenna arrived, and after they'd spent a few minutes together, one of Bryant's assistants slipped up to the group and gestured to Janssen. "We need to begin."

As he made his way to the door, he noticed Evie standing with her chin cocked, looking up at Charlie sideways. Charlie smoothed her jacket over her slender hips, turned, and said something to Evie. Jenna was watching him, her mouth closed tight above her square jaw, apparently trying to stay out of the scenario unfolding beside her.

The small room beyond the door was painted yellow, but the large room visible beyond a glass enclosure was pure white. Even the assistants' clothes were bleached and spotless. One of them greeted him as he entered.

"You must thoroughly bathe yourself with the special soap you'll find in the bathing area." She pointed to a door on his left. "It's important you not carry any germs or bacteria into the past, which might alter events. When you've bathed, put on the robe, underwear and shoes you will find in this package. They're made of a protein material that will dissolve when the time womb inserts you into your mother's womb. Your pills are in the pocket."

She handed Janssen a package containing the garments to be worn. "When you've disrobed, put your clothes on the chair outside the stall. Someone will remove them while you're in the shower. When you leave the shower, exit from the other side, and you'll enter the White Room."

As Janssen began to undress, his mind returned to the mission which the president, the secretary, and the world were relying on him to accomplish. The importance the president placed on the mission was reflected in the enormous expenditure of money and resources his administration freely gave to save Janssen's life.

Janssen's mind drifted to the name Jocko had emailed him the night before.

Tahad Abdul Azzadafa. The palms of his hands grew sweaty as he realized he hadn't given the name to anyone.

I should have called Secretary Tomlin.

He looked at his Q watch. No. Calling by Q would be insecure. He should have called from his satellite phone that morning. His mind had been too full of everything. He'd forgotten.

He stared around the room, then rummaged through the pockets of his pants. No pen or paper. Barefoot, with his belt unbuckled and shirt untucked, he stepped back outside the door. "Um, ma'am?" He waited until the assistant came around to where he stood.

"Yes?"

"Could I have a pen and a sheet of paper?"

The perky middle-aged woman smiled knowingly. "Leaving your wife a love note?"

"Hmm. Give me two sheets of paper, if you will, and—say, can I hang onto my Q watch for a while—until I leave? I'd like to do a little work while I'm waiting. I can soap it down."

"Here, let me have it. We have a special way of cleaning instruments and mechanical devices. I'll put it in the other room for you."

"Thanks. I'd appreciate that."

Quickly, he scribbled the name "Tahad Abdul Azzadafa" on one sheet of paper. On the other, he wrote a short note to his family.

Just in case I don't make it back.

He folded the first sheet into the last one, folded them both again, and placed them carefully in the pocket of his pants.

After Janssen finished undressing, he placed his clothes and the pen on the designated chair, then took the package of special garments with him to the shower, pulling the robe out and hanging it over the edge of the stall. Turning on the water, he let it run over his skin, enjoying the massage of the warm spray and the luxury of the moment while his mind switched back and forth between his mission to Tajikistan and his present plight. Life had taken so many twists and turns in the last few days. He knew whatever lay ahead was in the hands of providence and out of his control. He scrubbed his hair and felt the soap foam trickle over his face. He heard someone come in to retrieve his clothes, then walk out.

His mind switched back to the message from Jumakhan. Why the cryptic message? Who was Tahad Abdul Azzadafa?

As he soaped down his neck and chest, his wet fingers slid up against something hard and uneven. It was the gold chain he always wore around his neck. *The medallion. I forgot to remove the gold medallion.* He was so used to wearing it, he'd forgotten about it. Looping it over his head, he slipped the chain from around his neck and cupped the medallion in his hand. *Now what do I do with this?* He looked around, saw the robe hanging over the edge, and fumbled in the soft folds. He found a small pocket and slipped the medallion into it.

CHAPTER TWENTY-ONE

Janssen was glad he'd asked to have his Q watch. The wait for Scout to arrive was longer than expected. After he left the bathing area for the White Room, Drs. Bryant and Pruitt, now dressed in white and looking quite professional, showed him the time womb, describing for Janssen how it would work and what he could expect. Janssen craned his neck to see beyond the glass, wondering if his family had stayed. He spotted them standing near the window talking to Randall Robertson, who had obviously been sent to check on the progress of the enterprise.

When Bryant and Pruitt finished their demonstration, Janssen sat in a plastic chair beside his vehicle, took out his Q watch and checked his messages. Several standard department memos downloaded. There was another from Danny asking when he could schedule an interview with Newsweek, then an email from a sender he failed to recognize. He highlighted it and watched his screen fill up with what appeared to be a playing card of the four of clubs. *What the ... ?* He scrolled down to see if there was an explanation. *Nothing.* Puzzled, he rubbed his fingers over his chin and through his mustache, then saw another message from the same sender enter his mail box. He quickly highlighted it and read the message. "Iraq 2003."

He stared at the words and switched back to the previous screen. Four of clubs. "Iraq 2003" the other said. *Hmm. That's a bit of history.* He recalled the accounts of the Iraqi war in his history books and vaguely remembered the conflict that had dominated the news when he was just a boy of eight. He looked at the four of clubs again.

"Of course," he said aloud. *Wasn't there something called the Iraqi Deck of Cards listing the US most wanted from the Iraqi conflict?* Yes, one of his friends at the Embassy actually had an Iraqi deck of cards. They had played gin rummy with it. Why would someone send this to him now? And anonymously? He looked at the sender's address and hit reply. A message box appeared. "Undeliverable." *Just as I suspected. Scrambled. 2003 was 50 years ago.* Either someone was trying to confuse him or trying to tell him something—someone who wanted to remain anonymous. He looked back at the screens, trying to make a connection. *Four of clubs. Iraq 2003.*

He clicked on his search menu and typed in "Deck of Cards" and "Iraq". When a list of options appeared, he picked one that looked like it would provide the most exhaustive material. Janssen skipped through the general information explaining how the Deck of Cards was used among coalition forces to aid in finding and capturing former Iraqi leaders considered dangerous or guilty of crimes, until he came to pictures of the cards themselves. He scrolled down to the Four of Clubs and caused it to enlarge. The picture and name of the Ba'ath Party leader filled the screen. Janssen stared at it, frozen. Beneath the card was the name of an Iraqi leader once deemed one of the most dangerous individuals in the world. He had been captured by the US, tried, and found guilty of terrible crimes. Janssen riveted his eyes on the name, overwhelmed by his mental connections forming at light speed. The name he was looking at, printed under the Four of Clubs, was Sayad Radazon Azzadafa.

Janssen's mind raced. He clicked on the picture again for more detailed information and quickly scanned a summary of the man's role in the Ba'ath Party, along with his capture and trial. In the biographical section, Janssen read at the time of the Iraqi war, Sayad Radazon Azzadafa had a ten-year-old son. Janssen noted the boy would have been about his age at the time. Nothing further was known about the boy after his father had been taken into custody. He read through it again, looking for the son's name. Not there. He scrolled through the rest of the personals, but still found no mention of the name of Azzadafa's son.

From the corner of his eye, Janssen saw a flurry of activity around the time womb and sensed his time for departure was near. His heart thumped wildly as he scrolled through other pages of information. The name had to be somewhere.

He found one more reference to Azzadafa and clicked on it. Impatiently, he read through much of the same information he'd seen previously, with a large portion about other Ba'ath Party leaders. His hands were sweating. Everything was written in long, detailed paragraphs. Finally, in the middle of a tedious portion of text, he discovered references to family. Reading through the lists of names, he at last found mention of Azzadafa's wife and son. And then, at last, there it was—the name of Sayad Radazon Azzadafa's son.

Tahal Abdul Azzadafa.

Janssen heard a shout coming from the monitors in the other room, then an animated voice over the loud speaker.

"Scout has arrived at his destination." The awaited signal had come. Drs. Bryant, Pruitt and the rest of the research and scientific team were jubilant.

Janssen looked to the window where Charlie, Evie and Jenna stood waiting and talking. Evie caught his eye, smiled, and spoke to the others as she pointed at him. Jenna and Charlie turned and gazed in his direction. One of the lab assistants strode toward him.

"We're ready," she said.

Janssen let out a sigh and nodded. He licked his lips and walked over to the three women. Through the glass they said their last goodbyes.

"Uhh, check the pocket of my pants," Janssen said. "There's a note there for Secretary Tomlin ... and one for you too. I love you." He went to each one, put his palm against the hands they held up to the glass, then blew them a kiss and smiled. "Just don't be jealous now ... that you guys don't get to go back to your roots like I'm doing. I'll tell you all about it in a few days."

Evie's eyes were moist. She shut her eyes, then opened them and smiled.

Charlie stood between Evie and Jenna with an arm around each and nodded encouragingly to him. "Don't worry. We'll be fine." Janssen was glad to see Charlie and Evie had apparently made up.

Jenna tugged nervously at the collar of her shirt and winked at him.

"You know, we may have more to tell you about your trip than you have to tell us. We'll be watching you the whole time, you know."

Janssen shook his head, smiled, and made his way back to his transport.

Bryant's assistants carefully strapped Janssen in, then lowered the windowed hatch. He had a 360-degree view of his surroundings. He was excited, apprehensive, and incredulous all at once. Whatever else happened, it was bound to be a fascinating journey. Even if this was the end, his life would close at a climactic moment. He would have an experience no other human had ever known. Slowly, smoothly, his vehicle began to move forward. He looked toward the window. Evie, Jenna and Charlie were waving. He blew them a kiss. His journey to the past was underway.

The time womb entered a tunnel and proceeded down a tubular steel track toward what looked like a wall at the end. Fleetingly, it reminded Janssen of a ride at Disney World that appears to be heading for a crash into a barrier, which opened at the last second. However, the time womb was not moving fast like the rides at Disney World—rather, it moved slowly, deliberately. As the lip of the time womb touched the wall at the end, the wall fell away, and a powerful vacuum drew him inside.

But was he inside? Or outside? Tiny pinpricks of light studded the blackness as Janssen spiraled through an invisible passageway to somewhere—or nowhere. The lights fuzzed over, blurring into a haze. He seemed to be spinning, or perhaps the space around him was spinning. He couldn't be certain. For some time, Janssen couldn't tell how long, the capsule catapulted through space. Then everything was still around him, and he was floating. A vast, silvery hue stretched out in every direction.

Janssen sat transfixed by the scene around him. Up ahead, the silver-gray that surrounded his passageway appeared to narrow as dark shadows encroached upon the path from left and right. Janssen had no sense of speed, only a sense of moving forward into the narrowing path. Intermittently laser beams shot past him, crisscrossing through the constricting tunnel of gray. After a while he became hypnotized by the monotony of the colorless dusk surrounding him and closed his eyes.

Although he didn't sleep, his mind roamed back to the slumbering ghosts of the last few days. His illness, the pain, dizziness, the horrible sensation of tumbling. The lenses of television cameras as they converged on him. Then, like lightning streaking from a cloudless sky, the name Tahad Abdul Azzadafa streamed across his mind, locking in and grabbing hold. *Tahad Abdul Azzadafa.* Restlessly Janssen wrestled with the name, repeating it over and over until it lulled him into a half-conscious state of sleep.

Rising vaguely within him was a strange awareness of images from the past—not dreamlike, but palpable and solid. His eyelids flickered as he tried to shake off a growing sense that not only his body but his mind was returning to his earlier years. He resisted, struggling against it in vain, groping to hold onto the present, until at last weariness overtook him. He gave in to the yearning memories beckoning to him from another place.

… And he was back there, groping in another time, groping on the side of a mountain, reaching for a branch to pull himself up. Several boys were with him. Two up ahead, three more behind. The two in front were laughing.

"You can make it, Janssen."

He looked behind him, down at the rocks and the slim ribbon of water winding between the crevices below. He saw the other boys farther down the side of the cliff struggling to find a foothold, something to hold on to. Then he looked up toward the laughing face of his uncle Jocko on the ledge above. "Come on. You're almost here."

Janssen grabbed the end of a branch. It splintered in his hands, and he pressed his body against the cliff to keep from falling. Plastering himself against the side of the mountain, he held with all his might to a rock with his left hand, his right hand flailing for something to catch hold of.

Jocko held a tree limb over the side of the cliff near Janssen's right hand, and Janssen took hold of it. The boys behind him were closer now, coming up the side of the mountain.

"Let him fall," said an older boy beneath him, whose accent was noticeably different from his Tajik friends. "American. *Pfffft*. Let him go. Better off dead."

"Tahad Abdul Azzadafa, he's my nephew. How can you be so hateful?" Jocko peered down from the top of the cliff and pointed an accusing finger at the boy who had spoken. "Is that what your father taught you? You're in Tajikistan now. Your aunt and uncle will teach you better."

Janssen's eyes snapped open. *Tahad Abdul Azzadafa. Yes. That was his name. Tahad Abdul Azzadafa.*

CHAPTER TWENTY-TWO

"This is Michael Quigley." Michael strode about his cubicle as he spoke into his Q, addressing the receptionist in the Secretary of State's office. "I need to meet with the secretary as soon as possible. Do you have a time available when I could meet with him?"

"Sounds urgent."

"It is."

"Would you like to speak with him by phone?"

"It would be better in person."

"Very well. Let me check."

Michael tapped his fingers impatiently as he listened to *The Star Spangled Banner* and waited on hold.

"The secretary said you could come now."

"I'll be there in ten minutes."

Michael Quigley paced back and forth before the secretary's desk as Secretary Tomlin leaned back in his leather chair and gazed at him through steepled fingers.

"I don't think I follow you, Quigley. What do you mean the coordinates have changed?"

Michael stopped in front of the Secretary's desk, bringing his large hands up in front of him to gesture emphatically.

"I mean they've moved. First, they disappeared from my system completely for two hours. Then, when they reappeared, they'd moved." He began pacing again. "I don't know if the weapons have actually been moved physically, or if someone is screwing with the signals."

He stopped again and looked Secretary Tomlin in the eye. "What has me most concerned, however, is we don't know who our adversary is. If this is a scrambling of signals, he's more sophisticated than we think. If not, then he's right there—in Tajikistan—messing with the weapons."

Secretary Tomlin crossed his arms, rubbing his hands along the sleeves of his upper arms. "Looks like we need to get you over there."

"Yeah, and fast. I tried to call LaMarche to give him a heads-up for his negotiations with Rajanov. But his people there were incredibly vague as to how I could get in touch with him. He needs to know what's going on."

Secretary Tomlin stopped rubbing his arms and patted his fingers against his lips. "Yes-s-s." He picked up a pen, then set it down and lined it up beside a pad of paper so they were parallel. "Can I trust you to keep your mouth shut about something?"

"Of course."

"You're not going to be able to reach LaMarche for at least two or three days."

Michael scowled. "Two or three days? I thought we were in the middle of negotiations? What the—where is he?"

"If I told you, you'd never believe it. It's a very long story. The short version is LaMarche is extremely sick. He's undergoing some intense treatments and won't be available for two or three days."

Michael froze at the corner of the Secretary's desk. "Extremely sick? Janssen?"

Secretary Tomlin raised his chin and looked at Michael sideways. "Janssen?"

Michael shifted uncomfortably from one foot to the other. "Uhhh, Janssen LaMarche. I ... he's sick? It's serious?"

"Very. Without these treatments, he would not be able to continue. We're hoping for the best, but the outcome's far from certain."

Rattled, Michael inched backward toward the door. "Well, sir. I'm not sure what you want to do about the signal, then."

"We'll have to consult with President Gelford and explore our options. Keep your phone on. We may need you."

Jenna blinked and sat up straight in the chair. The relative quiet of the room had exploded into an abrupt buzz of conversation and exclamations. Workers, lab technicians, and researchers scurried across the lab to the control monitors. Drs. Bryant, Pruitt and the master technician hunched over the instrument panels. Although Jenna could not hear what was being said, she detected agitation in their rapid exchange. She rose quickly from her chair and hurried to join the group, listening to their words and trying to understand what was being said.

"Why is it jerking like that?" Bryant asked.

"The jerking seems to be related to the emergence of particles," said Weston, the engineer.

"What do you mean?"

"Whenever a particle is detected on the screen over here, the time womb appears to lurch in that direction."

"I don't like it. I don't like it one bit," Bryant said.

Pruitt turned to the middle-aged woman who had come up behind her. "Clarissa, you did make sure Mr. LaMarche was clear of any metal, didn't you?"

"He was wearing only the decon robe, underwear and slippers. He showered. I didn't do a body search."

"The capsule is reacting as though there is metal on board," Weston said.

"I don't know." Clarissa shook her head. "I don't know. He was looking at his Q watch while he was waiting, but he gave it to me before he left. And I had it thoroughly sanitized before he used it."

Dr. Bryant was studying the monitor. "Do a scan of the interior cabin."

David Weston touched a control button, and wavy lines marched across the screen. A window shot up: "Warning." A red light flashed beside it.

"It's positive, Dr. Bryant. There's metal in the cabin."

Dr. Bryant pulled at the strands of his whiskers closest to his neck. "Not possible. Not possible. How did this happen?"

"Dr. Bryant, the capsule is approaching the throat of the wormhole. Unfortunately, there are a number of particles in the vicinity. What do you want us to do?"

"We'll have to override automatic control and steer him through the field. We've got to get him through the throat. Weston, take over."

"Yes, sir."

Jenna watched in horror as her brother's transport dodged through a mass of bursting particles strewn along its path. She looked over at Evie who still slept on the red couch, a pillow under her head. Charlie was not there to talk to either, having taken leave for an hour to take care of matters at the office. Jenna looked at her watch. Charlie was due back before long.

Something black and ominous swept past Janssen's capsule, causing him to jump. As he did so, his vessel lurched to one side. The ride had suddenly become erratic, jerking this way and that.

With his left hand, he steadied himself against the side of the small craft. Small particles popped and burst near his capsule, and he shrank back into his seat. The tunnel was growing narrower, the walls closing in beside and around him. In the rearview mirror, a fiery missile-like projectile approached from behind. If it maintained its current speed, the projectile would reach him just about the time he went through the tightest part of the tunnel. He tensed his body and nervously ran his right hand along his thigh. His fingers struck against something hard and round in the pocket of his robe.

Oh, no! The medallion. Metal.

Janssen's breathing quickened and his heart raced. He let out a desperate moan of self-reproach, then reached his hand into his pocket and curled his fingers around the gold medallion he had dropped into it a couple of hours earlier. They had warned him, but he'd forgotten. Echoes of Bryant's words to Jenna seared his mind.

What are the dangers? Jenna had asked.

Virtual particles popping up around the time womb and damaging it. But we are taking every precaution to eliminate anything that would attract them—like metal.

Janssen stuffed the medallion back into his pocket and braced himself as he watched the fireworks explode close to his window. Ahead, the narrow throat of the wormhole began to envelop him. Behind, the large chunk of orange and red closed in and slammed into the back wall of his craft. The impact pitched him forward, then into a back-

and-forth seesaw. His craft lurched to the right, shook and gyrated and then spiraled, whirling into the dark gorge ahead. He could not move, could see nothing but a numbing gray spinning haze.

He was sinking. Everything blurred as inky blackness enveloped him.

CHAPTER TWENTY-THREE

Michael Quigley stared at the computer screen hologrammed against the wall of his cubicle.

"Can't be. Just can't be."

He lifted the plasma gloves from the sides of the Da Vinci ball and placed them on his hands, then moved his fingers within them to recheck the calculations he'd made. He ran his palm over the Da Vinci ball and frowned at the screen.

"What the—?" He slouched into the back of his chair, folded his arms, and grunted.

The daylight outside his window had long ago dispersed, as had the other workers in the building. With only his cubicle light plus the one in the hall, the shadows in the outer offices made it seem later than it was.

Michael rose and paced about the small enclosure he called his office, then sat back down and readjusted his numbers.

"No. I don't see how this can be." He plucked off his virtual gloves, rose, and paced once more, stopping at the threshold to his work area to lean his elbow against the wall and cradle his head in his hand.

What are they trying to do? Who's messing with this over there?

Taking a deep breath, he crossed his arms and stretched his neck upward to gaze absently at the ceiling.

Into his mind came the dreaded image that had haunted him since he was eight years old.

Streams of black smoke billowing up into the air through the New York city streets. People running, screaming. Skyscrapers hovering helplessly above the chaos. And there, at the farthest end of the boulevard, the top of the twin tower crumbling, collapsing, burning from the top down.

He stood frozen for a moment staring at the nightmare unfolding before him. Trembling, Michael fled into the restaurant where his father was drinking coffee and talking to the manager. Tears streamed down his face as he stood at his father's elbow.

His dad looked at him with alarm. "What's happening out there, Michael?"

"The towers. The twin towers. One of them fell down. The tower where Carey works."

His father stared at him for a moment that lasted an eternity. Then he jumped up, raced into the street, and stood there staring, mouth open, eyes bulging, an unlit cigarette dangling from his fingers. Michael ran to him and buried his face in his chest, but his father nudged him away. He took out his cell phone and punched a number. Waited. Punched it off, listened, punched it again—over and over. Michael heard him say the name Jesus. But it wasn't a prayer.

"What about Carey, Dad?" Michael asked through his tears. "He's okay, isn't he?" He tugged on his father's arm. "Dad! Where is Carey?"

His father didn't answer.

Michael never saw his older brother again. The brother who'd breakfasted with them at the downtown café that morning, the brother he'd idolized and worshipped, was gone. Stolen from them.

His father took up drinking. His mother never got out of bed. Before Michael's next birthday, his parents divorced.

Michael's body tensed as he stared again at the computer screen. A rippling watercolor image of his brother's face drifted silently across the mental screen behind his eyes.

What about Carey?

Terrorists.Terrorists, that's who. He shook his head and bolted for the desk. He dropped back into his seat and replaced the gloves.

"You guys over there think you can outfox me?" The words came out in a growl. "Well, I'll let you in on a secret. You geeks just messed with the wrong American."

His strong fingers speedily entered numbers and calculations on the virtual keyboard. Then, slowly, he rotated the Da Vinci ball. He looked at the configurations on the screen and ran his tongue along his upper lip. "Okay, now, wimps. Deal with that."

He sat back in satisfaction, then arched his back and stretched. After removing his virtual gloves and reattaching them to the Da Vinci ball, he clasped his hands behind his head.

A furtive smile crept over his face as he reached out and shut off the computer. He got up, positioned his chair under his desk with deliberate care, and walked to the door. Leaning against the doorpost, he studied the small cubicle and drummed his fingers on the wall. He left and headed toward home.

By the time Charlie returned, Evie had joined Jenna at the monitors, where the two women huddled together watching Janssen's module spiral and hurtle through the narrow throat of the wormhole. Evie's initial alarm seemed to turn to more of a somber pensiveness. While Jenna scurried back and forth between monitors and control panels, alternately watching Janssen's capsule on the screen and listening to the conversation of the scientists, Evie resolutely stationed herself at the monitor, her dark brown eyes fastened on the image of her father's capsule.

Jenna motioned to Charlie to join them, and pointed to the spinning vehicle on the screen.

"What's happening?" Charlie asked, eyes wide. "What caused this?"

"It's too awful. There's something metal in there attracting the particles."

"Metal? He had metal ...?" Charlie's mouth dropped open. "Why would he have metal?"

"Metal attracts these particles, and that's evidently what caused the capsule to be hit."

Charlie's face went ashen. "Metal? No!" She stopped and stared at the screen. "Where're the clothes Janssen took off?"

"It's not here," Charlie said a few minutes later, as she drew her fingers from the pocket of Janssen's pants. She looked at Evie, then at Jenna, and nervously raked her fingers through her waves of ash blonde hair. "It's not here."

Jenna looked at the pile of items on the bench which Charlie had just removed from the pockets. A comb, keys, papers, receipts, paper clips.

"What, Mom? What are you looking for?" Evie asked.

"Dad's chain with the gold medallion. Don't you remember? He wears it all the time. You must have seen it at the beach last summer. He never takes it off ... even in the shower."

"Oh, yes. I never did know what that was. You don't think he would have taken it off?"

"Well, it's not here," Charlie said matter-of-factly. "And he's got metal on board. It's a logical conclusion."

"Why wouldn't he take it off?"

"I never understood it. It was something special his mother"—Charlie looked at Jenna—"your mother ... gave him, right before she died."

Jenna gazed at her in surprise. "The gold medallion Mom always wore? The one with the rose engraved on it?"

"Yes."

"So he has it. I wondered what happened to that. I looked for it ... after Mom was gone. I didn't know Janssen had it."

"I was always curious why she'd give it to Janssen rather than to you, her daughter. But then it's not for me to say."

"You think he's wearing it now?" Evie asked. "I mean, he knew he wasn't supposed to have metal on board."

"I don't know. I only know it's not here with his clothes."

"Couldn't he have taken it off at home, Mom?"

"I guess it's possible.

Jenna eyed the items on the bench again. "He may have left it at home if he was afraid to lose it."

"That makes sense," Evie said.

Charlie shrugged her shoulders. "I hope you're right." She stuffed the items back into the pockets of Janssen's pants, stared at the monitor once more, then carried the clothes back to the Yellow Room.

Jenna wrung her hands, then crossed her arms and swayed back and forth, trying to work out her jitteriness as she and Evie continued to watch Janssen's capsule spin through the wormhole's narrow throat.

Evie put a comforting hand on her aunt's arm. "I think he's going to be okay. I just feel it."

Jenna looked at her skeptically. "I wish I were that optimistic." Her shoulders heaved in an enormous sigh. "It doesn't look good to me right now."

"I know, but ..." Evie regarded her aunt with a steadfast gaze. "I just think he'll be all right."

"You've been praying?"

Evie nodded. "Yes, and I just feel a peace ... like he'll be safe for at least this part of the trip."

A yelp of hilarity went up from the group in front of the instrument panels. Jenna and Evie turned to face them.

"He's out!" They were gleefully slapping Weston on the back. "Good job, Weston." They wheeled around to the women and the others in the lab. "He made it through the throat. The capsule is straightening out."

A surge of relief washed through Jenna's body. Evie's eyes brimmed with unshed tears, and Jenna reached out and hugged her. "Oh, thank goodness you were right." She glanced toward the monitors. *But how is Janssen after all that?*

"Can you tell if Janssen is all right?" she asked Pruitt, when she had made her way to the instrument panels.

"On the cameras he appears to be asleep," Pruitt said. "His eyes are closed."

"Is he conscious?"

Pruitt rubbed her fingers across the milky whiteness of her forehead and moved closer to the assistant who was rotating a trackball and watching signals march across the screen. "I believe he's okay. We're checking him now."

"He made it, Mom," Evie called out as Charlie hurried up to join them. "He's out of the throat."

Dr. Pruitt looked at Charlie. "We're checking his pulse and heart rate now."

One of the assistants spoke up. "He's unconscious, but monitors show his pulse is strong and his heartbeat's good."

Jenna dropped her head in her hands. "Oh, what a relief."

"Thank you, God," Evie whispered.

Jenna smiled and put an arm around Evie's shoulder. "I'll second that one."

"I'm thankful for science and skilled technicians," Charlie said.

Evie nodded. "It all works together."

"In a few minutes," Pruitt interrupted, "Mr. LaMarche will enter warp time. From this point on, he will be going back into his earlier years. You'll be able to see him change on the video monitor."

Jenna and Evie inched toward the screen.

"You won't see any change yet. It'll take a while. Changes will take the form of sporadic scenes, snapshots that'll be captured in his process of cycling back. A reverse editing device enables us to see these action sequences in forward motion."

"How fascinating," Evie said.

"He'll lose about five years each hour."

"Maybe I ought to try this," Jenna said.

A couple of the women assistants turned around and chuckled. After the tense afternoon, Jenna sensed everyone was glad for the opportunity to laugh.

"What will it be like for my dad as he goes back in time?" Evie asked. "Will he actually feel younger? Will he feel like a child again?"

"I imagine Mr. LaMarche will experience his progression back in time as a sequence of dreams, revisiting particular moments in his past in a dreamlike state. It will probably be late morning or early afternoon when he reaches his destination."

"Janssen ... Janssen." It was his mother's voice, soft, weak, plaintive—the way he remembered it on the morning she died. She was reaching a hand out to him. Her eyes were glistening. "I'm so glad you're here."

Janssen took her hand, cupping it between both of his. "Of course I'm here, Mom." He was fighting to keep back tears, wanting to be strong.

"I'm going to be fine ... you know." Her eyes were shining with that mysterious confidence that tended to unnerve him, especially now.

He let his breath out slowly and nodded his head, managing to muster a wry smile. He wanted to say something comforting, but this morning he could think of nothing.

Weak though she was, his mother was the one with the words.

"You were my biggest blessing," she said. "You gave me life."

"No, Mom, I think you have that backward." Janssen tenderly rubbed her hand and smiled into her pale face. "You gave *me* life."

A flicker of a smile crossed her lips.

"Yes, I did." She seemed to kindle with a light from within, and Janssen watched his mother's eyes grow brighter with a radiance that lit up her entire face. "Yes. I did."

She gazed at him for a few moments, then reached her hand up to her neck and groped for the gold chain that always hung there, picking at it weakly. She frowned, then looked at Janssen with pleading eyes. "Janssen, help me."

"What are you trying to do, Mom?" He leaned forward and lifted it off her neck so she could hold it in her hands and view it more easily. She looked down at the medallion hanging there, then attempted to raise the chain over her head. It caught on her chin.

"Here, Mom. Do you want to take it off?"

She looked at him appreciatively and nodded.

Janssen gently raised it over her head, then with his left hand, turned her palm up and carefully dropped the gold medallion into it, the chain looping on top.

She held it toward Janssen. "Here, son. I want you to have it."

He looked into her eyes, trying to capture the meaning of her gesture. There was a depth there he could never understand. He looked at the medallion, then studied her again and knew the answer. Heaven itself was shining through her eyes.

He accepted the chain and closed his fingers around it. His mother smiled, and her eyes clouded over with tears. "I love you, Janssen."

"I love you, Mom. You're a wonderful mother."

He reached over then and gathered her frail body into his arms, holding her close. Her thin arms clung to him as though she never wanted to let go. His heart felt it would burst. No longer able to contain the ache that pierced through him, he allowed his tears to fall unashamedly onto the dark hair tumbling down around her shoulders. He couldn't let her go.

This tenderest of moments, one he would carry in his heart forever, had caught up with him once again as he traveled back through the shadows of time.

CHAPTER TWENTY-FOUR

A swinging metal sign creaked in the light breeze. Beneath it, four figures waited in the darkness as a fifth man strutted toward them through the narrow alleyway. The youngest of the four tossed a cigarette butt to the ground and crushed it underfoot. The tall older man in the group spat in the dirt of the dry roadway, then grunted and narrowed his eyes at the unhurried figure advancing their way. The watchful eyes of the third, a middle-aged man with curly hair, darted from one to the other.

"Patience," he said. "They'll be in our possession soon."

"Not soon enough," said the fourth, an older man with a scarred lip. "We're fifty years overdue already." He took a prolonged drag on his cigarette and fixed his gaze on the man emerging from the alleyway. Exhaling cigarette smoke into the face of the newcomer, he grabbed up a knapsack with his left hand.

"You're late." With his right, he flicked the cigarette into the road and gestured with his head toward the mountains beyond the far end of the lane.

They marched down the road, passing by the market area and then by a two-story house, larger than the rest. In the house's unlit doorway, a husky older man leaned on a cane.

Without altering his gaze, the leader signaled him with a jerk of his head, then forged on toward the heights that beckoned beyond.

Curtains parted in the second story window above a ledge lined with potted plants. Dark eyes watched, then retreated behind white cotton lace.

The man with the cane slipped through the door behind him.

The village slept then until early morning, when the ringing sound of gunfire shattered the silence of dawn.

Throngs of reporters gathered on the steps of the State Department the next morning when Danny arrived for work. As he attempted to squeeze through the crowd to get to the front entrance, a rumpled-looking reporter eyed him curiously.

"What's up?" he asked the reporter, who continued to stare at him.

"Three guards at the weapons cache were shot and killed last night, and another wounded. We're looking for a statement from LaMarche."

Danny tugged at his collar. "I see."

The reporter edged closer. "Say, didn't I see you at the press conference? Aren't you on LaMarche's staff?"

"That's right." Danny stuck out his hand. "Dan Saunders."

Reporters from the other side of the entrance began to swarm his way.

"Brad Turner with the New York Times," the reporter said as he shook Danny's hand. He tapped a window on his Q watch. "Where's LaMarche? We've been trying to reach him, but his secretary won't tell us where he is, and the guards won't let us inside."

The crowd of reporters converged like flies at a Kansas picnic as Danny stammered out his answer. "He's, uhhh, traveling."

"Where has he gone?" asked a female reporter with a yellow scarf.

"I—I'm not at liberty to say right now—but here, let me make some calls. Maybe I can get some information for you." Danny raised his arm to speak into his Q watch and stepped to the side.

Three of the more tenacious reporters followed.

"Give me a few minutes," Danny said, "and I may be able to come up with answers."

Grumbling, the reporters moved back with the others.

"Office," Danny said into his Q.

Leslie Ann sounded harried when she answered the phone.

"Have you heard from LaMarche this morning?" he asked.

"No. And the media are driving me crazy. We've also gotten calls from President Rajanov and Prime Minister Oqilov in Tajikistan." Leslie Ann's voice was shrill. She was obviously under a lot of pressure. "Everyone's trying to find Mr. LaMarche, and I have *no* idea where he is."

"Have you tried his wife?"

"I got her secretary on the phone, but she said Mrs. LaMarche isn't expected in the office today either. I don't know what's going on. What shall I do, Danny? I don't know what to tell these people."

"All I know is I've got a crowd of hungry reporters out here. Do what you can to locate him. I'll hang on here till you do."

When Charlie's Q phone rang, Jenna looked toward the sound with a jolt of surprise that the real world outside still existed. The events in the lab had become all-consuming.

"My secretary," Charlie said to Jenna and Evie. "Hello ... Mr. LaMarche's office? All right. ... mhmm ... I understand. I'll call them immediately."

"What is it?" Jenna asked.

"Leslie Ann called my office, said it was urgent." Charlie punched in numbers as she spoke. "Hello, Leslie Ann?"

Charlie listened, then straightened her shoulders and pursed her lips. "I'm sorry, he's not available. Can I help with something?" She slipped to a chair and sat down.

Jenna saw Charlie frown as she listened to Janssen's secretary on the other end. Even from where she stood, Jenna could hear excited tones coming from the voice patch behind Charlie's ear.

"Oh. No, I hadn't heard ..." With a look of agitation, Charlie raked her fingers through the wavy hair at her temples. "Yes, I'm sure the media is in a frenzy ... President Rajanov called too?" She looked at Jenna and Evie, who were both listening intently. "And Prime Minister Oqilov? Yes, I understand why you're so distraught. I'll see what I can do. The media needs an answer. We'll, ahhh ... I'll let him know as soon as I can get in touch with him ... okay, patch me through to Danny if you would."

Charlie put the phone on mute and turned to Jenna and Evie. "The weapons cache was attacked last night. Three guards were killed. The media are in a frenzy, and Rajanov and Jumakhan both called this morning."

"Oh, no, Mom."

A chill ran through Jenna's body. "What timing. Unbelievable."

Charlie unmuted the phone. "Danny, handle the media the best you can. I'll get word to Janssen as soon as I'm able. Just stay cool, and let Secretary Tomlin know what you're doing."

She disconnected from the call, then rose and shook her head. "Danny's surrounded by reporters on the front steps of the State Department. He doesn't know what to tell them."

"What can we do?" Jenna said.

"Hopefully Secretary Tomlin is dealing with it, and, of course, the president."

The ominous fear Jenna felt at the first mention of the attack caused the blood vessels at the side of her head to pulsate and throb. "But Janssen has their ear. They trust him."

"You used to know Jumakhan pretty well, Jenna. How do you think he'll react?" Charlie asked.

"I think if he could get hold of Janssen, it would be okay," Jenna said, "but obviously he can't. There tends to be a certain distrust of the US over there in that part of the world. This isn't good."

Evie walked toward the video screen in the lounge area, where the faces of news commentators occupied the screen. She turned up the sound. Emily Cross was addressing her colleague as they sat around a desk.

"Do you think these hostilities will mean a setback for US negotiations with Tajik officials in working out an agreement about the weapons cache?"

"I don't know, Emily," Mat Christopher said. "This morning Secretary Tomlin told reporters he believes rogue militants are to blame for the killings, but no one knows the motive, as Tajik authorities haven't been able to confirm if any of the weapons are missing. The strangest thing is, no one's been able to get hold of Janssen LaMarche, and he's the honcho who's supposed to be handling this. I don't see this as a time for him to do a disappearing act."

Evie sighed as Jenna and Charlie walked up beside her. "This is just too much. I've got a headache."

"You're not the only one," Jenna said.

On the ITV, Emily was responding. "Let's hope Janssen LaMarche *is* in contact with Tajik officials. Meanwhile, we have a live feed from the steps of the State Department, where reporters have been speaking to one of his aides."

The face of Danny Saunders appeared on the screen. He looked poised and confident in his gray suit and burgundy striped tie.

"We know hostile factions are trying to acquire the weapons." His voice was solid and unwavering. "And they will go to any length to get them. I think this demonstrates we are probably closer than we thought in reaching an agreement with the Tajik officials." The camera zoomed closer to Danny's face. "Someone over there is restless."

Jenna smiled at Evie in spite of herself. "Not bad."

Evie looked a little bewildered. "He handled that well, didn't he?"

"Yeah," Charlie said. "But the positive spin will only hold things at bay for so long. What I'm really worried about is what Rajanov and Oqilov will think when they can't get hold of Janssen."

"And they won't for about another thirty-six hours at least," Jenna interjected.

"A lot can happen in that time."

CHAPTER TWENTY-FIVE

"How cute," Evie said as she joined Jenna at the central monitor to watch the progress of the time womb. "Do you remember Dad looking like that?"

On the screen before them, a twinkly-eyed young boy around two with dark wavy hair looked up and stretched out his chubby little hand as if reaching for something.

"Yes, wasn't he adorable?" Jenna answered. "Of course, sometimes I thought he was a pest—like when he'd come into my room and knock over my blocks and laugh like he was the cleverest thing."

Evie laughed. "Dad would do that?"

"Every chance he got. He thought he was really funny. I used to get so mad."

"I bet."

The scene on the screen abruptly changed, and Janssen, now a toddler, tottered across a carpet. He wavered, wobbled back and forth, then lost his balance and tumbled onto the rug. In minutes, he appeared on the screen again as a sleeping baby with thumb in his mouth and cuddling a floppy-eared stuffed dog.

The picture on the screen disappeared, and a stream of wavy lines blanketed the monitor.

Jenna looked toward the elevators, hoping to see Charlie returning. "I wonder when your mom'll be back."

Evie threaded her fingers through the strands of blonde hair tumbling over her shoulders. "She's got a lot going on at the Department, I guess."

"What are the reporters saying now? Anything new?"

"No," Evie said. "Just rehashing the same thing. And they still don't know if any weapons were taken or not. They're interviewing lots of different people with different opinions, and wondering where Dad is."

Jenna pressed her thin lips together and sighed. *Wondering where he is. If they only knew.*

Several of the doctors and scientists came to stand behind them to watch Janssen on the bigger screen as he approached his prenatal environment.

"Oh, look!" Evie pointed at the monitor. A perfectly formed fetus, curled up in a sleeping position, was sucking his thumb.

"That was fast." Jenna said. "How old is he there?"

"He's about five and a half months," Dr. Meyers responded, stepping up beside her.

"We're nearing the final destination now," Weston said over the loudspeakers.

A few minutes later an automated voice boomed above their heads. "Ranger at destination. Time womb secure. Date is May 12, 1995. First half of Mission LaMarche now complete."

"That means Scout and Ranger have connected," Bryant explained. "They're programmed to make that announcement only when their magnets have linked together."

In the first half of the journey, the speakers connected to the audio monitors had been largely silent, with only an occasional pop or bleep. But during the last few hours, while the time womb was actually going backward in time, a variety of sounds came and went. Voices spoke and ran together, with an occasional word breaking through the stream of sound. Every now and then Jenna would catch a hint of applause, laughter, music, engines roaring, or a baby crying. But the automated voice of Ranger was the first intelligible message she or the rest of them had heard.

Now they stared at a tiny baby before them, swimming and waving one of his arms.

Charlie was wiping her forehead with the sleeve of her blouse as she walked up to join them. "It's really humid out there, even with my thermo ring."

"Oh, there you are," Jenna said.

Charlie pushed damp strands of hair off her face and looked at the screen. "Now don't tell me that's Janssen."

"It is," Jenna said.

"He must be—what? Four months?"

"No. He's arrived. He's eleven weeks."

"Eleven weeks? He's pretty developed for a fetus."

Evie started laughing.

"What's so funny, Evie?" Charlie asked.

"He just did a somersault. And look, he's got the hiccups."

Dr. Meyers edged closer to the screen at Evie's words. "She's right. He's hiccuping. Could be the abrupt change in environment. It might take a minute for things to settle down." He turned back to the doctors. "We'd probably better wait a minute before releasing the medicine into his bloodstream. When are the nanobots scheduled to administer it?"

"About thirty minutes from the time of arrival," Pruitt said.

"That should be about right."

From the speaker, a woman's muffled voice resounded in their ears, immediately grabbing everyone's attention.

"Turn up the amplification," Dr. Bryant instructed.

The woman's voice increased in volume, but it was still muffled as though filtered through water.

"It happened very suddenly," the voice said. *"I was fine. Then all of a sudden I got this—this horrible nausea."*

Jenna gasped. She stared at the monitor, then the speaker.

"Mom!" The word escaped her lips in a puff of breath, barely audible. Jenna shook her head, then stepped back and dropped onto the cream-colored cushion of the sofa. "This is unbelievable. That's Mom's voice."

"You mean that's Grandmother?" Evie asked, looking at her aunt. "How weird."

"Sit down, dear." The second voice was faint and had a broken accent.

"Who's that?"

Jenna blinked in reflection and rubbed her hand along the contours of her square chin. "Maybe my grandmother. I'm not sure."

"Where are those voices coming from?" Charlie asked, joining Jenna on the couch.

"From the speakers," Jenna said, and pointed them out.

"I know. But how are we hearing them?"

"Through the womb. Don't you remember? Janssen has an embedded audio chip."

"I'll have to admit—I'd forgotten that."

"I'll make you some tea, Anna."

"That sounds good, Mama."

A tiny, high-pitched child's voice whimpered through the speakers. *"Hold me, Mommy, hold me."*

"Oh, my gosh." Jenna closed her eyes and leaned her head back against the seat.

"Is that you?" Charlie asked.

"It must be."

"Mommy doesn't feel very good, darling."

Dr. Bryant looked at Dr. Pruitt with alarm. "You don't think the mother is experiencing a physical reaction to LaMarche's arriving in the womb, do you?"

"I don't know."

"Her words indicated the nausea came on suddenly," Dr. Meyers said.

"The metal ..." Dr. Bryant pulled on his beard and dropped onto the sectional a few feet from Jenna and Charlie. "I've been afraid ..."

"Where's the metal now?" Pruitt asked. "The time womb is dissolved."

The scientists all turned to stare again at the viewing monitor.

"Is that a shadow behind the baby's right side?" Meyers questioned. "Or, no, it's solid, spherical. What is that?"

Pruitt frowned and peered at the screen. "I see it ... behind his shoulder. It's moon-shaped."

Bryant removed his glasses, cleaned them with a cloth he retrieved from his pocket, and put them back on to study the images on the screen. "No, it's part of a circle. The baby appears to be leaning into it."

With palm pressed flat against the top of her denim dress, Jenna leaned forward, trying to see what the scientists were looking at.

Charlie rose and inched closer to the monitor. She shook her head. "I can't believe this."

Pruitt bent forward and tilted her head to the right, then pointed at the screen. "What's that he's gripping? There's something floating from his hand ... a string, or cord ..."

"A gold chain." Charlie folded her arms in front of her and shook her head. "He always wears a gold medallion around his neck. Is that what you see?"

Pruitt turned back to the screen. "I believe there *is* a shine to it. That may be it."

"How could that get by inspection?" Bryant's eyes darted around the room as if looking for someone.

"Are you sure that's what it is?" Meyers asked.

"Enlarge the picture," Bryant ordered, looking back at the screen. "Zoom in on that round object—and the string or chain or whatever it is in his hand."

The lens closed in on the baby's right shoulder and arm, which was immediately magnified until it filled the screen. A shining round gold object, a little larger than the baby's head, drifted behind him near his shoulder. Attached to it was a thin gold chain floating freely in the amniotic fluid. The chain was wrapped around the baby's wrist.

Bryant swore. "That chain!" He looked at the women behind them then stormed across the room to the control booth.

Pruitt followed, along with the rest of the research team. A feeling of dread clutched at Jenna's heart. She hurried to catch up with them, Evie and Charlie at her heels.

Pruitt studied Bryant as his fingers navigated the keyboard, punching buttons. "This isn't good."

Meyers moved to the instrument panel. "How will this affect things?"

"If anyone acts in a way contrary to their original actions in real time, the possibility exists that everything else will get thrown out of balance. Like dominoes. One change can potentially cause other changes. The whole system can be thrown into disarray. We will not be able to count on a predictable outcome. Anything can happen. And the baby ... that chain." He looked at the women and shook his head.

"*Do you feel any better, dear?*" Anna's mother's voice came over the speakers.

"Not really. I think I'd like to lie down a minute."

"Up, up," the high-pitched child's voice urged persistently.

"No, Jenna Lynn. Not now, honey."

"Come here, darling. Let Grandma hold you."

Suddenly a boy's voice blared through the speakers. *"Zoom, zoom, zoom. Here he comes. He's after you, Jenna Lynn."*

They heard feet scuffling across the floor. Then the sound of crying. *"Mommy."* A scream. *"Mommy!"*

"Phillip. Be nice to your sister. Phillip, don't do that!"

Evie looked at Jenna. "That must be your older brother Phillip. I've heard you and Dad talk about him."

Jenna nodded, memories beginning to play through her head. "Yes, it is."

"That's so sad."

"Yes. I remember Mom crying a lot when he died."

"How did he die?" Charlie asked. "I don't remember."

"He drowned in a neighbor's pool when he was seven."

"And how old were you then?" Evie asked. "How much older was he than you?"

"He was three years older. I was three and a half when he died. Your dad would have been about one. He never really knew Phillip."

Evie blinked and shook her head. "What an awful thing to happen."

"Yes," Charlie said. "And they called you Jenna Lynn?"

Jenna grimaced. "Yes."

"I can't do this. I just can't do this." Jenna heard her mother beginning to cry.

"I know, dear. It is hard. If you could only feel good, it would help. Do you have medicine for upset stomach?"

"No," she sniveled. *"I think I'm out."* They heard the rattling of bottles. *"No, I'm out."*

"Why don't I go get something for you?"

"No, Mama." Her voice sounded strained and agitated. *"You don't know your way around."* She began to sob.

"I know the way to Safeway. I take the boy. Give you chance to rest. I think I know how to get to store."

"No, Mama. It isn't safe."

"I will be okay, Anna."

"Do you even know how to drive my car?"

"I can drive. I feel certain I can reason it out. Now give me keys, Anna."

They heard the clanging of metal against metal.

"Come on, Phillip. You and Grandmother go to store."

"Can I buy some candy?"

"Yes, we will get you candy. And some for your sister."

"Remember to put on the hand brake when you park. The hill is awfully steep at the Safeway."

Evie turned from the speaker and looked at her aunt. "How can she be out of her meds? Wouldn't her auto-shopper keep her supplied?"

Jenna chuckled. "They didn't have that back then."

"Well, then why don't they just order something to be delivered from an online store?"

"They didn't have those back in 1995 either. Not the way they do now."

Evie shook her head and looked perplexed. "Hmm. Times do change, don't they? Where did you live then, Jenna? What are the hills she's talking about?"

"Sausalito. Just north of San Francisco. It's on the other side of the Golden Gate Bridge."

"She certainly sounds emotional. I don't remember her being that way."

"Women sometimes get emotional when they're pregnant, Evie."

Pruitt turned confidentially toward Bryant and spoke under her breath so as not to be overheard. But Jenna heard their conversation clearly.

"They're changing their behavior."

"Yes."

"What will this mean?"

"I don't know. We will undoubtedly know in thirty hours. But for every action, there is a reaction. I don't feel good about this ... especially because of that chain." He looked up at Pruitt. "The baby could strangle to death on it."

CHAPTER TWENTY-SIX

As Michael crossed the plaza at the entrance to the State Department Building, he was surprised to find himself thinking about Jenna. The unexpected encounter had been a little unsettling—but it also awakened something in him.

He pictured Jenna's coquettish, pixie face, funny response, and teasing green eyes as she lifted her shoulders in her characteristic sassy swag.

He didn't understand his failure to appreciate her during their sixteen years of marriage. Worse, why he was drawn to the shallow glamour of what seemed exotic and out of reach ... until the unreachable boomeranged on him and had him in its ugly grip.

After divorcing Jenna and marrying Wanda, Wanda's flattering words, and what he'd interpreted as love, quickly soured into an insatiable craving for prestige and money. When her anger turned almost violent, their nasty divorce almost ruined him financially.

Seeing Jenna again was like a fresh breeze blowing off the Pacific.

But whatever feelings might stir within him now, he'd wronged her too much for any kind of forgiveness. He shuddered as he recalled his icy response to her beseeching eyes before their divorce and the muffled crying he often heard behind closed doors. No, he'd hurt her too deeply. There was no turning back.

Now she'd be suffering again—devastated by Janssen's illness. If only there was something he could do to help.

Michael pushed through the glass doors of the State Department Building and headed toward the elevator, then stopped and looked at the building directory. Secretary of State—Seventh Floor. Janssen LaMarche—Sixth Floor. *I could swing by Janssen's office on my way up to see Tomlin. Try to get Jenna's number to send her a note. I could at least do that.* The elevator doors opened and Michael stepped inside. He reached toward the buttons and paused. His finger hovered beside the seven, then drifted back to the six. He pushed it.

When Michael entered Janssen LaMarche's office, a lanky young man with sandy brown hair stood at the front desk talking to the receptionist.

The young woman at the desk looked up. "Hello. May I help you?"

"Yes, I'm Michael Quigley." He removed his card from his wallet and handed it to her. "I'm the weapons analyst on the mission to Tajikistan. I uh, I used to be a close friend of Mr. LaMarche—and his sister. I guess he's not in."

"No, he's not."

"I'm sorry to hear about Mr. LaMarche. I wanted to get in touch with his sister, Jenna. I saw her briefly the other day outside Secretary Tomlin's office, but I neglected to get her address or phone number."

The receptionist and the man standing at her desk exchanged glances. The young man straightened to his full height.

"What do you mean, you're sorry to hear about Mr. LaMarche?"

Michael hesitated. "I'm sorry. I didn't get your name."

"Danny Saunders, Public Relations Director for Janssen LaMarche." Danny took a business card from the receptionist's desk and handed it to Michael. "This is Leslie Ann."

"Good to meet you, Mr. Saunders ... Leslie Ann."

"Likewise. What were you saying about Mr. LaMarche?"

Michael sensed he was venturing into deep, forbidden water. "I said I'm sorry to hear about his—his illness."

Danny and Leslie Ann's eyes bored into him with unusual interest.

Danny shifted from one leg to the other, looked at Leslie Ann, then back at Michael. "We— ah—aren't talking about that, you know. Where did you *hear* about Mr. LaMarche's illness?"

Michael was cutting his luck a little too thin. Coming here had been a mistake. He feared betraying the confidence he'd been given. But then Janssen worked with these people, so surely they knew he was ill.

"Say, I, uh, I didn't mean to interrupt your day. Maybe I should check back later. Just give my regards to Mr. LaMarche."

"No trouble," Danny said. "So you're on the mission with Mr. LaMarche?"

Leslie Ann joined Danny at the front of her desk. "I think I remember seeing your name on some correspondence. You're a friend of Mr. LaMarche and his sister?"

Michael stepped toward the exit. "Yes. I was hoping to get in touch with Jenna."

"I could give you her social email."

"Terrific. I'd appreciate that."

She looked at Danny and walked back to her chair. "Have a seat." She motioned toward the chairs beside her desk, then pulled on her computer headset.

"I can't stay. Have an appointment upstairs."

The young, fresh-faced PR Director sauntered over to one of the seats Leslie Ann had directed Michael to, motioning for Michael to join him.

"I guess you heard what happened last night in Tajikistan ... the killing."

"Yes. Not good."

"We've been fending off the media all day. Particularly difficult, since we've had a hard time getting in touch with Mr. LaMarche. But with the illness ... "

"Yes, he wouldn't be able to handle that."

"We've been in the dark as to where he is."

Michael placed a hand on the back of one of the chairs. "Afraid I can't help you there."

"We talked to Charlie—Mr. LaMarche's wife—"

"Yes, I know Charlie."

"She didn't say much about how he is." Danny frowned. "We're concerned. If you know anything more ..."

They were digging for information. "I don't really know much myself. Just that he's—quite ill—same as you, I guess." He watched Leslie Ann writing on a strip of paper. "I don't envy you having to work with the media under these circumstances. They need to hear from Janssen. Things could get more out of control without his face on camera to answer questions."

Danny nodded. "My concern exactly. Look. You've got my card. Let me know if you hear anything more. We're really at a loss here."

Leslie Ann gave him the strip of paper. "I think you can reach Jenna here."

"Thanks. You've been really helpful." He extended his hand to Leslie Ann, then to Danny.

Danny shook his hand. "Remember, let me know if you hear anything."

"Right."

After the door closed behind Michael, Leslie Ann scurried over to Danny. "I knew it. I knew something was wrong."

"Well, now we know. What do we do?"

"What *can* we do?"

"Handle it the best we can, I guess. Why are they being so secretive about it?"

"Do you think it's serious?"

"It's either serious for sure, or it may sound serious to the public. They probably don't want the media to get wind of it, whatever it is." Danny took a few steps toward the hallway leading to his office. He turned around. "We need to keep this to ourselves, Leslie Ann. Not a word to anyone."

"What about Shannon?"

As Michael entered Secretary Tomlin's office, Tomlin's secretary looked up at him and punched off her phone. "I was trying to get in touch with you. With everything that happened in Tajikistan last night, President Gelford called an emergency meeting. Secretary Tomlin left a few minutes ago for the White House. He wants you to join him."

When the guard escorted Michael into the Oval Office, the president waved Michael over. "Quigley, we were just talking about you. Grab a chair and join us."

Secretary Tomlin and Randall Robertson scooted their chairs to the right to make room for Michael as they huddled in front of the presidential desk.

"Tomlin here tells me either the weapons have been moved, or your signals for locating the weapons have been scrambled by someone."

Michael pulled a striped chair over to the desk. "They were scrambled, but last night I managed to decode them again. I do have a reading on the weapons now."

Gelford straightened in his seat and leaned back. "Good job. But I'm afraid our situation is still too precarious for comfort. It looks like we need to get you over to Tajikistan pretty quickly so you can evaluate things on the ground."

"Yes, sir. Just tell me when and how."

"Inform Bradley. He'll go with you."

Tomlin shifted his body and rubbed his right hand along his left sleeve. "Mr. President, we need to think this through. Quigley needs diplomatic backup. I'll call Rajanov myself and see if I can make any headway. However ..." He shook his head and looked the president directly in the eyes.

Michael crossed one leg over the other and leaned forward to look at Tomlin. "When will LaMarche be back in circulation?"

Tomlin shook his head. "We don't know." There was an impatience in his voice. He was still looking at Gelford. "We have to keep our options open, Mr. President. This thing with LaMarche could go either way. We need to have some kind of backup in place. Preferably diplomatic, but ... " His eyes remained fixed on the president as his voice trailed off.

"You're thinking military action?" Gelford asked.

"If necessary, yes."

"Tomlin, you know our policy of soft power."

"It's your call, Mr. President, but these Tajik people are awfully squirrelly. If LaMarche is out of the picture, I don't know which way their tails will quiver."

"What's happening with LaMarche?" Michael asked. "What do you mean, out of the picture?"

A total and uncomfortable silence ensued until Randall Robertson jumped into it.

"I don't think Secretary Tomlin meant to imply he *is* out of the picture. Just that there are problems. LaMarche made it safely back in time, but there were problems with the time womb. And there apparently was metal on board ... which poses a risk to the mission and his safety."

Michael's head felt as if it had disconnected from the rest of him. *Time womb? Back in time?*

"Where is LaMarche?"

"Walter Reed Hospital Annex," Robertson said.

Tomlin cleared his throat.

"Quigley wasn't privy to that information, Robertson. He didn't know about the time thing." He rubbed his chin and turned to Michael. "Quigley, you'll need to be extremely discreet. If the media get hold of this, or the Tajiks—we're toast."

"I'm afraid I don't know what you're talking about."

"Let's just leave it at that," Tomlin said. "How accurate are your calculations in locating the weapons? If we were to deal with this militarily, how close could we come?"

"I've got a pretty good read on it, but backup information is advisable. I would suggest satellite photos. Penetrating laser photography probes pretty far underground. Or we could drop in a robotic land vehicle or even roach recon spies. I personally think it would be better to back it up with on-the-ground verification."

The president leaned back and crossed his arms in front of his chest. "How would China, Russia, and India respond to our acting militarily?"

"If that's a direction you want to consider, Mr. President, I'll look into it."

"It's not a direction I'm considering, Tomlin. You know that's not how I want this to go. But I'd like to have the bases covered. We need to know how our allies feel. How far they're willing to go."

"We'll do some talking, check it out."

"Carefully, Tomlin. If we use military force at any level, we'd first have to involve the whole Cabinet and the leaders in Congress. It's a last-resort issue."

"I understand, Mr. President."

"For now, I think we need to get Quigley over there to check things out on the ground. You and Neely will have to do the best you can on the diplomatic front until LaMarche gets back here."

"It's too bad we have to rely so heavily on LaMarche," Robertson mused. "It would be good to have someone else involved who has connections over there, but I guess there isn't anyone else."

Michael shifted in his chair and uncrossed his legs. "There *is* one other person ..."

All three men stared at him.

"Someone else with close connections in Tajikistan?" the president asked.

"Yes." Michael nodded. "His sister, Jenna LaMarche."

"His sister?" Tomlin said. "Does she have diplomatic experience or training?"

"No official training, but Prime Minister Oqilov adores her. Plus she has a very cool head."

President Gelford pursed his lips and looked at Tomlin, who leaned back, wrinkled his forehead, and steepled his fingers.

"How exactly do you know so much about the LaMarche family," Tomlin asked, "and Oqilov's relationship with them?"

"Years ago, we used to be quite close."

"Not anymore?"

"No. We had a falling out several years ago."

"I see." Tomlin sat up more erect in his chair. "Well, I don't think we're so desperate we need to pull civilians in off the street to freelance as diplomats."

The president rolled his chair closer to his desk and straightened his back. "For now, let's just get Quigley over there." He looked out the window. The sky had darkened, and the wind whipped leaves along the ground. "This weather is pretty threatening. I think we need to act fast. Quigley, prepare to leave tomorrow morning. Tomlin, do your best with the negotiations. Just make sure Quigley's got safe passage into the country and into the area where the weapons are located."

CHAPTER TWENTY-SEVEN

The slam of a door followed by uncontrolled sobbing erupted from the overhead speakers. A childish voice arose over the top of it.

"Mommy—hurt? Jenna Lynn kiss. Make Mommy better."

Evie and Charlie smiled at Jenna, who responded with a shrug and a shake of her head. "Why is Mom crying like that?"

Charlie sat on the bench in front of the monitors. "I guess you didn't know back then either."

The baby was still now. Not moving at all. Jenna stared at the sleeping child in her mother's womb on the screen before her and listened intently to the distant, oddly personal conversation.

"Thank you, sweetie." Anna's voice was strained. "Mommy will be okay. Why don't you rock your baby? I think I hear her crying."

"Oh."

Little feet pattered loud at first, then softer.

Anna blew her nose. A minute later there were the alternating tones of a telephone being dialed, followed by faint ringing.

"Cindy, it's Anna."

Against a low vibration, a second woman's voice came through.

"How are things going?"

"Awful. On top of all the other, I have nausea now."

"That was one thing I thought you had going for you, babe. You haven't had nausea before, have you? Aren't you in the third month?"

"Yeah, the third month is almost over, and I was fine up until today," Anna said. "I don't know why I'd start having nausea at this point." The nasal tone in her voice was interrupted by a sniffle. Her voice cracked. "I don't know what I'm going to do. The children—I can't handle this. I feel like I'm going crazy." She gasped as if trying to hold back tears. When she spoke again, her words were whiny and shrill. "How will I handle three children?"

"You don't have to make it so hard on yourself," Cindy said. "Remember what I suggested when you first told me about everything."

"Yes, yes, I know. And I'll have to admit it's crossed my mind."

"Do you want me to check into it for you?" Cindy asked.

"No, that's all right."

"I'll be glad to do it if it's hard for you. I'm here for you, girl. You don't have to be alone in this."

"Well, if you want to make some calls." Anna paused. "But I don't know."

"I'll call around, Anna. You can let me know."

The phone clunked onto its cradle, and then there were footsteps, as if Anna were pacing back and forth.

"I don't know. I just don't know." There was a long silence, then more footsteps and the rustling of paper. The phone dialed again.

The child's voice reemerged. "Mommy ..."

"Just a minute, Jenna Lynn." Anna's voice was sharp.

"But Mommy."

"Be quiet, Jenna Lynn. I can't hear ..."

A woman's voice was heard on the other end of the line, but Anna and Jenna Lynn's voices drowned out her words.

"Hello. Be quiet! Hello, where are you located?" Anna asked.

They heard the rattling of pencils, a shuffling of papers, then scribbling. Jenna Lynn began to whimper.

"What are your hours?" Anna asked.

"I feel like an eavesdropper," Charlie said.

"This feels sooo strange," Jenna said. "I wonder why she's so upset."

Charlie folded her arms over her chest and leaned back. "Probably the hormones."

"What's she doing?" Evie asked.

"Shhh. Let's listen," Jenna said, holding her palm up.

The child began to blubber.

"Jenna Lynn, stop crying. There's nothing to cry about...." Anna's voice was tense. She was almost shouting. Jenna Lynn's blubbering turned to a wail. "I just can't take this," Anna whispered. A pencil dropped and bounced along a hard surface.

"I'll call you back later." The phone clanked against the receiver. "Come here, Jenna Lynn. Let's you and your baby and I go lie down on the bed. Your baby needs a nap. Let's go love on your baby."

The speakers were quiet. On the monitors the fetus kicked his legs and jumped, his whole body arching, then floating in the expanse of amniotic fluid surrounding him. He repeated this activity several times, then yawned. He pulled his hands up to his face, curled up in a fetal position, and began sucking his thumb.

Jenna smiled. It was one thing to see her children on a 3D live enhanced sonogram before they were born. But to see her fifty-six-year-old brother once again in their mother's womb was unbelievable. And to hear herself as a one-and-a-half-year-old!

Shaking her head, she stood and walked to the lounge area. She wanted to check in with her intern at school, look at her messages, and take a nap. Jenna laughed at the idea. *Both me's can take a nap at the same time.*

Across the room Charlie walked around talking on her Q, looking calm and collected.

On a nearby couch, Evie was speaking to Helen at Sweet Peas.

"The computers went down *again*? I don't believe it. Call that repairman back. Things were supposed to be fixed by now." Evie paused in her conversation. A frown stole over her face. "What do you mean he's a little creepy? Did he do anything inappropriate? Oh ... well ... I see. Maybe you should have someone in there with you when he comes, just for a precaution. Be careful, Helen. And be sure to set the alarm monitors and cameras."

Jenna angled her arm into speaking range and spoke into her Q.

"Jill. School."

A few minutes later she clicked off the phone and smiled in satisfaction. *Glad the kids are enjoying the play. Jill seems to be doing fine.* She tapped the screen on her watch and saw her messages begin to download. Several posts in her social email, but nothing significant. As she was about to disconnect, a new one downloaded. She stared at the name as though it were written in Chinese. *Michael Quigley.*

"Michael?" She shook her head. "Now that's a rare one." She highlighted it and read the message:

Jenna,
Great seeing you again the other day. Glad you appear to be doing well. Heard about Janssen's illness, and wanted you to know how deeply sorry I am. I don't know much about it—guess it's being kept under wraps for obvious reasons. If there is anything I can do to help, please let me know. And I really mean that!

Yours,
Michael

She clicked off her phone, clenched her teeth and sighed, her nerves prickling her into a shiver. An email from *Michael*. A *nice* email from Michael.

Now that requires food. Preferably something rich and gooey. Besides, I'm getting a headache.

She spotted the sign to the cafeteria at the far side of the room, past Janssen's glass enclosure where the time womb had been. She shook off her stress as she rose and made her way to the automatic glass doors. Vending machines lined two of the walls with their displays of edibles. Sandwiches in one, full course meals in another, beverages, breakfast items, a variety of ethnic cuisines— ah, desserts. She headed toward a dessert dispenser and waved her hand twice over the glazed doughnut.

Actually I don't think two is enough. Think I'll get four. Yes, Michael is definitely a four-doughnut case.

She waved her hand two more times over the doughnut and pressed HEAT. A few seconds later, four shiny doughnuts emerged on red plastic plates.

After adding a cup of coffee to her tray, Jenna sat down at a small round table and took a big bite of doughnut, savoring the sticky sweetness as she tried to discard Michael's message from her mind.

He'd signed it *Yours.*

Yeah. Sure. I wonder what Michael wants from me.

She sipped her coffee and pictured Janssen's time womb moving toward the partition, saw the wall separate and the time womb disappearing through the opening. She'd feel so much better when this was all over.

She picked up a napkin and began crumpling it together on her lap. Why did Michael have to enter her life again now? She saw his face as she'd seen it outside Secretary Tomlin's office, thought of his words in his message. Where was that familiar brashness she remembered?

Michael had just wedged his underwear into a corner of the suitcase when his satellite phone rang.

It was Jordan in Secretary Tomlin's office. "Mr. Quigley?"

"Yes."

"Secretary Tomlin wants to speak to you."

Tomlin's gruff voice came on the line. "What are you doing?"

"Packing."

"Stop. We have to think this through again. One of our CIA agents was just apprehended in northern Tajikistan. He's been accused of murdering the three guards last night and confiscating some of the weapons."

"Tremendous."

"What about Bradley and the others?" Tomlin asked.

"We're all booked on a plane early tomorrow morning."

"I've got a call in to Rajanov," Tomlin said. "Let me see what I can find out. I'll call you back. Things are going south fast."

Michael dropped onto the edge of his bed. "Do you want me to call the others?"

"Just put them on hold."

"Done."

Michael clicked on the GITV. The plasma screen covering much of the wall in his bedroom came to life. Michael pushed the channel button.

The picture changed to a reporter in Khujand, Tajikistan, standing in front of the pillared entrance to a gray stone building.

> About an hour ago, Chet, officials took into custody an American whom they accuse of murdering three guards last night, guards assigned to protect the weapons cache. They've also charged the American in the disappearance of some of the weapons. At this time, we do not know the individual's name. All we've been able to gather is that he was apprehended inside the house of a member of the National Assembly and leader of the IRP party. Unofficial witnesses say one of the leader's sons saw him break into the house and called police.

A small inset in the bottom right-hand corner of the larger screen displayed the concerned face of Chet Robbins.

> Brent, do you have any word from government officials in Dushanbe? How will this affect negotiations?

> We have received no official word from the Tajik government on their position, Chet.

The cameras switched from Tajikistan back to the newsroom and Chet Robbins.

> And once again we still have not been able to reach diplomat Janssen LaMarche. He seems to have disappeared off the face of the earth.

Back in the lab, Jenna was curled up sleeping on one of the couches when the muffled sound of children screaming jerked her awake. She blinked her eyes and looked over at Evie and Charlie, who stared at the overhead loudspeakers. Jenna shook her head to fluff out her matted hair and sat up. "What's happening?"

"Things are lively again," Evie said. "You're not very happy."

Jenna looked toward the speakers.

"No! My candy!" Jenna Lynn shrieked, then broke into a wail. "Mommy!"

A boy's rough voice responded. "I bought it." Jenna heard the sound of scuffling, then a loud crash.

"Phillip Junior!" Anna's voice. "Look what you've done. The lamp is broken."

Jenna Lynn was crying. "Phillip ate my candy."

Jenna heard a whacking sound, a scuffling of feet.

"I didn't mean to do it," Phillip cried.

"Go to your room."

Another clattering noise. "Phillip, pick that up."

"I thought buying them candy would make them happy," Anna's mother said. "I didn't know it would cause all this."

"It's not your fault."

"Anna, I will watch the children. You lie down again. You need to rest."

There was a loud sigh. A door slammed and clicked against a threshold. For a couple of minutes there was silence, then the rustling of paper and a series of high electronic pitches. Anna was dialing the phone. She spoke quietly, soberly, deliberately.

"Cindy ... I've decided to do it. Did you make those calls?"

A deep vibration accompanied Cindy's voice as she responded through the phone wires. "Yes, I did."

"What did you find out? Did you find a place?"

"There's one in San Francisco. And they're open tomorrow. I could take you, if you want. You'll need someone to give you a ride. You can't drive afterwards, you know."

A pause, then another sigh.

"All right. What time will you pick me up?"

"How about seven? It's best to get an early start. Have you told your mother?"

"No. She wouldn't understand."

"But you're sure? You've thought about it now?"

"Yes, I've thought about it. It's the only way, Cindy. I can't handle all this. I'm going to have an abortion."

CHAPTER TWENTY-EIGHT

Jenna stared at the speakers, her mouth open. Panic gripped her heart.

"What did she say? What is she doing?" She watched the fetus float like a tiny astronaut in the amniotic fluid. "She can't do this. She *can't* have an abortion. Not now. Janssen's a—a—*person*."

"Mom, an abortion?" Evie's face contorted in an expression of horror as she turned to her mother. "Mom, she's going to abort *Dad*!"

Charlie shook her head, a blankness glazing her eyes. She turned toward her sister-in-law. "Jenna, do you have any idea? Did your mother ever ... ?"

"No. I don't know anything about this. This is unbelievable."

Charlie frowned and licked her lips. "She seems to be overwhelmed at the thought of having three children. I always thought of her as a much stronger person than that."

"She *was* a strong person," Jenna said. "I don't understand this."

"Even if the medallion has caused a change, I can't imagine her behavior deteriorating this drastically over a bout of nausea." Charlie narrowed her eyes at Jenna. "Why would having a third child cause her such hysteria?"

"I don't know, Charlie. I really don't." She took a deep breath and let it out. Fear spread through her body like flood water through a mountain hollow.

Evie covered her face with her hands, her fingertips digging into her scalp. "Oh, God. Grandmother, of all people. *Grandmother* having an abortion. And aborting *Dad*. I didn't think she even believed in abortion."

Charlie straightened and squared her shoulders to her full height above the other two and crossed her arms in front of her, shaking her head. "People can say one thing and then do another when it actually affects *them*."

"But Grandmother wasn't like that. I can't believe this."

As Jenna reached over to stroke her niece's shoulder, Evie's fearful gaze seized her own. Against the immensity of the high-tech lab, Evie in her grief-stricken state appeared to Jenna like a little girl—frail, alone, afraid, the waves of her cornsilk hair caressing her face with childlike winsomeness.

Drs. Pruitt, Bryant, and Meyers hurried toward them. Charlie turned at the sound of their approach, her forehead creased with worry.

"Can you do something about this? Can we get him out of there?"

Dr. Pruitt, her face ghostly white, gazed at her for a moment with mouth open and eyebrows raised to their maximum height.

"It would be difficult. The process of removing him takes time, particularly since the time womb must be reassembled. Mr. LaMarche is scheduled to return in slightly more than twenty-four hours." She frowned in thought. "We could possibly accelerate the timetable to a small degree. But if we did bring him back early, he'd die of Ichiban Syndrome. The medication wouldn't have time to take effect."

"Twenty-four hours is not a long time," Dr. Meyers said. "Perhaps if we ride it out, he'll come back before she goes ahead with it."

Bryant cleared his throat and coughed. "LaMarche's health is only one of the considerations. The mother's possible alteration of history is a huge concern to me. And I don't know if removing him would stop what has now been set in motion."

Meyers's face paled.

"Dr. Bryant, are you saying even if we should bring LaMarche back, whatever decision the mother has made now would continue back in 1995 and affect us here in 2052? In other words, his coming back before the abortion occurred wouldn't stop the process?"

"I can only conjecture at this point, Dr. Meyers. There has been no scientific evidence to prove the matter one way or the other. I'd like to think if we were able to extract him before she went through with the abortion, his being alive at a later point in time would preclude her ability to abort him *in utero*. But the effects of time travel are still untested. We can't say anything with certainty. Once you start unraveling history, theoretically anything can happen." Bryant looked at Evie above the rims of his glasses. "Weston is doing some research now."

Meyers turned to Jenna. "Does it seem reasonable for her to respond this way at the prospect of a third child?"

"No, absolutely not! She was a wonderful, caring mother. I can't imagine her doing this."

"Where's her husband?"

"He ... I don't know. I'm sure he's there somewhere," Jenna stammered, gesturing toward the monitor.

"But you had a father?"

"Yes, yes, of course I had a father." Jenna tensed as she saw everyone's eyes on her. She tried in vain to keep her voice level. "Yes, we definitely had a father, and yes, he lived with us." She shrugged her shoulders and waggled her head nervously. "He dominated the family."

"Where is he now? Is he still alive?" Meyers asked.

"Yes, my dad ... " Jenna stopped abruptly.

Dr. Meyers stepped closer. "Would he know about this?"

"Dad. Yes. Dad would know." Jenna twisted her wrist and spoke into her Q-watch. "Dad—home."

Phillip LaMarche's dignified, unsmiling face billowed above the phone.

"Dad. Hi. Dad, I've got to ask you something."

"Just a minute, Jenna. I need to set my glass down." Her father's face disappeared, then returned a minute later. "My neighbor was just over here and she'll talk your ear off. Talks about everything from gardening to ..."

"Yes, I'm sure. But I need to ask you something." Jenna hesitated. "I know this is going to sound weird, but—did Mom ever consider having an abortion when she was pregnant with Janssen?"

There was a long silence. Jenna peered up at the hologram. Her father's face showed no expression. "Dad? Did you hear me?"

"Of course I heard you, Jenna. That has to be the most absurd question I've ever heard in my entire life. What on earth are you talking about?"

"I know it sounds crazy. But bear with me a minute. I need to know. Think about it." She drew a breath and spoke slowly, deliberately. "Did Mom ever talk about aborting Janssen? Was she overwhelmed at the thought of having a third child?"

"Pffff. Mom didn't have an abortion, Jenna. Janssen wouldn't be here if she'd had an abortion."

"I know ... but she must have talked about it ... or had a reason to have an abortion."

"You aren't making sense, Jenna. Janssen is fifty-six years old. What is all this talk about an abortion?"

Jenna pushed her right hand deep into the pocket of her denim dress and began to pace. "Dad, she scheduled an abortion."

"What? Jenna, make sense! Mom is gone. Janssen is alive."

Suddenly his frown disappeared, and concern flickered into his gray eyes. "How is Janssen, Jenna? Wasn't he going to have an operation of some kind?"

Jenna swayed to a stop. "Yes, Dad. He's in the middle of the procedure right now. That's why I'm calling you. That's why we need to know."

"Jenna. You're talking in riddles. What's going on? What's happening to him?"

Jenna raised her eyes and gazed directly into the hologram, as if she were looking at her dad in the same room with her.

"I know you don't understand. It's very complicated. We didn't tell you the whole story about the medical procedure because we didn't want to worry you. The doctors told us the only known cure for Ichiban Syndrome has to be administered before birth while the baby is still in the womb. Janssen had to be sent back in time—back to the womb—to be healed."

"Back in time? What do you mean back in time? Blast it! What will you think of next? Try to make sense, Jenna."

"Ichiban Syndrome is a fatal disease, Dad. An incurable, congenital disease." Jenna rubbed her nose in agitation. "Janssen was in the final stage. He was dying, Dad. This procedure could save his life."

"Jenna, where is your brother?"

"He's back in time now—in 1995. Janssen is back in the womb, in the eleventh week of development. Right now."

"How can that be?"

"It wasn't low-tech, Dad, I'll tell you that. It's a very sophisticated setup. Janssen is to remain there for thirty-six hours till the medicine takes effect. Then he'll be back."

She paused and curled her lips inward as she reflected on how her dad was responding to what she said. He was no longer debating her. After giving him a few seconds to let her words sink in, she continued. "We can hear what's going on around him. And Mom just scheduled an abortion."

Again, there was a long silence on the other end. The hologram jerked and shifted. It appeared Phillip LaMarche had decided to sit down.

When her father spoke again, his voice was subdued. "Where are you?"

Jenna inhaled deeply. "At the Walter Reed Annex."

"I'm coming down there. How do I get there?"

"It's late, Dad. You shouldn't be driving. And there's a storm coming."

She heard Evie's Q watch ringing. Evie stepped aside to answer it.

Jenna was sure her father had to know if her mother had contemplated abortion, and why she might have chosen it. But the more she tried to pry the information out of him, the more Phillip protested, insisting he come there so he could see everything for himself. She and her dad were in a deadlock of wills.

Charlie tapped her on the shoulder. "If he's insisting on coming over, we can ask Danny to pick him up. He's on the line with Evie."

A feeling of relief loosened the knot of confusion in her head. Jenna nodded to Charlie. "Dad, if you really want to come, there's a young man who might be able to pick you up."

Charlie beckoned to Evie. Evie edged slowly toward them. "Ask Danny if he could pick up your grandfather and bring him here," Charlie instructed.

Evie stared at her mother, then Jenna. She screwed up her face and sighed.

"Danny, I might have a job for you after all. We need someone to pick up my grandfather and bring him here. We're in the annex of Walter Reed Hospital."

Michael's satellite phone was ringing. It was Secretary Tomlin. In the hologram cloud before him, Tomlin's forehead was furrowed, his face strained. Hardly taking a breath between sentences, he spoke rapidly and intensely, continuing the conversation they had started hours before as if no time had elapsed.

"I had Neely call Rajanov to test the waters. Rajanov is blaming the US, saying we're behind the violence the other night. Later I got through to Oqilov. Oqilov wants to talk to LaMarche. 'Where's my nephew?' he says. They're suspicious. He says he feels there's something wrong."

"How are things going with LaMarche now?" Michael asked.

"More complicated by the minute. Not looking good." Tomlin paused. "Twenty minutes ago I got a call from our Ambassador to Uzbekistan. CIA operatives spotted heightened activity among suspected members of terrorist cells there, and they've heard increased chatter. They think something's going on."

Michael stood, and carrying his glass of merlot, paced to the ITV screen. The talking heads of news reporters continued their discussion of the Tajikistan crisis.

Little do they know.

"What do you want me to do?"

"Hang tight. If you're going over there, we need assurances you'll be welcomed and given safe travel to the north to inspect the weapons. Without that, we could just be aggravating the situation. It's either diplomatic backup for you or military backup. One or the other."

"I'm packed and ready to leave whenever you give me the go."

"That's what I wanted to hear. Meet the president and me in the Oval Office at eight tomorrow morning. We're putting Special Forces down in Uzbekistan tonight to see what's happening. Hopefully we'll know more by dawn."

Michael set his glass down on a nearby table. "Why is Rajanov accusing the US of being behind the shooting of the guards?"

"The one guard who made it out alive says they were attacked by a group of four Americans. He heard them speak English. Later they found an American cigarette stub."

"What about cameras?"

"The men were masked, but dressed in western clothes."

Michael frowned. "So did we do it?"

"Absolutely not."

"Then it was a plant."

"Exactly."

Evie felt hot. *An abortion?* Her father was back in the womb, and her grandmother was talking about the unthinkable. Evie's mind whirled. Her grandmother was talking about aborting not a baby, not a fetus, but her dad, whom Evie loved with all her heart, a grown man who'd been her grandmother's beloved son, a man who was pivotal in world affairs. But, of course, Anna back there in 1995 didn't know her actions could actually change the course of history. She would never do this if she *knew* what she was doing—actually killing the son who had been her shining star. Evie shuddered. And if he were aborted, what would happen to his children? Evie's own existence, as well as her dad's, might hang on the thread of her grandmother's unwitting decision.

Evie was standing by the beverage machine in the lounge with a bottle of water when her grandfather and Danny arrived. She set the water on a table and walked over to greet her grandfather. She was glad he was here. Maybe he would have some answers.

In a surge of emotion, she hugged her grandfather with unusual warmth.

He patted her back and looked around as he slowly disengaged himself. He cleared his throat. "Where's Jenna?"

Evie pointed toward the monitors on the other side of the room where her aunt stood, hands on hips, listening to her mother. Jenna's lips were drawn down to a thin line. Charlie shrugged her shoulders.

"She's over there."

Clarissa scurried over to the elevators and asked for introductions, then spoke briefly to the guard who had escorted Danny and her grandfather from the unsecured part of the building. After checking their identifications and having them fill out paperwork, she seemed satisfied with their legitimacy and returned to the control station.

"Jenna, please explain this to me," Phillip said when his daughter arrived from the other side of the room.

Jenna slipped her arm through her father's and ushered him toward the couch in the sitting area near the elevator.

"Let's sit down. I'll tell you about it from the beginning."

Danny stood glued to one spot, pivoting his head slowly as he gawked at the impressive technology and sophisticated apparatus located across the enormous lab.

Evie crossed her arms in front of her and stared at the marbled pattern of the shiny tile floor, then sighed. She raised her head and looked at Danny. He was trying to be nice. She needed to be polite. "Thank you for bringing my grandfather here."

Danny's face colored as his eyes flickered back toward Evie.

"My privilege. It's the least I could do after what happened the other day. Look," he said, shrugging uncomfortably, I don't usually do things like that. I was just daydreaming, listening to music, not paying attention. It's no excuse, but ..."

Evie waved a dismissive hand. "It's okay, Danny. I understand. I've done the same thing before." She blushed, recalling her drive with her grandfather and the balloons a few days before. "By the way, thank you for the flowers."

"Don't mention it," he said.

"No, the flowers were beautiful."

His look of discomfort faded. "I'm glad you liked them."

The dancing light in his brown eyes grabbed Evie's attention and temporarily lifted her spirits. "I did," she said.

They smiled awkwardly at one another. Danny shifted his lanky body from one foot to the other and gestured toward the glassed-in area, the screen, and the monitors. "I had no idea what was going on here. In the car, your grandfather said Mr. LaMarche had gone back in time?"

Evie rubbed her fingers across her lips, subconsciously reminding herself of the secrecy of her father's venture. "I don't know how much you should know about this, Danny. I'm sure your job's been rather difficult these last few days with my father's sudden absence. But …"

"Look, you don't have to tell me anything you don't want to." Danny took a step backwards. "In fact, if you don't need me anymore, I should probably go. You probably need to get back to … " He waved toward the lab.

"Yes. Thanks for understanding, Danny." Evie walked with him to the elevator. "How's the weather out there?"

"It's getting pretty windy. Started to drizzle when we came in."

"What's happening with the hurricane?"

"Still a few miles out at sea. Heading farther up the coast. But we're due for some rough weather." Behind him, the elevator doors opened.

Evie cocked her head and gave Danny a smile. "Stay safe."

Danny's face colored again as he stumbled backwards into the elevator. "Let me know if you need anything. Sandwiches or—something to eat—anything. Let me know."

The elevator doors closed, and Evie drifted back to the couch where Jenna and her grandfather were sitting together. She could hear Jenna explaining what had been happening over the last few days.

"And what we don't understand is we heard Mom schedule an abortion. Obviously, she didn't get an abortion, but why would she be considering it? I can't imagine Mom feeling so overwhelmed by the idea of having a third child. She loved children."

"Seems like a moot point to me. She didn't get an abortion before. She won't get one now." Phillip looked toward the big screen in the middle of the room. "Why should something happen now that didn't happen before?"

"If one thing is changed because of the person's going back in time, then other things can change as well. There's a domino effect. And we think something did change."

"What do you think changed?"

Jenna's expressive green eyes grew more focused as she carefully studied her father. "Dad, did Mom have nausea when she was pregnant with Janssen?"

"Uh—I don't remember, Jenna. It was a long time ago."

"Think, Dad. Because that's what we believe is different. Janssen had metal with him when he went back. He wasn't supposed to, because it can disrupt the magnetic forces in the time continuum, but he did. Somehow he had that gold medallion of Mom's. And when it went into her womb with him, she immediately had a bout of nausea."

Evie saw her grandfather's eyes glaze over with a thin veil of alarm. He stared at Jenna with a look of dazed confusion.

"Do you understand what I'm saying?" Jenna said.

In the bright light of the lab he looked more frail than usual. His eighty-four years were beginning to tell on him. "Grandfather," Evie said, "you look tired. Are you all right?"

Phillip nodded. "I ... yes ... I just don't understand how this could be happening."

"Dad, it would help if you could tell us if Mom had nausea when she was pregnant with Janssen. Try to remember."

"I—I really don't know. I was away a lot."

"When I was pregnant with Todd, it seemed like Mom told me she'd never had a problem with nausea," Jenna said.

Phillip's shoulders fell. He swallowed hard and raised his chin. "She had three pregnancies, you know. It's hard to keep all that straight."

Jenna pressed her lips into a thin line and heaved a sigh of annoyance. She pushed herself off the couch and stood staring at the screen.

From watching Jenna, Evie knew she believed Phillip was being evasive or stubborn, as he often was. Evie didn't think that was it. Studying Phillip, Evie felt sorry for him. It was late, and he was probably tired. It *was* a long time ago for him to remember, and men didn't always pay a lot of attention to things like that.

Phillip slowly pulled himself up to join his daughter. "What's the plan here now? How much longer is Janssen going to be back there?"

"Another twenty-two hours or so."

"Couldn't they bring him back before then?"

"Possibly. The techs are looking into it." Jenna turned to him. "But then he would die of Ichiban Syndrome."

"What should we do, then?"

"Hope and pray she doesn't go through with the abortion, I guess." Jenna's gaze drifted to Evie with a helpless eye-roll.

Evie's skin prickled. "I already am," she said. "I've been praying all along."

Someone behind her cleared his throat. She turned to see David Weston, the engineer, a short stocky man with a goatee. He looked at Phillip, then Jenna. "I understand this is your father?"

"Yes," Jenna said.

"Mr. LaMarche, if you would give us a few minutes, Dr. Bryant, Dr. Pruitt and I would like to speak with you."

CHAPTER TWENTY-NINE

When Danny reached the unsecured area of the building, he paused and listened, believing he'd heard voices coming from the direction of the front entrance. When he got to the circular stairway and looked around, he was alone.

He knew he'd heard someone, and for the past couple of days, he'd sensed someone following him. He couldn't put his finger on anything concrete. But yesterday a black Chevy had made all the same turns he made when he left Mr. LaMarche's office and went to the Pentagon. And tonight, after he picked up the senior LaMarche, a set of headlights in his rearview mirror stayed with him until he pulled to the curb and turned off his GPS and front beams. Danny waited until the car passed, then made a U-turn, drove down a side street, and wove in and out of some neighborhood streets for extra security. The senior Mr. LaMarche thought Danny was lost. Not wanting to worry the elderly gentleman, Danny told him it was a shortcut.

Had he led someone to the lab?

Now the wisdom of LaMarche and the others was clear—better not to let too many people know what was going on. And if all the facts were known, their misuse could be devastating to the US mission. Going back in time? Maybe that was more than he needed to know.

He opened the outermost door of the Annex, and at the same time a car with its headlights off pulled away from the building, tires swishing on the pavement. He tensed. Maybe he should let someone know he might have been followed.

Danny hesitated at the door, peering at the street through the drizzling rain. The trees across the way were bending in the wind. His car was parked in front, only a few steps away, and he made a dash for it.

Two cars in front of his, a dark figure emerged from behind a van and darted toward him in the darkness.

It was late now. But with the talk of abortion, the uncertainty of what might happen, and the worsening weather outside, everyone was leery of leaving the lab. After a conversation with Bryant, Pruitt and Weston, they decided to take Robertson up on his offer to stay in the guestrooms reserved for visiting scientists.

Evie felt light-headed and sick to her stomach. The scientists' speculations confirmed her worst fears about the question of her own existence if her grandmother proceeded with the abortion. Her grandfather had not shed any more light on the situation. Bringing her dad back early didn't seem to offer any actual advantages, given the strong possibility once changes were set in motion, it wouldn't matter whether her father was still back in time or on his way back. They'd decided to ride things out. The whole situation seemed surreal.

When they headed upstairs, her Q rang. It was Danny.

"Yours was the only number I had available," Danny said. "Sorry to bother you, but I need to let someone know I was followed to the Annex."

Evie's response sounded soft and restrained in her own ears. "Who was it?"

"I don't know. There were two cars. One left with its lights out, and the other waited for me. A man came at me in the dark, but I managed to jump in the car and get away. I didn't really want to wait around to see what he wanted."

"Smart fellow. Where are you now?"

"In the car. I just wanted everyone there to know."

"Is he still following you?"

"I don't think so. I think I lost him. I'm afraid someone's trying to find your father, and they could be getting close."

"Maybe you should call Secretary Tomlin, or Randall Robertson."

"Do you have their numbers?"

"Let me find them." Evie tapped her Q watch and sent the information to Danny. "But you don't think anyone's following you now?"

"Doesn't look like it."

"Be careful, Danny."

"I'll do my best."

She turned off the phone and ran her fingers through the strands of hair at the nape of her neck.

"What was that?" Charlie asked.

"Danny," Evie said in a subdued voice. "He thinks someone followed him here."

Jenna bit her lip. "I shouldn't have said so much on an insecure phone when I called Dad."

"It was a traumatic moment," Evie said. "Any of us would've done the same thing."

"Someone may have been staked out at Phillip's house," Charlie added.

"Staked out at my house? What do you mean?" Phillip said, outraged.

Charlie turned in his direction. "Phillip, everyone's trying to find Janssen."

"So they'd look for him at my house?"

"You're his father, Phillip. They're undoubtedly checking out all the angles."

"Who's *they*?"

Charlie squared her shoulders. "Let's hope it was the media."

Jenna had been worrying a fingernail while the others talked. "You know, I think I might've been followed the day Janssen had the bad seizure, when I was supposed to have lunch with him," Jenna said.

Charlie frowned disapprovingly. Her voice was strident. "Why didn't you say anything about it before?"

To Evie, the tension between her aunt and her mother was palpable. Why did her mom take that overbearing, self-righteous tone? It was not helpful at the moment, with the grim prospects of what might happen.

"Actually, I forgot." Jenna stared at Charlie, her mouth set in a thin line. "There was too much else to worry about. And it might've been my imagination anyway."

"What happened?" Evie asked.

"I was at the Smithsonian, preparing for a field trip with my class next month. A Middle Eastern man kept appearing in every room I was in. He kept staring at me, and I think he may have taken pictures of me with his Q. It made me nervous."

"We just really need to be careful," Charlie said, "and to remember what we're up against."

The guy's really creepy.

Evie shuddered, remembering Helen's words about the computer repairman at Sweet Peas earlier in the day. Was everything okay there?

"We should let Secretary Tomlin know about this," Charlie said.

"I gave Danny his number."

Charlie nodded, then turned and took Phillip by the arm.

"We need to get you to your room, and we all need to get to bed and get some sleep." She looked at Evie and stopped, her forehead creased with concern. She slipped over and squeezed Evie's shoulder affectionately. "We'll get through this, Evie. Try to get some sleep."

Evie watched her mom and grandfather as they headed down the hall. Everything seemed so out of control. Taking a deep breath, Evie leaned against the wall. She needed to pray. She bowed her head and clasped her hands tightly beneath her chin.

God, I don't understand this. Help us. Please help us. Everything is so out of control. Don't let Grandmother have an abortion. Take care of Daddy. And me too, Lord. God, I know you see both the past and the present at the same time. You're omnipresent, God. You can do anything. You know what will happen to Daddy, and me, and my brother. You created us, God. You have a plan for our lives. I know you do. But I'm scared. Please, God. Please. Help us.

She shivered.

And God, keep Danny safe—and Helen. Lord, please make everything turn out all right.

Jenna came up beside her. "Come on, young one. You need to get some sleep too."

Evie sighed. "Yeah, I guess."

They turned to walk down the hall together. Jenna folded her arms in front of her. After a few seconds of silence, Evie watched Jenna tilt her head toward her with an air of scrutiny as she lowered her arms to her side. "Evie, what made you the way you are? You know, all the praying and stuff?"

Evie eyed Jenna's reflective expression. Jenna had never seemed particularly interested in God.

"I used to go to church with Grandmother when I was young. I loved all the things I learned there," she said. "That's why I can't imagine she'd get an abortion."

Jenna nodded. "I know. It's hard to understand. But why's all this religious stuff so attractive to you?"

"Because it's truth, Jenna." Evie wrinkled her brow and slid her hands along the thighs of her jeans before stopping to gaze into Jenna's eyes. "But it's not really about *religion*. It's not about rules and such." She took a breath. "Don't you think it's kind of exciting Dad can have a personal relationship with President Gelford?"

"Yes, I do. It's pretty amazing."

"It's amazing to think the president of the United States cares what happens to Dad personally and can use his authority to watch after Dad. Well, I feel I have that kind of relationship with the one who has even more authority, who can protect me and Dad from any harm, the one who holds the power over everything—even more than the president."

"You mean God?"

"Yes."

"Hmm. That's an interesting way to look at it. You really believe you have a relationship with God?"

Evie nodded. "Yes. I know I do." She crossed her arms and hugged them into her chest. "I have to admit I don't understand what's happening with all this right now. But I trust God. I do. Somehow I know he's in control of this— even though it doesn't seem like it."

There was a sadness in Jenna's eyes as she shook her head and sighed. "I hope you're right, Evie. I really hope you're right." They turned to continue walking. "I wonder why Mom didn't take me to church more. I went a couple of times, but ... " She stopped mid-sentence, then answered her own question. "No, I take that back. I know why we didn't go."

"Why?"

"Dad didn't want us to go. He always made fun of Mom for going. Janssen and I kind of took his side, I guess."

When Jenna crawled into bed, she found herself staring at the ceiling. In the haze of her thoughts, she saw her brother climbing into the time womb, workers lowering the hatch, and Janssen's face dimly appearing in the window of his transport, ghostlike and distant. She shuddered. Was that the last she would ever see of her brother?

She turned on her side and gazed at the darkened window, listening to intermittent drops of rain striking the pane. If Janssen was aborted, not only would he have never been born, but Evie and Alexander wouldn't be born either. History would be rewritten.

What have we all gotten into?

Jenna raised her head from the pillow and stretched her neck, shaking her short locks to ease the tension. She needed to get some sleep. She thought about Evie praying in the hallway. Did prayer really work? It was comforting to know Evie believed it did, and maybe—just maybe—it did.

She dozed off for a short time. When she awoke, she once again found herself staring at the ceiling.

Twice she got up and went down to the lab, checking in with the midnight shift and going to the monitors to see if she could hear anything from the speakers. But all was quiet. The second time, as she headed back to her room, she ran into Evie.

"You can't sleep either?"

"No, and I need to," Evie said, rubbing at her face. "My eyes feel like they're burning holes in their sockets."

"Well, nothing's happening. If you're going to get some rest, now's the time to do it."

Evie closed her eyes and took a deep breath.

"Are you all right?" Jenna asked.

Evie nodded. "I'm okay. This is just all so unbelievable."

Jenna put an arm around Evie's shoulder and gave it a gentle squeeze. "Your faith will see you through."

Evie bit her lip. There were tears in her eyes. She nodded again.

"I wish I were a praying person like you so I could encourage you." Jenna paused. "But who knows? Maybe I'll give it a try, just for you."

Evie looked up at her and smiled. "I'd like that."

Faint rays of light stole through the coverings on the window beside Jenna's bed in the early dawn. The rain had ceased, but the wind continued to gust against the panes. Opening her eyes and catching the light, she realized she had finally managed to fall asleep for a couple of hours. The heaviness of her lids urged her to close them again and drift back into the amnesia of sleep. But a nagging anxiety deep in her soul compelled her to get up and return to the lab. She looked at the clock. 5:30.

Evie was already there, dressed in loose sweats and a knit top, standing before the monitor where a tiny infant kicked his legs and swam with his arms. Evie turned and pointed to the speakers when Jenna came up behind her.

Above their heads came the sound of sobbing and wailing. A heaviness gripped Jenna's heart. "She sounds hysterical."

"What's going on, do you think?" Evie asked.

"I wish I knew."

"Do we know what time it is there?"

"Not really. San Francisco time would be three hours earlier than ours, but this is not real time."

Evie blinked a couple of times and frowned. "What do you mean?"

"Something about time travel taking him somewhere else in space."

"Huh?"

Jenna brushed her hand against her nose. "It's confusing. I don't really know. But the gist is it's hard to know what time it is in the place we're listening to."

Evie shook her head. Her flaxen hair hung in clumps down her back from tossing and turning in bed. "I'll be so glad when this is over."

Jenna sighed and looked at her. *I hope we'll be glad.*

Evie lowered her head in her hands and swallowed hard.

"You're scared," Jenna said. "So am I. Have you gotten any sleep yet?"

"A little."

From the speakers they heard a clock striking in low vibrato. Once, twice, three times.

"Hmm. Must be three o'clock there. Well, now we know." Jenna fluffed her hair. "Why don't you go back to bed? This sounds like a lonely, middle-of-the-night kind of crying. She may be agonizing over her decision. The best thing you can do is pray she changes her mind."

A few hours later, after two more changes of the guard between Jenna and Evie and one encounter with Charlie, the three women, joined by Phillip, settled in at the center of the lab. Clarissa handed out cups of coffee from a cart laden with doughnuts, bagels, and cream cheese.

Evie, still in her sweats, had twisted her hair into a loose bun. She sat on the couch propped against her mother's shoulder. Charlie dabbed at the dark circles under her eyes, revealing her own lack of sleep. Leaning back against the cushions, Phillip sipped his coffee. Beside him, Jenna reached for her second doughnut just as a burst of music followed by a man's voice blasted from the speakers. An underlying static created an uneven vibration of sound.

> *And that was R.E.M's big hit from 1987, "It's the End of the World As We Know It." It is now six o'clock on a cold and foggy Saturday morning in beautiful San Francisco. You are listening to KABL 92.1. In the news today, one more person died last night as a result of the March 20 sarin terrorist attack in Tokyo's underground railway. With this latest death, twelve people have now died from the sarin exposure, and several others are reported to have permanent brain damage. Now that Japan has suffered two deadly sarin attacks by the same terrorist group in the past year, precautions and guidelines are being prepared so hospitals can quickly identify toxic agents such as sarin and other nerve agents, which rapidly penetrate intact skin.*

The voice abruptly ended with a click, and Jenna heard the shuffling of feet, the clinking of hangers in a closet and the sliding of a drawer.

With her hand still outstretched toward the plate of doughnuts, Jenna shivered. "Did he say sarin?"

"Yes, he did," Phillip said. "The sarin attack in Tokyo was one of the earlier terrorist attacks."

Evie sat up straighter and set her cup of coffee on a nearby table.

"Sarin. Oh, my. It's like history is suddenly right here."

Charlie cleared her throat and nodded.

"History. Yes, it is here. We don't realize how much history is actually part of our present lives. We're constantly affected by things in the past. I see it continually in my work in the Interior Department."

Finally grabbing a doughnut from the cart, Jenna settled back against the cushions. She stared at the monitor where the baby flung an arm to his side. She sighed and took a bite of the sweet, sticky pastry.

Once again voices came from the speakers.

"You are dressed already? This is early for you."

"Yes. Mama, could you watch the children for a few hours this morning?"

"Where are you going?"

"A friend is picking me up."

"Where are you going?"

"I ... I just need a break, Mama."

"Yes, yes. This is all such a difficulty ... Anna, you been crying ... Anna?"

Sniffling came from the speakers.

"Anna." Her mother's voice was soft, gentle and soothing, but more distinct. She sounded very close. "I'm so sorry all this happen, darling Anna. Men can be so selfish."

Phillip uncrossed his legs, then shifted in his chair and recrossed them. He set his coffee cup on the table beside him.

"How could he do this, Mama? How could he leave me like this?" Anna's voice rose in volume and pitch. "Me ... and the children too?"

"He does not deserve you, Anna. You are too good for him."

Deep sobs issued from the speakers. "I don't know what to do. I want to die. I can't do this." The weeping continued.

"You are strong woman, Anna. You will do fine."

"How will I do fine? No, Mama, I won't do fine. How will I do fine when he's gone off with another woman while I'm carrying his child?"

"Oh, sweet Anna."

"Phillip Junior and Jenna Lynn are enough. What will I do with another child? Raise three children all alone? No, I can't do it. I can't go another six months carrying this child knowing he's off with that awful—that woman."

More sobbing.

"Anna. Anna."

"I'm like trash. Me and the children. He's thrown us all away—for her. Everything is her. He's obsessed with her. And we're nothing."

Shock waves stiffened Jenna's body. Her head pounded. She turned to her father and stared at him in unbelief.

Not this. Not now.

Phillip paled and got up from his seat. He shuffled a few feet away and paced back and forth behind the couch, rubbing his neck with both hands. The agonized crying from the speakers continued.

"You are beautiful woman, Anna. Another man will come along, and ..."

"I don't want another man."

"You could come back to Tajikistan. Your father take care of you."

"I don't want to go back to Tajikistan. I'm an American now." More weeping. "I wish I could die."

"Don't talk like that, Anna."

"I mean it. I want to die. And I'm not going to have this child."

"What you mean—you are not going to have this child?"

A doorbell rang.

"Anna? What do you mean?"

"Just what I said, Mama. I'm not going to have this child."

There was a click, and a door banged against a wall, then Cindy's voice. "Are you ready?"

"Let's go." Anna's voice was broken.

"It's pretty cold. You may want a jacket."

"No, Anna. Anna. No. Anna."

Anna's mother kept calling after her. Then a door slammed shut, and the speakers went silent.

CHAPTER THIRTY

Overhead lights in the lab blinked off, then glared back on as a crash of thunder echoed through the underground chamber. Weston looked upward at the windowless walls.

"Ophelia. The hurricane must be strengthening and moving north."

Another sharp crack. A gigantic peal of thunder rolled and crackled and plowed through the air.

Against the wail of the wind outside, the sound of a car engine cranking echoed from the overhead speakers.

Jenna shivered, then turned her attention from her father and the storm to the sound of the car. The engine ratcheted, then roared. It idled for a minute, sputtered and stopped. On the monitor, Jenna saw the baby jump at the sudden noise. He began flailing his arms and kicking his tiny legs. Once more the car erupted into life, then died. The third time the engine was cranked, it finally caught. They heard the shifting of gears and the slow idling of the car as it began to move, then nothing except the engine's low hum and the moaning of the wind outside.

SAN FRANCISCO, 1995

The engine purred now as the Camaro cut through the hovering patches of morning fog. The car negotiated the hillside curves, finally emerging from the cloud cover on the heights above to turn onto the street leading into town. Neither of the women spoke.

Anna stared straight ahead. Her jaw was set and resolute as she dug her hands deep into the pockets of her fleece jacket.

At the stop sign, the car hesitated, then moved through the intersection past a cluster of small buildings. Ahead of them, spires of the Golden Gate at the other end of town peeked through the white clouds billowing above the Bay.

Just before the bridge, Cindy pulled to the stoplight, drummed her fingers on the steering wheel, and looked at Anna directly. "You're all right with this now?"

"Yes."

She nodded as the light turned green. "Okay, here we go. No turning back. Right?"

"Right."

They spiraled up to the bridge that spanned the waterway in a graceful sweep of copper and latticed steel. Anna looked across the Bay to the city of San Francisco, where tall rectangular buildings punched their roofs into the sky.

"You said it's on Hyde?" Cindy asked as they left the bridge and turned onto Highway 1.

"Yes, your directions say it's on Hyde—off Market."

"You look pretty grim."

"I feel pretty grim."

"I heard shouting when I came to the door."

"I'm just upset, Cindy."

"I know. Men are jerks."

"I didn't think Phillip was a jerk. I—I thought he was different. I don't think I'll ever be able to trust anyone again."

"Welcome to the real world, sugar."

Anna looked down at her hands and began rubbing her forearms. "You've done this before, right? It was—okay?"

"Not a picnic, but it's over in a snap. I was in New York at the time. Four years ago. Guy wouldn't even pay for undoing the mess he caused me."

"I never thought I'd do this."

"The first time is the hardest."

"First time?" Anna spun in her seat and stared at Cindy in alarm. She felt her heart squeezing into a tight ball.

"That's what people tell me. You don't have to look at me like that."

WASHINGTON, DC, 2052

Rain pelted the garden outside the window of the Oval Office. Tomlin leaned forward in his chair and narrowed his eyes at Michael.

"The pot is quickly coming to a boil," Tomlin said.

Frowning, President Gelford looked from Tomlin to Robertson to Quigley. "In other words, the situation has intensified. In Uzbekistan last night, Special Forces discovered a cave recently inhabited by a terrorist cell. They found detailed designs and specs for sophisticated delivery systems for WMDs, particularly suitable for chemical and biological weaponry. There was heavy machinery and equipment ..."

"And signs of sudden movement in and out of the place," Tomlin interjected.

"They apparently left in a hurry," said Gelford.

"Whew." Michael shifted to the edge of his seat. "If they know what they're doing, the kind of systems you describe could launch the weapons over long distances and disperse their contents—chemical or biological or both—over larger areas, increasing their kill rate." He looked toward Tomlin. "That was what I was trying to talk to you about the other day."

Tomlin nodded. "The CIA told us the same thing. The technology they found is made to order."

Michael sat back again and crossed his arms over his chest. "So Uzbekistan is involved in this."

"Terrorist cells from Uzbekistan anyway," said the president.

"Who else?"

"That's the million-dollar question," Tomlin said.

"The worst part is the maps they found," the president added.

"Maps?"

"Detailed city maps of DC. New York. And Chicago, Los Angeles, San Francisco and Tokyo, along with fragments of surveillance reports discussing the vulnerabilities of landmark areas."

"God help us."

"Have you communicated this to Rajanov?" Robertson asked.

"He doesn't believe us," Tomlin replied.

"What about Oqilov?" asked Michael.

"He wants LaMarche."

"Without LaMarche, we're in deep trouble." The president rolled his chair closer to the desk. "I don't want to resort to force or threats. We've got to try everything possible before we get to that."

"How is he now? LaMarche?" Michael asked. "How long's it been now? Three days?"

"Doesn't look like he's going to get back here in time, if at all," the president said. "The procedure has become more complicated than expected."

Gelford's eyes moved from Michael to Tomlin to Robertson. He fastened his gaze once again on Michael. "Tell me more about his sister, Quigley. What's she like, and how close is she to Oqilov? If she could at least slow things down ... give us time to come up with another strategy."

Michael shifted his weight to the side of his chair and crossed his legs.

"Oqilov's her uncle, her mother's younger brother. He's only about three years older than Jenna, and she's two years older than Janssen. Jenna went with Janssen and their mother to Tajikistan on the visits LaMarche spoke of, and as children they all used to play together. Prime Minister Oqilov has always been extremely fond of Jenna."

"Hmm. What's she like personally?"

"I met her," Robertson said. "She's a very nice woman. Seems levelheaded."

"She's a quick thinker, witty, a schoolteacher. Teaches third grade," Michael added.

"Married?"

Michael felt the color rising in his cheeks.

"Divorced." Slowly, he uncrossed his legs and arms and straightened up. "Look, I might as well level with you. She was my wife. We've been divorced for seven years."

Both Gelford and Tomlin blanched as if they'd been hit in the face. The president leaned across his desk. "You and LaMarche—brothers-in-law?"

"We were."

"Why didn't you tell us before?" Tomlin asked.

"You didn't ask. I didn't think it mattered."

"Sounds like our security investigation was a bit lax, to say the least." Gelford looked hard at Tomlin, then Robertson.

"I can't believe this." Tomlin rose and walked to the glass door leading to the porch. He stood with his back to the others for a moment before turning again to the room. "I was going to suggest Ms. LaMarche accompany you to Tajikistan. But now it sounds like that might be awkward."

Michael took a deep breath, a mix of apprehension and excitement somersaulting within him. "It probably would be. But if necessary, I think she'd agree to it. Anyway, I hope she would."

"How should we go about this? Robertson, you want to contact her?"

"Things are pretty intense in the lab right now," Robertson said. "I don't think I could get her away from there till after we find out what's going to happen with the abortion."

"Abortion?" Michael frowned. "Who's getting an abortion? I didn't think people got those anymore, with in-vitro adoption technology being so common."

"It's a long story," Robertson said.

"Actually, I'd be willing to talk to her first, if you don't mind," Michael said. "She may be a little intimidated if you call her cold like that, without any warning."

"Are you two on speaking terms?" Tomlin asked.

"I think we are. I'd like to give it a try, anyway."

"Well, hurry it up then. We've got to move, and quickly."

SAN FRANCISCO, 1995

The Camaro turned off Market onto Hyde. Ahead of them, Anna saw several people walking up and down the sidewalk with signs above their heads.

"There's picketers," Anna said.

"Looks like it. This must be the abortion clinic. Don't those people have a life?"

PIECES OF DARK, PIECES OF LIGHT

Three women and a man paced along the sidewalk with brightly colored signs. On a yellow one, "Choose Life" was scrawled in large black lettering. A red sign reading "Abortion Stops a Beating Heart" obscured the words of the third one, carried by a man in a brown hat.

Cindy slowed the car as she neared the building's driveway. When her left turn light began to blink, a middle-aged woman with a pleasant smile approached the corner where they were about to turn. She had no sign, but carried a small stack of leaflets. The woman locked eyes with Anna.

Anna flung her hand toward Cindy.

"Stop. I can't go in there." She drew her hand back to her throat and pressed her fingers against the top of her cobalt blue turtleneck. "Not with all those picketers."

Cindy put on the brake and looked at her curiously.

"Go on." Anna gesticulated toward the street. "I don't want to turn in here. We can come back later."

Cindy let the steering wheel spin back, then directed the car out onto the road.

The woman on the corner with the pamphlets relaxed her hands to her side. Her face brightened.

"I wish those people would mind their own business."

"How long are they out there?"

"I don't know, but don't think for a minute they do abortions all day either. You're going to have to make up your mind. If you're going to do it, you've just got to do it."

"Let's drive around a few minutes. Let me get used to this." Anna turned to look through the back window at the picketers who had stopped to watch their car continue down the road. "I don't know if I have the nerve to cross a picket line."

"Don't let a few fanatics intimidate you, Anna."

"Is that what they are? Fanatics?"

"Do you want to go get a cup of coffee?"

"No. I'm fidgety enough already. Just drive around a little."

"Where?"

"I don't care. Anywhere. Driving calms me down."

Cindy turned up California Street and put the car in first gear as the Camaro strained up the steep incline. At the top of the hill, Anna gazed down at the Transamerica Pyramid towering above the city, then closed her eyes and listened to the tires swishing on the pavement. Opening her eyes, she saw they were winding past neat rows of pastel Victorian-style houses joined side by side, and she said, "It'll take a few minutes, but I'll get my courage up. Then we can go back."

"Wait a minute. What's that?" Anna pointed toward a small pink one-story building with a sign out in front.

"'Center for Women,'" Cindy read. "'Pregnancy counseling.'"

"Is that an abortion clinic?" Anna asked.

Cindy slowed the car. "Looks like it."

Anna sighed. "And no picketers."

Cindy pulled into the parking area in front and parked beside a white Camry.

Anna's heart beat faster. Her palms were clammy. Nervously, she fidgeted with the handle of her purse.

Cindy put on the hand brake, then turned to Anna, who stared at the front entrance to the building without moving.

"Well? You going in?"

CHAPTER THIRTY-ONE

The room was decorated in soft pastels, with large white wicker chairs dressed with pink cushions. Behind the counter a woman with a round face, frizzy brown hair, and very little makeup handed her a questionnaire.

Anna took the clipboard from her and gazed around the room. Although furnished tastefully, the sizable room felt empty. She wondered if she should have had Cindy come inside with her, and then thought better of it. Cindy was a little too intense.

She wiped her sweaty palm against the front of her jacket and sat down to fill out the form. Thankfully it was short and asked only for basic information.

Anna filled out the questionnaire, handed the clipboard back to the woman, and felt her heart pounding in her throat as she opened her mouth to speak. "Are you … doing abortions today?"

"We don't do abortions here," the woman said. "But we can give you a free pregnancy test and information on the nine different kinds of abortion so you can make an informed decision. Everything's confidential."

Anna felt the tension in her body increase a bit. It was another delay. "Nine different kinds of abortion?"

"Yes. Would you like to get a free pregnancy test?"

"I already did one."

"A home kit?

"Yes."

"You're welcome to double check it. They're not always accurate. Some women have come in thinking they were pregnant, and it turned out they weren't."

Wouldn't that be nice.

The woman gave her a cup and directed her to a restroom behind her desk. When Anna handed it back to her a few minutes later, the receptionist indicated an office down the hall.

"It'll take a few minutes to get the results. You can wait in that room with the blue wallpaper. Sunny will join you in a minute to go over the results."

Anna walked past two closed doors to the room at the end of the hall, a clock ticking away in her head. She didn't want to waste too much time here. She needed to get back to the first abortion clinic they'd seen, but she welcomed the idea of getting more information. Maybe she would have more courage to face the people in the picket line if she knew exactly what she was getting into.

The room was all blue. On the far side of the room Anna spotted a table with a display of plastic models of fetuses in graduated stages of development. The caption underneath said they were life-size models. Anna walked to the table, curious to see what the one looked like at eleven weeks.

Do abortion clinics have things like this? But then this place doesn't do abortions. It's an information center. A doctor's office? A counseling center? Planned Parenthood? The twelve-week fetus already looked like a baby, even though it wasn't much longer than her thumb.

"It's fascinating to see how quickly they develop, isn't it?" The cheerful voice came from behind her.

Anna turned around to see a pretty blonde woman standing in the doorway.

"I'm Sunny," the blonde said, taking a couple of steps closer. "You must be Anna."

Anna stared at her. Sunny. The name was perfect. She looked like a vision of sunshine with her bright face, warm brown eyes, and engaging smile.

Sunny motioned toward the couch. "Why don't you come over and have a seat so we can go over the results of the pregnancy test? Then perhaps we can chat a minute."

Anna sat on the edge of the cushion and fingered the corner of her jacket while Sunny took a seat in one of the white wicker chairs opposite her.

"The results indicate you're pregnant, Anna, just as you suspected."

Anna nodded and looked at the window draped with blue flowered curtains. "I was sure I was."

"Stacy said you came in for an abortion."

"That's right."

Sunny looked down at the questionnaire on the clipboard in her hands. "This says you're married."

Anna sighed.

The woman placed the clipboard in her lap and regarded her. "How long?" she asked.

Anna spread the fingers of her left hand and stared at her diamond. "Seven years."

"Do you have other children?"

Anna nodded. "I have a boy four and a half, and a girl who's two."

"And no previous abortions?"

Anna thought of Cindy's comment earlier that morning and cringed. "No."

"Is your decision to have an abortion something you've discussed with your husband? Or is this something you're choosing on your own?"

Anna took a deep breath. "I'm doing this on my own."

"Hmm. I'm sure you have a good reason. You don't look like a woman who would make this kind of decision lightly. Have you considered other options?"

"Other options. You mean …?" Anna stopped without finishing her thought.

"I mean like keeping the baby—or placing him for adoption."

Anna winced. "I could never give my baby away."

"What about keeping the baby, then? Is that possible?"

"No."

"You're certain? What if you had help? Would keeping the baby be a possibility if you had help?"

"What kind of help?"

"We can refer you to various agencies that can assist you financially. We can help you with prenatal care, maternity clothes, and baby supplies. We have a food pantry, parenting classes, and we can even assist you with housing if you need it. Or help you find a job or learn new job skills."

Anna sighed. "No, that's not the kind of help I need. I just can't raise three children by myself. That's the thing, and that's all there is to it. There's too much going on in my life. I just can't handle it."

"By yourself?" Sunny looked at her questioningly. "What about your husband? Won't he help?"

Anna felt her emotions churning inside her. She bit her lip. "My husband left me and the children." She picked up a blue-flowered pillow and clutched it to her bosom. "He's involved with another woman."

Why had Phillip done this to her? She shouldn't have to be dealing with this by herself. But there was no point thinking about that now. She was by herself. "The woman at the desk told me you would give me information about abortion—the different kinds and all."

"Yes, Anna. There are nine different kinds of abortion, and I'll tell you a little more about the actual procedures in a moment. But first I think you should know about the possible side effects. There are a number of risks, both physical and psychological."

"Risks? I thought it was pretty simple."

"It's a surgical procedure, Anna. And unfortunately, even when local anesthesia is used, ninety-seven percent of women do report experiencing pain during the operation. More than a third of them say the pain is intense, even more painful than a bone fracture."

"Well, even having a baby is painful, so I guess that's to be expected to some degree. My friend said it was a short procedure though. That it didn't take very long."

"The procedure itself doesn't take a terribly long time, but there can be some long-range complications. I want to make sure you're aware of these, Anna, because they can affect you for some time."

"Really? What are they?"

"After an abortion, some women experience bleeding or hemorrhaging. Sometimes the uterus is perforated. There can be other physical damage as well."

Anna wrinkled her nose and grunted.

"A lot of women end up becoming infertile or sterile as a result of an abortion, or they have later miscarriages."

"Well, I don't have to worry about becoming infertile because I don't intend to have any more children. As for the rest, well, I guess there's always a risk. But thanks for telling me about them."

Sunny frowned. "Yes, it's something to consider. But beyond the physical complications are the psychological ones. And these are even more common." Sunny picked up a blue brochure from the table beside her and handed it to Anna. "This will tell you more about it."

On the front were the words, Before You Make The Decision. Anna opened the flaps. There was a list of physical effects on one flap, and an even longer list of psychological effects on the other.

"When a woman is in a hurry to get rid of her problem," Sunny continued, "she's often not thinking through all the facts. But afterward it begins to hit her, and she realizes she aborted a real baby, a baby who was alive but is now dead. A very, very large number—some reports say ninety-three percent—have what is called post-abortion trauma. Symptoms range from nightmares, flashbacks, tremors, or uncontrollable crying to becoming hostile and angry, or going into deep depression. Some women become promiscuous. In more severe cases, they might start drinking heavily, taking drugs or have thoughts of suicide. They are overwhelmed with guilt."

Anna tensed. She drew her hands to her throat and stared at the pillow in her lap. She thought of Cindy. Angry. Promiscuous. Cindy had not always been like that. Anna looked up and saw Sunny studying her. Her eyes were warm and compassionate.

"Abortion is not the quick, easy fix many people think it will be, Anna. After having an abortion, many women begin thinking about the baby and have regrets. Because it is a live baby inside you, you know." Sunny glanced at the fetal models on the table beside her. "You saw the models over here. I don't want you to be deceived into thinking you'd just be removing a blob of tissue. And according to what you put down as the date of your last period, he's eleven weeks." She reached over and picked up the twelve-week fetal model. "Your baby is completely formed now, as you can see here. He even has fingernails. He breathes, swallows, makes a fist, kicks, and jumps."

"The baby can do that? At eleven weeks? But it's so small."

"Yes, Anna, he's very small, but he's already very active. He has a heartbeat and brain waves, and he's even capable of bending his fingers around an object or sucking his thumb. In fact, he might even be sucking his thumb right now."

Anna felt a knot in her stomach. The pressure at her temples was strengthening into a throb.

"I can't believe he can do all that. I thought it was just ..."

"A blob of tissue?"

"Yes."

"Well, no, Anna. He's much more than that. He's a little tiny person who needs to grow."

Anna rubbed her fingers along the base of her throat. She was breathing hard. "I don't know what to do."

"As I said, we're here to help you in whatever way we can."

"But you can't help me raise three children."

"No, but God can."

"God?"

"Yes. God cares very much about both you and your baby, and he can take care of you."

Anna knit her brows together and let out a little laugh. "I'm afraid I can't really see God helping me raise my children. That sounds a little strange."

She flipped the brochure over and looked at the back. Halfway down the page was a question in boldface print. 'Can the fetus feel pain?' Anna swallowed hard and looked up at Sunny. "Can the ba—fetus feel pain when the abortion is done?"

"Studies show the baby can definitely feel pain at thirteen weeks, and some scientists believe they feel pain as early as the eleventh and twelfth week."

"And my baby is eleven weeks." Anna stared at the fetal model on Sunny's lap. "What are these different kinds of abortions? How are they done? Are they painful for the baby?"

Sunny sighed. "The most common procedure done in the early part of pregnancy is called suction aspiration or vacuum curettage. In this type of abortion, a powerful suction tube with a sharp cutting edged device is inserted into the womb through the stretched open cervix. The suction dismembers the baby and tears it to pieces, then rips the placenta from the wall of the uterus. The medical staff are required to reassemble all the parts of the baby afterward to make sure nothing has been left inside that could cause infection."

Anna's eyes had been widening in horror during Sunny's description. She screwed up her face. "That's horrible!" Her heart was pounding.

"I had hoped I wouldn't have to get into that with you—because it is horrible."

"Isn't there a pill I can take or something?"

"They are in the process of developing a pill called RU486, but even when it becomes available, it still will be a terrible procedure for the baby and the mother. It takes thirty-six to forty-eight hours for the baby to die, and he is basically starved to death. Then you deliver a dead baby."

Anna's hands were sweaty. Her head throbbed. She picked up the pillow and hugged it close to her. "I don't want to kill my baby."

"I know you don't. And you don't have to."

"But what can I do?"

"There's always adoption."

Anna shook her head. "I can't give my baby away. I can't carry it for nine months and then give it to someone else."

"Many girls say that. And it isn't easy, but adoption can be a beautiful alternative for everyone involved. You can know you've given your baby the chance for a good life, and you can even pick out the parents."

"No, no. There's no way. I can't give my baby away." Tears welled up in Anna's eyes and spilled onto her cheeks. Sunny came over and sat beside her, putting a supportive hand on her arm. Through wet lashes, Anna looked into the lovely face of the woman next to her. Sunny was looking at Anna with an expression of deep compassion.

"I can't have this baby. But I don't want to kill him, and I don't want to give him away." Anna buried her face in the pillow and began to sob. "Why did Phillip leave me and go off with that awful woman? I don't know what to do."

Sunny squeezed her shoulder supportively, then grabbed a square tissue box from the table beside the couch and handed it to her. "I know this is very hard for you."

Anna put the pillow on her lap and blew her nose, then shoved the tissue into the pocket of her jacket. Crying was not what she wanted to do. But what did she want? There weren't any good answers. She liked this woman. Could she help? She was so gentle and caring.

Sunny waited, then looked deep into her eyes as if searching for the right words. "I'm so sorry you're having to deal with this, Anna. You walked through this door looking for an abortion, but I somehow feel there may be another purpose to your being here."

"Another purpose?" Anna sniffled. "Like what?"

"You're going through a lot of pain. But Anna, you don't have to suffer like this. There is an answer I don't think you've thought about—maybe you don't even know about."

Hearing those words from this woman's lips somehow caused her to relax. Sunny had an answer for her. "Something besides adoption?"

Sunny smiled. "Yes, something besides adoption." Sunny looked back at the clipboard in her hand. "I note on the form you filled out you don't have any religious affiliation." She set it on her lap. "Is there a reason for that?"

"Not really," Anna took the tissue from her pocket and blew her nose again. "My father was Muslim by tradition, my mother Russian Orthodox. Neither were very religious. So, I just never ..." Anna shrugged her shoulders and stopped.

"Never really thought about it much?"

"That's right."

"I see. What I have to say might be helpful to you then. You're apparently going through a really tough time in your life right now, and you don't have the advantage of knowing about the peace that comes from having a relationship with Jesus Christ." She paused. "If you'll allow me, I'd like to tell you about it."

Jesus Christ? A relationship? Anna felt so lost, so confused. She didn't know anything about the Christian Jesus. It was just another religion, but in some intangible way, Sunny's words and the warmth of her eyes managed to soothe Anna's agitated spirit. She wanted to hear the answer Sunny had for her.

"Can I tell you what I've learned in my life about God?"
Anna nodded.

"From the beginning of time, God has desired a relationship with man, but we just always go our own way. We sin. We do things we shouldn't. And God is so holy he can't have a relationship with us when we choose to do things he told us not to. I learned about Jesus at an early age, but I chose to stray from him for many years. I wanted to do things my own way. The Bible says, 'No one is perfect, no not one,' and that certainly applies to me. Have you found that to be true too?"

Perfect? Anna felt a pinching of her heart as she pictured her mother's horrified face that morning, heard her pleading words. No, Anna. No. No, Anna. Anna lowered her eyes and nodded. Perfect? She definitely wasn't perfect. And she wasn't even a good mom any more. She'd become impatient with her kids, and here she was wanting to get an abortion.

"Yes, I know that's true."

Sunny nodded. "But you know, Anna, he loved us so much and wanted so much to have a relationship with us, he decided to let his own son take the punishment we deserve. His son paid the price for our sin, so we could have a relationship with God in spite of our sin. His son Jesus died for us. All we have to do is acknowledge he did that for us and ask for his forgiveness. If we accept his gift, and if we desire a relationship with him—just as he desires one with us, then we can enter into a relationship with the almighty God, who is our Father—our heavenly Father. And he'll watch over us and show us the way."

"I've never heard that before."

"It's true. And when this happens, he will give us peace."

"Peace?" Anna shook her head. "There's no way I'm going to have peace—not now. No matter what I do, my life is a mess."

"You know, I used to think like that too. But God knows things we don't." Sunny shifted a bit, turning more toward her.

"Anna. You're a beautiful woman, and I know God has a wonderful plan for you and your life, if you can just learn to trust him. I know things look impossible now, perhaps even hopeless, but you're just seeing one part of the picture. Life is like a puzzle, and we're like little ants walking along the pieces of the puzzle. We only stand on one piece at a time, and we can't see how the whole puzzle fits together. But there's someone who can see the whole puzzle. And when we put our trust in him, he can guide us along those puzzle pieces so we can see how it's all connected. Some pieces are dark, and some pieces are light. But when they all fit together, they make a beautiful picture."

"A beautiful picture. How can what's happening to me now be part of a beautiful picture?"

"One of my favorite verses in the Bible says, 'All things work together for good, to those who love God and are called according to his purpose.' All things, Anna. God loves you. He wants to make things beautiful for you. But you have to trust him."

"God really cares about us? About me?"

"Yes, Anna, very much. He loves you. That's why Jesus gave his life for you. Would you like to have a relationship with him? Would you like to see him turn all this around for something good?"

Anna nodded. "Yes, I would. Of course I would. What do I have to lose? Even if you're wrong, what could I lose now?"

"Do you believe?"

Anna gazed into Sunny's brown eyes. There was a look of caring and honesty that gave her confidence in her. "Yes, I think I do."

"Would you like to take this step of faith, then? Would you pray with me?"

Anna nodded. "Yes."

Sunny reached over and took Anna's hands. "Then say this prayer with me."

She bowed her head and said a simple prayer, and Anna repeated it, thanking God for his forgiveness and acknowledging Jesus as her Savior, then asking him to become Lord of her life.

Sunny then prayed another prayer. It was beautiful, with words and phrases that wrapped a feeling of warmth around Anna and made her feel as if she were almost floating above the ground. She felt a lightness, and an inner peace she'd never experienced before. When Sunny finished praying, Anna looked up at her and smiled.

"Thank you. You're right. I feel peaceful. It's amazing."

Sunny hugged her. "You also have a brand new life."

A gold medallion dangling from Sunny's neck swung out and snagged a button on Anna's jacket. "Oh, I'm sorry."

Sunny disentangled it and let it drop at her throat above her pink sweater. It had a rose engraved in the middle and was quite striking.

"How pretty," Anna said.

Sunny lifted the medallion in front of her so they could both look at it more easily. "It is a lovely medallion, isn't it? The rose represents life."

"Oh."

Sunny let the necklace drop back into the opening of her sweater, then leaned forward. "How do you feel?"

"So much better. Peaceful, like you said."

"And what about your baby?"

The dark dread crept back into her being. What would she do about the baby?

"Actually—" Anna began stammering. "I ... I ..." She looked at Sunny directly. She liked this woman. What would she tell her to do? "What do you think?"

"I think God will give you the strength to take care of this child. Or if you really don't think you can handle it yourself, you could place your baby for adoption. If you trust God, he will show you the way."

"Anna, I believe you'll make the right decision. Follow your heart. God has put the answer there. You are his child now. Follow your heart, not your fears."

They stood up together and walked down the hall toward the reception area. Anna scanned Sunny's radiant face, then studied the medallion once more. "The rose stands for life?"

"Yes, new life." Sunny smiled. "I'm looking at two new lives right now. Yours and your baby's."

A weight fell from Anna's heart. Her face broke into a smile.

"Thanks to you." Anna placed her hand on her stomach. "Both of us ... thanks to you." She put her arms around Sunny, hugging her close.

"Here." Sunny reached for her necklace. "I want you to have this medallion." She lifted it off her neck with one hand and pulled the chain up over her head with the other. "This will be a remembrance of today and two new beautiful lives."

"No, no. I couldn't."

"I insist. I feel God wants me to give it to you."

Reluctantly, Anna accepted it and looked at it. "Thank you."

"Do you want me to put it around your neck?"

"All right." Anna bent her head and allowed Sunny to slip it over the blue turtleneck. "Thank you so much." She hugged her again.

"Call me," Sunny said, "if you need to talk." She picked up two cards, wrote something on one of them, then handed them both to Anna along with a cassette. "Here's my cell phone as well as the office phone. I'm also giving you a card telling about a Bible study you can attend to learn more about Jesus and the decision you just made. And this is a tape I think you'll appreciate."

Anna looked at the cards and the tape, then put them in her purse.

Cindy was in the waiting room when Anna emerged from the inner offices.

"This isn't an abortion clinic," she said.

"I know."

"What happened in there?"

"We talked."

"You look funny."

"Funny?"

"Different."

Outside in the parking lot, drizzling rain splashed against Anna's face as they walked to the Camaro. The wind had picked up. Anna pushed her collar up around her neck and pulled the flaps of her jacket closer.

With car keys jangling, Cindy quickened her pace. "This rain may have driven the picketers away."

They drove through the streets, up the hills and once again past the rows of houses. Anna watched the rain splattering against the windshield as the wipers droned back and forth.

In a few minutes, Cindy began to slow the car and put on her turn signal. "We're in luck. They're gone."

Anna looked up to see they had arrived back in front of the abortion clinic. The picketers had left. Anna fingered the medallion at her neck.

"If you trust God, he will show you the way," she whispered to herself.

"What did you say?"

"I was repeating something the woman said back at that place."

"What was that?"

"If you trust God, he will show you the way."

"The way to what?"

"The way to a beautiful life."

Cindy frowned and began to turn into the driveway of the clinic.

Anna touched Cindy's arm. "You needn't go in there."

"What do you mean? We're not going through this again, are we?"

"I've changed my mind."

Cindy looked at her strangely.

Anna blushed, then took the cassette from her purse and slipped it into the tape player. "I'm not getting an abortion."

CHAPTER THIRTY-TWO

As the story unwound from the speakers overhead, Evie sat cradling her forehead in the palm of her hand. When Anna declared her intention to keep the baby, Jenna saw Evie's lips moving. Evie turned and hugged her mother. She rose with tears in her eyes and came to Jenna. They embraced silently.

Jenna stroked her fingers through her niece's soft golden hair, then turned to look at her father, who sat slumped in a metal chair behind her.

Earlier, when Phillip LaMarche first rose from his seat beside Jenna, he'd paced for a few minutes, then dragged the chair within earshot of the speakers where he sat alone listening to his wife's incriminating words. A couple of times during the unfolding drama, he rose and strode about in agitation. Now, with none of his former self-righteous and aristocratic air, he sat quietly, his face gaunt and empty.

Disappointment settled over Jenna like a dark cloud, invading the joyful relief of her brother's rescue. Her father's integrity was tarnished in her eyes. She'd never thought of her father as perfect—but this?

Not this. Not like Michael.

She turned and dropped back against the couch.

"All those years ago," Charlie said, "and now ..."

"And now it all comes out," Jenna said despondently. She eyed Charlie defensively. "But she did have a reason for considering it."

Charlie shrugged her shoulders and let them drop in a sigh.

"It must've been a very hard time for her," Jenna added, hoping her sister-in-law's sigh indicated regret over her earlier accusations against Anna.

"All this reminds me of a verse in the Bible," Evie said. "'There's nothing hidden that will not be made known. What you have said in the dark will be heard in the daylight.' Even though this happened so long ago, here we are. We never really get away with things."

"I don't know, Evie. Sometimes, it seems like people do," Jenna said bleakly.

"But maybe only for a while."

Jenna sighed. "Maybe."

Charlie adjusted the scarf at her neck. "Well, I guess that explains why Anna gave the medallion to Janssen. What a drama."

"And the abortion wasn't something she was going to do just because Dad went back in time," Evie added. "The medallion proves she really *was* going to do it."

Jenna quirked an eyebrow and gazed at Evie, then shook her head. "What if she'd had the abortion originally? Janssen never would have been born. And neither would you. Our whole lives would have been different."

"Well, thank God she didn't," Evie said.

Jenna peered at her father again. He still had not moved from his seat.

Phillip's eyes met Jenna's. He pushed himself out of his chair, then trudged to the monitor where the child slept peacefully with his thumb in his mouth. He shifted uneasily from one foot to the other, his gaze unwavering as he watched the infant for a long minute. Finally, as if he'd made a decision, he turned and shuffled around the end of the long three-piece couch, easing himself onto the cushion beside Jenna. Instead of his usual appearance as a handsome elderly gentleman, he looked old and haggard.

No one spoke. He rubbed the deep lines in his forehead.

"I didn't know," he said. "I never realized what I did to her until now."

Jenna studied the remorse written on her father's face with mixed feelings of anger, sadness, and sympathy. How could he have done that to her mother, her sweet, kind mother? Michael's face flashed before her. It was hard to know how to respond. But she had a lot of questions.

"What happened afterward, Dad? Obviously you two got back together."

Phillip's gray-green eyes, glazed over with regret, flickered toward Jenna as he raised his head.

"It was Phillip Junior," he said. "When Anna was about five months pregnant, Phillip Junior told me Mommy had a baby in her tummy. I confronted Anna about it, and she admitted it was true." He paused. "I guess the pregnancy brought me to my senses."

"So who made the move to get back together?" Jenna tried to suppress the terseness she felt edging into her voice.

"I told her I thought it would be appropriate."

"Appropriate?"

"Yes, with the baby and all."

"And she just agreed?"

"Well, she was pregnant." He squirmed and shifted his position, then crossed his left leg over his right. "I'll have to admit, I was a little surprised Anna took me back."

"Grandmother was a very forgiving person," Evie ran her palm along her neck. "She talked a lot about forgiveness—the importance of it and all."

Charlie cleared her throat. "I always wondered why Anna walked on eggshells around you. Now I guess we know."

Phillip drew his lips together in a tight line and darted an angry look at Charlie as he thrust himself off the seat. "I feel like I've been stripped naked," he snapped.

Jenna's Q watch was ringing. She looked at the caller ID, groaned, and abruptly turned off the ringer. "What timing."

Charlie and Evie looked from Phillip to Jenna inquisitively.

"It's Michael." Jenna watched her father make his way toward the other end of the seating area.

"Really? What would he be calling about?" Charlie asked.

"I don't know. He's been acting weird."

"Weird?"

"Well"—Jenna screwed up her face—"friendly."

Charlie snickered. "Men."

A beep signaled a message on Jenna's phone. She shook her head impatiently. *What is he calling about? I don't need this just now.*

She pushed the button to listen. Michael's voice sounded strained and anxious. "Jenna, it's important I talk to you. Call me ASAP."

Jenna watched her father standing at the end of the semicircular couch, leaning against the back of it with his head bowed forward. She thought of Evie's words. *Nothing hidden that will not be made known.*

Her Q watch rang once more.

"Michael again?" Jenna shook her head to reduce the tension in her neck, then pushed back the short wisps of hair tickling her forehead. She deactivated the video, stood up and pressed talk. "Yes?"

"How are things with Janssen?"

"Better."

"That's good to hear." He paused before moving on.

She waited impatiently for him to continue, then paced past her father into the open spaces of the lab.

"Jenna, I need to talk with you."

She rolled her eyes. "What about?"

"I can't talk about it over the phone."

"How about a teeny-weeny hint?"

"It's important. Official."

Janssen flashed through her mind. *The mission.* They were on it together. Was it about the mission? About Janssen?

"Hmm. You mean *official* official?"

"Yes."

"I see. When did you want to meet?"

"As soon as possible."

"We're in the middle of a hurricane, you know."

"Yes, I'm aware of that. I'm soaking wet already. No need for you to get wet. I'll come to where you are. Are you with Janssen?"

Michael's question caught her off guard. How much did he know about Janssen? "No."

"Well, let me phrase this in a different way. Are you in the same place you've been for the past several hours?"

Jenna stopped pacing and looked toward the elevator. "Yes."

"I'm going to take a stab at it. I think I know where you are. In half an hour, meet me inside the front door of wherever you are. If I've guessed right, you'll be there. If not, I've wasted a half hour. Deal?"

"I guess."

"You guess?"

Jenna turned to stare at the glass enclosure where she'd last seen her brother.

The mission.

"I'll be there."

Half an hour later, Jenna was waiting in the front lobby of the Walter Reed Annex when Michael Quigley pushed through the heavy front door. He was dripping wet.

"How did you know I was here?" Jenna asked.

"I've been in meetings with the President and Secretary Tomlin. Randall Robertson let it slip. I guess I wasn't supposed to know, but don't worry. It's safe with me." He studied her face. "How's Janssen?"

Unprepared for his question and show of concern, Jenna felt her eyes unexpectedly filling with tears. She blinked them away and swiped at the corner of one eye. "Things look a lot better than they did an hour ago. We may have made it over the biggest hurdle."

"That's good to know." He crossed his arms and leaned back on his heels. "I'm sorry about this. I know how much your brother means to you."

"Thank you, Michael." Jenna cleared her throat. "What did you want to see me about?"

"Is there a place to sit down?"

"It's pretty bare up here. We've been in a part of the building that has very tight security. I don't know what's on this floor."

Michael tried a door a few feet away. It was locked.

"Well, why don't we sit on the stairs over there. The place looks pretty deserted." He turned and motioned for Jenna to precede him in the direction of the stairway, then peered cautiously down the empty hallways and up at the platform between the floors. Apparently satisfied they were alone, he helped Jenna take a seat on the second step, while he settled himself on the first. His long legs forced his knees to angle awkwardly on the low stoop.

Jenna stared at him. He seemed so different. Gallant, actually. Not in a showy way, just polite. What did he want?

"Jenna," he began, "I know you're familiar with our mission, the one Janssen and I were to go on together."

"Were?"

"Hopefully, we still will. It's just that ... Janssen apparently is sick. I don't know all the details. What I've heard sounds pretty wild. I've just gotten bits and pieces. But the bottom line is he's incapacitated for the moment. You probably know better than I for how long."

"Hopefully not much longer. Maybe a day or two."

"Okay. That helps. Sounds good. But the problem is, things are deteriorating very rapidly in Tajikistan. We're in a near-crisis situation."

"You mean the shooting of the guards?"

"That, and one of our CIA agents is being held for killing them and confiscating some of the weapons."

"No!" Jenna frowned and grimaced. "I can't believe it."

"Now, this is confidential." Michael perused the platform above them, then stood and scanned both halls before sitting again. "We've also gotten word from our ambassador in Uzbekistan—there's increased activity among terrorist cells over there. More chatter on their phone lines and so on. Last night Special Forces hit a cave that had been held by a terrorist cell. They found signs of sophisticated delivery systems for weapons of mass destruction—especially chemical and biological, like the ones in the weapons cache found in Tajikistan. And there were maps of New York, DC, and other cities, along with surveillance reports. Really chilling. Something serious is going on. We need Janssen desperately, but we can't have him."

"Oh my. What are Jocko and Rajanov saying?"

Michael smiled. "Good girl. Just the right question. They want to know where Janssen is. Not being able to reach him makes them suspicious. They don't believe Secretary Tomlin. They think we're the aggressors, that our intentions are hostile."

Jenna shook her head. "What are we to do?"

Michael laughed. "Bingo. The perfect question again. You're scoring one hundred today."

"Hopefully this is not a game, Michael. Why are you telling me all this? What does this have to do with me?"

"Three out of three." Michael grinned at her.

Jenna stared at him, her mouth drawn back in a tight, thin line. She stood up and moved away. "I don't have time for this. I need to get back downstairs."

Michael stood and reached out to her. "I'm sorry. I don't mean to be offensive. Just trying to be funny."

"You're not succeeding." She turned to go.

"I'm sorry." He stepped toward her. "Sit back down. Please. I have something very important to ask you."

Standing there, facing the man from whom she'd been divorced for seven years—the man who betrayed her and broke her heart—Jenna wanted to leave, to walk away and forget about this conversation.

"Jenna, President Gelford himself asked me to talk to you. Please." He motioned toward the step once again.

Outside, the wind howled, straining against the doors of the massive edifice. Jenna sighed, then walked back to the stairs and sat down. "Please get to the point."

"You know Jumakhan well. He respects you. I would even go so far as to say he adores you. I believe he'll listen to you almost as well as to Janssen. You can let Jumakhan know there isn't anything fishy going on—assure him there is nothing afoul here. Tell him what you want about Janssen, but he must understand he can trust us."

"The President wants me to call Uncle Jocko?"

"Yes. If you agree to it. He and Secretary Tomlin would like to meet with you and talk more about it. We don't have any time to waste, Jenna. If Tajikistan sells the weapons to whoever it is they're talking to, it may be all over for us."

Suddenly a picture flashed through Jenna's mind. She saw Janssen standing on the other side of the window in the lab where the time womb had been. He was telling them about a piece of paper. "Give it to Secretary Tomlin," he'd said.

Jenna stood up abruptly, her face flushed. "Oh, my gosh. We never gave it to Tomlin. We ... forgot." Jenna turned and raced down the hall, leaving Michael staring after her.

"What are you talking about? Where are you going?" Michael called.

Jenna turned around in mid-stride. "I forgot something. Stay there. It ... it's important. I'll be back in a few minutes." She hurried farther down the hall, then turned again. "Tell them yes. I'll call. I'll do what you asked."

CHAPTER THIRTY-THREE

Back in the lab, Jenna rummaged through the pockets of Janssen's trousers. "I can't believe I forgot about this."

"I can't believe we *all* forgot about it," Evie echoed.

"There's just been too much going on," Charlie said. "We can't be too harsh on ourselves."

"Here it is." Jenna held up a note with all their names on it and tore it open. She wasn't prepared for the personal message. She took a deep breath and bit her lip to keep her emotions in check.

"What is it?" Evie hung over her shoulder and read aloud. "'Thank you for your love and support through the years. Please know if I'"—her voice cracked—"'don't return, I have no regrets. Carry on—hold me in your heart, and don't look back. I love you all. Janssen.'"

Jenna turned and placed a hand on Evie's arm. "He's coming back. He'll be fine."

"I know. It's just that …" She gasped for breath as a tear trickled down her face. "He almost didn't."

Feeling her own eyes growing hot, Jenna laid Janssen's note down. "That's obviously not for Secretary Tomlin. What's this?"

She unfolded another paper that had been wrapped inside the first. She rotated it in her hand.

"'Tahad Abdul Azzadafa.' It's a name. That's all it says. This must be the paper meant for the Secretary."

She folded the paper and put it in her purse. "I've got to go back upstairs. The President wants me to talk to Uncle Jocko. Things have gotten pretty serious. Uncle Jocko and the other Tajik leaders think the US is responsible for those murders." Jenna grabbed her purse and coat and turned to face them. "Jumakhan and Rajanov want to know where Janssen is. It's bad. I've got to see what I can do."

"You're the one now, Jenna," Charlie said. "I'm glad you're going to talk to him."

Charlie's uncharacteristic comment took her aback. Did she really think Jenna could do any good? She threw her coat over her shoulders and hurried to the elevator.

Michael was waiting on the stairs.

"Okay, let's go," she said.

"It's pouring out there. The storm has let up a little, but you'll be drenched."

"I've been wet before. Can we meet with the President now?"

"I'll let them know we're coming. Here. You can use this." He took a wand from his pocket and opened his umbrashield.

If Jenna had ever pictured herself having an audience with the president of the United States in the Oval Office, the reality of this day's meeting would have been far beyond anything she could have imagined. With the drama of the presidential seal in the center of the room staring up at her as she entered, her eyes came to rest on the imposing desk nestled in the arc of the oval room.

President Gelford was seated there with the Secretary of State. They were watching her.

She reached up and dabbed at her hair. Water dripped down her neck. Running her fingers through her short brown locks, she tried to fluff it up. She laughed. "Nothing like making a grand entrance."

"You look beautiful," Michael said.

Her mind did a flip at his words. In spite of the rollercoaster of events that had whipped her around over the past few days, Jenna was still unprepared for compliments from her ex-husband. She frowned at him. "I don't know about you."

"I mean it. You are beautiful."

What on earth was going on with Michael?

The whole situation seemed surreal—being invited to the Oval Office by the president in the middle of a storm, arriving dripping wet as she entered one of the most impressive and influential rooms in the world, and having her cheating ex-husband tell her she looked beautiful.

Maybe I'll wake up and find out this is all a dream.

"Welcome." The president, with collar loosened and sleeves rolled up, rose from behind his desk and made his way to Jenna as she stood transfixed in the doorway.

Jenna blushed and stuttered, then put out her hand. "Hello, Mr. President. I'm sorry I look so awful. The rain—"

"You look wonderful, I assure you. This isn't a time for formalities. We have some pressing issues before us. How's your brother?"

"Things are looking more promising today," Jenna said. "I think the worst is over."

"Fantastic. That is extremely good news for all of us. I hope he'll be back here and ready to travel to Tajikistan soon."

"Yes, I do too."

"Until he is ready to complete this mission, however, we need someone to fill the gap. I understand you may be able to help us."

"I'll do what I can." She ran her fingers through her wet hair again, trying to give it some body.

"This is Secretary of State Tomlin. I guess you've already met Randall Robertson."

"Yes. Nice to meet you, Secretary Tomlin. Mr. Robertson." She shook hands with both of them, then followed them toward the couch in the seating area.

"I guess Quigley explained what is going on," Gelford said, settling into his chair. He reiterated much of what Michael had told her earlier on the Annex stairway. "Would you be willing to place a call to your uncle on our behalf?"

"Certainly. Just tell me what I need to do."

"We don't expect you to resolve the entire crisis, Ms. LaMarche. Just get us a little negotiating room. Explain whatever you want about your brother. We'll leave that up to your discretion. You know your uncle best." He stopped, cleared his throat. "Right now, I think they must believe we're holding him hostage or something. They're extremely distrustful."

"Yes, I think I can help straighten that out." Jenna nodded, then turned to the Secretary. "Secretary Tomlin, I need to give you this." She pulled the slip of paper from her purse. "Janssen instructed us to give it to you before he got into the time womb, and I'm sorry to say we all forgot. It has a name on it. I have no idea what it means. Hopefully you'll know more about it."

Tomlin unfolded the paper and read it.

"Tahad Abdul Azzadafa. I'm not familiar with the name. You say you don't know where he got it, or anything more about it?"

"Nothing."

"Interesting. He obviously thought it important. We'll check it out. Thank you, Ms. LaMarche." He studied the note for a second, then folded it and tucked it into his coat pocket.

The president gazed at the rain streaming down the windows and tapped the end of his pen against the polished surface of his desk. He turned to Michael and Jenna. "One other very important thing we'd like you to accomplish in your phone call to Jumakhan. We need him to promise safe passage for Quigley to travel to Tajikistan and examine the weapons. Do you think you could do that?"

Jenna looked at Michael with a crooked smile. "Make sure Jumakhan will keep Michael safe?" She raised her chin a little, keeping her eyes fastened on him. "Now that's an interesting request." She looked at the president, then Tomlin, and winked. "There's some history here, you know."

"Yes, we know about it." Gelford laughed. "Hopefully you're a merciful person."

Secretary Tomlin cleared his throat. "I hate to add this at this particular time, but if your call to Jumakhan is successful, we would like you to consider making one additional commitment."

Jenna looked at him expectantly.

"We'd like you to consider traveling to Tajikistan with this first envoy. Neely, Bradley, and Quigley will be going, along with a few other weapons specialists. Once your brother returns, we will send him there immediately, but in the meantime, we need someone to help the Tajiks keep a cool head."

"When would we leave?"

"Tonight, after the storm clears."

CHAPTER THIRTY-FOUR

Evie had not gotten a response from Danny all day. Twice she'd tried his Q phone and then sent messages. Now it was almost two in the afternoon, and still no word from Danny. What had happened after he called last night? Had someone still been following him?

The muscles in her neck twinged tight. She walked to the lounge area and got a bottle of water from the beverage machine. Although the water cooled her throat, it had little effect on the tension rising in her body. She tried to shake out her shoulders in an attempt to relax. Why was she so nervous?

By the time Michael dropped Jenna off at the Annex, the driving rain had eased into a steady drizzle. She wasted no time getting back to the underground laboratory and filling the others in about her meeting.

"I hate to leave now before Janssen comes back," she said.

"You'll be a lot more helpful to Janssen by running interference in Tajikistan," Charlie said. She nodded toward Evie and Phillip. "The three of us will hold the fort down here."

Jenna peered at Charlie questioningly. She was being so nice, so—complimentary. But she was the political one with a good head on her shoulders. "Will you promise to keep me up to date on what's happening with Janssen?"

Charlie nodded. "You needn't worry about that."

Evie raised her right hand in a scout's-honor gesture. "Promise."

"I don't know what good I can really do there," Jenna said.

"Don't underestimate yourself," Charlie said. "You only need to keep things smooth and steady until Janssen joins you. Jumakhan has a lot of respect for you. Just try to slow things down."

"Get Jumakhan in a good chess game. That will slow him down," Phillip said, joining the conversation. "He loves chess."

Jenna laughed and looked at her dad. His face held an unusually inviting vulnerability. She reached over and hugged him. When she began to pull away, he stopped her and held her at arm's length. Phillip gazed at her and nodded.

"I'm proud of you, Jenna."

"Thanks, Dad."

His eyes flickered away, then back, as he continued to grip her arms. "I'm sorry I wasn't a better father. Or husband." He let go and looked away. "Charlie was right. Your mother did walk on eggshells around me. And I let her. She thought I'd leave again, and I took advantage of that." He paused, shifted his weight from one foot to another, and sighed. "It's too late to apologize to her. But I can apologize to you—all of you. I don't mean to keep you, Jenna, but I just wanted to say that before you left."

"Thanks, Dad. That means more than you know."

Jenna embraced her father again and felt a sigh shuddering through his body. He patted her on the back. This moment of closure with him felt good, but time was growing short.

"Well, I need to go." Jenna hugged Evie and squeezed Charlie's shoulder. "Remember to keep me informed." Jenna looked at Evie and cocked her head to one side. "You look a little peaked, young one. Are you okay? I think you need to get some sleep."

A familiar tune began playing on Evie's Q watch. She looked at the display and felt a flood of relief. She clicked on the phone and attempted to sound nonchalant.

"Danny?"

"Yeah. Sorry I didn't call you back sooner. It's a long story."

"Is everything all right?"

"I hope so. But something is going on."

"What do you mean?"

"Well, this morning, it was pouring rain ..."

"Yes, I know." She resisted the temptation to say *get to the point*.

"... so I waited a couple of hours to go into the office, hoping the sky would clear up." He paused. "Finally, I decided I couldn't wait any longer and went out the front door to get in my car. Well, the minute I walked outside, the doors to three vans slid open. A bunch of reporters and cameramen ran at me. Those guys don't care what the weather's like, I'll tell you. Of course, they all were covered by rain paraphernalia, but the wind was blowing like crazy."

Evie rose from her seat and paced about the room. Why in heaven was he rambling on about the weather?

"They ran up to me and wanted to know what I was doing at"—he cleared his throat—

"well, you know, the place I was last night."

"Yes," Evie said.

"Some of them saw me there. Then they wanted to know who was in the car with me. I'm trying to be careful what I say here, you know, Evie."

"I understand."

Get to the point, Danny.

"They thought they knew who it was, and they wanted me to confirm it. Then they asked me every other conceivable question they could come up with. In the meantime, of course, I was getting drenched."

"What did you tell them?"

"I said it was personal business. What else could I say?"

"And about—the person in the car?"

"I said it was an old friend of mine."

Evie laughed. "Mhmm."

"I know. I know. But the serious part of all this is one of the reporters pulled me aside and told me he and another reporter had been—where I was last night, and that someone else had been there too. Someone who was following me. Somebody not from the media."

A wave of fear passed over Evie, rendering her momentarily speechless. It took her a moment to respond.

"Did he have any idea who it was?"

"All he said was, it was a short, muscular man with a swarthy complexion."

"You need to let Secretary Tomlin know."

"I already did."

"What did he say?"

"He thanked me for the information."

Secretary Tomlin paced between his desk and the front door.

"Something sinister is going on here, Quigley. You be careful over there. Stay alert."

"What do you think it is?"

"I don't know. But someone's very interested in LaMarche's whereabouts. Too interested."

"It's the negotiations," Michael said. "What do you think they're up to?"

"What I want to know is *who* it is. I don't like the looks of it. Not at all."

"We'll be over there soon. Hopefully our being on location will help."

"You stay sharp. I like your ex-wife, by the way. Tell her to watch her step. You're not the only scoundrel she needs to be wary of."

Evie plopped beside her mother at a table in the lounge. "I'm so ready for this to be over. How long have we been here? A week?"

"Three days," Charlie said.

"Is that all? When will they start bringing Dad back?"

"I've lost track of the time. Shouldn't be long now." Charlie idly swirled her near-empty cup.

"I hope not. And how will they keep the medallion from causing problems on the way back?"

"Good question. And I have some other questions on my mind. Let's ask."

Charlie and Evie found Drs. Bryant, Pruitt, and Meyers at the instrument panels, absorbed in intense conversation. Evie and Charlie stood behind them and listened. The subject of time was on their minds too.

"It's been almost thirty-two hours now," Meyers said.

"Yes," Bryant answered.

"Can you tell if the medication is working yet?"

Dr. Pruitt clicked her Da Vinci ball several times and looked at the screen. "Doc-H3 is just now running tests to see if the disease has been successfully eradicated."

"Doc-H3?" Dr. Meyers said.

"The nanobot swarm assigned to carry out the medical procedure."

"How long will the tests take?"

"About twenty minutes."

"So we should know in twenty minutes if my father has been healed?" Evie asked eagerly.

"I believe so." Pruitt turned in response to Evie's query. "Of course, we need to run further tests when he returns. But if these preliminary results are favorable, we can start bringing him back shortly. We've already begun preparations for his return."

"Will the medallion cause problems on the way back like it did before?" Evie asked.

Pruitt and Meyers eyed Dr. Bryant, who remained absorbed in the instrument panels. Bryant looked up at them and slowly shook his head without changing position. "The nanobots have sophisticated camouflage capabilities." He continued scrolling through some calculations on an overhead screen. "I've instructed them to mass themselves about the locket. That should keep the particles from detecting the metal on the way back."

"Thank God," Evie said.

"I think the thanks really go to you three." Charlie said. "Thanks for being on top of this. You've all done a great job. But Dr. Bryant, I have another question—something else has been on my mind."

Dr. Bryant closed the screen and turned, looking at her with a vacant expression.

"Since the time womb was damaged on the way back in time, how will you make sure it will work properly when it returns to our time?"

Dr. Bryant smiled broadly. "That is the delectable part of all this. Don't you wonder where the time womb went? Where it is, now that the subject is in his mother's womb?"

Charlie flushed. "You know, I can't believe I hadn't thought about that, but now that you mention it ..."

"There are teams, hives, swarms, whatever you want to call them—I like the term hive myself—of nanobots accompanying the mission. Some hives are dedicated to taking care of the time womb. Did you notice as the time womb went back in time, it shrunk to the size of the subject?"

"Why, yes. It was very gradual, wasn't it?"

"Nanobots were assigned to deflate the time womb in proportion to the subject's size as he got younger and smaller. When the time womb was no longer necessary and became an obstruction, another hive of nanobots dismantled the time womb, molecule by molecule, and stored these molecules individually on themselves, to hold until his time to return home. They are now beginning to reconstruct the time womb, and of course, as they rebuild, they will restore it to its original undamaged structure."

Dr. Meyers was listening intently. "Where are the nanobots now?" He frowned in thought. "I've been curious about that dark film surrounding the fetus, and I'm wondering ..."

"You mean, what causes it?" Dr. Bryant nodded. "Yes, the dark film is made up of nanobots. The nanobots are invisible to the naked eye, but grouped together they resemble a dark cloud—or film, in this case. Have you read much about nanotechnology?"

"Not much. I've just read a few articles in medical journals and such. It's a fascinating science."

"With unlimited possibilities."

"Almost too unlimited, from what I understand," Dr. Meyers said. "Could be a little dangerous."

"With the opportunities of science come the responsibility of ethics."

"Yes, to be sure."

As Evie and Charlie left the lab's master control area, they passed beneath the speakers above the large screen at the center of the room.

"I think I'll go lie down a minute," Charlie said. "I'm tired."

"Are you going upstairs?"

"Yes."

"I think I'll come with you."

Music sounded from the speakers above, and they stopped to listen to the haunting lyrics. Over the music they heard Anna's voice.

"The woman at the pregnancy center gave me this music tape, Mama—about a baby in the womb, asking what he was supposed to be. The baby is a real person already, just like the song says. And he has a future. Who knows he could grow up to be somebody important. A doctor, a scientist, or a hero who saves the world ..."

"Oh, my," Charlie said. "If she could only see him now."

"I think she does, Mom."

CHAPTER THIRTY-FIVE

As the plane lifted off the ground, Jenna watched out the window as the Capitol City and landscape below shrank to miniature proportions. To the north, heavy clouds—the remnants of the hurricane—moved along the northeastern coastline into Canada. Resting her head against the seat, she closed her eyes, exhausted. What day was it? The last few days had all run together until it seemed like a blur. She'd gotten little sleep. Now here she was on a fourteen-hour flight to Tajikistan, assigned the job of keeping the lid on a boiling kettle of international conflict capable of exploding any moment into a world crisis. Was she up to the job? She didn't know. For the moment, she wasn't sure she even cared. Her eyes burned in their sockets. She'd think about all this tomorrow. All she wanted to do now was sleep.

She awoke a few hours later to a sinking feeling in her stomach. A tremor shook the cabin. The plane dropped, then pitched back and forth. The captain's voice came over the loudspeaker.

"Sorry, ladies and gentlemen. We just hit turbulence. I'm taking us up to a higher elevation. We'll be fine in a minute."

Jenna leaned her head back again and closed her eyes. She was no longer sleeping, but her mind continued to turn over, hovering in the twilight world between sleep and wakefulness. She glanced over at Michael in the seat across the aisle. He had his trans-information receiver open on the food tray. He scrolled through several screens, then looked down at some papers. A cloud of depression crept into her heart. She shook her head and tossed her hair to sweep away the gloom, then grabbed a magazine from the pocket before her.

At her sudden movement, Michael looked over at her. Out of the corner of her eye, she watched him curiously while she flipped through the pages of the magazine.

He stared at his TIR for a minute before snapping it shut and repositioning his tray. He glanced again at Jenna, unbuckled his seat belt, then stood in the aisle with his hand on the top of her seat. "Mind if I join you for a minute?"

"That's fine," Jenna said.

Michael slid into the seat beside her, angling his long legs in her direction, his knees pressing into the foam seat in front of him.

"I saw you sleeping. Brought back memories."

Memories? What is this all about?

"Thanks for coming on this mission on such short notice," he continued, "and for intervening on my behalf. You're a good sport."

"Just answering the call of my country," Jenna said flippantly.

Michael smiled. "Yeah." He was silent for a moment. "Jenna ..." He looked at her with a pained expression. She waited for him to finish his sentence, but the swishing of the approaching food trolley seemed to break his concentration. "Here's breakfast," he said. "Hungry?"

"Actually, yes. Come to think of it, I'm starved."

"Mind if I stay here and have breakfast with you?"

"Suit yourself."

Whatever serious thought had been on his mind seemed to vanish as he began talking about their son, Todd, and the house he was designing. After stewards picked up the breakfast trays, Michael excused himself and went back to his seat.

Lasers flashed around Janssen in the darkness as his vehicle hurtled through space. He had a sense that considerable time had passed, but he couldn't recall anything but the frightening race through the wormhole's throat. It seemed as if he were waking from a deep sleep. Strange memories crouched in the recesses of his mind. He looked at the soft ivory substance surrounding him. The crack in the front window was gone.

He wondered how much of what was in his mind was real, and how much was mere dreamstuff. He looked down at his body. Had he been healed? The mission to Tajikistan ... what was happening there? How long had he been gone? His experience—and the encroaching real world—had left him with nothing but questions.

The craft began to slow until he had a sense of floating. The time womb was heading toward an obstruction at the end of a long passageway. He tensed, bracing for the crash. Inches before impact, the wall parted into a wide portal. The unrestrained dimensions of infinite space gave way to concrete walls on both sides as his vehicle shifted onto a track and continued to move forward. A glass door ahead opened to greet him.

He was home.

As the time womb slowed to a stop, white-coated doctors and crew hurried toward him. The top of the time womb lifted, and a lab assistant clasped his hands to help him disembark.

Beyond the partition, he spotted Evie. She smiled and waved to him. Beside her, Charlie nodded. Then he saw his dad. He struggled to remember—had Dad been there when he left? He didn't think so. He searched the figures on the other side of the glass for a glimpse of his sister, his eyes traveling from one face to the next. No Jenna.

Dr. Bryant extended his hand. "Congratulations on a successful mission, Mr. LaMarche."

Successful?

Janssen couldn't remember anything. His mind was still in a time warp. "How soon will I know whether I'm healed?"

Dr Meyers clapped him on the shoulder. "According to what we could see from the monitors, the medication worked perfectly. We believe you *have* been healed. But we need to do an actual physical exam to make sure."

"You've made scientific history." Pruitt's round mouth curled upwards.

"I'm afraid I can't remember much of what happened. It's kind of a blur."

"That's understandable. But we have it all recorded," Dr. Pruitt said. "You can see or hear any part of it you'd like."

The bustling activity and voices all talking at once attacked Janssen's still all-too-fragile sensibilities. He stood slightly dazed, feeling out of control. Everyone knew more about what had happened to him than he did.

The doctors and uniformed aides ushered him to the doors leading to the yellow preparation rooms. Dr. Meyers walked beside him. "We'll let you greet your family and friends before we do the physical."

Janssen entered the bright yellow rooms, and as doors opened to the outer sector, he saw Evie and Charlie on the other side, with his father behind them.

Smiling, Charlie hastened toward him.

"I'm so glad you're safe." She put her arms around Janssen's shoulders and kissed him. He held her for a long moment.

"It's a relief to be back. Thanks for still being here."

Then he gathered Evie into his arms. She was crying.

"Daddy! Oh, Daddy. I can hardly believe you're actually here." She clung to him, then looked up into his face, smiling through wet lashes.

"That's my girl." He reached up to wipe a tear from her eye. "I need those smiles."

Over Evie's shoulder he spied his dad.

"Welcome home, Janssen," Phillip said.

"Dad."

"I expect you're surprised to see me here," Phillip said. "I got into the act halfway through the show. They—ah—needed some explanations."

He grabbed the old gentleman's hand, then clasped him to his chest. "Explanations?"

"Yes, son. It's been quite an ordeal. Venturing into your past can bring about some unwelcome revelations."

Into Janssen's mind burst the fleeting memory of loud noises, crying, and shouting. A vague sense of dread shivered through the fibers of Janssen's nerves, and then it was gone—as if some frightening recollection from the distant past had been stirred, but not fully dredged to the surface. "What do you mean, unwelcome revelations?"

Charlie scooted up to him and grabbed his arm. "It's a long story. We can talk about it later."

Clarissa appeared beside him and held out a medallion with a long chain attached. "Dr. Bryant instructed me to give this to you. We found it in the time womb. The techs have already scanned it, but they want you to keep it available for them to look at if they need to study it further."

The color drained from Janssen's face as he remembered the jarring of the time womb and the horror of discovering the medallion in his pocket. What had transpired after that?

He shuddered as he picked it up. "I forgot to take this off. Did it cause any problems?"

Charlie and Evie looked at each other. He couldn't tell if they were about to laugh or cry. Clarissa cleared her throat.

Nodding, his dad crossed his arms. "It exposed us to a few bombshells and almost changed the world, but other than that …"

Evie reached out and turned the round gold piece over so she could see the rose engraved on top, then smiled up at him. "It has quite a history."

Janssen felt off balance, unnerved. He gazed at Evie uncertainly, then at his dad. What did everyone know that he didn't?

Charlie squared her shoulders and nodded. "The dangers of the familiar."

The sense of dread returned. "What happened?"

"Do you want to hear about it now or later?" Charlie asked.

"I don't know. I'm mystified. My mind feels scrambled."

"It's a long story," Charlie said.

"That's right," Clarissa said, "and we don't have time for it now. Everything turned out okay. The most pressing thing now is your physical."

"That's right, Daddy," Evie added. "Then we can all breathe a sigh of relief, and we can talk."

Feeling he'd already lost control, he allowed Clarissa to steer him toward Dr. Meyers, who waited in the doorway. He'd only taken two steps, however, when an inexplicable fear seized him. He swiveled on his heels and looked into the faces of his family.

"Where's Jenna?"

"Jenna's fine. She's gone on to Tajikistan."

Tajikistan. What was happening there? Jenna in Tajikistan?

Throughout his physical, Janssen's mind raced with questions.

"Hold still," the nurse said, as she scanned him with her wand.

Finally, with a sense of relief, Janssen emerged from the examination rooms in a sport shirt and khaki pants. Secretary Tomlin waited with his family outside the door, talking with one of the technicians.

"LaMarche!" Tomlin bellowed. "Are we ever glad to see you in one piece." He clasped Janssen's hand and jubilantly slapped his shoulder. "I hear you're in good shape."

"Thank you, sir. I'm glad to be here, believe me."

"How soon till we have the results from your physical?"

"In about an hour for most of them. Forty-eight hours before the final one."

"Hmm." Tomlin pursed his lips. "We have a lot to fill you in on." He searched the room with his eyes. "Let's find a place to sit."

"Over here." Charlie motioned to a door leading to the cafeteria.

"I'm anxious to hear about everything."

Evie came up to join them as they moved toward the glass doors. She handed her dad a large glass of iced tea.

"A girl after my own heart." Smiling, Janssen accepted the tea from her hand and took a long swig. The cold liquid tasted refreshing with a sweet tang. "Ahh, it's minted. Wonderful." He turned to Tomlin walking beside him. "What's happening? Why is my sister in Tajikistan?"

Secretary Tomlin signaled for Clarissa to pull some of the tables and chairs together. As Clarissa assembled the sitting area, Tomlin jumped immediately to the events in Tajikistan, briefing Janssen on the urgency that had required Jenna to serve as his surrogate. He grabbed the back of one of the chairs and stepped around to the front, then dropped into it heavily. The chair scooted backwards.

"We can't put our finger on who's behind this," Tomlin said, "and we don't want to make accusations. But somebody is determined to keep us from getting those weapons. And your uncle is falling for it."

A restive fear churned Janssen's insides. Tomlin's remarks triggered a name in his mind.

Tahad Abdul Azzadafa.

He stopped and stared at the floor to gather his thoughts, then moved to a chair and sat. He rubbed his chin and raked his fingers through his mustache before he spoke.

"I think it's possible there's some connection between the weapons found in Tajikistan and the WMD from the Saddam Hussein regime at the turn of the century."

Tomlin furrowed his brow and stared at Janssen quizzically. "You've been back in time longer than I thought, LaMarche. That was fifty years ago."

"I'm serious. I put it together just as I began going back in time. Tahad Abdul Azzadafa. Did they give you the name?" He cast an anxious look at Charlie and Evie.

Tomlin cleared his throat. "Yes, just yesterday. Jenna brought it to me."

"He's the son of Sayad Radazon Azzadafa, an Iraqi Ba'ath Party leader, one of the most dangerous men during that time. Do you remember your history from the Iraq war of 2003?"

Tomlin lifted his chin with a faint nod of dubious acknowledgment. "How did you make this connection?"

"Some messages I got on my phone. One from my uncle. One anonymous. It all fits together."

"We've been looking into the name." Tomlin tapped his phone and scrolled through his screens. "He lives in Kanibadam in the northern part of Tajikistan. Has a textile business in Khujand, is a member of the House of Representatives, and very active in the IRP. Quite influential."

Janssen stroked his mustache as he listened intently.

"He also has a financial connection to Uzbekistan. Haven't yet been able to find out much about it, so we'll have to keep digging." Tomlin scrolled down and continued to read. "He has a son and two married daughters. Wife died. A female cousin still lives with him. Apparently he grew up in the home of an aunt and uncle. Nothing about his early history, however—mother, father—nothing like that."

Janssen nodded and leaned forward in his chair. "Yes, that's the one. His father was captured during the second Gulf War. The son came to Tajikistan when he was about nine or ten."

"How do you know that?"

"He was in a group of boys I played with when I was about eight. An angry cuss. Cold-blooded. Belligerent. I didn't know who his father was, though—not until I read it on the internet a few days ago."

"I thought you were mainly in Dushanbe."

"My grandfather took Jocko, Jenna, and me to the north with him when he traveled there to negotiate water rights between the neighboring countries. We used to climb around the mountains with some of the children there. He was one of them." Janssen shuddered. "He was mean even then. Hated Americans. Hated me."

Dr. Meyers strode toward them from the examination rooms with a look of satisfaction.

"What's the report?" Evie asked anxiously. "Will he be okay?"

"All the tests are perfect. According to the first battery, he's as clean as a newborn babe. But he won't be completely clear until we have the results of the final test, forty-eight hours from now." He scratched his head. "You can go ahead with your plans, though. Do what you need to do. I don't anticipate any problems."

A collective sigh of relief rose from the tables.

Evie touched his arm. "Dad, when you get a break, I promised Jenn you'd call her."

Janssen's face brightened. "I'd like that."

Charlie looked at her watch. "She's undoubtedly still on the plane."

In the hologram during Janssen's call to Jenna, his sister's smiles and tears at his safe return warmed his heart. His expedition had obviously been quite a strain on her. She expressed relief when he told her he would catch a flight that night and arrive in Tajikistan only one day after she did. As he clicked off the phone, he chuckled with pride at Jenna's grit in agreeing to proceed to Tajikistan ahead of him with Michael in her company.

What a trooper.

CHAPTER THIRTY-SIX

For the past two hours since changing to a smaller plane in Helsinki, Jenna's intermittent snatches of sleep proved to be unsatisfying. She was overtired and her mind unsettled, spinning from one thought to another.

A dark dread hung over her. How heavy a hand would she have to play in Tajikistan? Could she succeed in transferring Jocko's personal trust in her to her country as a whole?

She sighed.

I'm an elementary school teacher, not a diplomat.

She hoped she'd be able to prevent them from selling the weapons to whatever country was vying for them for at least one day. But a lot could happen in twenty-four hours. Surely she could hold things together for such a short period of time. Then Janssen would be here.

Janssen. The memory of their earlier conversation brought a thrill of exhilaration. She stared clear-eyed into the airplane's darkened cabin. In one day, she would see Janssen again.

He's made it out of the time womb. He's well.

Jenna felt the plane's engines pull back to commence descent. As she raised the window shade and looked out on the night sky, bright memories spiked her thoughts. She pictured Uncle Jocko and the familiar sights and places in Tajikistan she'd grown to love as a girl. What fun they'd had climbing the rugged hillsides, collecting eggs at the dairy farm, riding horses and chasing sheep on the Northern slopes.

Beneath the moonlit sky outside her window, large shadows passed under the plane as they flew over the mountains. Minutes later the lights of Dushanbe appeared.

Pockets of anxiety jumped up to dim her excitement, but she brushed them from her mind as she watched the plane descend over the city. Her spirits continued to lift. *Things have to work out.* After all, this was Dushanbe and Uncle Jocko, a city and uncle she loved.

Michael came and sat beside her and looked out at the city.

"Brings back old times, huh?"

She screwed up her face and peered at him. "For me, it does. Yes."

As the ladder was lowered and they descended the steps, the familiar blare of longhorns rang out loud, clear, and shrill, celebrating their arrival. From the top of the steps, Jenna saw the row of musicians under the floodlights. She hadn't seen horns like that since the last time she'd been in Tajikistan fifteen years ago, the one time Michael had accompanied her there. In the shadows across the tarmac, Uncle Jocko stood with his petite wife Sheela and their four grown children with spouses and little ones.

Michael descended the steps behind her. "Quite a reception."

Nodding, she pushed the button on the handle of her carry-on to activate the aircushion. "A Tajik welcome. I love it." She waved at Jocko and Sheela, who approached the plane with stately dignity.

Strap in hand, Jenna hurried toward her uncle with her carry-on surfing above the ground behind her. Michael stopped her and reached toward her suitcase.

"Here, let me help."

She looked back at him, momentarily bewildered. "Thanks."

She handed him the strap and crossed the asphalt, where she received a warm hug from her uncle. She turned and embraced Sheela, who introduced each of her children, in-laws, and grandchildren.

While she met the family, Ambassador Neely introduced Jumakhan to Randall Robertson, Bradley Jones, and the others on the team.

Jocko dutifully shook each of their hands, then hurried back to Jenna's side, offering her his arm.

"Ahhh, my Jenna. You still seem the girl. Happy and smiling."

"I feel like the girl again, just being here," she said. "I'd forgotten about the horns. I love their greeting. They always make me feel so welcome."

Jocko smiled at her. "You *are* so welcome."

Jenna climbed into the car with Jocko and Sheela, while Ambassador Neely's aides provided alternate transportation for the others to lodgings provided by the US consulate. Michael handed Jenna's carry-on to one of Jumakhan's helpers and nodded to Jenna. She acknowledged his action with a quick smile, then turned to her uncle.

Jocko patted her hand. "It will be good having you back in our home again."

In a few minutes, they pulled up to the charming two-story brick house Jenna had always loved—now aglow in warm lantern light. Jenna walked to the French doors opening onto the central courtyard and sighed contentedly.

The fountain and rock garden were still there. Lights from surrounding rooms glimmered against the uneven stone walkway. She felt at home.

"It's beautiful," she said to Sheela.

Sheela bowed her head meekly, her long, gray-streaked black hair tumbling around her shoulders. "Thank you, Ms. Jenna."

Tilting her head, Jenna gave her a warm smile. "Please just call me Jenna."

Sheela excused herself and went to the kitchen, returning with a plate of strawberries and wedges of ripe melon. She offered the plate first to Jumakhan, who took a slice of melon. Then she went over to Jenna, who still stood surveying the house and garden. "I thought you might like some refreshment."

"Oh, thank you." Jenna picked out a large red strawberry and took a seat in a comfortable chair alongside her uncle's wide armchair.

Jocko's face suddenly became grim. "Tell me about Janssen. I could tell you were unable to say much on telephone. Will he be well again?"

Nodding, Jenna briefly outlined the seriousness of Janssen's illness, his need to undergo extensive medical treatments, and the welcome new results of recent procedures. "Everything went as they'd hoped, and the doctors believe he is completely well. We are waiting on one final report."

Jumakhan ran his palm over the top of his head. "I heard very little. No mention in media."

"That was intentional, Uncle. This is very confidential. In our country, if the media hear about something like this, they're relentless. They follow people around and shout questions at them. They try to interview everyone who has the least bit of information. They're invasive.

Because of the precariousness of the situation, we told them nothing."

Jumakhan frowned. "Very difficult."

"Yes, the timing of all this has been very bad for us as a country—and for you as well, perhaps." Jenna regarded him thoughtfully. "Janssen has been completely inaccessible for four days now. I'm afraid it's made you distrustful—even suspicious, maybe."

"Yes. My countrymen do not trust US. They didn't before. And now is worse. If they could see and hear from Janssen, it would make big difference."

"They will see him very soon, Uncle Jocko. He should be here tomorrow night. You should get an official call any time now."

"I look forward to that, Jenna. We all look forward to that." He leaned over and took Jenna's hand in his. "I am sorry for Janssen's illness. But I am glad he is better and glad you are here too. It is very good to see you again." Jocko rose from his seat and offered to help Jenna up. "I know you are tired after long trip. Sheela will show you to your room. We will see you in morning for breakfast."

"Thank you, Uncle." Jenna hugged him and followed Sheela down the hallway at the west end of the living area.

Without taking time to unpack, she undressed and crawled under the thick layer of covers. The down pillow felt luxuriously soft against her cheek, and she fell quickly into a deep sleep that held her till morning.

"We invited Ambassador Neely and the rest of your team to join us for breakfast," Jumakhan said when Jenna entered the living area the next morning. "We will eat in courtyard."

In a few minutes Ambassador Neely, Michael, Bradley Jones, and the other men on the munitions team arrived. Sheela brought thick, round loaves of fresh homemade bread into the courtyard on large trays.

Even though the other three men had been on the plane with Jenna, she had been exhausted and had not become acquainted with them. Now they sat with her around the big wooden table in the courtyard, eating warm bread and strawberries, melon, apricots and apples. A fresh breeze stirred the air and brushed against Jenna's face as they talked. It was a pleasant way to start the day.

Bradley Jones, an amiable African American man from Montgomery, Alabama, was a former Ranger who had left the service to get a master's degree in chemical engineering at Georgia Tech. His present position at Sandia Labs had led him into being "a chemical munitions expert hunting down clues to WMD from the early 2000s." His humble spirit and generous attitude were impressive.

Mo Jackson was a rough man's man and former Marine from Colorado, who worked now as a contract security guard for the State Department.

Kevin Donahue, a slightly built middle-aged man, had a sad countenance and quiet manners. Because he was a CW4 from the Army Chemical, Biological, Radiological, and Nuclear School at Ft. Leonard Wood, Missouri, his expertise was especially needed now.

After they breakfasted, Jumakhan cleared his throat and tapped his spoon on the table three times.

"Time now to talk about procedure for today."

He cast a long look at Michael, Bradley Jones, Mo Jackson, and Kevin Donahue.

"We have agreed to allow you to inspect weapons. In an hour, official helicopter is scheduled to take you near town of Khujand, where you will be met by officers who will escort you to area where weapons were discovered. The leader's name is Amirali Talamov. A translator called Hiskim Gupova will also accompany you." Jumakhan held up a tablet. "I have written their names on this paper. They will stay with you while you inspect weapons and return with you when you are finished. Helicopter will bring you back here. If you need more than one day to inspect weapons, you can stay in humble accommodations in Khujand." Jumakhan glanced at each of the four men, then looked back at Michael. "Any questions?"

"Will the helicopter take us directly to the site?" Bradley Jones asked.

"No. You will take helicopter over mountains to village north of Khujand, then you travel short distance by motor vehicle. The last part of trip is by foot."

"How long is the part on foot?" Donahue asked.

"One or two miles."

"In the mountains?" Michael asked.

Jumakhan nodded. "Yes, it will be mountainous terrain. Wear hiking boots. And weather will be warm. Best to use thermo rings to keep cool."

"If we should run into any problems, is there a number where we can reach you?" Michael asked.

"Yes. I'll send it to your phone. Here is a paper with the information too." Jumakhan made a note on a sheet of paper with the names on it and pushed it across the table to Michael, then caught Michael's gaze and gave him a long, deliberate look.

"Mr. Quigley, I understand you are in charge. Please do all you can to cooperate with officials. We desire to keep everything peaceful."

"I understand, Prime Minister Oqilov," Michael said. "We desire the same."

Jumakhan studied him for a few more seconds, then took his napkin from his lap and placed it on the table in front of him. "Good. Then everything is understood."

When the other three headed for the car with Ambassador Neely, Michael lagged behind. Jenna saw him lingering in the living room on the other side of the patio doors. Earlier during breakfast, she had caught Michael watching her from the opposite end of the table. He was acting so strange.

Now Michael stood in the doorway. With anxious eyes, he cleared his throat and motioned to Jenna. His voice was mellow. "Could I talk to you a minute?"

Jenna excused herself and strolled to the spot where Michael was waiting. "Yes?"

Michael flexed his jaw and straightened his body. "What I wanted to say yesterday on the plane ... I know this is a little late, and maybe it doesn't make any difference to you now anyway, but I need to say it."

He paused and looked at his feet. When he lifted his eyes, his face appeared strained and drawn. He took a deep breath, then spoke softly but deliberately. "I'm sorry."

"Sorry? Sorry for what?"

"For everything. For seven years ago. For the hell I put you through." He paused again. "For being a jerk."

His words hit her like a brick. She was stunned. She felt the blood drain from her face.

"You're right." She stepped back toward the courtyard. "It *is* a little late."

"I know. But I need you to know. I don't deserve your forgiveness. I don't deserve anything from you. But I wanted you to know."

"Thank you, Michael. Hope everything goes well up there in the north." She wheeled around toward Sheela.

Hearing the front door shut, Jenna turned and gazed after him. She shook her head. *How absolutely bizarre.* A refreshing rush of satisfaction washed over her. She felt lighter. After all these years, she was gratified to know Michael Quigley had finally realized he was a jerk.

CHAPTER THIRTY-SEVEN

Although the day was sunny and cool, the blinds inside were drawn tight against the light. Seven men huddled around a table in the corner of the darkened room.

The oldest one stood with the aid of a cane and limped to an armchair a few feet from the others, easing himself onto the seat. "You understand, then, what to do."

The youngest man leaned his chair back on two legs and rocked back and forth. "Yeah." He lifted a rifle above his head. "Got it."

The older man frowned. "Wait until you are away from the road, Solbatov. Don't get anxious. Wait for Abdul."

"Yes, Solbatov. There's no hurry." A man with a scar sneered. "Who knows, maybe a couple of them'll fall over a cliff and save us the trouble."

The six men around the table joined in derisive laughter, but the man in the armchair remained somber. "I've waited too long for this, Talamov," he said. "Don't mess this up. Abdul, make sure you take care of Popyev and Gulov first. No room for mercy. No witnesses. It's got to look like the attack came from the Americans, just as you did the other night."

"Understood, Father."

"When do we get our weapons?" another asked.

"After we get rid of the Americans," Talamov said.

"Yeah, Zodov." Abdul rubbed his hands together. "Finally, we'll get the weapons that are rightfully ours."

The man in the armchair turned to a distinguished-looking older man at the end of the table. "Zayd."

The man acknowledged his name with a nod toward the speaker.

"How are things on the other front?"

Zayd leaned forward. "All in place. The Uzbeks are right on schedule. They have their eye on a sweet little backup plan in the US. Cyber warfare will add the finale if anything goes wrong."

"This'll be easy," Solbatov said. "They'll be—how do Americans say it—like sitting ducks." He snickered.

"They'll be roast ducks before too long."

"Allah be praised."

"Forget Allah," the man in the armchair said. "Zayd and I are the ones who conjured all this up. Praise us." He tapped his cane against the compact earthen floor. "At last, my father can smile from his grave."

Evie watched her father's plane roll down the runway. The roar of the engines beat against the stillness of the night air. She breathed deeply in relief, drawing in the pungent smell of engine grease mixed with the lingering wetness from the previous day's storm.

Nearby, Emily James spoke into the lit GITV cameras, giving her on-site report to the nation.

> Tonight, the mysterious Janssen LaMarche reappeared just as suddenly as he disappeared three days ago." With her back to the retreating plane, she stood on the wet asphalt and continued. "At a news conference given just

minutes before his departure to Tajikistan, LaMarche told reporters recent health problems demanded he take time to recuperate before embarking on his mission. No specifics were given, but according to LaMarche, he is now recovered. So as he and his entourage take off to Tajikistan, we wish him well. Hopefully, it is not too late for LaMarche to resolve the escalating crisis.

Among the throngs of reporters who came to share a glimpse of the elusive Janssen LaMarche with their viewers, Evie spied Danny distributing press packets and attempting to answer questions. Bethany Chambers and the chosen few press elite had already boarded the plane now headed for Tajikistan.

She saw Danny look her way. Their eyes met, and he smiled and nodded. A few minutes later, he was at her side, the remaining press packets neatly tucked under his right arm.

"This has been quite a day," he said. "Bethany and I have been working like crazy getting ready for the media. But thank God, Mr. LaMarche—I mean your father—is back and on his way to Tajikistan." He looked up at the dark sky where the plane's lights banked to the right. He gazed back at her, his eyes bright with expectation. "How are you doing?"

"Happy and relieved, but tired."

"Been quite an ordeal for you, hasn't it?"

"Yes, but it's interesting to see how things work out. Along with the bad, there's been some good."

Danny's expression softened into one of reflection. "Mm. I'd like to hear about it sometime."

"How would you like to get some dessert when we leave here?" Danny asked. "I know this little Italian restaurant that has the best tiramisu you ever put in your mouth."

"I love tiramisu." She gave him a teasing smile. "You make it hard to resist. Sounds scrumptious."

Evie'd never been conscious of Danny's height before. Now, as he walked beside her toward the parking lot, she suddenly felt small and vulnerable. He was slight of build, but with an understated strength along his shoulders. His crooked smile held an appealing playfulness. The honest, straightforward look in his blue eyes was refreshing. How had she gotten such a negative impression of him?

At the car, Danny popped the lock and zipped around in front of her to the passenger door. Just as he reached for the handle, Evie stopped in front of the bumper.

"I don't know if I can ride in a car with a University of Kansas sticker on the back."

Danny paused in mid-reach and stared at her.

"It reminds me of that car that cut in front of me at Burger World."

Her comment appeared to catch Danny off guard. He hesitated with his fingertips still on the handle, his body tilted forward.

Evie grinned, trying hard not to giggle. Her eyes danced.

Danny relaxed his shoulders and laughed nervously.

Evie tilted her head mischievously, allowing a tantalizing smile to spread across her face. She chuckled.

"I'm forgiven, then?" he said.

"Yes, you're forgiven."

When the plane leveled off, Janssen spread his things on the empty seat beside him and positioned his trans-information receiver on the tray in front. He turned on his TIR and highlighted the jigsaw puzzle program that routinely helped him relax on long flights. He needed to unwind and get his thoughts together. Of the ten puzzles on his program, he selected one of a hunting scene. He studied the picture for a minute to see how it fit together before splitting the screen to look at the puzzle pieces.

Janssen split the screen in two, then perused the pieces, quickly finding the corners with which to anchor the hunting scene. After finding several of the straight edges, he methodically began to build a frame. Gradually, he worked the puzzle until he began to differentiate between the colors, which subtly melted into one another. One by one the pieces interconnected. The picture was taking form.

The stewardess stood beside him. "Would you like to order a drink?"

"Yes. A glass of Australian chardonnay, please."

From the window of the helicopter, the mottled mountain landscape below reminded Michael of a Persian rug woven with threads of moss green, camel, and khaki. Over the thwocking of chopper blades, the pilot informed the men they were crossing the Hissar-Alai range. Continuing past a number of ridges and peaks, they finally saw a lush valley spreading out beyond the mountains.

"Khujand," the pilot bellowed, trying to be heard above the rumble of circling rotors. He pointed at the city beneath them. To the east, a large body of water glinted in the sunshine.

In the foothills, they spotted another smaller congregation of buildings. "You meet here, near *qishlaq*." He motioned toward the village. A few minutes later, the pilot began lowering the chopper onto a flat plain. The updraft buffeted them about, rocking the cabin and pitching it to one side.

The helicopter vibrated and shook, then finally set down. Eagerly, the men disembarked, climbing awkwardly from their cramped quarters. A cloud of dust particles kicked up by the churning rotors caused Michael to cough and blink. He brushed himself off and surveyed the area.

Donahue pulled a remote from his pocket and clicked a button. A narrow black tractor robot with an elevated claw and sensor tower appeared in the helicopter's hatch. Donahue and Mo lifted it onto the hard-packed earth.

Two bearded men wearing turbans and loose trousers with overhanging shirts stood on a slope beyond the landing field. With hands cupped over their mouths, they whispered to one another as they watched the Americans exit the plane.

Michael waved and ambled toward them. The men looked at him blankly, then turned to walk away.

"Wait, are you"—Michael tore the paper from his pocket and read the name—"Amirali Talamov?"

The two men shook their heads, saying something he could not understand, and shuffled off.

The Americans looked at each other, then at the pilot. "Do you know the men we're meeting?" Michael asked. "Will you recognize—"

The sound of a car's loose throttling and tires spinning on gravel interrupted his words. A scabby red truck pulled around the corner of a rundown brick building at the end of the field and braked a few feet away. Out jumped four men in garb more fit for rough terrain. Dark shirts hung over white trousers that hugged their legs. The three younger men had dark wavy hair. Two had short, neatly cropped beards and thick sideburns. The third had a long goatee and wore a skullcap. The fourth man, more advanced in years, had a scar on his lip. He stepped forward and approached the group of Americans.

"Michael Quigley?"

"That's me. Are you Amirali Talamov?"

"Yah. We take you up mountain." His voice was gruff, his attitude less than enthusiastic.

"Wherever the weapons are, that's what we're here to see."

"Weapons, yah," he said in a guttural tone, almost spitting out the last word.

"Is this everyone?" Michael asked.

Amirali Talamov put up his hand and shook his head as though he did not understand Michael's question. "Interpreter come."

Moments later, an old gray van rumbled down the road. The door slid open, and two older men climbed out, both with gray beards and leathery faces. They looked around at the others who had arrived by truck and spoke to one another in a local language. Michael supposed it was Tajik.

Michael looked back at his comrades. "Do you have the equipment bags ready?"

Donahue nodded and held up one of the bags. "Ready."

"And Droster G9?"

"Yup," Donahue clicked the remote. The robot rolled out from the base of the chopper and waited behind them.

The Tajik guards gaped at Droster G9 with looks of astonishment, while the two men from the van bent their heads together in a flurry of whispering.

Michael approached the van. "Which one of you is the interpreter?"

"I am interpreter," the taller of the two answered.

"You're Gupova?"

The man lifted his head in a kind of nod without changing expression.

"Well, we're ready whenever you are," Michael said.

Gupova narrowed his eyes and pointed to Droster G9. "What is that?"

"It's a robot to help carry equipment and analyze weapons."

"It stays here with helicopter."

"No, it's coming with us."

"No." Gupova looked at his comrades, three of whom came to stand beside him. Talamov, the man with the scar on his lip, grunted and frowned.

"We can't take weapon." Gupova said.

"Droster G9 is not a weapon," Michael said. "It's an unmanned ground system."

Gupova shook his head. "Looks like weapon."

Michael screwed up his face and shook his head impatiently. "We're not here to fight a battle. We're here to inspect weapons."

"We hike through high mountains, travel in car. Robot cannot go."

"Droster G9 can climb mountains better than a man. And we can fold him up so he'll fit in the truck."

Talamov stepped back to the van, cocked his arm toward his mouth, and disappeared around the back. Michael could see he was making a call on his Q watch.

"Robot? We didn't know of robot. Tell how it looks?" The man with the cane was still sitting in the armchair, his eyes fastened on the younger Abdul while he spoke on the phone. "How big? Size of a man?—I see picture you sent." He frowned. "It climbs mountains?" He squared his shoulders and gripped his cane more tightly, then banged it against the leg of the desk beside him. "After you leave in van for mountains, send Zodov back here in truck. We add fireworks to the party to take care of robot. You drive slow up the mountain and wait for the truck to catch up." His forehead furrowed in thought. He stared into Abdul's lean face and deep-set eyes as he clicked off the phone. "You been practicing with that gun?"

"Yes, Father."

"Make those first shots count. No mistakes. Your grandfather didn't bring weapons all the way from Iraq so Americans could wrench them from our grip forty-nine years later."

"I understand, Father. I won't disappoint you."

"The American ducks won't be helpless, but if we act fast, we will catch them off guard."

Abdul nodded and stood up.

"Watch your step."

Rejoining the group, Talamov whispered to Gupova, then spoke aloud to the others. "We can't take robot in truck."

"Why not?"

"Against orders."

Michael shook his head and spun on his heel to look at Bradley Jones and Mo, then turned back. "Then we'll fit him in the van. We can dismantle the claw."

Not understanding what Michael said, Talamov leaned his head toward Gupova. The two conferred together again.

"You Americans—cramped together," Gupova said, motioning with his hands to show how scrunched together they would be if they took the robot.

"We'll deal with it." Michael turned to Donahue and Mo. "Let's get Dros ready for travel."

After they disassembled the claw and sensor tower and placed it in the back of the van, Michael saw Talamov pointing, giving orders to Gupova and the other Tajik with the long goatee whom Talamov called Solbatov.

Solbatov approached Michael and the others with heavy cloths in his hands. Gupova followed behind.

"What's that?" Michael asked.

"One of conditions for taking you to see weapons," said Gupova, "is you not see how we go. We blindfold you."

Michael stepped backwards, thrusting out his hand in protest. "Wait a minute. This is not what we were told. You've got your instructions all wrong, pal. We're not going to be blindfolded."

"Well, p-a-l," Gupova said, exaggerating the pronunciation, "It seems you are one with wrong instructions. We make agreement with President Rajanov."

Closing ranks with Michael, the other three Americans mumbled in protest. Mo was swearing.

Michael raised his Q watch to his mouth and touched the screen. "We'll resolve this one real quick." The phone began to ring.

Jumakhan answered.

"Prime Minister Oqilov, this is Michael Quigley."

"Yes, Mr. Quigley. I surprised to hear from you. Have you not met up with Tajik officials?"

"Yes, we did, but the men who met us here are giving us all kinds of problems. Now they're telling us that before they'll take us to the weapons cache, they've been ordered to blindfold us."

Jumakhan drew in his breath. "Only while you are in van, Mr. Quigley. I should have told you before."

"Yes, if that was part of the agreement, you should have told us. We did not agree to that."

"We had to make concessions. Many do not trust US. After all, your spy already shot and killed three of our Tajik guards and stole some weapons."

"Prime Minister, with all due respect, I'm not sure you know that to be a fact. Anyway, we are not here to steal the weapons or harm anyone. I am a scientist. We are here to see the weapons and verify what is there. That is all."

"I very sorry, Mr. Quigley. But President Rajanov and I had to make agreement with IRP officers in that region. If you want to see weapons, you will have to comply."

Michael slapped off the phone. His anger grew hotter by the minute. He needed to stop talking before he caused an even bigger wedge between the two countries.

This is why some people are scientists, some are soldiers, and some are diplomats. I am not a diplomat.

Bradley Jones was beside him, listening. "No go, huh?"

"You know what makes this whole thing completely ludicrous, don't you?"

Jones studied Michael for a minute, then smiled and nodded. "Yeah. We already know where the weapons are. I thought they were more sophisticated than this. Didn't we get interceptions and mixed signals?"

"Exactly. There's more than one set of brains at play here."

CHAPTER THIRTY-EIGHT

For at least an hour the van bumped along the rock-strewn road. Every curve jostled the blindfolded passengers, throwing them against one another and the walls of the vehicle. Dust blew in their faces through the open windows. The cramped quarters reeked with body odor.

"This is crap," Mo said. "You'd think we were criminals."

Seated beside Michael, Donahue shifted restlessly in his seat, poking Michael in the thigh with his knee as he recrossed his legs. "It's sweltering in here."

"Yeah," Mo agreed. "I'm sweating like a pig, even with my thermo ring."

Beads of perspiration clung to the nape of Michael's neck. He reached up and adjusted the cushiony ring at his throat to allow more ventilation, then rotated his shoulders to relieve his tension.

Wedged between Mo and Michael, Jones plopped his head against the seat back and slithered into a more relaxed position, causing the seat to jiggle. After several minutes Michael heard him breathing heavily.

"Jones, are you sleeping?" Mo asked.

"Trying to."

"How do you do it?"

"Well, when no one's talking to me, I just close my eyes, and the rest comes naturally."

"In a situation like this? You can sleep?"

"No need to stress. We have a job to do. Might as well get ready for a good climb. We'll get our exercise, no doubt."

"Pretty rugged terrain, I guess," Donahue said.

"Yeah. You in shape?" Mo asked.

"The Army keeps you in shape, like it or not. But I've had pretty light duty lately," Donahue said. "You do much climbing, Jones?"

"Had to do a lot of climbing during my years as a Ranger. My work with the lab's taken me on some interesting excursions, too, so I keep in shape. The Ranger mentality gets in your blood."

"Yeah? What about you, Quigley?" Mo asked.

"Don't ask. I've got a desk job. But I've always liked hiking for recreation."

"How far will we hike?" Donahue asked.

"Good question," Mo said. "Is our interpreter in the car? What's his name?"

"Gupova." Michael lurched into Donahue as the car bounced over a large obstruction in the road. Pieces of debris flew in the window. They shook their heads vigorously to clear the bits of rubbish from their faces.

"Crap," Mo said. "Hey, Gupova."

The low hum of voices from the front seat continued. Gupova didn't answer.

"Hey, Gupova," Mo called a little louder.

The chatter ceased.

"You talking to me?" Gupova asked gruffly.

"How far will we be hiking in these mountains?"

Gupova said something to the other guard in the car. Raucous laughter erupted between them.

Gupova's voice came clearer and louder as he turned around toward the Americans. "Not too far. Couple of miles—is most."

The guards snickered.

A few minutes later, the tires bumped over some large rocks, and the van skidded to a rough stop.

"You can remove blindfolds now," Gupova said.

Michael reached up and tore off his blindfold. He looked over at the others. Mo jumped from the van and headed to the back to retrieve the robot just as the truck drew up behind them.

As Jones climbed from the van, he handed the blindfold to the younger, more muscular guard with heavy sideburns who had strolled over from the truck behind them. The guard smiled and said something in a polite manner, which Michael assumed was a thank-you.

Michael looked around at the high, jagged cliffs surrounding them on both sides of the road. A few short scruffy trees dotted the hillside. Clumps of underbrush and scrub peeked out of the gray rocks. The air brooded, hot and still.

The three older men—Talamov, Gupova, and the one they called Zodov—hovered together with the young Solbatov with the long goatee, talking in low voices.

The two younger guards stood apart looking curiously from the Americans to the others huddled together. They spoke and shrugged their shoulders. The more muscular one looked puzzled and shook his head.

Talamov motioned to the young guards and spoke something in Tajik.

Gupova approached the Americans.

"We go now." He snapped his head toward the mountain, threw his knapsack over his shoulder, and trudged toward a path flanked by two large boulders. Michael and Bradley followed.

Talamov took the lead, motioning for Gulov, one of the young guards, to follow. The tall Gupova walked up behind him while the others stood back and waited for the Americans to get in line. The goateed Solbatov, the muscular young guard called Popyev, Droster G9, and Zodov brought up the rear.

Pushing beyond the boulders, Michael saw a rocky path angling to the right, then plunging into a deep ravine. On the other side, it continued up a steep hillside.

A blazing sun beat against his face. He squinted in the intense brightness and stopped to put on sunglasses, then plodded on, grinding the loose gravel beneath his feet.

Close at his back, he heard Bradley's heavy steps, and Michael sensed with Bradley's stamina and long strides, it was an effort for him to stay behind. Michael moved to one side and nodded for Bradley to go ahead.

"Go on, Jones," he said. "I can tell you're faster than I am. You take the lead after the Tajiks."

Bradley looked at Michael questioningly, then hiked past and crunched along the rock-laden path. Michael fell in behind.

As the men descended into the ravine, Michael picked his way through dense clusters of increasingly large rocks, looking for footholds. Donahue stumbled at his back.

"Can we stop a minute?" Donahue asked. "I need a rest."

"We keep moving," Gupova said gruffly.

Popyev said something to Gupova, prompting a terse reply from Talamov. When Popyev spoke again, Talamov answered angrily, his sneer causing the scar beside his lip to protrude in a thin, menacing line. Michael sensed the young guard had been thoroughly put down.

The path narrowed. The underbrush thickened. Branches and thistles snagged Michael's pants, tearing at the fabric and scratching his legs.

Michael looked back at Donahue, who struggled to keep up. "Are you all right?"

"I'm hot. Really weak." Donahue pressed his hand against his forehead. "My head feels light. The sun's getting to me, I think."

Michael halted, calling out to those in front. "We need to stop for a minute and rest."

"No, we keep going," Gupova said.

"No, we stop," Michael repeated testily.

Up ahead, Bradley turned around. "Getting tired?"

"Some of us need a breather."

Michael darted his eyes at Talamov and Gupova. The two men exchanged a few words. Gupova scowled.

"Ten minutes we stop. Then we go."

Donahue wiped his arm against his forehead. His face was flushed.

"Isn't your thermo ring working?" Michael asked.

"I dunno. Maybe not. Just need to rest a minute." He dropped onto an outcrop of rock and took a long drink from the straw that extended from his hydrating backpack. He removed the flask from his pack and poured water over his face. The water splashed down his shirt and quickly soaked into the ground at his feet.

Popyev stood apart watching. Of all the guards, he seemed the only one sympathetic to Donahue's plight.

Michael strode up to the guard and extended his right hand, then pointed at himself with the other. "Name's Quigley."

The guard smiled. "Me Popyev." He gestured toward the sun. "*Garn*." Hot.

As they resumed climbing the hill on the other side, the loose gravel slipped beneath their feet, causing Michael to slide. Ahead of him, the surefooted Bradley loped up the hillside like a mountain goat, and behind him, Mo clumped along, planting each step firmly against the hard earth. At the back, Michael heard Donahue skidding on the rock-strewn path, and the droning hum of Droster G9 moving steadily forward.

Finally they reached an open spot and proceeded along a wide ridge on the face of the mountain. From across the valley, a gust of warm air blew in Michael's face. Although the wind was hot, it fanned the scorching wetness that clung to his skin, offering welcome relief. Michael looked back at Donahue. "Feels a little better now."

A sudden explosion rocked the hillside and reverberated off the canyon walls. Michael saw Droster G9, at the end of the line, burst into pieces. A loud blast from a rifle rang out.

Michael heard a scream of pain.

Janssen took another sip of wine. The puzzle picture was beginning to take shape.

But where's the muzzle of the gun?

Janssen had assembled the frame and was working inward. He locked another piece into the puzzle and leaned back, the foam seat floating with his sudden movement. He stretched out his legs and stroked his mustache, staring out the window into the darkness.

He could put this puzzle together, but what about the bigger puzzle he needed to solve? Tajikistan. What about that?

He clicked *save* on his TIR, then closed it and glanced at members of the media in the back of the plane. Bethany Chambers was asleep with a black coat pulled over her.

Janssen reached for a pad of small index cards and began scribbling a few words on each.

"4 of Clubs in the Iraqi Deck of Cards ... Tahad Abdul Azzadafa." This he noted as #1.

"The weapons cache." #2.

He held them up side by side. The two suggested the weapons cache could originally be from Iraq—one of the caches that had been the subject of so many searches and controversy in the early part of the century. If so, Azzadafa would undoubtedly assume ownership of it. And if he hated Americans as much as he did when he was a youth, his hatred could have fueled the violence that broke out in recent days along with the blame placed on the US.

Then there was the recent economic boom in Tajikistan, brought on in part by Iranian investments in the textile industry. On a third note he wrote "growth in economy," "Iran," and "Textiles."

Jumakhan's reluctance to mention the other party wanting to purchase the weapons, but admitting Tajikistan's more prosperous economy, was a factor in their decision. "Jumakhan's reluctance." #4.

And why had Jumakhan given him Azzadafa's name, but cautioned Janssen not to mention it in response? This he noted as #5.

Michael's discovery of sophisticated interception and scrambling of his signals. #6.

Then the most recent developments—the killing of guards at the weapons cache. # 7.

The accusation by one guard that Americans had raided the cache, and the apprehension of the American spy, Sali, who'd been charged with the murders. #8.

Finally, the maps and delivery systems found in Uzbekistan—delivery systems perfectly suited to enhance the mass destruction capabilities of the chemical and biological weapons allegedly found in the Tajikistan weapons cache. #9.

How do these things connect?

He shuffled the cards on the tray before him. If Azzadaffa was involved, who else was involved with him? How many tentacles did this monster have? Many questions. Few answers. A lot of pieces that weren't fitting together.

He turned on his TIR again and clicked his DaVinci Ball to pull Shannon's report up on the screen of his information receiver. What had she found out about textile companies in Iran? She had listed three major companies and two minor ones. He studied the names of the corporation officers and executives, then clicked on each to view their histories.

One was a devoted father of three sons and two daughters, involved in dozens of activities with his children.

Another traveled frequently to the US to indulge his weakness for horse racing. The third CEO appeared to be building a virtual business empire, owning a number of corporations.

Janssen was tired and having a hard time focusing. He scrolled down the list of the CEO's business dealings, only half paying attention to the screen. The word Uzbekistan flashed on the monitor and he stopped to read further. Interest in a gold mine in Zarafshan.

Hmm. Near Tashkent. Interesting connection.

Janssen was too tired to read more. He quickly scrolled through the rest, but in the middle of the list, something flashed on the screen that again grabbed his attention. He reverse-clicked and went back to it.

There. A member of the Expediency Council in the Iranian government. Hmm. That might be interesting. Soheil Morashi. I'll have to make a note of that.

He highlighted the bio and saved it in a special folder.

Janssen leaned back against his seat and closed his

eyes, then opened them again. One more thing. The American spy, Sali. What did he know? He reached for another card and scribbled # 10—Sali.

Janssen's eyelids felt like lead. Deciding to check the other two companies later, he shut down the TIR. He'd let the pieces of this puzzle marinate in his mind awhile. He needed to sleep so he'd be fresh when he arrived in Tajikistan.

CHAPTER THIRTY-NINE

Another clap of gunfire split the air. Michael felt his insides tighten. His lips trembled.

The guard at the front of the expedition clutched his chest, stumbled over the rocks, and fell to his knees.

"Gulov is shot," Gupova cried from the front of the line. "Americans."

A third shot rang out. Michael flattened himself on the gravel. The side of his chin stung as he scraped against the rocks.

The gun blasted again. Michael saw Popyev jump behind a six-foot boulder, but not quickly enough. Popyev flinched and grabbed his arm.

Donahue, still dazed by the sun, stood alone on the crest of the hill in his red tee offering an easy target. He gaped in bewilderment toward the sound of the gunfire.

Desperation and helplessness overtook Michael as he watched.

"Donahue! Get down. *Get down!*"

His warning came too late. Donahue moaned and grasped his stomach, then swayed and toppled to the unyielding earth.

Terror seized Michael. He froze. From his position he couldn't see Donahue, couldn't see if he was alive and moving. Then, only inches from where Donahue lay,

Popyev peeked out from behind the rock. He crawled to the injured older man, loosened his shirt, and felt his pulse. With his good arm, Popyev began dragging him back behind the rock.

Michael was suddenly ashamed of his own inaction. He felt powerless, impotent.

If only I had a gun.

Lifting his head, he saw his friends had scattered and gotten out of sight. To his left, Zodov appeared to be heading from the back of the line toward Popyev's place of concealment. Solbatov, shouting, removed a gun from his belt and headed toward the cliffs behind them. At the front of the line Talamov stood in the open, eying the scene. Gupova jerked Gulov's body over and knelt to feel his pulse, then rose and charged into the brush.

Michael dragged himself behind some scrub. *Who* was shooting at them? Targeting both Americans and Tajiks alike? They needed help. He needed to let someone know what was happening.

Michael raised his Q watch to his mouth. "Robertson." He heard the phone ring, then a voice mail greeting.

He clicked it off as the gunfire continued. He was seized with desperation and fear. He tried to think of who he could call or message—someone who knew their situation, someone who could summon help. Whose number did he have?

"Jenna," he said into his phone.

Jenna's heart constricted. She could hear shots in the background and men yelling in the Tajik language. Panic gripped her as she clicked off the phone.

She called Randall Robertson. The ringing went to voice mail.

"This is an emergency." Her voice quivered. "I just got a call from Michael Quigley. They've been ambushed in the mountains. Call me back. Please." She hung up, messaged him, then called Neely. When she heard his warm, real-life voice, a lump caught in her throat. She could hardly talk.

When she repeated what Michael told her and what she heard herself, Neely promised to find Robertson, but suggested she let Jumakhan know.

A shiver ran through her body. She was now part of the loop. The crisis had escalated, and she was expected to help solve it. This was why she was here—to be the go-between, to talk to her uncle. And Michael was in serious danger.

She found Sheela in the kitchen making tea.

Sheela looked up when Jenna entered. "Would you like some tea, Jenna?"

"Not right now, Sheela." Jenna felt the agitation vibrating in her voice. "I was looking for Jumakhan. Is he here?"

"Yes, he is in study." She poured the hot water from the kettle into a teapot and replaced the lid.

"Could I talk to him?"

"Certainly." She set the teapot on the counter and turned around. "Is everything okay?"

"No," Jenna said honestly. "I need to talk to him right away."

Sheela pivoted toward the door and motioned for Jenna to follow. "I take you to him. This way."

Together, they scurried down a long hall on the east side of the house. "This is study."

The door to Jumakhan's office was cracked, and Jenna heard him talking on the phone. Her uncle's voice was loud and decisive. "Tahad Abdul Azzadafa is the one who has been talking to him. He's the one with the connection. Ask him."

Despite her feeling of panic, at the mention of the name Azzadafa, Jenna's ears perked up. *The name. The one Janssen wrote on the slip of paper.* Jenna darted a look at Sheela. She was listening to the conversation also.

"I don't like the tension either," Jumakhan continued. "But we need to give it a little more time. At least give my nephew a chance ... I know. The US has investors, too. Janssen mentioned something in one of our conversations about a refrigerator manufacturer ...."

Jenna's stress level rose with each moment she delayed. She needed to tell Uncle Jocko what was happening, but she suspected what she was hearing was valuable. She felt torn. She looked at Sheela quizzically. "Who is Tahad Abdul Azzadafa?"

Sheela's face reddened. "Very important man—member of Majlisi Oli—like your House of Representatives. He is representative elected by people—from northern province." She screwed up her face in an unpleasant manner. "I do not like him—don't trust."

"No? Why?"

Sheela shook her head. "Not honest. Mean." She frowned and squinted.

"Does Uncle Jumakhan trust him?"

"Sadly—I believe he does."

Jenna glanced through the crack in the door. He was still talking. "Have you told Jumakhan how you feel?" she asked.

"A little. Not a lot." Sheela said.

"Why not?"

"I am woman."

Jenna blanched in surprise. "Jumakhan thinks like that too?"

"It is our culture," Sheela said in a hushed voice. "Jumakhan good man. He listens to my opinion about family, house, many things. But when it comes to government and politics, I am only woman." She smiled ironically.

Jumakhan seemed to be finishing up. "That's where they are now. We'll talk again when they return from the expedition."

Jenna grimaced, then glanced at Sheela anxiously.

Taking Jenna's cue, Sheela pushed open the door a little more and stuck her head around the opening. "Jenna needs to talk with you."

"Bring her in." He rose from his chair and met them at the door, a smile spreading across his face. "Ahhh. How is morning going for you, Jenna? Have you unpacked yet?"

Jenna's heart thumped wildly. "Not good, Uncle. I just got a call from Michael …. "

Michael's mind raced as he surveyed the situation.

Along the ridge to his left, Mo had just sidestepped an attack from the goateed Solbatov, then grabbed the gun from him and tripped him, sending him flying.

Not far from them, Zodov stood, shoulders hunched, scanning the area where Donahue had been shot. A trail of blood led through a crevice between the boulders where the two men had retreated. Chin jutting forward, Zodov raked his fingers through his thick hair and sprinted over the rocks toward them.

Holding his bleeding arm, Popyev peered around the edge and called to Zodov. Michael could tell from his tone he was pleading for help with the dying man.

Instead, the older Zodov sprung his knife and lunged toward Popyev. The younger guard ducked and rolled away, then grabbed Zodov's wrist with his good hand and yelled at him. The older man cursed. Michael watched, horrified.

Farther down the path, Talamov yelled a command to Zodov, who jerked his hand from Popyev's grasp, quickly sheathed his knife, and reached for a gun. Popyev's face paled. He recoiled with a look of fear. Zodov aimed his weapon at the young guard.

A wave of adrenaline surged through Michael's body. Popyev had proved to be a friend, and he was injured. Michael grabbed a rock and hurled it. The missile struck Zodov in the back. The man turned.

Like a *deus ex machina*, Bradley Jones appeared out of nowhere and sailed into Zodov from behind, sending the gun flying from his hand.

The two men scuffled in the dirt. A cloud of dust scattered through the heat of the summer air as Zodov flailed and shouted. Jones sent a fist into Zodov's belly and another into the soft underside of his chin. Zodov lashed back, trying to fend him off. In a sudden motion, Jones seized a large rock and crushed it into Zodov's skull. The older Tajik wavered and crumbled, then lay motionless.

Shots whistled over Jones's head. Another bullet skimmed low past Michael's prone body. Talamov headed toward them. Casting about for a safer place to hide, Michael spied a crevice in the rock behind him. He made a dash for it. "Jones! Over here."

Bradley swept the gun from the ground and turned just as Talamov fired at him. The bullet missed. Bradley scrambled toward Michael and jumped in beside him.

Near a patch of scrub, Mo and Solbatov still hammered each other with their fists. Mo rammed him with his knee, then chopped the back of his neck. Solbatov stumbled and fell.

Talamov ran at Mo with his gun cocked, but the burly former Marine dove for the older man's knees and took him down. The two men clawed at one another as they rose to their feet. The Tajik raised his gun again. Mo ducked beneath him, grabbed his forearm, and flipped him over his shoulder. Talamov lay splayed in the dirt, unconscious.

Solbatov charged Mo again, and the two men tumbled to the ground.

Bradley pointed to a clump of trees on a ridge parallel to the trail they'd been following.

"The shots are coming from there. I'm going to circle around behind them." He touched Michael's arm. "Make yourself conspicuous on the other side of this opening here, and while they're aiming at you, I'll run out the other side. Shout at Mo or something."

"Thanks," Michael said sarcastically. "How conspicuous do I have to be?"

"Enough to be seen. Not enough to get shot."

"This whole thing has been a setup from the start. You know that, right?"

"Sure do. Question is, who are the good guys, and who's bad?"

"I guess we know when one of them tries to kill us."

Bradley tensed into a sprinting position, then threw out his hand. "Okay, run!"

Bending in the middle, Michael lurched to the edge of the crevice, raised his head, and yelled.

His bellowing accomplished its purpose. Two bullets screamed over his head just as he pulled it back. He scanned the other end of the fissure. Bradley was gone. Leaves rustled in a distant tree.

He looked again at Donahue and Popyev behind the boulder. The muscular young guard slapped Donahue's cheek to revive him, then placed his ear against his chest. Painfully removing the vest from his bloodstained uniform, Popyev folded it to form a pillow and placed it beneath Donahue's head.

Gupova dashed from Michael's right, brandishing a gun. He looked toward Michael, then headed toward the rock where Popyev tended to Donahue.

Michael shouted. The young Popyev glanced up just as Gupova emerged through the opening in the rock. Popyev slithered further back, abandoning Donahue. Gupova aimed at the young guard, and Popyev rolled as a shot rang out. Michael heard the pinging of the bullet striking stone.

Then, in a moment seared forever into Michael's brain, the dying Donahue, struggling to a semi-sitting position at Gupova's feet, pulled a gun from his jacket and aimed at Gupova's chest. He pulled the trigger.

Gupova froze, eyes staring straight ahead, mouth open, then collapsed.

With dirt clinging to his beard and sideburns, Popyev raised his head. Holding his bleeding arm close to his body, he pulled himself along the ground to Donahue just as the soldier fell back again. Popyev felt for a pulse at Donahue's throat, then moaned and cradled his head in his hands.

Momentarily forgetting his own danger, Michael stared in awe until a bullet hissed over his head and brought him back to his danger. He peeked over the edge of his hiding place to see a recovered Talamov rushing at him, pointing a forty-five in his direction. Michael pulled himself back into the crevice, then half-scooted, half-crawled along on his belly to the far end.

At the opening of the crevice where Michael had been, Talamov leaned over the top, pointing his gun. Seeing Michael at the opposite end, he cursed and shot wildly into the crevice. Michael leapt from the hole and sprinted to an embankment of trees as Talamov fired again.

Shouting at Talamov to stop, Popyev picked up Donahue's gun. Talamov whirled around toward the gentle guard and opened fire. Bullets ricocheted off the boulder.

Popyev aimed and shot, yelling angrily. The bullet flew wide, and Talamov ran at him.

From among the trees, Michael circled, then dashed through the open space and fell on Talamov from behind. He felt a crush of pain along his chest as they plunged to the ground. The gun fell and skipped along the earth. They fought, grabbing and punching one another.

Talamov wrenched Michael's arm backward. A sharp pang ran along Michael's upper arm as he leaned onto his side and kicked Talamov in the ribs.

Popyev leaned against the rock, blood dripping from his shoulder onto his gun as he watched them fight.

Once more Bradley Jones appeared, now shirtless. He wrestled Talamov away from Michael and held him down, holding him by the hair and hammering his head into the ground until Talamov hung limp.

"Give me your shirt," Bradley said to Michael, "and help me keep this guy down."

Bradley tore Michael's shirt into strips, then tied them around Talamov's wrists. "This will do till we get back to the van."

"How many men did you find across the way?"

"Only one. The main enemy was in our midst."

Mo and Solbatov were still tumbling over the rocks, pummeling each other with stones, their clothes now torn and filthy. Solbatov reached for a gun lying a few feet away. Mo thrust his fist deep into the young Tajik's gut. Solbatov writhed back in pain.

With Michael close behind, Bradley sprinted toward Solbatov, forcing him to the ground.

While Solbatov thrashed about unsuccessfully beneath the force of Bradley's grip, Michael and Mo shredded Mo's shirt and tied Solbatov's wrists and ankles.

A vibration in the air caused them to pause. A rhythmic thumping sound thundered overhead, growing louder by the second. Above the tree tops, they saw two helicopters, rotors spinning, hovering above the hills. Michael's spirits brightened. The one in front had a red, white and blue insignia and said *USAF*.

Zodov, Gupova, Gulov, and Donahue were dead.

When the entourage of helicopters and land vehicles pulled into Khujand an hour and a half later, they were met by two more helicopters from Dushanbe. One of them carried Jumakhan and Rajanov, who had come for first-hand accounts. Michael watched Neely and Robertson disembark from the second, then gaped in surprise when Jenna poked her face into the opening of the hatch. He warmed at the sight of her.

She took Robertson's hand as she jumped to the ground, then turned with a face streaked with worry to scan the group who came to meet the chopper. Her eyes met Michael's. Her face relaxed.

Michael threaded his way from the back of the throng to greet her. "Jenna."

Her voice was soft when she spoke, her eyes wide with concern. "You're all right?"

"Just a few scratches. I'm surprised to see you here."

Jenna bristled, then shrugged and tossed her head. "Just following through on what I was sent here to do." Her face softened again, her forehead knit in a frown. "It looks like you've had an absolutely awful experience. Is everyone else all right?"

Michael shook his head and stared at the ground. "Donahue's dead."

"Oh, no!" Jenna's hand went to her mouth, and the color drained from her face.

Watching her reaction, a wave of emotion swept through Michael as he once again pictured the mortally wounded Donahue raising up on one elbow and drawing the pistol. His voice cracked. "He was one brave chief."

Robertson clapped him on the shoulder. "Sorry you've had such a grim day, Quigley."

Michael twisted his mouth in acknowledgement. "Yeah. Thanks."

"Ambassador Neely and I want to hear about this from you and Jones." Robertson nodded to the former Ranger who had slipped up to join them. "Then the ambassador is going to talk to Sali, our man who's been arrested. I understand some of the locals who were involved in the attack in the mountains have already been locked up in jail."

He turned to Jenna. "The President and Prime Minister are going to the cell to speak with them in a few minutes. It might be good for one of us to listen in. I don't speak Tajik, of course, so my presence wouldn't mean much, but I was wondering if you would feel comfortable going. I could accompany you if you'd like ... " He glanced over at Michael. "Unless—"

"I'd be glad to go with her"—Michael turned to Jenna—"that is, if you wouldn't mind."

Jenna glanced back and forth at the two men, then addressed Robertson.

"It would probably be more productive for you to go with Ambassador Neely." She quirked an eyebrow at Michael. "I'll be fine."

"Sounds good." Robertson eyed Quigley. "But tell us what happened today."

Quigley and Jones filled him in on the details. Then the three joined Jumakhan to listen to Popyev, who was giving an emotional rendition of the story.

Popyev spoke angrily and shook his finger in the direction of the town jail where Talamov, Solbatov, and the man who attacked them from across the ravine were being kept. He teared up when he looked at the body of Donahue and his friend Gulov, and spoke proudly and authoritatively when he directed his gaze at Bradley Jones.

Jumakhan grimaced and ran his hand over the top of his head. "Quigley, I don't know what to say. Apparently, we've all been set up. There are not words enough in either of our languages to apologize to you appropriately. This is terrible day for Tajikistan."

"Yes, Prime Minister. I can agree with you there. This *was* a terrible day."

CHAPTER FORTY

"Abdul Radazon Azzadafa, what are you doing here?"

President Rajanov peered through the steel bars of the holding cell where three prisoners sat on the stone floor, leaning against the back brick wall. "How are you involved in this?"

Beside Rajanov stood Jumakhan Oqilov. Two police officers hovered behind them. Another was posted inside the cell, hand on the gun in his holster. Jenna and Michael watched from the rear near the entrance to the small building. Jones, Mo Jackson, and Popyev stood beside them.

"I did nothing. It was the Americans."

"Then why are you here, Abdul?"

Abdul motioned to the Americans behind Rajanov and Jumakhan. "They attack."

"Sir," Popyev said, stepping forward, his arm wrapped in bandages, "the Americans did not attack. Those three plus Gupova and Zodov attacked. Gupova and Zodov tried to kill me. Abdul ambushed us on our way to see the weapons. The Americans saved my life."

Rajanov turned at Popyev's words, his eyes carefully studying the young guard's demeanor. "You have an honest face, Popyev. I believe you. Why would you lie?"

Jumakhan cleared his throat. "As I told you before, President Rajanov, Popyev went into great detail describing the incident to me earlier. His story has been consistent and verified by the other witnesses. According to him, Donahue—the American who died—Bradley Jones, and Michael Quigley saved his life. They acted only in self-defense."

Rajanov turned back to the three men in the cell.

"Abdul, how could you betray your father like this?" Rajanov continued. "Do you know how this will make him look in the eyes of his peers? Your father is an important man. His reputation will be tarnished."

Without meeting Rajanov's eyes, Abdul raised his head defiantly, looking past him to the Americans. He said nothing.

"Abdul, speak to me. Why did you do this?"

Abdul crossed his arms over his chest, looked at his cellmates, and grunted.

The officer inside the cell with the prisoners shoved Abdul with the flat of his left hand while brandishing his gun with the right. "Who do you work for, Azzadafa? Speak!"

"Hold off a minute, Mehrak," said Jumakhan. "I have called his father. He should be here any minute. Perhaps he can get his son to talk."

At the mention of his father, Abdul gaped at Jumakhan, then at Rajanov. Mehrak stepped back.

"Talamov, Solbatov. What do you have to say for yourselves?"

"I have nothing to say," Talamov said.

Solbatov glanced at Abdul. "Americans started it."

"We're not getting anywhere here," Jumakhan said to Rajanov.

The roar of a car pulling up outside drew everyone's attention. An engine switched off. Moments later, a distinguished-looking man, leaning on a cane, walked uneasily through the doors. Abdul rose to his feet, his eyes brightening.

Jumakhan nodded to the man as he entered.

"Azzadafa, I'm sorry to bring you bad news. Perhaps you can bring your son to his senses."

"Yes, perhaps." Azzadafa elbowed his way through the throng and approached the jail cell. His face was stern, unflinching. "Let me inside."

One of the guards outside the cell unlocked and pulled open the door to the small enclosure. Azzadafa poked his cane through the entrance, then pulled his body in after it. Uneasily, but with determination, Azzadafa marched up to his son, stopped inches from his face and stared at him. He switched his cane to his left hand, and with his right brutally slapped his son's cheek.

"You disgrace our family name."

Abdul winced and grabbed the side of his face.

"I am ashamed," Azzadafa growled. "*Ashamed.*"

"Please, Father."

"Have you told them who is behind this? Why you did such a thing? Why you disgrace your family in such a way?"

"I have said nothing, Father."

"Tell them who put you up to this," Azzadafa shouted furiously.

Abdul seemed dazed by his father's actions and stared at him in dumb silence.

"Tell them, Abdul," Azzadafa yelled again. "Who put you up to this?"

Suddenly, as if snapped into alertness, Abdul blurted, "The American spy."

"The American spy?" Azzadafa questioned with a gentler demeanor.

"Yes, the American spy," he repeated. "He—promised me money."

"Why would he want to kill the Americans?" Jumakhan asked.

Abdul shrugged. "Don't know. He promised me money. I agreed."

Tahad Abdul Azzadafa let his head droop forward, then shook it back and forth as he unsteadily inched his cane around to turn back toward the exit.

"Americans. I knew it. Even my own son contaminated by filthy American money."

"How was your visit with Sali?" Jenna twisted in her seat beside the helicopter pilot as she addressed Ambassador Neely and Robertson, seated behind her.

"What did you say?" Robertson asked her.

She readjusted her headset so they could hear her more clearly. "I said, how was your visit with Sali?"

Ambassador Neely glanced at Robertson, then cleared his throat.

"Good. We're convinced he's innocent of any wrongdoing. He told us he thinks some of the men who attacked our guys today were the same ones who shot the guards at the weapons cache. It was five men then, and five today."

"I wouldn't be surprised. They seemed a rough group. But why does he think that?" Jenna braced herself as the chopper banked into a circle. It quickly leveled off.

"The night of the attack, after he heard the gunfire, Sali went into the streets to see what was happening. He saw two of them, Solbatov and Abdul, carrying suspicious-looking boxes into the house of Zayd Azminov, one of the IRP leaders. The next day, when Sali thought no one was around, he went snooping for the weapons. That's when he got caught."

"Did he find anything at the house?"

"He said he didn't have time."

"But you think we can trust him? You think he's telling the truth?"

Robertson nodded. "Secretary Tomlin checked his background carefully. He has superior ratings and has done good work for us in the past. The accusations against him are ludicrous." The chopper lurched, and Robertson steadied himself against the front seat. "Nothing pans out except his being found at the house. And he told us the reason he was there."

Jenna twisted farther to see Robertson more clearly. "That man, Abdul, accused Sali of paying them to attack. You think there's any truth to that?"

"None," Robertson said. "They're using Sali as a scapegoat."

"Whom do you think Rajanov and Jumakhan will believe?"

Neely frowned. "That's the unanswered question. We think they do believe Popyev—the guard who was with our munitions team. The one they apparently tried to kill."

"Yes," Robertson interjected. "He may be one of the keys to Rajanov keeping an open mind. And you can help with Jumakhan too."

Jenna blanched. "I don't know. I feel so inadequate."

Ambassador Neely patted her shoulder. "You just have to do the best you can. That's all anyone can ask of you."

When embassy aides dropped her off at the house, Jenna trudged up the walkway to the front entrance, the heaviness of her responsibility weighing upon her. Too much was happening now. What could she possibly say to Jumakhan that would help?

Especially since I'm a woman.

The thought soured in her mind as soon as it surfaced.

She entered and looked toward the courtyard where they'd gathered that morning. How quickly the situation had deteriorated.

Poor Donahue.

She remembered his face, and the tiredness in his voice as she listened to him talking at breakfast. She rubbed her hand over her creased forehead. Tears clouded her vision.

How could they have foreseen what happened today? She paced across the living area to the small sitting room, then back to the dining table. In retrospect, it had clearly been a trap. But now that the man who attacked Michael and the others was blaming Sali, she didn't know who Uncle Jocko and Rajanov would believe. She was here to help her uncle see the truth, but she didn't actually know Sali herself. What would Janssen tell her to do?

Janssen. She raised her wrist and tapped a number on her Q watch. Perhaps she could get through to him on the plane. The ringing went to voice mail. She sent a brief message and looked at her watch. Four-thirty. He was due to arrive in three hours.

Jenna padded to the French doors leading to the courtyard, pushed them open, and stepped outside. She dropped listlessly onto a bench and stared at the fountain bubbling up and spilling onto the blue iris at its border.

I'm just not up to this.

Sheela appeared at the French doors and tiptoed into the courtyard carrying a tray.

"Would you like some tea?" Although slender in build, she handled the large tray with ease and grace.

"Yes, I think I would. Thank you."

Sheela set the ceramic teapot on a small table near the bench and poured the tea into porcelain cups. "Do you want sugar and cream?"

"Just sugar, thank you."

Sheela stirred a teaspoon of sugar into the tea and handed it to Jenna. She picked up the second teacup, held it in her hand a moment, then perched delicately at the other end of the stone bench. With the steam rising into her face, she gazed at Jenna over the rim of her cup. Deep in the soft brown eyes, Jenna discerned unspoken words, words that longed to feel the substance of sound.

"There is trouble?" Sheela said at last.

"Yes. I guess you heard about it, right?"

"A little. It is very sad."

"Yes, very." Jenna sipped the tea and set the cup back on its saucer. "What do you think about it all, Sheela?"

Sheela's eyelids fluttered nervously. She bit her lip and stared into her teacup, then raised her eyes to meet Jenna's. "I think Tahad Azzadafa is responsible."

Jenna looked at her quizzically. "You do? Tahad, the father? Why?"

"I hear things. People talk."

"What have you heard?"

Sheela frowned. "Things I cannot say." She looked at Jenna pleadingly. "Try to understand. I want to help, but I must be careful not to hurt others."

"I see."

Sheela picked up the teapot, leaned toward Jenna, and began to pour more tea into her cup.

Jenna put out her hand. "No, thank you. I've had enough."

Sheela filled her own cup. "My daughter will be here soon," she said, a sudden lilt in her voice. "You met her when she was young and at airport, but I would like you to know her better."

"I'd like that. What is her name?"

"Anna."

"Anna? Like my mother. I'd forgotten that."

"Yes, she was named after her."

Jenna smiled. "I'm sure Mother was pleased with that."

"Yes, she was. Your mother was very special to me."

"I guess I didn't realize you knew her that well."

"I knew her very well." Sheela gave her a sad smile. "One summer after you and Janssen were grown, she came to visit. I was very sad. I had had two little boys, but then afterward, I kept having—what you call it—miscarriages. My babies died before they were born. Every time it was little girl who died. I wanted little girl very bad. You know, our men want sons, but for women, daughters are special."

Jenna nodded. She had sons, and she loved them dearly, but she missed not having a daughter. Perhaps that was why she felt so close to Evie.

"Your mother saw I was sad. We talked."

"Mother was a very sensitive person."

"And very wise. Your mother Anna's words—and her faith—brought new hope to me. And to others also."

"Oh? How was that? Did she talk to other women here?"

Sheela fingered her cup. When she answered, she spoke in a whisper. "No, she did not talk to them. I passed her words along to others. And it helped them."

"Hmm." Jenna nodded and smiled. "Her words must have been very special. So you talked to your friends about my mother?"

"Well, one friend, at least."

"That's interesting. Is it a friend here in Dushanbe?"

Sheela lowered her eyes, replaced her cup on the tray and ran her fingers along the handle of the teapot. She took a deep breath and straightened her shoulders. "No, she not live in Dushanbe." Her words were terse.

Jenna sensed displeasure in Sheela's changed attitude, as though she'd said something inappropriate. Jenna didn't know how to respond next. She didn't want to be nosy—just sociable.

"Yes, your mother was big help to me after I lost my little girls," Sheela said, turning the conversation back to where they were before it became uncomfortable. "She prayed with me, and year later, Anna Sunny Oqilov was born."

"Sunny?"

"Yes."

"Hmm. That's interesting. Is that a Tajik name?"

"No, Sunny is English word."

"Oh. You mean, sunny, like our sunshine. And it's Anna's middle name?"

"Yes, Sunny was friend of your mother." Sheela brightened again, apparently glad to have changed the subject.

Jenna's mind flipped back to a few days before when she'd overheard the conversation between her mother and a woman named Sunny through the speakers at the lab. *Strange.* "Hmm. Yes. I think I may know who you mean."

Sheela reached for her teacup and took a sip. "Sunny helped your mother—like your mother helped me—when she was very sad, before Janssen was born. Your mother smiled *big* when I told her Anna's middle name."

"Yes." Jenna was pleased. How special for her mother to have had that affirmation. She nodded. "I think I know the story."

"It was when you were very young. Only two or three, I think."

Jenna sighed, remembering the drama she'd witnessed days earlier. How much had Mom told her? Did Sheela know her mom almost aborted Janssen, the man they all loved and counted on to help them now? What had Mom told her that was so helpful?

Jenna studied the glow on Sheela's face. *She prayed with me ... oh, of course.* "Are you Christian, then?"

Sheela beamed in response. "Yes. Come." She set her teacup on the table beside her, then took Jenna by the hand and led her back through the French doors and into a room off the living area. She pointed to an end table in the corner beside a wooden rocking chair. A Bible sat on the lower shelf.

Jenna picked it up and leafed through it. The pages were worn with much reading. "And what of your friend? Is she Christian too?"

Sheela nodded uncomfortably. "Yes."

Sensing she'd ventured onto thin ice again, Jenna hesitated. "Being a Christian in Tajikistan must be hard sometimes."

"What?"

"I mean, so many here are Muslim. Is it sometimes hard to be a Christian?"

Sheela's eyes engaged Jenna's. "Tajikistan allows freedom of religion. It is not hard for me. Jumakhan is very understanding. But for some people it is very hard."

"I see."

When Jumakhan returned at dinnertime, his usual easygoing demeanor was gone. His troubled countenance betrayed his inner agitation.

Anna Sunny Oquilov was a lovely, charming woman. Her bright eyes and enchanting smile reminded Jenna of a slightly darker version of Evie. Under normal circumstances, Jenna would have loved getting to know her cousin. But her uncle's conspicuous silence over dinner constantly drew her attention.

Finally, when Sheela and Anna rose to clear the table, Jenna was able to approach him.

"You are worried by today's events, aren't you, Uncle?"

"Yes, Jenna. Very much so."

"What do you think brought on the violence?"

"I wish I knew answer, Jenna. I hesitate to speak my thoughts. I am afraid I do not trust young Abdul Radazon Azzadafa. I believe he lied to us, and to his father."

"That was the young man at the jail? The son of the representative?"

"Yes. He has disgraced his family and his country." Jumakhan took his napkin from his lap and laid it on the table. "But most of all, it made me realize we must make decision about weapons. We cannot wait. Our country is being torn apart by violence because weapons remain here. Rajanov presses me to join him in making decision."

Jenna studied his expression. "You mean deciding whom to sell the weapons to?"

"Yes."

"But you'll wait till after Janssen arrives tonight, won't you?"

Jumakhan sighed and looked at the clock on the wall. "That is what I have been holding out for. I want to hear what he says. But Rajanov might not be swayed. His mind grows firm. And we cannot wait much longer."

Janssen awoke to the captain's voice announcing their descent into Dushanbe and requesting passengers to turn off all electronic equipment.

As Janssen began to comply, he noticed a message from Jenna. After reading it, he pressed the off button on his Q watch.

Too late now, I'm afraid.

CHAPTER FORTY-ONE

The blowing of the longhorns at the Dushanbe airport signaled a much-anticipated celebration for Jenna LaMarche. Seeing her brother disembark healthy and smiling from the airplane brought a joy to her heart that had seemed impossible only a few days earlier, when he lay on the couch in his office, his life ebbing away.

Breaking free from the traditional formal decorum customary for her uncle and his family, Jenna hastened over the tarmac toward the arriving passengers, tears and laughter joining together as she clasped her brother around the neck and smiled into his eyes. Janssen hugged her tenderly and ran his fingers through the short locks of hair at her neck.

Having already seen cameras and media poised for pictures and taping, Jenna quickly composed herself. She leaned on Janssen's arm.

"I've never been so happy to see anyone in my life. I can hardly believe what my eyes are telling me. You look wonderful."

He squeezed her hand affectionately. "And I feel wonderful. Even slept on the plane. Believe me, life never felt like such a gift before."

Two reporters slipped through a loose barricade provided by members of the Tajik police and began shouting questions to Janssen in the Tajik language. As one policeman pushed the intruders back, another officer interjected himself into the milieu and guided Janssen and Jenna toward a protected area off the field where Jumakhan and Sheela waited.

Reluctantly Jenna released Janssen to the welcoming salutations of his Tajik family.

Although Jocko had been cordial during the ride home, Janssen sensed a distance, an awkwardness. All the time they were talking about family, his uncle's mind seemed somewhere else. After joining the others, Jenna seemed to become uneasy also. He'd heard the agitation in her voice in her Q phone message, but in the elation of their happy reunion, he still hadn't thought to ask her why she was trying to reach him.

As they followed Jumakhan and Sheela toward the front door of the house, Jenna took his arm and held him back from entering.

"Janssen, some things have happened you need to know about." She quickly told him about the attack on the munitions team, the death of Kevin Donahue and the two Tajiks, and Ambassador Neely's conversation with Sali.

A dark dread crept over Janssen as he listened to her words. "They apprehended the perpetrators, then?"

As Jenna was about to respond, Sheela beckoned to them from beyond the threshold. "Please come in and make yourselves comfortable."

Janssen turned to face her. "Thanks, Sheela. We're coming. Just having a little brother-sister chat."

He took Jenna's elbow and steered her into the house. "Thanks for the update. We'll talk more later."

When they had at last all assembled in the front room, Sheela brought out tea and refreshments. Jumakhan set his teacup resolutely on the side table and turned to Janssen.

"Janssen, long have I looked forward to your coming to Tajikistan. But now you are here, I find I cannot have leisurely conversations as I would like, for other matters press upon me."

"We have much to discuss, Uncle."

"Much has happened. I fear weapons cause much harm to our small country. Every day more violence. Tension and fear grow daily among the people."

"I am here to help."

"Janssen, it appears to many here that US presence does not help." The discomfiture Jumakhan had displayed during the ride home was now replaced by uncharacteristically stark directness. "With US presence, danger grows. Rajanov presses for decision. We no longer want weapons in Tajikistan."

"That is exactly what I think as well. That is why the US wants to purchase the weapons from you ... because they bring danger. We want to dispose of them so no one will be harmed by them."

"Rajanov does not trust US. I am not sure I do either. I trust you, Janssen, but I do not know if I trust your country. US presence continues to cost lives."

"I understand your concern, Uncle. Jenna just told me what happened today. Were you able to apprehend the perpetrators?"

"Three men are in jail. One is in hospital. But motive is unclear. Abdul Radazon Azzadafa says American spy hired them to attack, but I don't know if I believe him."

Janssen, who had been thoughtfully stroking his chin, jerked his head up at the mention of the name. "Azzadafa?"

"Yes."

"Is he related to Tahad Abdul Azzadafa?"

"He is his son."

"Well, then, Uncle. That's it."

Jumakhan looked at him quizzically. Sheela began removing the empty cups to take them to the kitchen.

"What, Janssen?"

"It all goes back to Tahad Abdul Azzadafa—just as you indicated to me in the email."

Jumakhan stared at Janssen blankly. "Email? What email?"

"The email you sent me."

"I did not send you email."

"Don't you remember? You sent me an email with the name Tahad Abdul Azzadafa—just a few days ago."

"No, Janssen. You are mistaken. I did not send email. I would have no reason to send email with that name."

Janssen returned Jumakhan's stare, then rotated the screen on his Q watch to email and brought one up from a few days earlier. He stepped to Jumakhan's side, positioning the watch before his uncle's face and projecting the email into a holographic image.

"Here," he said. "See for yourself."

The email displayed, indicating the sender to be jumakhanoqilov@tajik.gov.

The subject line read: *CONFIDENTIAL*

The text said:

Tahad Abdul Azzadafa

Please no response by phone or email.

Jumakhan's eyebrows knitted together with a look of confusion. "Not understanding this. I did not send email." He turned his head toward the chair where Sheela had been sitting. "Where is Sheela?"

Jenna spoke. "She took the cups and plates to the kitchen."

"Sheela," Jumakhan called abruptly. "Sheela, come here."

In her typically modest demeanor, Sheela peeked through the door of the kitchen. "Yes, Jumakhan?"

"Sheela, you use my computer sometimes, no?"

"Yes, Jumakhan."

"Did you send email to Janssen LaMarche?"

Sheela cast her eyes downward, her face coloring. She glanced at Jenna, then Janssen. When she answered, her voice was almost a whisper. None of them could hear her words.

"Sheela, answer me. Speak up," Jumakhan ordered. "Did you send email to Janssen LaMarche?"

Sheela bit her lip and shut her eyes for a moment. Janssen saw her lips move before any words came out. Her eyelids fluttered open.

"Yes, I did."

Jumakhan flew off his chair toward Sheela where she stood at the kitchen door. "Woman, why you do such a thing? You send email about Azzadafa?"

"Yes, Jumakhan. I did send email." Sheela's voice was bolder now, although Janssen saw a tremor in her fingers. She stepped back and pressed her hand against her throat.

"Why? Why you do this?"

"Because—because someone needs to know." Her voice was hoarse and plaintive. She cleared her throat. "I thought Janssen Aryan LaMarche might listen. Maybe look into it more, investigate, learn truth."

"Look into what?"

"Tahad Abdul Azzadafa. He is cruel man. He plans violence toward many."

Jumakhan scowled. "You do not know this."

"Yes, I do, Jumakhan."

"How do you know?"

"People talk."

"What people? Women?"

"Yes."

"Women do not know about such things ..." His voice trailed off as he caught Jenna's look.

Janssen could not stay seated any longer. He rose and joined them beside the kitchen door. "Actually, I did investigate, Uncle. Do you remember the violent Iraqi regime that was overthrown by the US in the early part of the century? The one controlled by Saddam Hussein?"

"Yes."

"Do you remember the Iraqi Deck of Cards that listed the dangerous leaders from that regime?"

Jumakhan rubbed his hand over the top of his head and frowned in thought. "I believe I do, now that you mention it. That was very long time ago, Janssen. I do not understand what you try to say."

"Jumakhan, did you know Azzadafa is the son of the Ba'ath Party official listed as the Four of Clubs in the Iraqi Deck of Cards? His father was one of the leaders in that bloody regime. Did you know that?"

"No, I did not know that. But Azzadafa is respected man—member of Majlisi Oli."

"Perhaps so. But why did his son attack the Americans today?"

"Azzadafa was very outraged by his son's behavior," Jumakhan said. "He struck him in the face and told him he was ashamed."

"Hmm." Janssen looked at Sheela. "What do you think, Sheela? Why did Azzadafa strike his son in the face?"

"He deceives many," Sheela said, relaxing her hand down to her side. "He is not what he seems to be."

Janssen pressed his fingers against his mustache, drew them down over his lips, and rubbed his chin. He closed the screen on his Q watch, causing the time to reappear. Nine o'clock. Janssen took a step backwards, then moved toward the sitting area and glanced at Jenna. He began pacing about the room.

In his mind, the puzzle pieces began dropping into place.

"Uncle, does Azzadafa have anything to do with the negotiations with the other party who wants to purchase the weapons?"

At his question, Jenna straightened her back and sat with rapt attention.

"I am not at liberty to share the details of those negotiations," Jumakhan replied.

"I see. Does the other party know the US is trying to purchase the weapons?"

"I expect they do, since there has been much talk on the news—CNN and others."

"So they know about us, but we are not permitted to know about them. Seems like we are on somewhat unequal footing, Uncle."

Jenna had now risen to her feet. Reflectively, she crossed the room to join the others. "Pardon me, Uncle. But I believe earlier today I overheard part of a conversation." You mentioned Azzadafa's name. It sounded like you may have been talking about the weapons. You mentioned Janssen also—and the US."

Janssen listened with interest, then raised an eyebrow and looked at Jumakhan. Sheela cowered in the kitchen door, her eyes fastened on her husband.

Jumakhan's eyes traveled from one face to the other. He looked up at the ceiling, then down at the floor and crossed his arms. Janssen took a step toward Jumakhan, then stopped and walked to a game table with an antique chess set on display. With his back to the others, he picked up one of the pieces, set it down again, and turned around. "When we were boys, we used to like to put jigsaw puzzles together. Remember?"

"Yes, Janssen. I remember."

"Uncle, I feel like we are putting another puzzle together now. Only you have some of the pieces and I have others. But until we put all the pieces together, we are not going to be able to see the whole picture. You are afraid for your people. I am afraid of great danger that could affect the entire world."

Jumakhan shifted, angling his body away from Janssen, and ran his fingers over the top of his head.

"Do you see what I am saying?" Janssen continued.

Jumakhan studied Janssen's face and turned his eyes away. His lips drew down to a thin line. He nodded.

"Azzadafa is involved in negotiations. He is main contact with—other party."

Two of the puzzle pieces suddenly locked together in Janssen's mind. A picture was emerging.

"And do you completely trust Azzadafa?" Janssen asked. "Is he a man of integrity? A man you admire?"

"He is man to be respected, man of influence. I do not agree with all his politics. He is in IRP party. He can sometimes be—mm, overbearing—manipulative. But I try to work with people of all parties, to bring about consensus."

"That is noble and good, Uncle. I have always admired that in you—as well as in Grandfather Oquilov. That was his strength in working with the people. But is it possible Azzadafa could be deceiving you?"

Jumakhan studied the floor, silent for a long moment before answering.

"I do not know."

"Uncle, do you feel you can trust me? Do you believe I would deceive you?"

"I trust you, Janssen. But I know you have great allegiance to your country. It is possible you too could be deceived."

"Six people have died here. You are worried. I am worried. I trust you, but you do not seem to trust me. We have a great puzzle. If we could put all our pieces on the table, together we may be able to solve it. I want the truth. I believe you do too."

"Yes, Janssen. I want truth."

"Then help me."

Jumakhan tilted his head to stare at the ceiling. With his eyes averted, he lumbered over to the sitting area and sat down in a straight-backed armchair.

"Sheela. Get us some more tea, please."

"Yes, husband." The tension that had visibly gripped Sheela appeared to drain from her body as she disappeared into the kitchen.

"This conversation must remain between only us." Jumakhan looked from Janssen to Jenna with an expression of great concern. "That is agreed? You do not tell anyone what I tell you."

"Agreed," Jannsen said.

Jenna nodded. "Agreed."

"The other party is Iran."

The revelation assaulted Janssen's mind with a barrage of new questions. He slipped to a chair opposite Jumakhan and perched on the edge. "So Iranian leaders are the ones who want the weapons?"

"Yes."

"Who in Iran are you dealing with?"

"Soheil Morashi is the man involved with negotiations. I have not spoken with him. Rajanov spoke to him once to confirm."

Janssen frowned. Where had he heard that name before? "So Azzadafa is the one dealing with him?"

"Yes."

"How was the first contact made?"

"Again, Azzadafa was the contact person. They approached him."

"Doesn't that seem a bit unusual? That they would contact Azzadafa, rather than you or Rajanov?"

"He has broad connections throughout the region. It did not seem unusual."

"But neither of you have spoken to President Kharrozi or other persons higher up in the Iranian government?"

"No. It did not seem necessary."

Sheela entered the room with her teapot and fresh cups on a tray. After handing them out, she set the tray on the rectangular table in the middle and took a seat on the sofa.

Janssen spooned sugar into his tea and held the cup in his hands. "Thank you, Sheela." He sipped from it, then set it down and looked again at Jumakhan. "What are the advantages of selling the weapons to Iran instead of the US?"

"Iran made large investments in textile industry here in Tajikistan. It helped our people put food on table. They are angry we have not yet sold weapons to them. They think US intends to use weapons, not disable them. They threaten to withdraw investments that help our people."

"Did Morashi say that to you? Or Rajanov? Or Azzadafa?"

"Rajanov spoke to Morashi once. I am not exactly sure what was said." Jumakhan drank from his teacup. "Other conversations have taken place through Azzadafa."

"Uncle, doesn't that sound a little suspicious?"

"Azzadafa represents us, just as you represent US. He reports conversations."

"But Iran has not told you *directly* they will withdraw investments." Janssen leaned forward in his seat and gazed directly into Jumakhan's eyes. "Do you believe the US would use these weapons? Don't you believe us when we tell you we want to disable them so no one will be hurt?"

"I do not know, Janssen. I do not trust US. American spy killed guards protecting weapons cache."

"I understand the evidence for that was pretty circumstantial. Cigarettes, American dialect, and so on."

"Not circumstantial he broke into house of Majlisi Oli representative. He was caught in act."

Janssen frowned. A Majlisi Oli representative? "A different member of the Majlisi Oli?"

"Yes. Zayd Azniov."

"Hmm, is he also in the IRP?"

"Yes."

"Well, I certainly agree the break-in needs to be looked into. That is not good, and Mr. Sali may be guilty of that, but I don't believe he shot the guards protecting the weapons."

"Then who did?"

Jenna leaned forward in her chair. "Didn't Popyev say the men who attacked our weapons inspectors were trying to make it appear Americans were responsible for the attack?"

"Yes, I believe Popyev did say that," Jumakhan said.

"Do you believe him?"

"He seems very honest man. I think I do believe him— even though young Azzadafa said American spy paid him to attack."

"If the young Azzadafa is dishonest enough to kill people for money, do you think he is honest enough to be believed in other things?"

Jumakhan cleared his throat. "I feel young Azzadafa deceives us."

"I would like to talk to his father, Tahad Abdul."

Jumakhan blanched. "That would not be good."

"Are you afraid of him?"

Jumakhan frowned. "Not afraid. But I do not want to insult him. He is man of influence, particularly in IRP. We need coalition for government to work. He is not forgiving man."

"And I suspect you've just hit on the key to all this," Janssen said. "I have a feeling he has also not forgiven the US for capturing his father—for invading Iraq fifty years ago." Janssen moved further forward in his seat. "Uncle, do you remember when we were boys? We went climbing in the Tian Shan Mountains, and a branch broke in my hands when I was near the top. I was right behind you. I could have fallen. You held another branch down to me and helped me up. But Azzadafa was down below and shouted up to you to let me fall. You were angry with him."

Jumakhan scratched his head as if trying to remember. "I do not know."

"He hated me because I was an American. Is there any reason to believe he has changed?"

"I do not believe he likes America. Yes, I think you are right in that."

"Let us both talk with Azzadafa tomorrow, Uncle. We need to know the truth. Invite Rajanov along if you like."

"I do not know what to say. First, I need to talk to Rajanov. It is very uncomfortable request. Let me think about this, Janssen." He shook his head again. "I do not know."

CHAPTER FORTY-TWO

"Jenna, may I talk to you?"

"Of course, Sheela. Come and sit down."

Sheela sat gingerly on the edge of Jenna's bed as the early morning light filtered through the sheer curtains at the window. "I am worried."

"What about?"

Sheela sighed. "I am worried about my friend."

Jenna caught the cautious look in her eye—the same expression she'd seen the day before when they talked together in the courtyard. "Your Christian friend?"

"Yes."

"You've been reluctant to talk about her."

"Yes. I am very afraid for her now. I think she may be in great danger."

"Oh?"

"Male head of her family is very important man—evil man."

"Do you think he will hurt her?"

"Oh, he already hurts her. He beats her. What I fear for is her life."

Jenna blanched. "He beats her?"

"Yes."

"Shouldn't she leave? Aren't there people who will help?"

"In our culture, man is allowed to hit his women."

Jenna shook her head in disbelief and gently took Sheela's hand in her own. "And now you're afraid for her life? Has something happened to bring about these fears?"

"When things go wrong for him, he becomes angry with her." Sheela looked down at her hands, then up. She locked eyes with Jenna. "I believe things will go very wrong for him today."

It was 10:19 a.m. when Janssen, Jumakhan, Bradley Jones, and Hamasa Kandarov, Chief Officer of the Tajik Police, knocked on Tahad Abdul Azzadafa's door.

A long, impassioned discussion between Jumakhan and President Rajanov the night before had ended with Rajanov reluctantly agreeing to Jumakhan Oqilov and Janssen LaMarche making the visit. His accompanying them was out of the question, in order to maintain a spirit of impartiality. But he insisted a third person, a Tajik, go along as a witness to whatever took place. He preferred Kandarov, who in his position as police chief could take whatever appropriate action might be necessary. Rajanov trusted Kandarov's judgment and demeanor.

Rajanov also insisted the visit be in the form of an inquiry regarding Azzadafa's son. Under the circumstances, that would seem appropriate. Janssen would be on a fact-finding mission to help the US learn what happened in the attack that caused Donahue's death, and to determine the official position regarding Sali, the American held in custody by the Tajiks.

For his part, after consulting with Randall Robertson, Janssen asked Bradley Jones to accompany him. At first,

Randall himself offered to go, but as they discussed it further, they both agreed even though Jones did not know the Tajik language, as a former Ranger he would be better equipped to handle a difficult situation should it arise. Before leaving for Kanibadan, Janssen asked Robertson to get the names of the other conspirators involved in the previous day's incident and have the CIA scour their files for any intel.

Jumakhan knocked a second time.

A moment later, they heard the latch click. When the door opened, they saw a petite woman peeking out at them from behind the veil of her burqa. She invited them inside and led them to the living area, where she, Jumakhan, and Kandarov exchanged polite greetings. Her name was Padua. She was Azzadafa's cousin who lived in the house with him. When Jumakhan introduced her to Janssen and Bradley, her eyes lit up above the veil.

"You are Janssen LaMarche?" she asked. "I hear about you. Your mother was wonderful woman. I am pleased to be acquainted."

"Did you know my mother?"

"No ... not personally. My friend tell me about her."

A man's loud voice boomed from the back of the house. "Who is it?"

"We have guests," she answered, in a restrained voice that Janssen doubted could be heard at the rear of the house. She motioned timidly toward the couch. "Please sit. I will summon Tahad Abdul."

A clicking against the wood floor drew Janssen's attention to the opposite end of the room. He looked up to see Azzadafa appear beneath the lintel of the doorway, leaning on his cane. In courtesy, the four men stood in greeting. Azzadafa extended a hand to Jumakhan and Kandarov. He nodded without enthusiasm as Jumakhan introduced Janssen and Bradley.

"I believe we knew each other as boys," Janssen said pleasantly in his best Tajik, trying to insert a certain cordiality into the meeting.

Azzadafa regarded him coldly. "I don't recall."

Jumakhan shifted uncomfortably from one foot to the other. "Tahad Abdul, Kandarov and I wanted to follow up with you on the incident yesterday. Mr. LaMarche and Mr. Jones here are gathering information on that too, so they can take reports back to their country. Also, they're collecting more details about the events involving the American we have in custody."

Azzadafa grunted acknowledgment.

Jumakhan cleared his throat. "Why don't we all sit down?"

Setting the tip of his cane down firmly behind him for support, Azzadafa worked himself back toward a straight chair and with considerable effort, settled onto a small cushion, then squared his shoulders and sat upright, his cane gripped tightly in his right hand.

As the others returned to their seats, Janssen studied Azzadafa's countenance for familiar traces of the boy he'd known. The thick, leathery skin of Azzadafa's face was deeply lined, a scowl permanently ingrained into his features. His beard was gray, neatly manicured and squared off at the bottom. The one thing that had not changed was the knife-edged glint of his eyes and soulless icy gaze.

Jenna was still in her bedroom when the front bell rang. Moments later, Sheela knocked on the door. "Mr. Quigley is here to see you."

"Oh. Okay. Tell him I'll be there in a minute."

When Jenna entered from the hallway, Michael was pacing back and forth in the living area.

"Michael?"

He stopped pacing and strode toward her. Jenna saw several scratches on his face. Two of his fingers were bandaged.

"Looks like you had a rough day yesterday."

"Yeah." He raised his eyes to hers. Their warmth caught her off guard. "I wanted to thank you for coming to our rescue yesterday."

"I wish I could have done more. I feel awful about Kevin Donahue."

"You did what you could. We all did." Michael cleared his throat. "But I wanted to thank you. And I hope I didn't offend you yesterday morning with what I said." He rested his hand on the back of a chair, and opened his mouth as if to speak again, then bit his lip. "I've been thinking a lot about things. You're a wonderful person, Jenna. And you didn't deserve what I did to you."

"Thank you, Michael. I appreciate that." She looked aside and rubbed her hands against the waist of her skirt.

"I suppose this comes way too late, but if there's anything I can do to make it up to you, I'd like to try." Michael watched her intently, his eyes fastened on hers, a look of genuine remorse etched across the lines of his face.

She felt uncomfortable. His words were those she'd longed to hear for many years, but now that he was saying them, she didn't know how to react. It had been far too long.

"I look back on those days," Michael said, "and I don't understand myself. I gave up everything ...."

"Apparently there was something you wanted more."

He shook his head and paced to the French doors, standing there for a minute as he stared out into the sunshine. "I was a fool."

The words washed unexpectedly through her like a clear, cool stream of fresh water. A crack that had formed in the shell of pain encasing her spirit the day before widened ever so slightly. Her heart felt lighter.

"Say that again. It sounds refreshing."

Michael turned and looked at her, then began to laugh. "I was a fool."

Her eyes brightened. She wanted to laugh too, but restrained herself. "Again."

Michael gazed at her standing there in the light, a buoyancy of spirit rising within him. He shook his head and smiled. Feelings stirred in him he had not known for many years.

Michael's eyes met hers once more. A ray of sunshine from the patio sent a glow across Jenna's face. Mesmerized, he walked slowly toward her, watching the sparkle in her expression begin to mellow. The closer he got, the more he longed to take her in his arms. He stopped in front of her and let his eyes caress her face. How had he missed her beauty. Again he stepped toward her, his gaze fastened on the light in her eyes that gradually changed from laughter to tears.

He reached out and took her hand.

"I was *such* a fool."

CHAPTER FORTY-THREE

"Tahad Abdul, we are concerned about your son," Kandarov began. "He is in serious trouble. What would be his motive for acting in such a violent manner?"

"You heard him. The American spy bribed him with money to do it."

"Even if that is true, Tahad Abdul, why would he consent to such villainy? Even for money?"

Azzadafa looked first at Janssen and then Bradley with disdain, apparently not realizing Bradley could not understand their conversation since they were all speaking Tajik.

"American money defiles the mind. I do not know what made him yield to such temptation. You must ask my son."

"What about the other men he was with?" Jumakhan asked. "What is his relationship to them?"

"Why do you ask me these things? Ask my son."

Jumakhan leaned forward. "Do you know those men?"

"Yes, I know them. Of course. They worked as guards." He shifted in his seat, then leaned back and crossed his arms in front of his chest.

"But you did not know them well?"

"They are acquaintances."

Jumakhan massaged his throat reflectively. "Did you have a good opinion of them?"

"I knew nothing disagreeable about them. As I said, they were acquaintances."

As Janssen listened to the exchange between Azzadafa and the others, he noticed Padua in her burqa hovering quietly beyond the far door behind her cousin. She had been there for several minutes. Azzadaffa seemed unaware of her presence.

"Do you know where Abdul Radazon got the rifle he used?" Kandarov asked.

"No."

"Doesn't it belong to you?"

Azzadafa uncrossed his arms, grabbed his cane tightly in one hand, and leaned forward. "What is this? Are you accusing me?"

"No, no, Tahad Abdul. We are just trying to help your son. We are looking for answers."

"Where was he the night of the attack on the weapons cache?" Jumakhan asked.

"Why do you ask? He had nothing to do with that. It was the American."

"We are trying to be thorough in our investigation," Jumakhan said. "There is some doubt the American is guilty after all."

Azzadafa's face paled. He leaned back and crossed his arms again. "How can you say that? The testimony from Fariad was conclusive."

"There are others who speak English and smoke American cigarettes." Kandarov said. "He saw no faces."

"Abdul Radazon was with me. At my home."

Kandarov looked at Jumakhan and nodded. "He confirms his son's story then."

"Yes."

As Janssen listened to Azzadafa, he saw Padua linger in the shadows beyond the threshold, a veiled specter framed in the jambs and lintel of the doorway. She was bowing her head now and moving her lips.

Janssen leaned forward and cleared his throat. "Representative Azzadafa, I know you are a man who travels much and has many connections in this part of the world. Do you have many ties to Uzbekistan?"

Azzadafa clenched his teeth. The muscles in his jaw flexed. He took a deep breath and straightened before answering.

"I know Uzbeks, yes, of course. Our lands are close. We have similar concerns." He frowned and let his eyes play up and down Janssen's body. "But what has this to do with incident involving Americans?"

"There are a number of related situations I am looking into."

Azzadafa stared at Janssen with contempt.

Ignoring the older man's belligerent attitude, Janssen continued, determined not to lose his one opportunity to question the man he felt was responsible for the recent violence. "Some delivery systems for chemical and biological weapons have been found in Uzbekistan. Do you know anything about them?"

Azzadafa grunted. "No. Nothing. I did not know there were such things."

"What do you know about the weapons cache found in the mountains? Do you have any idea where the weapons came from? How they got here?"

"How would I know this?" Anger rose in Azzadafa's voice. "How does anyone know this? The weapons are said to have been there many years."

"Could they have anything to do with your father?"

Azzadafa's face grew red as he pushed on his cane in an attempt to rise to his feet. "How dare you?" He glared at Janssen, nostrils flaring. "Get out of my house."

"Azzadafa, I don't believe Mr. LaMarche meant anything by that." Kandarov said.

"You don't know anything," Azzadafa fumed.

Janssen noticed Padua taking a step backward beyond the doorframe. Her eyes were large with a look of alarm. She vanished from the doorway, presumably retreating to the back of the house.

"Oqilov, are you going to permit me to be interrogated by this foreigner, this—*American*?" Azzadafa said the last word with great contempt.

"We are just trying to keep the peace, Tahad Abdul."

"I am insulted," he said sternly, attempting again to rise from his chair without success. "Oqilov, do not look to me for support from IRP after this ... outrage."

"I am sorry, Tahad Abdul. We thought you might have valuable information."

Suddenly, like an apparition, Padua again appeared in the doorway, holding a small old laptop in her arms. She stood boldly, her shoulders erect, no longer stooped and bowed. Janssen saw her standing there motionless in the darkened hallway for one full minute. Her voice shook when she finally spoke.

"I believe this is what you want, Mr. Prime Minister, Mr. LaMarche."

At the sound of her voice, Azzadafa turned in his chair to look at her. His eyes bulged. His face grew red.

"Woman, what is this? What do you do?"

He fought to push himself out of the chair with his cane, this time with success.

"Insolent, brazen woman." He hobbled toward her with surprising speed, lifted his cane, and swung it hard against her head.

Padua cried out in pain. The laptop flew from her hands.

Azzadafa grabbed for it in midair, pitching forward in an attempt to balance on his cane while intercepting the laptop. It struck the ground between them.

Padua clutched her head and slumped to the floor, her burqa falling from her face to reveal a large purple bruise across her right cheek. Another disfigured her mouth and chin.

Bradley vaulted from his chair, seized Azzadafa by the collar and threw him to the floor, then hurried to Padua and helped her up.

"Mr. Jones, it is best to leave this," Jumakhan said in English as he rose from his seat. "This is private business. She is his woman."

Kandarov was on his feet as well. He stepped solicitously toward Azzadafa.

Janssen slowly stood and faced his uncle. "You mean he has the *right* to beat her?"

"I do not agree with it," Jumakhan said feebly. "But each man must choose for himself. It is personal decision. I do not treat my women like this, but some men see it as their duty as means of discipline."

"Isn't she his cousin?" Janssen asked.

"Yes."

"He has control even over his cousins?"

"When she lives in his home. It is the way of the Prophet, peace be upon him."

Having struggled to a sitting position, Azzadafa tried to push himself off the floor. Kandarov leaned down to offer his hand.

With Bradley's help, Padua got to her feet, then stooped to rescue the laptop from its landing place not far from Azzadafa.

Azzadafa swung at her again with his cane.

She jumped to avoid it but tripped on her skirt and slid across the floor. Once more she got up and darted for the laptop.

Azzadafa swung again, then lurched for it himself.

Padua stooped, snatched up the laptop, and wrapped her arms around it just as his fingers brushed it. She hurried across the room and held it out to Janssen. Her voice trembled. "You find answers here."

"You're giving it to me?" Janssen looked at Azzadafa, then at Jumakhan and Kandarov before gazing once more at the battered woman.

"I am tired of living with lies. 'The truth shall set you free.'" She pushed it at him. "You find truth here."

Peevishly rebuffing Kandarov's help, Azzadafa raised himself to one knee and glared at Padua. "Rebellious woman. Give that back to me."

Janssen glanced his way, then bent toward Padua and whispered in her ear. "Is your cousin lying then?"

"Yes," she whispered back. "All he says is lies." She nodded toward the picture of the man in uniform on the shelf. "He is like his father, very cruel." She pushed the laptop toward Janssen's hands and looked pleadingly into his eyes. "Please take this."

"Janssen," Jumakhan said, "you interfere ..."

"She is giving it to me, Uncle."

"Give it back. We should leave here."

"Please." Padua's gaze embraced Jumakhan with desperation. "I will help you. Please take me and the computer with you."

Bradley crossed to her side. "We cannot leave this woman here. He could kill her."

A light flickered on Jumakhan's Q watch.

His uncle peered down at it, frowned, and pursed his lips. Turning away, he pressed an icon on his watch, then touched the patch behind his ear and grunted a faint greeting.

Tension spread across Jumakhan's face as he listened to the person on the other end. His countenance grew pale.

"Uhhh, one moment." He turned to those in the room. "Excuse me, please." Jumakhan stepped outside and shut the door.

Azzadafa pushed his way along the floor toward Padua, his cane extended treacherously.

Janssen stepped between them, shielding her from his advance. Through the front door, his uncle's muffled voice, laced with staccato expressions of alarm, held Janssen's attention even while he watched Azzadafa's approach.

Seconds later, Jumakhan barged through the front door again. Stress replaced his usually calm demeanor. His teeth were clenched, his expression outraged. He narrowed his eyes angrily at Azzadafa and turned abruptly to his Chief Officer of Police.

"Kandarov, take woman and laptop. And place Tahad Abdul Azzadafa under arrest."

"Tahad Abdul?"

"For treasonous activity."

"Treason?" Kandarov asked, visibly shaken.

"That was Rajanov on phone." Jumakhan's voice was terse, his face flushed. "Azzadafa has deceived us to believe Iran wanted to buy weapons. President Kharrozi of Iran knows nothing about it. We have been betrayed, made to look like fools in front of whole world."

A look of shock descended over Azzadafa's face.

Seeing Bradley scanning their expressions, trying to interpret what was being said, Janssen caught his eye, lifted an eyebrow and jerked his head toward Azzadafa, who was now inching backward and attempting to push himself up on his cane. Bradley took a step in Azzadafa's direction.

Jumakhan turned to Padua. "Woman, you want us to take this laptop. Why?"

"Because you will find truth there."

"What truth?"

Padua looked fearfully at her cousin rising to his feet. "I fear to say it."

"You needn't be afraid. We will protect you. Your cousin goes to jail. Tell me."

"You will see Tahad Abdul's guilt there."

"Woman, keep silent. You know nothing," Azzadafa growled.

"Guilt in what? Did he conspire with the men we are holding at the jail to attack the Americans?"

Padua glanced furtively at Azzadafa, lowered her head and stared at the floor, then darted a desperate look at Jumakhan. Her mouth opened as if wanting to speak, but she stood mute before him.

Jumakhan took a step closer to her. "You are free to speak, woman. You will be safe."

Padua trembled, then took a deep breath. As she exhaled, the word she struggled to utter came out. "Yes."

"That's all I need to hear," Jumakhan spun on his heel. "Tahad Abdul Azzadafa, you are under arrest for treason *and* for conspiracy to commit murder."

Azzadafa's nostrils flared, his eyes hot with hatred. His left hand groped to steady his cane. His right fumbled to the top of it. He pressed a button. The handle flipped open, and a derringer no larger than his palm appeared in his hand.

"I do not think so."

He snapped the gun toward Janssen and Padua.

"Deceitful, cursed woman," Azzadafa shouted. Padua raised the laptop just as he pulled the trigger. A bullet zinged through the air.

Janssen heard a crack and a squeal of fright, and saw Padua lurch backward. There was a splintering of glass as the bullet ricocheted off the edge of the laptop and shattered the far left window behind her.

Azzadafa raised the gun to fire again.

Bradley sprang at him from across the room. Azzadafa jumped back, and the gun fired wildly. A bullet gouged the ceiling. Bradley's fingers reached for him, but Azzadafa pulled away, escaping his grasp and quickly slithering out of range. He slipped through a door and into the back of the house.

The door slammed shut. The lock clicked. A low muffled voice. Azzadafa was talking to someone.

Bradley set his shoulders and threw his body at the door. The door held fast.

Janssen ran up beside him. "Let me help."

Padua pointed to the back of the house. "Back. He may go out the back door."

Kandarov shoved open the front door to circle around the side of the house while Bradley motioned Janssen to step back. He braced himself for another run against the inner door to the bedroom area. He hurled his body at it, breaking it open.

Through the opening, Bradley and Janssen saw Azzadafa scramble through a back exit. He turned to fire at them, but Bradley was already on him, grabbing his arm, bending it upwards and back.

The gun went off.

Azzadafa groaned in pain. Blood spilled from his neck. His left hand clutched at his cane for support. The gun dropped from his right as he groped vainly for something to grab onto.

Bradley took Azzadafa's arm and gently eased him to the floor just as Kandarov burst around the corner and Jumakhan emerged from inside the house.

Kandarov was beside him. "What happened?" he asked in Tajik.

"His gun went off in his hand. He shot himself in the neck. The bullet must have hit his jugular vein." Janssen said. "Better get an ambulance."

Jumakhan approached cautiously.

Azzadafa lay in a pool of blood. His piercing eyes glared at the Americans with hate.

Bradley reached over and touched Azzadafa's Q watch. "It's connected. He was talking to someone on his Q."

Azzadafa jerked his arm, struggling to wrench it from Bradley's hand. Bradley gripped it tightly, removed the wristband, and dropped the arm.

Bradley touched the screen on the phone.

"Hello?" he said into it. He looked at Janssen. "The phone just went dead." Rotating the icons on the screen, he looked at it again, then back at Jumakhan. "He was talking to a ... Zayd Azniov."

A mental screen clicked open in Janssen's head. A puzzle piece floated before his eyes.

"Wasn't it Azniov's house where Sali—the American you have in custody—was found? Didn't Sali accuse Zayd Azniov of harboring the stolen weapons at his house?"

Jumakhan paled. "Yes, and he is member of Majlisi Oli." Jumakhan dropped his head. He barely moved his mouth when he spoke, this time in his Tajik tongue. "Kandarov, have your officers go to the house of Zayd Azniov immediately. Hold him there for questions. You and I will meet them there."

"Yes, Prime Minister. Right away."

Padua stood in the doorway as Kandarov slipped by her into the main part of the house. She crept closer to her cousin and looked down at him. She lowered her head, raised her hand to her mouth, and closed her eyes.

When she opened them again, Azzadafa was glaring at her. He muttered ugly words, struggling for breath even as he spoke.

"I have no tears for you, Tahad Abdul," she responded, "though you are my cousin. No tears."

Kandarov returned. "My men are on their way. Also, an ambulance comes here for Azzadafa. I am going to Zayd's house now to ask questions."

Janssen related to Bradley what Kandarov had said. "You feel comfortable staying alone here without knowing the language? I'd like to go along with Jumakhan, if you don't mind."

Bradley looked at Azzadafa. "Don't think there's much danger. I've got my Q. I'll keep you posted." He nodded at Padua. "What about her?"

Janssen studied the battered woman for a moment and glanced at Azzadafa. "Padua, you should probably come with us."

Padua shook her head. "If you please, Mr. LaMarche, I prefer to stay for now. I go with you later."

"Are you sure? We don't know who else might be involved."

"Your man Bradley is here to protect me. I will be all right."

"We'll be back for you later, then. We'll need to ask you some questions too."

In the back seat of the car with Jumakhan and Kandarov, Janssen touched the patch at the back of his ear and spoke the name Randall Robertson. A moment later, he heard Randall's smooth voice on the other end.

He filled Robertson in about Azzadafa and the last call he'd made while running from the house. "Randall, how about seeing what else we have on Zayd Azniov?"

"Glad to. Incidentally, I was about to call you with the other information you wanted. You'll never guess what we found out about the ancestry of the other four men involved in the attack."

"Tell me."

"All of them are either sons or grandsons of the three terrorists captured in Afghanistan in 2003, the ones from Tajikistan sent to Guantanamo."

"You don't mean it."

"I'm dead serious."

"What a connection. The Iraqi Azzadafa and the terrorists from Afghanistan. Quite a legacy."

Robertson grunted. "Men who were bred to hate."

An hour later, Jumakhan's face was ashen when he and Kandarov emerged from Zayd Azniov's house.

Kandarov spoke feverishly to four officers who followed them out, pointing to the western mountains. The men walked to patrol cars parked in front of where Janssen had been waiting and continued talking for a few minutes. Kandarov spoke briefly into his Q watch, then jumped into the back seat of one of the cars just before it took off.

Jumakhan trudged back to the sedan he and Janssen had arrived in and climbed into the front seat behind the steering wheel. "They're gone."

"Gone? Zayd?"

"Yes. Zayd's house is in disarray. He left in a hurry. The dogs smelled something in a large bin in his basement."

"What dogs? What do you mean?"

"Dogs that find chemical and biological weapons. They sniffed some out in there. In Zayd's house." Jumakhan started the engine. "The dogs are still there with some of the other officers, but there's nothing there now. It's certain."

Janssen ran his hand through his mustache. "So Sali was right? They'd taken weapons to his house?"

"Yes, dogs smelled it. And now the weapons are gone, and so is Zayd." Jumakhan shook his head as he pulled the car into the road. "I fear what will happen."

"What are you doing about it?"

"We have alerted border guards. Activated faudoscopes to sniff out chemical vapors. Police are searching the roads. We think they may have taken the weapons through the mountains toward Uzbekistan." Jumakhan ran his free hand over the top of his head as he looked into the rearview mirror. "Who else is involved in this? That's what I want to know. What other surprises will we have?"

Janssen sighed and patted the laptop at his feet. "This should give us some of the answers."

The helicopter lifted from the pad, hovering clumsily above the ground, the blades clawing the thin mountain air. It rocked, then rose and banked to the south, turning in the direction of Dushanbe.

Janssen leaned back in his seat behind the pilot and Kandarov, angling his shoulders to the left to give more room to Jumakhan and Padua squeezed in beside him. His uncle twisted his body to get comfortable. It was a tight fit with six of them in the chopper. Padua, although rescued from danger, still appeared agitated.

Sitting behind them, Bradley adjusted his headset and leaned forward. "Would you mind repeating what Rajanov said on the phone? I couldn't understand it all earlier."

Jumakhan hesitated, looked at Janssen, then turned his head toward Bradley as he spoke. "President Rajanov called President Kharrozi of Iran to find more information about what Iran was prepared to do to obtain weapons. President Kharrozi said he knew nothing about Iranians buying weapons cache. He identified man Rajanov thought to be representing Iran as mid-level official, member of Expediency Council, whose authority does not extend over such things."

"Hmm," Bradley said. "So who is this guy, and what does he have to do with it all?"

"And if Iran was not putting up the money, who was?" Janssen asked reflectively. "Azzadafa certainly doesn't have access to that kind of money."

"Janssen, you were right, you know," Jumakhan said. "We have been very foolish. I guess we don't know who was trying to buy weapons. If Morashi is not authorized to speak for Iranian government, who is he? And how was he planning to finance transaction?"

Janssen stared at his uncle. "What was that name again?"

"You mean Soheil Morashi?"

"Yes. He was the man you were negotiating with?"

"Yes, Soheil Morashi."

Janssen stared again at his uncle and looked out the window at the rocky cliffs below where a herd of sheep wound their way along a rugged path at the foot of the mountain.

"That name's familiar somehow." He watched until he could no longer see the sheep, then continued to stare blankly at the miles of biscuit-colored terrain stretching out beneath them. In his mind he recalled scrolling through a computer screen, down a list of names.

"That's it," he said suddenly. He turned back to Jumakhan. "Morashi is the CEO of a textile company. His was one of the names I looked up on my way over here. He's putting together a financial empire. As I remember, I think he also had an interest in an Uzbekistani gold mine."

Jumakhan shook his head and pressed his palm against his scalp. "Janssen, I'm sorry I did not trust you. I am in such anguish."

"You were trying to do what was right for everybody. You didn't know."

Padua had been staring at Janssen for some time while he was talking. Her forehead was furrowed and her eyes anxious. Several times she parted her lips as if she wanted to speak, then looked down and closed her mouth.

Janssen smiled at her. "Are you okay, Padua?"

Her eyes widened with concern. "Sir, I don't like to interrupt ... "

"That's all right, Padua. You're not interrupting."

"I—I'm wondering. Do you know someone named Evie?"

Janssen took on the attitude of a proud peacock. "Yes. My daughter's name is Evie. Why?"

Padua knit her eyebrows together and stared at her hands. "I hear Tahad Abdul talking about someone named Evie a few days ago." She looked up at Janssen with foreboding in her eyes. "I fear she may be in danger."

CHAPTER FORTY-FOUR

Janssen's head was spinning. *Evie?* In danger? This had nothing to do with her. She was safe in her little world of Sweet Peas, children's resale clothes, and admiring boys.

"What do you mean?" he asked.

Padua's deep-sunk eyes were large with fear, her eyebrows drawn together with vertical furrows between them. "I heard talk on phone conversations about someone named Evie. Use Evie for back-up, they said. 'If LaMarche starts getting close, make sure we can get to Evie.'"

Janssen's heart froze. "What does that mean?"

Padua shook her head. "I do not know   only that they talked about weapons. They would do anything to get weapons back."

Kandarov turned around. "Back?"

Padua flushed. "Yes. The weapons belong to Azzadaffa. His father brought them here many years ago from Iraq, when he brought Tahad Abdul to live with my mother and father. The weapons were special. He used to brag about them. Tahad Abdul's father and another man formulated a preservative that would make them last for a very long time."

Jumakhan leaned forward. "Why didn't Azzadaffa get them before?"

"They were lost. His father left message telling where they were, but Tahad Abdul was only boy then, and message was lost. He has lived his whole life thinking about them, wondering where they were, angry at himself—and everyone else—for losing the message. He searched mountains every day, digging in caves, everything he could do. A bad fall in the mountains caused him to fracture hip. That is why he uses cane."

Janssen's heart raced, his breathing shallow and rapid as Padua's words seemed to lengthen with each second into a never-ending discourse. When she finally finished her explanation, he jumped in immediately.

"Who was he saying these things to, Padua, these things about my daughter? Who exactly is involved in this? Is she still in danger, now that Azzadaffa is under arrest?"

"Friends in Uzbekistan—Wahhabis. Very strict. They are what you would probably call terrorists. Very smart. Scientific."

Horror gripped Janssen's mind. How could anyone be savage enough to involve Evie? His pure, beautiful, precious daughter? His heart pounded.

"I heard them say it would be a distraction for you—'take LaMarche's attention away from Tajikistan,' they said. They fear you, Mr. LaMarche. My cousin and his friends fear your influence in Tajikistan."

"Do you have any idea what they plan to do? Or when?"

"No ... only they said, 'if LaMarche gets close.'"

Janssen turned to Bradley and interpreted the conversation for him.

"LaMarche," Bradley said. "You *are* close. I don't want to sound like an alarmist, but I'd say we've got no time to waste. We need to get to the bottom of this. We need to get into that laptop."

Janssen leaned forward to Kandarov. "We need to get into that laptop now to see if we can find out what the threat is concerning my daughter. How about giving Jones a crack at it?"

Kandarov swiveled in his seat and passed the laptop back to Janssen, who handed it to Bradley.

Janssen pressed a screen on his Q and entered a message. He sent it to Evie, then angled his wrist and spoke into his Q watch. "Evie. Q." He heard the phone ringing on the other end. It was only six a.m. in DC. Surely she was home.

After a few rings, the auto-answer kicked in, and the sound of her sweet voice ripped at his heart. "This is Evie. I can't come to the phone right now, but please leave a message. God bless you, and have a great day."

"Evie," Janssen said into her voice mail. "It's extremely important I talk to you. Stay where you are. Don't go anywhere until you talk to me. I don't want to scare you, but you might be in danger."

He clicked off the phone and spoke again. "Evie. Home." Again, no answer. He left the same message. Calling her work number produced the same results. As he texted her phones and email, he shouted to Bradley. "Any luck with the laptop?"

"No," he said. "I'm afraid I don't understand this keyboard."

Janssen turned to see what he was talking about. "Oh, yeah. It's in the Cyrillic alphabet." Janssen leaned forward. "Kandarov, are you computer savvy?" he asked in Tajik. "The laptop isn't compatible with English."

"Afraid not. Sorry."

Janssen looked at Bradley and shook his head.

"How far are we from Dushanbe?" Bradley asked.

Janssen repeated the question to the pilot, then turned to Bradley with the pilot's response. "Ten minutes."

"Call Quigley to meet us on the landing strip. If anyone can break into this, he can. I've never seen anything stand up against his hacking skills."

Janssen felt helpless. His daughter was in danger, and there was nothing he could do. He got hold of Charlie, but she didn't know where Evie was either.

"How about doing a GPS track on her car?" she suggested. "Wherever her car is, she's likely to be nearby. It would be a start anyhow."

"Great idea, Charlie. Do you want to contact the FBI and get that going, or should I do that?"

"It'd probably be easier from over here. I'll do it."

"Let me know what happens."

"I will, Janssen." She disconnected

Janssen switched off the phone and turned to watch Bradley trying different combinations on the keypad, all with no success.

"You don't remember anything else that might be helpful?" he asked Padua.

"No, sir."

Janssen heard the familiar tune on his Q watch telling him he had a call and anxiously clicked it on. It was Danny.

"Hi, Mr. LaMarche. Mr. LaMarche," he said in a somnolent drift of words. "I thought I should touch base with you about scheduling here. I still have a ton of requests for lengthy interviews when you return."

"Not now, Danny. I can't deal with that now. Sorry ..." His mind skidded suddenly into another thought. "But I'm glad you called. I can use your help."

"Sure."

"I'm very concerned about Evie. We've just brought down a key target over here. And now a relative of his tells us she overheard a conversation where they were talking about getting to Evie to distract me from our mission. And we can't reach Evie. She's not answering her phones."

Danny's mouth dropped open and his eyes widened in alarm. "She's not answering her phone? How about work? Did you send a text?"

Janssen shook his head impatiently. "No. She's not answering her phones or messages."

"If she's asleep I'd think the vibrate function would wake her."

"She takes it off at night. Says it itches."

"The other night she said she planned to spend a lot of time at work to catch up. They'd had a lot of trouble with the computer. But you did try Sweet Peas?"

"Yeah. Tried that, and our house too. My wife didn't know where she was either."

In the hologram beside him, Janssen could see Danny's head bobbing in and out of range while he spoke, as though he was scurrying around the room, preoccupied. He poked his left arm into the sleeve of his shirt, then his right. He bent over. Probably to lace his shoe, Janssen thought. He was obviously getting dressed.

"I'll go over to her house right now, Mr. LaMarche," Danny said. "See what I can find out."

"I appreciate that. How far away are you?"

"About twenty minutes, I think. But I'll get there faster than that."

When the helicopter came within view of the airfield, Michael Quigley was standing on the tarmac.

The music was blaring on Evie's clock radio. The backup alarm had apparently kicked in. She rubbed her eyes and looked at the time. 7:07.

"Ohhh!" She jumped out of bed and raced across the room. "I'll be late to meet Helen! I can't believe I overslept." She threw open the door of the closet, grabbed a long-sleeved blouse, a white shell top, and white pants—pulling them on as she hobbled to the bathroom.

Poking the last button through the hole of her blouse, she glanced in the mirror and ran a brush through her hair. She snatched her purse from the table and hurried out the door.

After Janssen's entourage disembarked from the helicopter, airport staff escorted them to a small conference room Jumakhan had arranged for them to use.

Michael set up the laptop and swore.

"This foreign crud doesn't help matters. Look at this keyboard."

Janssen leaned over his shoulder. "Yeah, it's not our alphabet. Can you get past that?"

Michael grimaced. "Hope so. Good thing I've got my Da Vinci." He removed a tool from his briefcase and pried off the keyboard, then retrieved his Da Vinci ball and set it on the table. Placing his hands against the exterior of the ball, he lifted off the plasma gloves adhering to its sides, allowing them to mold to his palms and fingers, then touched the side of the ball. A screen hologrammed before him. He quickly moved his fingers as though typing on a keyboard. Icons and a series of word combinations flickered across the Da Vinci screen. "Okay, that should get us started."

He shifted his hands to where the keyboard had been on Azzadafa's laptop and moved his fingers again. The plasma laptop screen flickered, and the operating system kicked into a startup sequence.

Janssen pulled a chair up beside him. "Did you get into it?"

"Not yet. But I got the laptop to accept my keyboard. Can't get anywhere without an intelligible keyboard to work with." He shook his head. "How do you read that stuff?"

Janssen chuckled at Michael's chutzpah. He'd always been amused by his brashness. "Interesting how you can interface the two like that."

"Now let me see if we can break into this."

Michael swore again as he worked his fingers in his virtual gloves without success.

Bradley came up and stood behind them. "Heavy encryption, huh?"

Michael grunted.

Janssen rose and paced about the room. His anxiety was getting the best of him.

Michael tore off one of the gloves, flung it on the table, and got up to walk about the room. Stopping at the window, he heaved a sigh and plodded back to his workspace. Dropping into his seat, he replaced the glove, then processed a series of commands.

The icon on the screen faded and the desktop displayed.

Janssen hurried to his side to look over his shoulder. "Get it?"

Michael air-punched his fist.

"Got it!" He looked back at the screen and worked his virtual keyboard again. "Okay now, where's the translator on this thing?" He flipped through a couple of screens.

Janssen pointed to an icon at the top. "Here, this one."

Michael selected it, and a list dropped down. "Is this the English?"

"Yeah," Janssen said.

"Okay, let's get into this creep's email." Michael brought up the search engine and entered "Janssen AND LaMarche OR Evie." A list of files scrolled onto the screen.

"You're a popular guy," Michael said sarcastically. "Quite a list. I'll filter the results."

Fortunately for Danny, it was still early enough that traffic had not yet thickened along Highway 237. By the time he got to the Rosslyn area, the main roads had come to life. He turned onto Fairfax and pulled in front of Evie's brick townhouse. After throwing the gears in park, he threw open the door and scrambled up the brick steps. With the forefinger of his right hand he jabbed the doorbell while pounding frantically with his left fist.

"Evie, open up. I have to talk to you."

The silence from inside gnawed at his nerves. Her driveway was empty, and there was no window into the garage. He looked at his watch. Seven-twenty. He scanned the curb along the street for signs of Evie's Volvo. Disappointed and perplexed, he jumped back into his car.

Michael entered "LaMarche" AND "Evie." Five entries appeared. "Here we go."

Michael perused the first three messages and grimaced. "I can't believe these scumbags." He looked at Janssen. "They've planted a bomb in Evie's computer."

Janssen stared at Michael, speechless. The words trembled in his mind, but refused to take hold.

A look of dismay swept over Michael's expression. His voice softened.

"Looks like they've set it to go off when the computer is turned on. But they've got to trigger it from their end first."

"At her home or business?" Janssen went cold as he gaped at the email. His heart pounded. "The day she came to my office—she mentioned her computer was down ..."

Shutting out the images of horror rushing into his mind, he went into action.

He called Tomlin first.

Then Danny.

CHAPTER FORTY-FIVE

Danny answered his phone on the first ring.

"Where are you?" Janssen's voice sounded desperate.

"At Evie's apartment house. She's not here."

"There's a bomb in her computer. Has she gone to work?"

Danny felt like someone had sprayed his brain with mace. "I don't know." He ordered the ignition to engage, yanked the door shut, and pulled his car onto the street.

"I'm heading for her shop right now." At the stop sign, he glanced to the right to see no one was coming, tapped the brake for ceremony, and spun the car to the left. "I bet she's gone to work. Like I said, she was trying to catch up."

"God help us," Janssen whispered.

At the stop sign at Clarendon, a young woman was crossing the street on her hover-glide with an armful of shopping bags. One of the bags began to slip off her arm. She slowed to adjust it and smiled at Danny, her eyes begging him to be patient.

"Come on, lady." He skimmed past her and charged around the corner.

She turned and glared at him.

"I'm going to try Evie again. I'll call you back." Janssen disconnected.

The traffic was heavy now, but moving. Finally, Danny passed the tall office buildings that signaled his approach to the Jefferson Davis Parkway and veered right onto it, tires skittering on the pavement. He overcorrected, and the car fishtailed. With the luxury of a multi-lane highway, he kicked in the thrust mechanism and swerved around a solar-powered vehicle. He was pushing the speedometer past his usual comfort zone and averted his eyes from it.

"Exceeding speed limit," a mechanical voice warned. "Please slow down."

His phone rang again. It was LaMarche. "Where are you now?"

"On the Jefferson Davis Parkway, just beyond the crosses of Arlington Cemetery. Almost to the Pentagon."

LaMarche groaned. "Still can't get Evie. No answer on any of her phones. And for some reason the Transportation Department can't pick up the signal of her GPS." His voice sounded strained and anxious. "Secretary Tomlin dispatched a bomb squad to Sweet Peas. But we don't know if it'll be in time."

"Would you like me to put you on companion mode on my Q so you can stay in touch?" He paused. "Or maybe there's something else you can do?"

"Not from here there isn't." Janssen's voice broke. "I've done everything I can."

Janssen's own words hit his ears as if somebody else had spoken them. In his mind he could hear Evie's voice continuing the commentary. "When you've done everything you can, let God take over."

He'd heard her say it time after time. His response had been to either sigh or smile patronizingly, or, worse, laugh. Now he was not laughing. Now her words washed over him again and again, like waves against the shore.

Let God take over.

Danny still spoke to him on the other end of the line. Janssen saw his face and his lips moving, but he couldn't focus on the words. "Danny, let me call you back."

Janssen wandered out onto the airfield and watched a plane speeding down the runway. The earsplitting whistle of the engine rent the air. The plane lifted and sliced through a low-hanging cloud. He stood and watched until it became a tiny dot on the horizon. His mind raced. His lips trembled— unwelcome tears burned the corners of his eyes.

"Oh, God." He dropped his head in his hands. "You know I'm not very religious. But it's Evie I'm asking you to help. She ..."

His eyes filled with tears. "She's one of your biggest advocates, God, and she's one of the most loving creatures on the face of the earth. Please help her, God ... if you're really up there ... don't let anything happen to her. Save her. Please."

He choked back a wave of emotion, let out a ragged sigh, and wiped the wetness from his eyes before it could spread onto his cheek. For several minutes he stared up at the sky.

He pictured Evie the way she looked when he peeked in on her in the bedroom and found her on her knees after she learned about his illness—her winsome expression, her eyes raised to heaven beneath dark lashes, a glow upon her face. "Please, God. Don't make her an angel yet."

"Oh. There you are." Bradley Jones came up from behind him. "We thought we'd lost you."

Janssen saw him scanning his face. *Strong men don't cry, Janssen.*

"They stopped Zayd," Bradley said.

Janssen nodded as he collected himself. "That's great. Did he have the weapons?"

"Twenty canisters. Ten of sarin—I think it's Sarin X50, and ten of anthrax. Appears we've found the enhanced weapons we've been looking for."

"Hmm. Congratulations, Jones. I know that's a good feeling."

"Any news about your daughter?" Bradley asked.

"No."

Bradley frowned and scuffed his feet along the ground. "Thought you'd want to know also—with good news comes bad. Looks like your daughter isn't their only target."

Janssen jerked his head and looked at him. "What do you mean?"

"They've planned a suicide bombing for Dushanbe. Same type of conditions ... like, 'If it starts looking like the US is going to succeed in securing the weapons ...'"

Janssen shook his head. "God help us all. What are Jumakhan and Kandarov doing about it?"

"Closing the borders, heightening inspections, putting robotic scanners and android guards at initial entry points. Plus Kandarov is erecting roadblocks on a number of key arteries. Hopefully, we're onto it in time."

Janssen put a hand on Bradley's back. "I'll go back inside with you now and see what's happening." They pushed through heavy doors and wound along a long vacant corridor. The door squeaked as they entered the small conference room.

Michael turned to look at them from his workspace. "This guy had tentacles all over the place. Look at this."

Janssen crossed the room and leaned over Michael's shoulder.

Michael pulled up an email from a sect in Uzbekistan coded WBIS. "Let me show you some of the most significant items first. This one was posted the day after Sali was arrested."

> Stage II of Project America is complete. Solid fuel delivery systems compatible with early millennium biosystems and chemical warfare. Will support payload. However, intercepts indicate detection from American source. Delivery systems being moved to safer location.

Another from WBIS read:

> Agents in target cities are ready with maps and schedules. Need to have primary locations identified.

"That one was copied to Soheil Morashi," Michael said. "And then there's this. It's an early email dated July 22:

> Where is money? Waiting to hear from Morashi. Cannot proceed until money in hand.

"Now, that last one clinches it in terms of the funding," Michael said.

Another one dated July 23 from Morashi:

> Trouble at mine. Engineers working out problems. Will have money in two days. Tell WBIS to proceed.

"This one was sent to Azzadafa from the Uzbek group the day after you were chosen as the point man in negotiations for the US."

> Need plan to provoke distrust of US motives and intentions. We will handle technological modifications and activate sleeper network. Morashi will finance operation. You, Zayd Azniov, and other Tajiks must implement on-the-ground operations to discredit US imperialism. Bring shame on the Great Satan. Demonize

them anyway you can. Janssen LaMarche has much influence with his uncle. We MUST undermine that.

"And this from Morashi to Azzadafa, Zayd Azniov and WBIS in Uzbekistan."

Threat of losing textile companies worries Rajanov, but Oqilov listens to LaMarche, and Oqilov's influence with Rajanov is significant. Decision could go either way. US promises money and investments. We must develop backup plans to distract LaMarche and undermine influence.

"And here's the Uzbek answer."

We will back up your bargaining position in two ways. In US, we will attack someone in LaMarche family. In Tajikistan, we will strike fear in the hearts of the leaders with suicide attack in Dushanbe.

"This one was two days ago."

LaMarche surfaced again. On his way to Tajikistan. Prepare to implement attacks.

Michael stopped and turned, a frown furrowed deeply across his brow.

"Janssen, maybe I shouldn't show you this next one. These scumbags! These rotten ... " He muttered a string of curses under his breath. "But you probably want to know just how these people think."

Janssen almost stopped breathing. What more could there be? But he had to know. He nodded apprehensively.

Michael swiveled back to the computer and swore again as he pulled up an earlier email from WBIS in Uzbekistan.

Surveillance reports from informants: Wife Charlie works for government. Too much security. Sister Jenna LaMarche lives alone in remote country house, appears harmless, but alert and watchful. Easy target for direct attack or kidnap. Daughter Evie LaMarche has own business. Lives alone. Unaware and naïve. Easy access. I recommend latter for targeting.

Janssen felt nauseated. He was afraid he might throw up. He groaned from deep within. "The innocent. They prey on the innocent."

He called all three of Evie's phone numbers and sent text messages again. No response.

Danny's Q watch was ringing again. It was his boss.

"Danny, I'll take you up on your offer." Mr. LaMarche's voice was shaky. "Go ahead and put me on virtual companion mode."

Danny flicked a switch on his watch, transferred the projection to the dash and saw the hologram balloon beside him. Janssen's image occupied the passenger seat. His eyes were flat and lifeless, his face pale.

"I've just passed the exit to the airport," Danny said, "and the traffic's slowing. Looks like an accident at Glebe. Still a couple of miles to the bridge."

The lane to his left began to open up. Danny put his foot on the accelerator and cut in front of a green Chevy Rhythm. He heard the screech of brakes, then a horn honk. The woman in the Chevy scowled and shook her finger at him. The traffic slowed again. He punched Evie's numbers in. Once more all three went to voicemail. His texts got no response. Danny lowered his window and craned his neck through the opening, attempting to see the cause of the slowdown.

He crawled along for what seemed an eternity, trying now to work his way into the right-hand lane and move to the shoulder.

If only he could get to the bridge.

With his right turn signal flickering, he gunned the car in front of a motorcycle, slipped between a GT Menda and a white Jeep, then sidled onto the shoulder and jammed the accelerator to the floor, spitting dust and dirt on the cars to his left. The steering wheel vibrated and his car began to shake as the Honda skidded through loose gravel and swerved toward the outer rail. He braked and heard the crunch of his tires as he tightened his grip and fought for control, allowing the steering wheel to spin slowly through his hands. The car straightened out, and he continued at a slower clip, moving steadily past the stalled traffic to his left.

When he passed the intersection at Reed a few minutes later, the lanes began to open up. Danny veered onto the highway, once again flooring the accelerator as he flew down the road, swerving between lanes. His eyes lighted on the speedometer ... ninety mph ... ninety-five .... He glanced away.

The car's mechanical voice droned its speed warning again.

"Shut up," he said.

"Sometimes you wish you could just turn those things off," Mr. LaMarche said from the hologram beside him.

"And how! Don't need that now."

"Keep doing what you're doing. We need to get there."

Ahead, Danny saw the parkway curving to the right as it crossed the small inlet toward Alexandria. He scanned the cars in front and looked across the water to the rooftops in town. Where was Evie? As he neared the bridge, he scrutinized the cars streaming across. The lanes were moving smoothly despite the density of traffic. The sun glistened against the shiny metal of different hues moving across the bridge—green, silver, black, red ...

Blue.

Danny blinked. He fastened his eyes on a splotch of blue winding around the bend of the bridge—a dark blue Volvo. A wave of exhilaration flooded his mind. He took a deep breath, afraid to put words to the hope that had materialized before him.

"Mr. LaMarche, I think I see her car. A dark blue Volvo."

"Dark blue?" Excitement resonated from Janssen's voice.

"Yes. Crossing the bridge—just about to make the turn."

"Pink sticker in the window?"

Danny narrowed his eyes and tried to scan the back window of the car, but a white truck was blocking his line of vision. The Volvo pulled ahead, and he saw it. "Yes, in the lower right corner. I think it's pink. There's a picture."

"An angel?"

"Could be. Yes. I think so."

"Yes. Yes."

"Then I think we've got her. I think it's her."

Evie looked at the clock on her dash. It was almost seven-forty. She was sure Helen was already at Sweet Peas. Helen was always right on time. Why had she forgotten her Q watch? She pictured it sitting on her dresser.

I could've called her and told her I was running late. I do the dumbest things. Why can't I be more organized?

Her car was wedged between a black Cadillac going ten miles below the speed limit in front and a white truck bearing down on her tail. She turned on her blinker to change lanes, but the cars to her left blocked her move. The white truck behind her aggressively darted into the left lane, barely avoiding a collision, then pulled away. Spying an opening in back of the truck, Evie began to move to the left when she heard the blaring of a horn behind her. She frowned. People were being particularly rude this morning.

She grimaced and shook her head as she began to edge over, but the car with the honking horn swerved from behind and cut her off. She peered into her side mirror and saw someone in a dusty black Honda waving at her wildly. It was Danny. What on earth was he doing?

As he pulled alongside her, she scowled. He was motioning for her to pull over. She didn't have time for this. She was already late. Evie raised her left arm and pointed to her bare wrist where she should have been wearing her Q watch. "I'm late," she mouthed to him.

He lowered his window and kept pointing to the right for her to pull over. He appeared frantic. And what was in the car beside him? A virtual. She leaned forward to get a better look. It was a virtual of her dad.

She cracked her window. "I'm late," she said. "Is that my dad in virtual with you?"

Even cracked open a little, the window muffled Danny's voice as he shouted from the opposite side of the car. "You're in danger."

She cocked her head and eyed him quizzically, then frowned as she slowed, put on her blinker, and edged to the right. Finally, she pulled into the parking lot of Potatoes, Etc. Danny zipped in behind her.

When Danny and her dad told her the story, Evie froze in fear. She pictured her computer at Sweet Peas and thought immediately of Helen.

"Evie, I'm so relieved we found you in time." Janssen said from Danny's speaker phone. "I'm sorry my work has brought all this—"

"But Helen! Helen's probably already at the shop. We're going over the books today. What if she's already turned on the computer?" She looked at her bare wrist. Her heart raced. "Danny, call Helen on your Q."

"I've been calling the store. No one answers."

"Call her Q."

"What's the number?"

Evie recited the number, and Danny punched it in.

Watching his face, she saw him start to speak, then stop. "She put me on hold," he called to her, "but she's apparently okay."

"Call again."

Danny hit redial. "It's ringing, but there's no answer. We've got to get over there. I'll keep trying. I'll send her a text too, but she won't know who I am." He turned the steering wheel toward the road. "You wanna come with me?"

"I'll follow you. Tell her you work with my father."

Danny sped off. Evie put her car in gear and turned back onto Henry Street. Danny was already two cars ahead.

"Lord, be with Helen," she prayed. "Don't let anything happen to her. Please, Lord, protect Helen."

They were still about seven minutes from the shop. She saw Danny draw up behind a truck and turn left at Princess. When Evie got to Princess, she sped through a yellow light and went straight to avoid waiting for oncoming cars. If she could make it to Cameron with the light still green and turn left, she'd only have two short blocks to her shop on Alfred. But at Cameron, the light was red, and a gold Cadillac blocked her in the turn lane. She pressed her palm against her lips and whispered a prayer.

When the light finally turned green, she whipped past the Cadillac, skimmed around a white convertible trying to parallel park, and raced to the next intersection. At

Alfred, she spied Danny's Honda coming from the left. He sped through a red light, and his car disappeared from view as he continued down Alfred toward Sweet Peas.

Evie's eyes filled with tears of gratitude at his reckless perseverance.

She turned right at Alfred and spotted Danny's car up ahead, passing King Street just before the light turned red. With several cars in front of her at the red light, she couldn't see beyond. She gripped the steering wheel with her left hand and rubbed her forehead with the other, then raked her fingers through her hair in utter frustration. The traffic began to move.

Danny's car was parked unevenly in a space in front of the small clapboard house. She pulled into the alleyway behind, threw the car into park and sprinted through the back door of the building.

The strong smell of coffee filled the air. Danny stood near the front door talking to Helen. The young freckle-faced girl held a wet rag. Evie glanced at the computer. It had not been turned on.

Relief washing through her body, Evie ran to her young assistant and threw her arms around her, tears choking her throat. "Helen, you're all right!"

Helen stammered as she glanced from Evie to Danny. "I—I spilled the coffee—all over—all over a rack of clothes and the rug. I ... I was trying to clean it up."

Evie started to giggle. A big tear rolled down her cheek. A burst of nervous laughter escaped as she bent toward Helen. She wasn't sure if she were laughing or crying. She looked at her dad in the hologram. He smiled at her. "Dad, we're okay. We're okay." She raised her face to the ceiling. "Thank you, God!"

"That's my girl. Yes, thank God," he said. "And thank you, Danny."

"Yes, Danny." Evie turned and stared at the lanky young man. He stood quietly, waiting. Sirens screamed in the distance.

Evie could see the picture of Danny's determined face, dimly outlined through the window of his car as he sped through the red light at Alfred and Cameron. She saw his pleading eyes as he motioned her car over to warn her of danger and cringed at her own sass.

She bit her lip and wiped away the wetness beneath her eyes.

"How can I ever thank you, Danny—after I've treated you so badly and all. You saved my life—and Helen's."

There was a ripple in his smile as he nodded at her affirmingly. "They were lives worth saving."

The look in Danny's brown eyes drew Evie to him.

"You're a really great guy, you know that?" She hugged him, lingering longer than she intended.

Danny wrapped his arms around her too. She felt a tingly feeling run up and down her back. When she finally pulled away, she was blushing. Danny stood gazing at her with a captivating expression. She couldn't take her eyes off him.

After the bomb squad arrived, Janssen disconnected and called Charlie, who had almost arrived at Sweet Peas herself.

When he returned to the airport conference room, Jenna met him at the door, her face lined with worry. "I was just coming to find you. How's Evie?"

Over Jenna's shoulder, Janssen saw Randall Robertson leaning over Quigley and Kandarov at the laptop.

Jumakhan was talking on his phone. Sheela and Padua huddled together in a corner of the room, intermittently embracing and crying.

Janssen took a deep breath and nodded. "She's fine. Danny found her in time. Everyone's safe at that end."

"Thank God."

"Yes." He gazed at Jenna distractedly, stroked his mustache, and nodded again. "Yes. Thank God."

Jenna sighed. "Now we'll hope God helps us on this end too."

CHAPTER FORTY-SIX

Azzadafa was dead.

Janssen paced down the hallway from Jumakhan's office, where he and his uncle had continued to speculate about the events of the day while they waited for reports from the border patrol and police. Now Janssen needed a break.

Voices in both English and Tajik drew him into the great room, where he found Michael and Bradley huddled at the dining room table poring over information from the laptop. Bradley's deep, resonant voice droned on. He appeared to be giving Michael a discourse of sorts.

To his right, Janssen saw Sheela and Padua on a sofa in the small sitting room off the living area, locked in deep conversation. Their high-pitched accents intermingled in a rapid Tajik singsong.

Jenna eased into the room, appearing especially happy. Michael's eyes met hers. Slowly, he rose, strode toward her, and extended his hand. Jenna took it, and he drew her to him as he playfully lifted the ends of her hair. The two began to laugh. As they stood talking face to face, Michael suddenly pulled her into the shadow of the hall. He brushed a stray hair from Jenna's forehead and leaned down to kiss her on the temple. Jenna laid her head against his shoulder.

Janssen heard Michael's low voice from across the room. Jenna nodded, and Michael kissed her again, this time on the lips. Janssen was pleased as he watched them together. If anyone deserved happiness and love, it was his sister, and the change he'd seen in Michael astounded him. Perhaps there was a future there after all.

Janssen moved toward the arched opening to the sitting area where Sheela and Padua leafed through a Bible. He moved near Padua, who was now looking like a new woman. The bruises on her face were partially covered with makeup.

"Padua, I want to thank you for saving my daughter's life. I hate to think what might have happened if you hadn't spoken up."

Padua blushed and cast her eyes downward. "It's nothing. Look what you did for me. I am now free woman."

"You're a courageous woman, Padua. I hope things go well for you from now on." Realizing he'd interrupted her conversation with Sheela, he excused himself and strolled back into the living area. He stood beside the chess set laid out on Jumakhan's well-used game table and picked up a knight made of olivewood, rolling it between his fingers as he gazed at the board. A lot had happened in the last few days.

Jenna came up behind him. "Have you managed to get all your puzzle pieces to fit together now?"

Janssen chuckled as he turned to her. Her face glowed. She looked lovely. And regardless of what was going on in her own life, his sister could read him like a book.

"I think so." He set the knight on the board and straightened his back. "After it became clear how Azzadafa was related to all this, everything came into focus. The other pieces fell into place. The only thing left now is to intercept the suicide bombers. But Rajanov and Jumakhan seem to have a pretty good handle on that. Dushanbe is swarming with police."

"Yes. That's good."

"What a legacy of hate," Janssen said. "Each generation of four separate families passing the hate onto the next generation."

Jenna shook her head, then glanced toward the dining area where Michael had returned to work on the laptop.

Janssen followed her gaze. "But how are you doing? Looks like things in your life are taking a turn."

Jenna flushed and fidgeted. "Yes, speaking of trying to understand puzzles." She chuckled. "Makes me think of the way Mom used to talk about puzzles—about how *life* was like a puzzle. I remember her saying everything all fits together in circuitous, unexpected ways. I'm beginning to see it. I would never have expected some of the things to happen that have taken place in the last few days."

Shouts came from down the hallway.

"Come here!" Jumakhan called. "Come here, everyone, and see this. We've got a live feed from the border."

In Jumakhan's office, Janssen and the others crammed in front of the wall-mounted intelligence monitor, where they saw a gray van, its doors flung open, with boxes strewn beside it. The low iron border gate was smashed in the center. Four men in jeans and T-shirts stood with arms raised while two uniformed guards and three plainclothes policemen pointed Glocks at them, motioning them to turn around. As three of them began to comply, the fourth lunged for the officer at the far end.

There was an ear-popping roar, and the man crumpled to the ground. Two guards grabbed him as he tried to roll away on the pavement. They snapped cuffs on his wrists and dragged him to a police car.

Jumakhan's face was jubilant. "Thought you'd like to see the group of Uzbeks they caught at border outside of Panjakent. They found cars loaded with ammunition and some suicide vests. Guards check boxes now, but seem pretty certain these are suicide bombers we look for."

"Congratulations, Uncle." Janssen said. "That's great news."

"So we set press conference for tomorrow morning?" Jumakhan asked. "How quickly can we get munitions out of here and taken to safe place?"

"Secretary Tomlin and a military contingent are already on their way. Should be here tomorrow afternoon. We'll get the agreements signed and the weapons out of Tajikistan as soon as possible. Hopefully everything will be done in a couple of days."

"I will be greatly relieved, Janssen. This too big for small country like Tajikistan." He turned to Padua and Sheela standing arm-in-arm. "Padua," he said, reverting to the Tajik language, "we thank you for your great courage. You saved many lives."

"I thank you for your commendation, sir. But your wife helped me be strong. She gave *me* life." She smiled at Sheela, then at Janssen. "And it began with your mother Anna and the woman Sunny. They brought life to us."

Jumakhan looked perplexed at her response, but smiled. "Yes, Sheela is good woman."

She gave me life. Janssen crossed the living room to stand before the French doors to the patio and watched the moonlight sparkle on the bubbling water of the fountain. Padua's words, and then his mother's from long ago, echoed in his mind.

You gave me life.

No, you have that backward, Mom. You gave me life.

Yes, I did.

He rubbed his hand over the medallion beneath his shirt. His mother had given him life because a woman named Sunny had introduced her to a deeper life—a life of faith that produced courage instead of fear.

Jenna came up beside him and pointed at his neck. "Can I see it?"

"You mean the medallion?"

"Yes."

He reached under his collar and hooked his finger around the chain, pulling it through the top of his sport shirt and over his head.

Jenna held it and turned it over to look at the rose.

"The legacy of the medallion. I've learned a lot through all of this. How many lives has it saved? I was thinking of what Padua said a minute ago. Padua was able to help because of the support she got from Sheela, and indirectly from Mom ... and the faith they shared with her. All pieces of one big puzzle. Many of the good things that've happened in the last couple of days are all related to what happened long ago."

In the recesses of his mind, Janssen saw that far-away look in his mother's eyes, that look that had always perplexed him—like looking through the clear waters of a vast ocean. The day she died, he'd seen it again, and for the first time, he knew. Heaven was shining through her eyes. But it still remained a mystery to him.

Janssen peered at the bookcase behind Jenna where he saw the picture of his mother gazing out over the ocean, then studied the medallion in Jenna's hand.

"In the puzzle of life, you don't always see all the pieces," Janssen said.

Jenna nodded. "Sometimes, not until much later."

She sighed and glanced toward Michael working at the table with Bradley. "But Mom used to talk about that too—remember? When we had problems of some kind, remember how she'd talk about the puzzle and say some pieces were light and some were dark, but eventually when you looked back, you'd see how they all connected to make a beautiful picture?"

Jenna fingered the medallion and lovingly ran a hand over it, then turned it toward the light. "I'm looking back at her life right now, and you know what I see?" Her eyes shone with a far-away look, a look he'd seen before. "A beautiful picture."

Life. You gave me life.

Janssen shifted his gaze from Jenna to the medallion. "All this has caused me to do some serious thinking."

"Me too."

WASHINGTON, DC
A WEEK LATER

Evie was sitting in the gazebo in Janssen's backyard when he arrived home.

He paused before stepping outside and admiring the scene cameoed before him. The late afternoon slant of the sun had chased the shadows from beneath the trees and spread a sheen over the dark green of the lawn. Roses were in full bloom. Daisies and snapdragons filled the beds beside the patio.

As Janssen pushed open the door, he heard her humming.

"You beat me," he said.

"Hi, Dad."

Janssen shut the door and crossed the lawn, then stooped beneath the latticed entrance to join her. "Thanks for meeting me."

Evie rose and gave him a hug. "I was glad to. It's given me such a warm feeling the last couple of days just knowing you're back in the US and safe and ... *well*." She emphasized the last word. "I'm sooo glad your doctor's reports are good."

"Yes." He held her for a moment, then gestured for her to sit beside him on the bench. "I know you've been busy getting things back in order at Sweet Peas, now everything's calmed down. And it sounds like you've got other things taking up your time now too." Janssen winked and grinned at her.

Evie blushed. "Danny? Yes, he's really a nice guy—and awfully understanding. I don't know why I gave him such a rough time."

"As I heard him say, you're worth it."

Evie laughed. "He's a very forgiving man. But what did you want to see me about? Something special?"

"Yes, very special for me. I think it will be for you too." Janssen took off the medallion. "I wanted to give this to you, Evie."

"Grandmother's medallion? But why? She wanted you to have it."

"It symbolizes life."

"I know."

Janssen stared at the ground, breathing in the scent of roses that perfumed the air. He wasn't sure how to say what he felt.

"I think it's only appropriate for you to have it. Because of you, I've made some significant decisions. I'd say, in fact, in your grandmother's words, I have life because of you."

Evie laughed. "No, Dad, I think you've got that a little confused. You and Mom gave me life. And you and Danny saved my life just last week. That's a double for you."

You gave me life.

443

Janssen nodded and ran his fingers over his whiskers.

"I guess that's true. But it's you who carried the true legacy of the medallion through all these years. You followed in your grandmother's footsteps of faith. I never understood what she was all about, never understood there's a deeper meaning to life. It's because of you I do now. Jenna too. We talked about it. I believe, and Jenna agrees, your grandmother would want you to have the medallion." He held it toward Evie. "Will you let me give it to you?"

Evie's eyes grew moist as she wrinkled her brow and gazed up at her father. She appeared to be searching his eyes.

Janssen met her gaze unabashedly. He smiled and nodded. "That's right. Grandmother's faith has finally been passed on to the middle generation that missed it the first time. Both Jenna and I. We finally get it."

Evie's tears began to fall.

"Oh, Dad." She reached her arms up around his neck and held him close. "You've made me so happy."

Janssen returned the hug. When she leaned back, he looped the medallion around the top of her head and drew it down to her neck, then studied it as it hung over the throat of her turtleneck. He nodded.

"The last piece. Now the puzzle is complete."

THE END

ABOUT THE AUTHOR

In her debut suspense thriller, **Linda W. Rooks** detours from her three earlier books, award winning *Fighting for Your Marriage while Separated, Broken Heart on Hold,* and *The Bunny Side of Easter,* to dive into a futuristic world of international politics and time travel where adventure and mystery reign, but hope remains king.

Linda is best known for her books on marriage and her ministry to those who are separated, inspired by her own marriage surviving the stiff challenge of a three-year separation and her desire to bring hope to others in marital crisis.

She writes because she loves it. But she also loves hiking in the North Carolina mountains, sculpting beauty from the wildness of her Florida garden, tinkering with new recipes in her kitchen, and sampling tasty dishes at a new restaurant or catching a good movie with her husband. She begins each day at breakfast with the *Wall Street Journal.*

Linda has a degree in creative writing from San Francisco State University and lives in Central Florida with her husband, a retired professor from Barry Law School. She has two daughters and five grandchildren.

To see some of the character backstories and follow Linda's blog, connect with her at:

http://www.piecesofdarkpiecesoflight.com.

And for some visual insights into Tajikistan, the characters, and other scenes in the story, follow Linda on Pinterest at:

https://www.pinterest.com/lindarooks1064/_saved/

www.ingramcontent.com/pod-product-compliance
Lightning Source LLC
Chambersburg PA
CBHW051521050726
47503CB00014B/332